Fire

Mima

iUniverse, Inc.
New York   Bloomington

Fire

iUniverse books may be ordered through booksellers or by contacting:

iUniverse
1663 Liberty Drive
Bloomington, IN 47403
www.iuniverse.com
1-800-Authors (1-800-288-4677)

ISBN: 978-1-4502-0308-1 (sc)
ISBN: 978-1-4502-0310-4 (dj)
ISBN: 978-1-4502-0309-8 (ebk)

Printed in the United States of America

iUniverse rev. date: 1/14/2010

Fire is dedicated to all the people I shared laughter and music with during the 90's, including those who left us much too soon.

CHAPTER ONE

▼

As she glanced around the room, Tarah Kiersey couldn't tell whether her body was shaking from fear or anticipation. While one side of her brain commanded her to run away—and *fast*—the other craved her few minutes on stage. Having all those eyes upon her was both frightening and gratifying at the same time. It was something that many people wouldn't understand. And maybe, she decided, they're the lucky ones. Maybe it was easier to go through life always playing it safe, never taking a risk. But was it worth it?

A legendary rock diva once compared the minutes prior to walking on stage to those just before snorting your first line of coke. She believed that although a part of you sensed the danger and feared the consequences, another part knew that the high would be so powerful and intoxicating that it would be worth it. Tarah was sixteen when she first heard this comment and had no experience with either doing cocaine *or* singing in front of an audience. Yet, even then she knew that those words were accurate. Both experiences scared her. Both peaked her curiosity.

Feeling nervous, she once again looked around the crowded bar in the hope of finding her boyfriend, but to no avail. She had met Jeff a couple of months earlier, back when the hot summer sun drove people into the downtown bars for a cold beer. His band had been playing at one of the city's most popular establishments when Tarah and her best friend stopped in for a drink. Jeff had started a conversation with her in between sets, and she immediately became infatuated with him. Later that night, they went to an all-night restaurant and talked until the sun rose over the dreary, southern Ontario city of Thorton. They had been together ever since.

But that was before the cool, September breezes brought students back to the college town, a city of four hundred and fifty thousand. Now it was not unusual to walk into the same bars that were low-key during the summer months and find them rocking up a storm. The music seemed louder and the people were always different, no matter where you went.

"Tarah Kiersey." The sound of her own name startled her. Feeling her stomach churning, she hid her discomfort with a smile and started walking toward the stage. It was her turn to sing.

As she made her way through a roaring crowd, the host spotted his next performer and automatically began to send compliments in her direction. "Now, don't be fooled; this lady may be small but she can *sing*." Noting the smile on Tarah's face as she climbed on stage, the announcer seemed encouraged to continue. "And we're in for a treat tonight, here at Jerry's Saturday night jam, because she has selected one of this year's biggest songs, 'Under the Bridge.' Great choice, Tarah!" He winked at the petit blonde and passed her the microphone before leaving her alone in front of a crowd of about two hundred people. To a seasoned performer, this would have been a piece of cake. But to someone like Tarah, who had very little experience singing in public, it may as well have been two thousand people.

Since the band had already started to play, Tarah had no time to second-guess herself. Although it seemed a little awkward in the beginning, the singing lessons she had taken earlier that year had prepared her to be professional. She knew that posture and proper breathing went a long way, not to mention being able to fake confidence. Looking past the faces in the crowd, the twenty-one-year-old wasn't even aware that she held a captive audience. No one who watched her would have guessed that her stomach was in knots and that she had broken into a sweat under the strong lights that beat down on her face. She sang like a pro.

Just as Tarah began to relax and found the courage to look into the faces in the crowd, something caught her eye. It was Jeff, her boyfriend. And he was with another girl—a tall brunette with big boobs.

It figures, Tarah thought. In fact, the woman was all over him, and judging by the smile on his face, he didn't mind. This, after promising Tarah that he had never cheated on her and that she was the only girl for him. After insisting that he'd be there for her that night, standing in the front row, since he was her biggest fan. It was a lie. He didn't even seem aware that she was on stage. She wanted to cry but instead continued to sing and pushed her feelings aside.

As she was about to finish, Tarah saw something that almost made her screw up the entire song. The brunette put her hand in Jeff's, gave him a sly smile, and led him toward the back of the bar. However, the crowd was thick and Tarah quickly lost sight of them. Trying to remain casual, her eyes scanned the many faces in the room. Her sadness quickly turned to anger, and it caused her voice to become stronger. This didn't go unnoticed by the crowd, who were becoming increasingly interested, impressed by the higher and longer notes that this very tiny woman was hitting. Many of those who watched her were musicians themselves and knew talent when they saw it. But Tarah was so caught up in her own drama that she didn't see their obvious acceptance. What she did see was her boyfriend walking into the men's washroom, hand in hand with the brunette. And as Tarah finished the song, she felt rage filling her body. Every lie he had ever told and every excuse he had ever made was now rising to the surface. Suddenly, the reality was painfully clear. As she stood on that stage, Tarah felt herself shake with anger.

Ignoring the cheering crowd and losing sight of the fact that she had just accomplished something big, Tarah felt engulfed in fury. Suddenly all the rumors she had denied in their two months of dating swirled around in her head. Feeling humiliated and repulsed, she abruptly slammed the microphone on the ground, causing a huge *thump* throughout the room, and then jumped off the stage. Her size was not a deterrent as she flew through the startled crowd of flannel shirts and ripped jeans, heading straight to the men's washroom where the stranger had taken her boyfriend. Only hesitating for a moment, she shoved open the door. Three guys at the urinals were oblivious to the fact that a woman was even in the room. Finding one lone stall door closed, Tarah used all her strength to kick the flimsy door open and felt a thud. The door swung back and revealed Jeff with his pants around his ankles and the brunette on her knees before him. Tarah felt her eyes sting with tears.

While the brunette attempted to chastise Tarah for not only interrupting them, but also hitting her with the door, Jeff quickly pulled up his pants. He had a deer-caught-in-headlights look on his face, and Tarah automatically knew that this wasn't his first indiscretion. Without even thinking, she lunged forward, her fist hitting the same face she had once adored.

Jeff automatically touched the cheek she punched, clearly stunned by Tarah's reaction.

"Baby, I'm sorry, I wasn't thinking …" He said the words as if they were rehearsed, like a child who misbehaves but always has his "forgiveness" speech tucked in the back of his mind. With downcast eyes and a soft voice, he continued to touch his face, "I deserved that."

Tarah could sense that a crowd was gathered behind her but didn't care. "You fucking asshole!" Her voice rang out through the room. "I'll show you what you deserve!" She lunged forward but felt her body being pulled back and eventually up off the ground. It took her a few seconds to realize that the bar's bouncers were dragging her out of the room and toward the exit.

"What are you doing?" Tarah began to cry and felt her feet once again touching the ground. She glanced toward the stage to see another performer was now singing for the crowd, although she still held her own captive audience. "I didn't do anything wrong."

"Miss, you started a fight," One bouncer was now leading her outside into the cool September evening. His strong hand was warm on her back as he talked to her calmly. "Now, I will admit, I saw enough to see where you're coming from," he said, walking with her to the side of the building and lighting up a cigarette at the same time. There were a few other people outside, but they were standing away from everyone else. "Trust me, I caught another guy screwing my ex once; let's just say that pretty boy wasn't looking too pretty when I was done with him."

Tarah felt herself laugh as she wiped the tears from her face. Her hand was starting to hurt.

"I understand why you reacted that way. But, in a place like this, they only look at who started the fight. Unfortunately, they don't look at who deserved to get decked," he inhaled his cigarette deeply and shrugged. "That's the way it goes. But I will say you are quite the boxer for a lady your size."

"Thanks," Tarah replied, and studied her hand.

"You're gonna want to put that on ice when you get home," he suggested. "As for your boyfriend, he's an ass. Trust me, I work in a bar. I can point them out one by one."

Tarah silently nodded, still trying to process everything that had just happened. She had managed to conquer a fear, only to be faced with disappointment. Could she ever just win?

"Anyway, I must get back in," he threw the cigarette on the ground. "Sorry for having to kick you out."

"It's fine." Tarah felt her head starting to ache, along with her hand, and she turned to walk home. She didn't have far to go and needed to clear her thoughts. After taking a few steps, she noticed that her hand was starting to throb with intense pain and feared that if she didn't get some ice on it soon, it'd be a mess the next day. Glancing toward some cabs parked nearby, she decided to splurge and get a lift home.

Feeling frustrated, defeated, and depressed, she jumped into an older white car and gave her address. As soon as she sat down, she noticed the mixture of stale air and BO that filled the vehicle. *Wonderful,* she thought. She couldn't even get a cab that wasn't disgusting.

"Have a bad night?" The driver asked as they headed in the direction of her apartment building. Looking up into the rearview mirror, she noticed the cabbie for the first time. In a way, Tarah almost wished she hadn't. He was an older guy, balding, but with a few long strands of stringy, blond hair falling onto his shoulders—as if having a few sprigs of long hair made up for what was missing on the top of his head. He was fat, wore unclean clothes, and had coffee cups thrown all through the car. She was slightly repulsed and started to feel she should have just walked home.

"Why?" she asked skeptically.

"I saw you gettin' thrown out of the bar." He winked at her in the rearview mirror. She didn't reply, just wanting the drive to be done.

"So did you get all rowdy and wild in there?" He winked at her again. She shook her head and glared at him.

"Maybe a little too much to drink?"

"No, I'm fine." Her voice was small. She felt so defeated at that moment. The entire night had been a disaster. Did she really need this shit now?

"Are you sure honey?" He turned around slightly just as they arrived at her apartment building. His hand touched her leg and attempted to move up her thigh when she abruptly pushed it off.

"How much do I owe you?" she said, suddenly very alert. What if this guy was a psycho and wouldn't let her out of the cab? Someone told her once that if you didn't pay, cabbies had the option to lock the doors and not let you out. What if he was a rapist? She felt ill even thinking about it. *Dear God, get me out of this situation.*

"Depends on how you want to pay." He raised his eyebrows. Tarah glanced at the big red numbers on the dashboard, pulled out a bill, and threw it at him before jumping out of the car and running up the concrete stairs toward the main door. Reaching into her pocket, she couldn't find her key.

This can't be happening to me! She saw the cabbie parking the car and turning off the lights. Tarah's heart was pounding violently in her chest as her hand searched the other pocket. She finally located the key and opened the main door. Flying inside, she didn't look back to see if he was following. The main entrance automatically locked behind her. For once in her life, Tarah was glad she had listened to her mother's constant nagging about moving into a security building. What if she hadn't? What kind of position would she be in?

Running up another set of stairs, she made it to the second floor of the small apartment building. Her hands shook as she unlocked the door and went inside. Locking it behind her, still in the dark, Tarah collapsed on the floor and started to sob, barely gasping for air. Feeling a pain developing in her chest, Tarah feared she was having a panic attack. Why were these awful things always happening to her? What did she do to deserve all this? What was wrong that all her boyfriends either cheated on her or didn't think she was worth their time? Why did other girls have men hanging on their heels while she had guys treating her like she was garbage on their shoes? Even the cab driver was treating her as if she was a two-dollar whore, rather than a respectable female. Did she send off some kind of message without realizing it?

Questions flowed through her head and her aching hand became less and less bearable. She stood up and glanced out the window. The cab was gone. Tarah turned on the lights and walked into the bathroom. Without looking in the mirror, she ran warm water into the sink, grabbed a washcloth, and roughly wiped away the tears and makeup. Looking into her own eyes, she saw a sorrow that filled her with a combination of self-pity and desperation.

Going back into the kitchen, she found a bag of frozen corn and wrapped it around her hand. It continued to hurt, but she almost didn't care. At least a painful hand was curable. But what about a painful life? How did you fix that?

After double-checking that her door was locked, Tarah turned off the bathroom and kitchen lights and went into her bedroom. Pulling off her jeans, she replaced them with a pair of shorts. Tarah left on the top she had specifically purchased for the bar that night. She wanted to wear a color that inspired confidence, and on a whim, chose the tight, red tank top that would only suit a figure as tiny as her own.

Collapsing on the bed, corn still wrapped around her hand, Tarah glanced at the phone and noted that her answering machine had a message on it. She listened. It was from Jeff. He was trying to justify what had happened that night, but somehow, he still managed to blame Tarah for everything. At first, his logic made her laugh hysterically, but then tears formed in her eyes. Glancing at the clock, she knew it was late, but decided to make the call anyway. She was desperate.

"Hi, I really have to talk." Tarah broke down on the phone. She had promised herself that she wouldn't cry, but the tears were running down her cheeks full force. "This has been the worst night of my life."

CHAPTER TWO

▼

They were set to meet at a trendy coffee shop the following morning. Tarah was the first to arrive, and after buying a very elaborate and overpriced specialty cup, which included whipping cream and sprinkles, she chose a seat at the back of the room. All around her, groups of friends sat together, talking and laughing over their drinks, while others sat alone, reading a book or newspaper. The staff appeared friendly and relaxed, the complete opposite of Rothman's, the discount department store where Tarah worked. She found her work environment to be stressful and unfulfilling to say the least.

Taking a sip of her drink, she quickly realized why it was so expensive. Unlike the coffee she grabbed at work every morning, this one was worth the extra money. She decided that her best friend was right to suggest this place. Glancing toward the door, then the counter, she noted that Wendy still hadn't arrived. *Fashionably late as usual,* Tarah thought, feeling uncomfortable as she sat by herself.

Just as Sarah McLachlan's song "Into the Fire" gently flowed through the room, Wendy Stuart finally made her appearance. Gliding through the doors, she waved at Tarah and headed toward the counter to place her order. It appeared that the staff was acquainted with the outgoing, young woman as they acknowledged her and rushed to make her coffee. Then again, Tarah considered, Wendy did work at a nearby bank. She probably dropped in daily for her morning brew.

"Hey, you!" Wendy was her usual bubbly self as she approached Tarah's table, pushing a strand of her caramel-brown hair from her eyes. Unlike Tarah, her friend had naturally wavy hair that always looked perfect. Her eyes were a deep, chocolate brown, and she had cute freckles on her face. These were all traits Tarah envied, while Wendy hated them. Placing her coffee on the table, Wendy removed a short, black trench coat and sat it on the chair beside her. She wore a plain, black T-shirt and a pair of Levi's. Plopping down in the chair across from Tarah, she studied her friend. "I hope you're feeling better today."

"I am."

"I told you everything would be better after a good night's sleep." Wendy pulled her chair in and took a drink of her coffee. It was in a tall, clear cup and looked rich and delicious. "You just needed some time to clear your head."

"It's not *all* better," Tarah objected, wishing her friend wouldn't make light of the whole situation. "I'm not as upset, but it was still a horrible night."

"I know," Wendy assured her. "But you really have to focus on the good here."

Tarah raised her eyebrows. *The good?*

"You sang in front of a bigger crowd than last time," Wendy reminded her. "That's a wonderful thing. Not a lot of people could do that. I couldn't."

"I suppose," Tarah reluctantly replied.

"And you found out what kind of person Jeff really is," Wendy said. "I know it was a horrible way to find out, but you had your suspicions all along."

Tarah knew she was right about that too. From day one, there were little hints and signs that made her weary of Jeff, but she simply assumed it was her own paranoia that caused her to worry. He always had great reasons for being late or canceling a date. There were always excuses.

"Plus, you got away from that creepy cab guy." Wendy made a face. "I really think you should report him to the company he works for."

"I can't remember the number on the cab or anything." Tarah sighed. "I was so upset that I just jumped out of the car and didn't really notice anything other than it was white."

"And driven by a creep."

"Yes, and driven by a creep."

"It's pretty scary when you think about it." Wendy sat back in her chair and glanced around the room. "What if you were drunk out of your mind and got in a cab alone to go home. God knows what kind of sick fuck might be behind the wheel."

"I know." Tarah looked down at her cup. It was almost empty but she could barely remember drinking it. "I just feel stupid over the Jeff thing. It's starting to seem like I have a dark cloud over me. Maybe nothing will ever work out."

Wendy tilted her head and frowned.

"I date idiots, I work at a horrible job that I hate, and I'm always broke." Tarah said.

Wendy nodded. Many people their age were in a similar predicament. Most wanted the freedom of being on their own, but that came with a big price. Even Wendy, who graduated from Thompson Business School earlier that year, was struggling to get by with her job at the bank. It was certainly not what she had dreamed of during her two years of college. It was difficult to find a good place to work without experience and impossible to get experience without a good job. And the dating world was a whole other ball game.

"It'll get better," Wendy assured her. "I can feel it."

Tarah attempted to share her enthusiasm, but just couldn't find it in herself to do so. Her friend's optimism came from a different background and belief system, so it was sometimes difficult for them to relate.

"You know what I was thinking?" Tarah pushed her empty cup aside. "Do you think my relationships with men are so fucked-up because I come from a family of divorce? I read that in a magazine and it does make sense."

"Maybe." Wendy considered for a moment. "Not necessarily though."

"I mean, my parents split up when I was fifteen," Tarah continued, "and my mom was in such a depression for *so* long." She would never forget those horrible days. Her father had quietly left in the middle of the night, and her mother was crying all the time and taking months off her work as a nurse to deal with the separation. Tarah had become the mother, looking after her younger brother, shopping for groceries—whatever needed to be done. Claire Kiersey just stayed in bed all day, only creeping out for food or to go to the bathroom. Meanwhile, David Kiersey's life and successful accounting career were not affected.

"I think it makes you sketchy on men," Wendy considered as she calmly drank her coffee. "But then again my parents are together, and I don't necessarily have luck with guys either."

Tarah nodded. Wendy had gone out with some real losers in the couple of years she had known her. She always dated attractive guys that ranged from the wild-child types to serious college boys. It didn't seem to matter who they were or where they came from, things never worked out in the end. It was something that Tarah just could not understand. Her friend had a charming and friendly personality, a perfect figure, a great job, and a cute apartment. Yet she fell in love with guys fast and furious, then everything would go up in flames.

"Maybe there aren't any great guys out there anymore," Tarah commented mournfully. "Maybe they're all losers."

"I don't know about that," Wendy's face was thoughtful, regaining its sparkle. "I did date a great guy way back when, but the timing was just off. It was when I was around sixteen, a year or so before I moved to Thorton for college. Which reminds me—"

Wendy grabbed her bag and dug through its many compartments, finally pulling out a yellow piece of paper, which she sat before Tarah. An ad for a band called Tanked announced that they were scheduled to play at a local bar on September 19, 1992. It was a Saturday night and Tarah's twenty-second birthday.

"To be honest, I'm not sure if I'll do anything this year." Tarah wrinkled her forehead. The idea of stepping foot in *any* bar had no appeal to her right about then. "Why did talking about losers you have dated make you think of this show? Do you want to date one of these guys?"

"No," Wendy grinned from ear to ear. "I *did* date one of these guys when I was sixteen." She pointed at one of the four young men in the black and white photo. "William Stacy, and *he* wasn't a loser."

"He's cute," Tarah commented as she leaned over the flyer. That was probably an understatement, she decided, after moving in for a closer look. He had dark hair that hung to his shoulders, reminding her of Eddie Vedder. His smile was welcoming, yet sexy.

"So, I was thinking that you and I could check out the show." Wendy raised her eyebrows. "And I can check out William."

Tarah pushed the bright flyer back to her friend. "When was the last time you talked to this guy? He may not be the same person he was when you were sixteen."

"I know." Wendy settled back on her chair with a hesitant expression on her face. "He may even be married with kids now, for all I know. I just want to check things out. He's the one guy I think I misjudged."

Tarah didn't say anything, but truly felt her best friend misjudged a great deal of guys. Unfortunately, she usually gave them too much credit. It was doubtful that this one was any better, but Tarah reluctantly agreed to go to the show. "But," she raised her finger in the air and hesitated, "I won't promise that I'll stay, especially if you two hit it off. I'm not being a third wheel on my birthday."

"You're never a third wheel." Wendy gave her a bright smile. "Besides, it doesn't matter because his band will be playing all night. We'll drink and celebrate your birthday either way, and if things are iffy with William and I, then we'll just take off and go somewhere else. Sound good?"

Tarah reluctantly agreed. After all, Wendy would do the same for her if she asked. She still couldn't help but feel a little disappointed that the fact of her birthday seemed to be merely a second thought. What if she had said no? Would Wendy have gone along without her? After all, her best friend's priority since Tarah met her was to find the love of her life. Unfortunately, she was kissing a lot of frogs along the way.

"So, he's a musician?" Tarah rolled her eyes. "Have you not learned anything from my experience with a musician?" She was referring to Jeff, who lived and breathed music. It was his life's passion.

"It's not fair to assume that all men in bands are jerks."

"Please, these guys not only want to play music, they want to live the rock star life style," Tarah warned her. "They want to be idolized and lusted after by their fans. Sex, drugs, and rock and roll all go together for a reason."

"That's not fair," Wendy repeated. "You shouldn't be so critical. Your standards for people are much too high sometimes."

Tarah thought back to the episode with Jeff the previous night and sniffed, "Obviously not high enough."

Wendy was taking another long look at the flyer before folding it and putting it back in her purse. "Don't dwell on it, Tarah. He's not worth it."

"I won't."

"Good." Wendy finally finished the last of her coffee. "We're going to go out next weekend for your birthday and I promise it's going to be the *best* night of your life."

Wendy was wrong, of course. It wasn't the best night of Tarah's life. It was, however, the night that changed her life.

Chapter Three

▼

After a long day at work, Tarah collapsed in her car. It had been another Saturday of retail hell for people employed in the industry—especially when working for a discount department store.

Every weekend tended to be the same thing. Parents would drag their crying, screaming kids up and down the aisles for what seemed like hours, while teenagers roamed the mall for what appeared to be a lack of anything better to do. People from outside of the city would make appearances at every major store in Thorton before heading back to their rural escapes. But the absolute worst were the consumers who still believed the absurd "customer is always right" myth. In the fast-paced world that consisted of mass production, million dollar corporations, and students who studied the science of marketing in schools, it amazed Tarah that people really believed that such an old idea was still in existence. It was like being fifty years old and still believing in Santa.

Turning her ignition, Tarah's '85 Sunbird loudly sprang to life. It carried such a force that an overweight woman who was pushing what appeared to be a twelve-year-old kid in a shopping cart turned to glare at her. Being at the end of her rope after a frustrating day at work, Tarah gave her the finger before tearing out of the parking lot. She had had enough.

She would have given anything at that point to go home and soak in a hot bath. However, Tarah had already promised to swing by her mom's place for a birthday dinner. Sure, it meant eating some real food for a change, *plus* cake, but it also would be an hour of verbal attacks by her mother and brother. It sometimes felt like the two of them were working together to make her feel as uncomfortable as possible. Bobby and her mom were very close, always had been. Somehow, Tarah didn't fit into the equation.

Arriving at her mom's house, Tarah noted that her brother and his girlfriend Sara were already there. She could see him through the window, where he sat in the living room. Bobby turned and watched Tarah get out of the car and walk up the steps. A sense of loneliness filled her heart as she opened the kitchen door and entered her childhood home. She was met with all the bad memories of her teenage years, but quickly pushed them from her head. All she had to do was get through one hour and then she could go back to her apartment.

"Happy birthday!" Her mother appeared at the door wearing a pair of sweat pants and an old sweater. The smell of baked ham filled the house. Tarah smiled uncomfortably while removing her boots. Still in her work uniform that consisted of black pants, a white shirt, and a burgundy smock, she felt a sense of dread as she noticed her mother looking her up and down. "Twenty-two years old today! Time sure flies." Although their conversation appeared to be pleasant enough, it was about to take a turn for the worse.

"Tarah, you really shouldn't wear those big, old boots," Claire Kiersey referred to her daughter's Doc Marten's. "There so big and chunky for such a small girl like you. You need a pair of cute little shoes."

"Mom," Tarah sighed, already feeling defeated. "I like them."

"I know that's what all you kids are wearing now," her mother continued as Tarah slid past her to enter the next room. She found Bobby sitting on the couch with a huge grin on his face, while Sara sat quietly in the corner. Tarah collapsed on the other side of her brother. "But they really don't suit a girl. You need to try something a little more feminine. I'm surprised they let you wear them at the store."

Tarah shrugged, knowing that Rothman's loved the fact that she wore their best-selling shoes to work. In fact, having a young, stylish woman modeling their most expensive footwear was just more encouragement for sales. "They don't care, mom."

Claire put her hands up as if to surrender. "I'm just saying that I don't think it's proper."

"Mom, come on." Bobby spoke up from the other side of Tarah, where he was leaning back against a pillow. The light of the September afternoon shot through the window and touched his face. Tarah thought about how he resembled their mother, with his dark eyes and hair. "That's what everyone wears now. Girls, guys, everyone."

"You don't wear them." Claire pointed out as she stood with her hands on her hip. "Neither does Sara."

"I can't afford them." Bobby sniffed. "Those are like hundred-dollar boots."

"I get my discount." Tarah jumped in before her mother could make a comment on the fact that she spent too much on footwear.

"At work the other day, this fifteen-year-old girl showed up wearing those shoes." Claire pointed toward Tarah's now bootless feet. "She was in to see the doctor on duty, well I can't get into why she was there and I'm not in the place to judge, but she was dealing with something no fifteen-year-old girl should be involved in, and let's leave it at that." She spoke dramatically and paused for only a second. "Anyway, the point is that she had on those big, clunky boots and this little mini skirt. She looked just *horrible*. Just a tiny thing like Tarah, wearing boots that were heavier than her whole body."

"Mom, it's *the style*," Tarah once again pointed out. She was used to her mother's rants and judgments with regard to things she saw daily at the hospital. For a woman who had been a nurse most of her adult life, it amazed Tarah that she was so quick to make assumptions on people. Claire had no idea that her daughter owned the same kind of outfit and wore it often.

Tarah's mother went on to complain about her recent schedule change at work, while Bobby discussed how exhausting it was trying to find a good job without having connections in most of the "worthwhile" companies. He was currently on welfare, living with Sara and her family in a trailer, just outside of the city limits.

"We're hiring at work," Tarah volunteered, thinking that there was no reason why her nineteen-year-old brother could not find a job. However, judging from the look of disgust on his face, clearly he wasn't appreciative of her help.

"I'm not working *there*," he spat out. "I can sit at home and make as much money as I would at Rothman's. They don't even give full time." Tarah knew that wasn't true. She worked over forty hours a week. "It's not worth it to come all the way into town for a job there."

Tarah shrugged and felt her heart racing. Talking to her brother did little more than frustrate her. But it was about to get worse.

"Oh honey, you can't expect your brother to work there," Claire quickly began to defend her son. "He'd be on his feet all day and his knees haven't been good since that hockey accident years ago." The particular incident that she was referring to happened when her brother was twelve. Apparently his body hadn't fully recovered yet. "It would just be too hard on him."

Tarah wanted to scream. Instead she looked at her watch and commented, "Is the food almost done? I have to be at Wendy's in an hour." Of course, that wasn't completely true, but she was at the end of her rope with her family. Also, her stomach was growling as the aroma of food filled the house.

"Yes, it should be." Her mother rushed to the kitchen, and Tarah followed to set the table, figuring it wouldn't hurt to push things along a bit. Thirty minutes later, the family finished a delicious meal. As much as her mother grated on her nerves, Tarah couldn't deny the fact that Claire Kiersey was a great cook. The dinner was followed by vanilla cake and chocolate ice cream. Finishing up her food, the birthday girl was glancing at the clock and ready to go when her brother suddenly decided to start a conversation.

"So Tarah, I hear you and Jeff broke up." A smirk crossed his face while his dark brown eyes began to dance. Sara looked uncomfortable. Tarah felt a sinking feeling in her stomach. "I heard that you caught him in a compromising position with another girl."

Feeling her face become hot with embarrassment, she didn't even have a chance to say a word before her mother jumped in. "Compromising position? Well, what does that mean?" she asked innocently, which made Tarah wonder if they had already discussed the Jeff situation before her arrival. How did Bobby know about the break-up, and for that matter, why did her family feel the need to take a stab at her, especially on this particular day?

"Do you want to tell her?" Bobby probed, while Sara grinned self-consciously at the opposite side of the table. Tarah shot her brother's girlfriend a dirty look and watched her expression become sober.

"What happened, Tarah?" Her mother leaned in closer as if they were sharing a secret. "What did Jeff do?"

"I don't want to talk about it," Tarah snapped. Feeling her heart race, she quickly added, "We broke up and that's it."

But her brother wasn't about to let it go. "Tarah caught him at the bar, with another girl in a stall and she punched him." He began to laugh and Sara quickly followed his lead. "Made a huge scene."

"What?" Claire looked completely stunned by this news. Her dark eyes were resting on Tarah. "He was with another girl in a public place and you punched him? Tarah, where did you find this guy? Oh my God, I wouldn't want to be dating some of the men out there now; you just never know what is going on with them. I hope you got an STD test, Tarah; he could've been with half the city, you just never know. And to punch him, I mean, that certainly doesn't make you look any better."

"I don't care!" Tarah snapped and pushed her chair away from the table. She felt her body shaking in fury. "I didn't come here to be attacked, especially not on my birthday."

"Oh honey, don't be so dramatic," her mother said, but it was too late. Jumping up, Tarah was already heading toward the door.

"Well mom, she *did* catch her boyfriend getting a blow job from the hottest girl in the room," Bobby said, and his laughter flowed into the next room. Tarah felt her stomach turn as she pulled on her Docs. Did he really have to go into so much detail? Feeling tears burning at the surface, Tarah held them back long enough to tie her shoelaces and return to the kitchen. Glaring at her brother as he laughed joyfully while his girlfriend did the same, Tarah couldn't even try to be nice at this point. She was now reliving the humiliation of the previous weekend, and it was like a knife through her heart.

"You know what, Bobby, you're hardly in the position to make fun of my life." Tarah watched the smirk disappear from both his and Sara's faces. "Considering you're living on welfare, with your knocked-up girlfriend, in a trailer. As pathetic as my life may seem, at least I'm not white trash."

And with that, Tarah turned and rushed out the door, leaving a stunned family behind. Up until that moment, Sara's pregnancy had been a secret from their mother.

Jumping behind the wheel of her car, she tore out of the driveway and headed home. That was when hot tears began to fall on Tarah's face. Her life was just a joke to everyone, including her own family. She wanted to crawl in a hole and die.

Back at her apartment building, she walked up the steps to the second floor and unlocked her door. It was now after seven o'clock, and the last thing she felt like doing was going out. She decided to soak in a nice, hot tub and think up an excuse to get out of going to the bar with Wendy. After all, it was clear that her best friend was only going to hook up with this William guy, what did she need her for? After the shitty day she had at work, then her birthday dinner, the last thing Tarah felt like dealing with was further disappointment. She just wanted to stay home, go to bed, watch some television, and forget all about her birthday.

However, she was barely out of the tub twenty minutes later when the phone rang. It was Wendy.

"What time are you coming over here?" she probed. "Or should I go meet you there?"

"Listen, Wendy, I had the worst day ever, and the last thing I want to do right now, is to go anywhere," Tarah blurted. "I'm really sorry, but I just had a huge fight with my brother, after being badgered by my mother. Work was hell and at this point, I can't imagine going out and actually having fun. As it is, I'm getting a headache."

"All the *more* reason to go out," Wendy insisted. "Come on Tarah, you know once you have a few drinks, everything will seem better. It sounds like you need to blow off some steam."

"Or crawl under the covers and forget this day ever happened."

"Don't do that," Wendy moaned. "It's your birthday, at least come out for one drink. If you don't want to stay, you don't have to. But just come out for a half hour, twenty minutes, ten, just come out."

Tarah reluctantly agreed, but only intended on staying for one drink.

After hanging up, she rushed around her room, attempting to put together an outfit for the night. Finally, she decided on a white belly shirt and long, black skirt that flowed perfectly over her hips. She found a pair of thick-healed, black shoes and slid them on her feet.

Glancing in the mirror, she decided to leave her blonde hair straight and just touch up her makeup. Unlike most nights that she headed out to the bars, she had no interest in spending too much time on her appearance. In reality, Tarah knew she was still mourning the break-up with Jeff, and her heart just wasn't into it. She had a sudden fear that he'd be out at the same bar that night. That was the last thing she needed. He hadn't attempted to call her since the previous Saturday night, which was slightly disappointing even after everything that happened. It just proved that she had meant nothing to him, which made her feel like a fool on top of everything else. She decided that he was probably happily dating the brunette from the bar by now.

The doorbell sprang her out of her thoughts of self-pity. Taking a deep breath, she ran downstairs to meet Wendy. Her friend wore a pair of jeans and a blue tube top that didn't hide the fact that she wasn't wearing a bra.

"Wendy, aren't you going to wear something under that?" Tarah pointed at the thin piece of blue material. "What if it falls down and everything flies out?"

"That won't happen," Wendy insisted as the two girls started to walk upstairs. "Plus, there is a built in bra in it."

"Are you *sure* about that?" Tarah asked, but her friend merely shrugged.

Once in her apartment, Wendy did about four shots and then had a beer. Tarah only had a few sips of some cheap wine that had been sitting in her fridge for weeks. It wasn't very good, but she didn't care. She just wanted the night to be over.

Just before eleven o'clock, they left the house. Wendy insisted on taking a cab, but since Tarah had no interest in drinking, she said they could bring her car. Plus, after the cab experience the previous weekend, she wasn't too keen on taking another taxi home alone. Especially considering she wasn't even going to stay for long.

They'd been to the college bar called Three AM a couple of times in the past, but it wasn't their regular hangout. It was small and catered toward music enthusiasts more than hardcore partiers. As soon as they walked in the door, Wendy was looking for William. She spotted him immediately. Tarah decided to stay at the bar while her friend went to reunite. She felt a little too vulnerable to watch their love suddenly rekindle. However, when Wendy found Tarah a few minutes later, she reported something completely different.

"How'd it go?" Tarah faked interest.

"I don't know." Wendy turned up her nose. "He remembered me, and was nice and all, but there was no spark."

"Maybe he has a girlfriend."

"No, he just broke up with someone," Wendy said. "He just didn't seem that interested in talking to me."

"Well, it looks like they're getting ready for the show." Tarah gestured toward the stage. "He probably was just busy."

"No, it wasn't just that he didn't seem into me, I don't really think I'm into him," Wendy said. "He seems, I don't know, kind of boring or something."

"But now, that guy," Wendy gestured toward a shaggy haired stoner on the other side of the bar, "now, *he* looks like my type."

"Really?" Tarah raised her eyebrow. The guy was staring at Wendy's chest but when she reported this back, Wendy didn't seem to care. "I'll be right back." She quickly moved around the bar, and Tarah turned to find the nearest exit. Enough was enough. If this was going to be her night, she was leaving.

But when she swung around, Tarah ran into someone. Moving back and feeling self-conscious as she apologized for her klutziness, she looked up into a humored, yet friendly set of hazel eyes. It was *the* William Stacy that her best friend had been so in love with only five minutes earlier, and for a second, Tarah thought she had forgotten to breathe.

CHAPTER FOUR

▼

"Oh, I'm so sorry," she repeated, feeling both awkward and shy. Tarah's face was getting warm and her voice seemed to catch in her throat. William's eyes curiously watched her speak. Although he towered over her, at about six foot two, there was something so approachable and welcoming about him that Tarah quickly could see why Wendy spoke so highly of her ex. Or at least why she had before that night.

He gave her a gentle grin and shrugged. "Hey, it could've been worse. At least you didn't have a drink in your hand. It's Tarah, right?" William pushed a strand of shoulder-length hair behind his ear. "Aren't you here with Wendy? She mentioned you earlier." His attention shifted to the other side of the bar where the woman in question now stood, flirting with the stranger. Tarah noticed that a darkness seemed to pass over William's eyes, causing her to wonder if he was jealous of the scumbag that Wendy was trying to pick up. However, turning his attention back to Tarah, his lips curved into another small smile. "Never mind, I think I figured it out. By the way, I'm William."

"Yes, Wendy mentioned you," Tarah heard herself blurting out, feeling even more awkward as the bar started to fill up. "Actually, I was about to take off. I'm not really in the mood to be out tonight. I've had a long day." She spoke apologetically.

"Oh no, you can't." William leaned in and his fingers briefly grazed her arm. "You have to stay and see Tanked play! It's the best music experience you'll have … ah," he rolled his eyes up at the ceiling, "well, it's the best music experience you'll have *tonight*."

Tarah laughed for the first time that day. "Well, I guess I can hang out for a bit," she reluctantly agreed, thinking his comment was somewhat lame, but at the same time, liking him. Wendy's ex definitely was charming and sweet, not to mention gorgeous.

She ended up staying for the entire show.

Watching William play guitar on the stage was mesmerizing. Tarah recognized that he was a talented and passionate musician. It was something you just couldn't fake. However, she wasn't necessarily as impressed with the rest of the band. For example, the bassist for Tanked was creepy. Maybe it was because his long stringy hair and dirty clothes reminded Tarah of the cab driver who drove her home the previous weekend. She quickly decided that her assumptions of him were probably unfair. The drummer appeared to be quite young but enthusiastic about every song they performed. Of course, these were all instruments that Tarah didn't play, so she was hardly an expert on any of their abilities. Something she did know about however was singing. And Tarah had no admiration for the lead vocalist of Tanked. He struck her as both pompous and talentless. There was a difference between singing and screaming, something he obviously didn't realize.

Regardless, Tarah enjoyed her evening more than she'd anticipated. Much to her surprise, she was capable of having fun at a bar without getting loaded. It turned out to be an okay birthday after all.

Wendy made few brief appearances throughout the evening, but she never stayed for long. It seems that her new love interest was buying her drinks all night, so it didn't surprise Tarah when she left the bar with him around midnight. Tanked finished playing shortly after one. Tarah glanced at the stage and gave William a quick wave before heading toward the door. He seemed like a nice guy, but he was Wendy's ex, which made her skeptical. Not to mention the fact that he was a musician, a trait that didn't impress Tarah very much since the dating disaster with Jeff. It was better to just move on and go home.

But before she reached the exit, she felt a hand gently touch her arm. She turned around and saw William smiling at her. "You keep wanting to run away, what's with that?" he teased. "I have to keep my eye on you."

"I guess you will," Tarah surprised herself when she made the blunt comment. William laughed.

"Why don't you stick around for just a bit longer? We're just packing up everything," he gestured toward the stage. Tarah noted that the creepy looking bassist was watching them intensely and she found it intimidating. "But after that, can I buy you a drink?"

Tarah really wanted to go home and sleep, but as she looked into his eyes, something made her say yes. He led her to an empty booth, told her to have a seat, and added that he'd be back as soon as possible. Even though he ended up not taking long, it may as well have been years for Tarah. Once her attention wasn't on the band, she felt self-conscious being alone in a bar.

William finally returned and sat across from her. "Sorry about that," he gestured toward the rest of Tanked who were carrying equipment off the stage and out a side exit. "We like to get it packed up and out to the truck as soon as possible, so nothing gets stolen."

"Does that happen?"

"Oh yeah!" William exclaimed. "I found that out the hard way. I used to be with this other band a few years ago, and we were actually here in Thorton playing at another place and someone stole my amp."

Tarah made a face. She knew how expensive that could be. She glanced at the rest of his band again. "Are you sure they don't need your help?"

William's eyes moved to the other side of the room. "Nah, they're good. I took some stuff out, they can get the rest for a change." He sat back in the seat.

Tarah nodded.

"So Wendy bailed on you?" He spoke gently while a smooth smile crossed his lips.

"Kind of."

"Considering that you've been alone most of the night, I'd have to lean toward a 'Yes, she did.'" William pushed a strand of hair behind his ear, displaying more of his perfectly tanned face. His eyes were red, and Tarah had noticed him yawn a few times during their short conversation. William gave her a playful look that showed he was teasing her. "At least that's how it looked from the stage."

"Okay, you're right, she did bail on me." Tarah grinned as she briefly studied her fingers on the table. "She begged me to come out tonight and pretty much took off as soon as we got here."

"Nice," William remarked sarcastically.

A waitress interrupted their conversation. William ordered a Sprite, and Tarah asked for a bottle of water.

"No drinks tonight?" William wrinkled his forehead.

"I could ask you the same thing," Tarah teased him. "I thought musicians were all about the partying lifestyle."

William rolled his eyes and laughed, "Not all of us." He had a boyish smile that seemed sincere as he studied her face. "At least, I'm not."

"No?" Tarah raised an eyebrow but continued to smile.

"Actually, I don't drink at all," William confirmed, much to Tarah's surprise.

"Wow."

"Yeah, it's not the norm for a musician, I'll admit it, but I just don't like how drinking makes me feel." He shrugged. "I used to drink when I was a teenager and got myself into a lot of trouble when I did, so now it just doesn't appeal to me."

Tarah nodded in understanding. She wondered what kind of things he did when he was younger but didn't want to ask. It was really none of her business. Chances were good that he hadn't done anything too outrageous.

"I'm impressed," she said. "I think that's great."

"It's not a big deal."

"I think it is," Tarah replied.

The two continued to talk until almost two in the morning. She found out his age (twenty-three), his birthday (March 16), and that he aspired to become a professional musician. She was starting to feel at ease talking to him when William announced that he had to take off for the night. "I still live in Springdale, so we have about an hour's drive home." Tarah recognized this as the small town where Wendy had grown up. She felt slightly disappointed that he didn't live in Thorton. "I've got to drive since the boys are drinking, and I'm getting really tired."

"I know the feeling," Tarah admitted. "I was so tired that I almost didn't come out tonight."

"Well, I'm glad you did." William offered her a warm smile and she returned it. They stared at one another for a long moment. "I'm glad we met."

"Me too."

The two exchanged phone numbers, and he promised to call her soon. Tarah was still feeling burnt over her last relationship, so wasn't getting her hopes up. Sure, he seemed like a great guy, but who knew? She had once thought the same thing about Jeff.

She watched him disappear into the crowd, and she made a dash for the door. Tarah rushed to her car and drove home. That night she had a dream that she and William were performing on a stage together. She woke up the next morning feeling hopeful, but wasn't sure why. Dreams were just dreams.

No sooner had she risen from her bed, when the phone rang. Tarah reluctantly answered it. Her mother was on the line.

"Tarah, I can't believe your brother went out and got Sara pregnant. She's just a child herself." Clair Kiersey started to rant. "I told them that there are ways to prevent that kind of thing, but I was clearly wasting my breath."

"Mom, I think that ship has sailed," Tarah couldn't help grinning at the thought of her mother lecturing Bobby and Sara on modern day birth control. It kind of made up for her shitty birthday dinner.

Ten minutes later, she was off the phone and eating a piece of toast and honey. The phone rang again. This time it was Wendy.

"I had the best time last night," she admitted to Tarah, who still felt a little offended that her friend had bailed on her for a man. But she once again bit her tongue. "Chris was so incredible. I think I'm in love."

"You just met him." Tarah assumed she was talking about the guy from the night before. Wendy had made no attempt to introduce them.

"I know, but we just had a connection," her best friend insisted. "We have everything in common." She continued on about her night, not really taking the time to ask about Tarah's birthday evening. It wasn't even an afterthought.

Twenty minutes later, Tarah was drinking coffee and looking out the window when the phone rang again.

"Hi, Tarah? It's William."

"Hi." Tarah felt her heart race. She hadn't really expected him to call, but she was excited that he did.

"I hope it's not a bad time."

"No."

"Cool, listen, can I come to Thorton and meet with you?" William sounded so casual over the phone. "There's something I need to talk to you about. Are you free this afternoon?"

She didn't hesitate to say yes.

CHAPTER FIVE

▼

Tarah sat on the front step of her building. Slouched over and feeling very small and irrelevant, she waited for William to pick her up. She wore a comfortable, black T-shirt, jeans, and a worn, blue sweater. She probably should have taken more care when dressing, but her heart just wasn't into it. Still feeling slightly depressed, she just didn't have it in her to try to impress a guy.

Lost in her own thoughts, Tarah almost didn't see the big, burgundy van parking in front of her building. Feeling someone's eyes burning through her, she looked up and saw William behind the wheel. Raising her eyebrows, she ran down the steps and opened the door to the awkward-looking vehicle.

"This is you?" Tarah asked without thinking. "I mean, of course it's you." Jumping inside, she closed the door behind her and turned to William. He wore a grin on his face as he slowly eased back onto the road.

"I know what you're thinking." He made brief eye contact with her before returning his gaze to the street. "Only people with kids or stoners drive around in vans."

"I was actually thinking child molesters or rapists," Tarah quipped, and both of them began to laugh as she was quick to add, "Not to suggest anything."

"Well thank you for *that*." His face pulled into a quick smile. "I'll be honest, this wouldn't be my first choice of vehicles. Unfortunately, the band has to get our equipment from point A to point B. So, I'm stuck driving this piece of crap around. I'd much rather be driving a Prelude."

"I understand."

"So, where are we going for coffee?"

"Doesn't matter," Tarah said.

"Hey, this is your neighborhood, not mine," he said mildly, while turning off her street. "You tell me."

Not thinking, she quickly suggested the same place she and Wendy went to on the previous Sunday. But as she walked through the doors ten minutes later, Tarah began to regret this decision. Suddenly, all the painful memories that filled her heart the previous weekend were recaptured, frozen in the walls of that same coffee shop. Every little thing was a reminder of her misery from that particular day. It suddenly hit her full force, causing her mood to deflate even further than it already had.

After they both ordered coffee, William signaled for Tarah to pick a table; she purposely didn't choose the same one she'd shared with Wendy the previous weekend. Time to change her karma. She attempted to put on a smile on her face as they sat down. But even though William didn't know her very well, he seemed to see through her act.

"I hope this wasn't a bad day for us to meet." He pensively studied her face and spoke with an even tone. "I promise to not take too much of your time."

"No, that's fine. I'm fine." She looked away nervously. "Just preoccupied. What did you want to ask me?"

"Um, okay, well when I was talking to Wendy last night, she was saying that you sing?" He took a drink of coffee and removed his jacket to reveal a Van Halen T-shirt.

"Yes," she said. "I mean, I'm not in a band or anything like that, but I sing a little bit."

"She said you sang in front of an audience a few times?"

"Yes." Tarah started to nod again. So *this* was what he wanted to see her about? She couldn't help but feel a little letdown. "Not much, but I have."

"Okay." He leaned forward on the table as if to confide in her. "Listen, our band is in the process of writing an album, and for one song we need a female vocalist. I was just wondering if maybe you'd be interested?"

Before she could answer, he quickly continued, "I'd have to audition you, not that I doubt that you can sing, but to see if you're right for the song."

Tarah suddenly felt the urge to get out of there. She just wanted to go home to her quiet apartment and avoid the world, so she abruptly said "Yes."

William stared at her for a moment. His eyes shifted to the other side of the room, and he sat back in his chair. He was clearly uncomfortable as he made eye contact with her again. "Listen," his voice remained calm. "It's up to you. Really, I don't want to make you feel pressured to do anything." He seemed to be checking his words carefully as he spoke, and Tarah automatically felt guilty.

"No, that's fine." She forced herself to calm down. Leaning against her hand, she looked toward a light that suddenly shone through a nearby window. "I'm sorry, I didn't mean to seem like a bitch to you. It has nothing to do with you. I just had a really bad night the last time I was on stage, and I was thinking about quitting the singing thing all together."

"Oh." William looked lost for words. "Did the audience react poorly?"

"No, not at all," Tarah said with a smile. "In fact, I did great. I sang in front of a large crowd at Jerry's, and it went really well. The audience was encouraging. I just had something really shitty happen to me after I sang. It's kind of a long, really screwed up story." It wasn't even about Jeff or the horrible incident of that particular night, it was the fact that her life felt like a joke. Her family, customers at work, and now boyfriends treated her like shit. And her so-called best friend was only around when no man was taking up her time. She felt defeated and alone.

William nodded and Tarah realized that he probably thought she was a nut. Maybe she should just stop talking.

"I think I understand." William nodded. "I just don't think you should let anything that happened *off* the stage, affect what happened *on* stage. It's all about the performance."

He spoke as if he had twenty years of experience in the industry, but yet William was her age. There was something about him that she trusted, so Tarah listened to what he had to say.

"You just have to move forward," he continued. "And I don't know how serious you are about the music industry. Maybe you just want to do jams or whatever and that's cool. But I'll tell you that if you ever want to get into this seriously, you can't dwell on small stuff. *Especially* when your bad night had nothing to do with being on stage. I did understand that correctly, it had nothing to do with being on stage, right?"

"I actually think I did the best I ever had that night." Tarah spoke honestly. "And you're right, I have to get over this other crap. Let it go."

"So, can I ask what happened?" William finished his coffee. "Not that it's any of my business, but it might help to talk about it. It's probably not a big deal."

"I got kicked out of the bar," she blurted out.

William tried to mask his surprise. "For?"

"Getting in a fight." Tarah looked away from him and felt her face getting hot. "It's a little embarrassing."

"Did you drink a lot and get into a fight with some girl?" William guessed.

"Actually, it was with a guy. It was my ex-boyfriend."

"I take it he wasn't an ex before that night?"

"No." Tarah shook her head and sunk down in the seat. "I was on stage singing and doing really well. He was suppose to come see me because he knew I was nervous, but he didn't show up. At least, I didn't think he showed up until I was on stage and saw him in the audience with another girl." She hesitated before telling him the rest of the story. Feeling humiliated, she avoided eye contact with him until she was finished.

William raised an eyebrow. "Oh … and you confronted them and they were … ah, doing something, right?"

"She was." Tarah forced another smile on her face.

"Oh, I think I got the picture," William said. "I understand. He did a horrible thing, and it's particularly disrespectful that he did all this while you were up singing. I did understand that correctly, right?"

"You did." Tarah felt relaxed. William seemed to really care.

"Okay, well we've established that you are a passionate person," William remarked, and Tarah laughed. "So, are you that passionate about music?" He seemed to purposely change the topic and she appreciated it.

Tarah considered his question for a few moments before she answered, weighing the pros and cons in her head. She did love the feeling of excitement when she was on the stage. If it hadn't been for Jeff on the previous weekend, her night would have been perfect. She loved singing, but did she want to do it in a serious way? Was she passionate?

"I think I am," Tarah finally answered. "I am."

When William dropped her off later that afternoon, he encouraged her to keep working on her vocal lessons and to get on stage as often as she could. "Listen, we're trying to iron out some details within the band right now, but I'll contact you after we do," he promised. "We're just at odds about a few things, so I'll keep you posted."

Tarah nodded, and she got out of the van. "Okay, you've got my number, so let me know."

As he drove away, she rushed into the building and upstairs to her apartment. Tarah's first instinct was to grab the phone and call Wendy, but something stopped her. William was her best friend's ex, and it didn't feel right to have a crush on him, let alone to share it with her. But he was so understanding and wonderful, she was dying to tell *someone*.

Tarah walked away from the phone and sunk down on her couch. Staring across the room at an unmade bed, she wondered what to do. It was Wendy who had told William that she sang, so it wasn't as if it was unthinkable that they had met to discuss music. However, Wendy probably didn't count on Tarah having a crush on her ex either. Suddenly, a simple situation seemed much too confusing.

Tarah decided to not dwell on it. The best thing to do was to keep her promise to William and continue singing. She'd just have to push her feelings aside till he contacted her again and see what happened. And although he had confirmed to Wendy that he was single, it didn't mean he'd necessarily be interested in her either. Maybe he just saw Tarah as someone to work with in the future.

There wasn't much to do but to wait.

CHAPTER SIX

▼

William called Tarah a week later. And that was only to tell her that his band was playing in Thorton on October 3, at a bar called The Tourist.

"You should come and check it out," he encouraged in their short conversation. Tarah sensed that William wasn't interested in anything beyond her singing abilities, since he hadn't really made any other effort to see her. She was disappointed.

The worst part was that when she mentioned the upcoming show to Wendy, her friend insisted that they should go.

"And Chris would love to come with us," Wendy gushed over the phone. "We had such a blast the last time we saw them play." Tarah wondered if Wendy even remembered that she was also there that night, let alone the fact that it had been her birthday. But she remained silent.

Tarah reluctantly agreed to join Wendy and her current flame to check out the band. She felt nervous and uncomfortable with the idea of seeing William again. And thought of being a third wheel with the new super couple of the year didn't help much either.

Going anywhere with Wendy and Chris was just embarrassing. The two of them were hardly shy about showing their lust for one another whenever the mood struck, with no regard for Tarah or anyone else. And even though Wendy attempted to make it sound cute by saying that it was like they were "the only two people in the world," Tarah would curtly remind her that they actually weren't alone at all. Not that it made a difference.

As soon as they arrived at The Tourist on the night of the show, Tarah spotted William on the other side of the room. Their eyes automatically met and she quickly looked away. Her face felt hot as Wendy grabbed her arm and pulled her close to the bar, where William and his band were standing. Chris swaggered along behind them.

"William!" Wendy rushed over to hug her ex-boyfriend. Tarah assumed that it was probably to make Chris jealous, but in fact, he actually appeared to be intimidated. Meanwhile, William looked completely baffled and just seemed to go through the motions. The rest of the band was looking Wendy up and down with interest. "When Tarah told me about your show, I knew we just had to come and cheer you on."

"Ah, thanks." He glanced at Tarah with a confused look in his eyes. "I appreciate it."

"So, when does the show start?" Wendy asked.

"Actually," William glanced at his watch, "pretty soon. We set up earlier, before the bar opened. We just need to do another sound check."

"Cool." Wendy almost seemed to bounce as she said the word. She grabbed Chris' hand and made some quick introductions before dragging him up to the bar. Tarah was about to quietly follow, when William touched her arm and carefully pulled her back.

"You always try to make an escape, don't you?" He smiled and gestured toward the guys who stood with him, who up until that point, were too busy checking out Wendy to notice that Tarah was even present. "I want you to meet the guys." He turned his attention to the other three band members. "This is Tarah, the girl I was telling you about. The one with the voice." Tarah felt a self-conscious smile slide over her lips as she glanced from one face to another. They were definitely a very unique group.

The first guy she was introduced to was Eddie, the band's drummer. At only seventeen, apparently the bars were making exceptions allowing him in their establishments in order to play. However, as he shyly stood aside with a bottle of water in his hand, it was quite clear that the freckled faced boy with the huge hazel eyes was not going to cause any trouble. In fact, after giving Tarah a fast smile to say "hi," he quickly put his head down, allowing his straight brown hair to cover his eyes. He was sweet and she liked him.

Next, she was introduced to Michael, the bassist, and much to Tarah's surprise, William's younger brother. However, the differences between the two were instantly clear. To begin with, Michael didn't even try to hide the look of contempt in his eyes as he turned toward Tarah. He didn't smile or show any gesture of good will, but instead glared at her and nodded. His dark hair was uneven and appeared to need a serious trim, while his beard only served to make him appear even less attractive. Although Tarah was pleasant to William's brother, he made her feel extremely uncomfortable.

The last person she met was the lead singer. Brian Thomas had dirty blond hair and dark blue eyes, and quite honestly was very attractive. And clearly, no one knew that better than him. He gave Tarah a once over and quickly started to flirt with her until Michael abruptly pointed out that it was almost time to go on. William shot her a nervous smile and the next thing she knew, Tarah was watching the four of them playing on stage.

"Aren't they great?" Wendy leaned over and asked. "I love that singer."

Tarah didn't agree. Once again, she found his performance fell flat. It just wasn't very good, he screamed rather than sang and it was annoying. Tarah decided that his looks were his biggest asset on stage. She was particularly offended by how he ruined one of her favorite songs, "Photograph" by Def Leppard. As her eyes flickered around the room, Tarah sensed a similar impression from other people at the bar. In fact, Wendy was one of the few who seemed to thoroughly enjoy the music.

"Hey," someone tapped her arm and she swung around to see John Duffy. He was once her high school counselor, but now he was simply her friend. Although he was quite skinny and his clothing caused him to easily fit in with the younger crowd, there was something in his face and eyes that quickly told another story. He was definitely a man who had seen and done a great deal of things in his day.

"Hi." Tarah was relieved to have another music enthusiast at her side, so they could critique the lead singer of Tanked together. "I haven't seen you in ages."

"I know, you'll have to call me one day soon and let me know how things are going," he yelled over the music. "We'll grab some coffee and catch up."

"I definitely will," Tarah agreed and turned her attention toward the stage. "What do you think of this show?"

Raising his eyebrows, his blue eyes gave her a questionable look. "It's like nails on a chalk board, Tarah, it really is. But I'm on my way out, I'll talk to you soon though?"

"Sure." Tarah gave him a quick wave and watched him rush toward the exit. He always had a bounce in his step, and his dark curls flapped around as he walked. Looking toward the band again, she noticed that Wendy and Chris were having an intense conversation. Her friend finally turned to her and blatantly announced that they were leaving because Chris wanted to have sex. "Do you want a drive home?" Wendy offered.

Tarah glanced at the stage; she doubted that William even remembered that she was in the room. He hadn't looked her way since the show began. Plus, getting a cab later was something she neither desired nor could afford to do. Maybe it was time to call it a night.

"Sure."

The next morning Tarah didn't feel like dragging herself out of bed. So, instead, she stayed curled up and turned on the television.

"—where she ripped a photo of Pope John Paul II. The outspoken singer was protesting alleged child abuse ..."

"Wow." Tarah was suddenly very alert, as she watched the reporter talk about the previous night's episode of *Saturday Night Live*, where Sinead O'Connor made a controversial and symbolic protest to the Catholic Church. They replayed the incident, showing the singer ripping the pope's picture. The audience was dead silent. And Tarah suddenly felt very alive. She could feel the intensity of the moment. Regardless of anyone's opinion, no one could dispute the fact that through her music, Sinead O'Connor had made a huge statement. She had created a moment that would be talked about for years to come because she was hitting a nerve. It was courageous and brave. It was beautiful. And it was at that very moment that Tarah discovered that she wanted to be on a stage—that she wanted to reach into people's emotions and challenge their beliefs.

A part of her wanted to call someone. William? She was just about to reach for the phone when it rang. It was Wendy. She was crying.

"I just woke up and Chris was already gone." She managed to get the words out before continuing to sob hysterically. "He left me a note saying that it just wasn't going to work out between us, because I was too flirty with other guys."

"Why? Cause you hugged William last night?" Tarah couldn't think of any other incident that would fit that category, at least not that she had seen.

"Well, that too," Wendy admitted and cleared her throat. "But every time I talk to a guy, he naturally thinks I am trying to pick him up." Tarah thoroughly believed there were three sides to this story, but she wasn't about to interrupt with her own theories. Like a good best friend, she just listened as Wendy went on about their wonderful night of amazing sex, those tender words shared in the early morning hours before dawn, and then *the note*.

Remembering the horrible end to her relationship with Jeff, Tarah tried to give words of understanding and compassion. Eventually, Wendy stopped crying, and Tarah told her about the Sinead O'Connor incident from the night before and how it inspired her.

"I don't blame her," Wendy sniffed. "All religion is corrupt."

"I think she was brave," Tarah said dreamily. "It makes me want to get out there and sing more than ever before."

"Then do it!" Wendy encouraged. "Call William, see what's up with the song thing." Tarah had confessed that part of the story to her. "Maybe ask him for me if he's still single," she giggled.

Tarah laughed with her friend but felt her heart sink. Chances were, if Wendy wanted him, she could get him.

Ending their conversation, Tarah decided to take her advice and call William. When a woman answered the phone, she abruptly hung up. Suddenly, she felt defeated. It clearly wasn't Wendy she had to be jealous of after all, and in a way, it made her feel closer to her friend. Had the crush on William pulled them apart?

The two girls became inseparable. Both single, they went for coffee, shopped at the mall, and had drinks together. When they were both broke, they sat around in each other's apartments and listened to Pearl Jam or Nirvana, while smoking weed. They decided that if they didn't have guys around, at least they had a strong friendship. With neither being particularly close to their families, both girls relied on one another for emotional support and advice. Tarah felt lucky to have Wendy as a friend and quickly forgot all the times that Wendy had ditched her when a guy was in the picture.

William didn't call after the show in early October. As the month came to a close, Tarah managed to push him out of her mind. She spent her days at work, at least one evening a week singing at a jam session somewhere in the city, and most of her other time with Wendy talking about their futures and dreams. While Tarah dreamt of being on a stage in front of a huge audience (and not being scared), Wendy simply wanted to move up in her banking career. Both were emotionally drained from the constant demand of customers who were never happy, and their dreams and friendship were what helped them through the toughest of workdays.

"Hey, at least you don't have to deal with people's money," Wendy pointed out one evening when they were comparing notes about their jobs while sitting in a tattoo parlor waiting room. Wendy had made an appointment to have her belly button pierced. "People get really fucking pissed when it comes to their money."

"I can kind of understand that," Tarah admitted. "But if you're bitching out a sales clerk 'cause they can't rip themselves in half and serve two people at once, it really doesn't make sense."

Wendy had to agree with that point.

But the beauty of friendship was about to be slightly tarnished. It happened when Wendy spotted a particularly attractive employee of the tattoo parlor. That was the beginning of the end. By the time the needle went through her skin, Wendy had already made a date and her next obsession began. Once again, she all but disappeared from Tarah's life.

In November, Tarah found the courage to return to Jerry's. Her performance was strong, and after singing a couple of songs, Tarah stepped off the stage feeling proud If anyone remembered the incident in September with Jeff, she had been forgiven. The supportive bouncer from that specific night gave her a nod and wink when he saw her on stage, causing her to almost laugh in the middle of an acoustic version of "I Was Made for Lovin' You" by Kiss. She thought of how much easier it was to perform before an audience now. Tarah still got the familiar butterflies in her stomach before a show, but she generally felt more confident. And when she doubted herself, Tarah just thought back to the inspirational moment when Sinead O'Connor tore up the Pope's photo on stage. Now, *that* was more courageous than singing in some unknown dive.

"Great job." She heard from behind. Tarah felt her heart beat a little faster when she turned to see William. His head was tilted slightly and he gave her a sincere smile. "You have an *amazing* voice. Wendy certainly didn't exaggerate. Love that version of the song, too."

"Thanks," Tarah said appreciatively. "I've been working really hard at my singing."

"I'm very impressed."

Tarah smiled and said nothing.

"You know, it's kind of funny, I was thinking of you today when I drove by and saw the jam session sign outside." William grinned. "Thought of your story about that night you were kicked out of here. Thought I'd come in and check out the live entertainment, whether it be music or otherwise."

Tarah laughed. Behind her, someone else was on stage singing a song by Pearl Jam.

"Which brings me to my next question," William shuffled around bashfully. "Um, I was actually going to call you."

Tarah felt her heart thumping loudly and anxiously waited for him to finish.

"How would you feel about being the singer of my new band?"

CHAPTER SEVEN

▼

"Needless to say, a lot has changed since the last time we talked." William was standing over Tarah's kitchen table, emptying the remainder of the coffee pot into his cup. He returned it to the nearby counter and carefully turned off the bright orange light on the coffee maker. "There, you don't have to worry about me burning the apartment building down."

Tarah gave him a tired smile and watched William return to sit down. His eyes were bloodshot and the aroma of coffee filled the room. Outside, the night was still and silent. Most people were probably in their beds, sleeping. Although she loved William's company, Tarah wished she were too. After all, it was almost five in the morning. It had been a long day, and he certainly gave her a great deal to think about.

"Well," William sighed loudly and glanced at his watch. "As soon as I drink the rest of this, I'll take off. And you can get back to me whenever you decide. You've got my new number?" He watched Tarah nod and he did the same. "Good. I hope you say yes." He gave a sincere smile.

Fifteen minutes later, Tarah stood looking out her kitchen window as William headed toward his van, which sat lifelessly on the side of the street. And then he was gone, and she was left with information that needed to be processed. Exhausted, she decided to go to bed and put the many thoughts that were swirling around in her head to rest. Maybe the morning would give her the answers she needed.

But the next day wasn't much better. At ten thirty in the morning, Tarah was staring at her clock and mentally reviewing segments of their conversation. William really wanted her to be the singer for his new band. If it were only as simple as that, but Tarah already knew it was so much more. Grabbing the phone, she quickly decided to call John. He'd know what to do.

"Would you like to grab a coffee later, Tarah?" John always spoke clearly, with great emphasis on each word. "We can meet wherever you choose."

"Oh God! I am so coffeed-out right now, you have no idea," Tarah began to laugh and briefly described how she and William had been up quite late drinking a pot of really strong, horrible brew. "Can we just meet at like, McDonalds? I'd love to have a cheeseburger right about now."

"Sure, wherever you wish," John was always so easy to get along with. He was such a nice man and someone who proved to be a good friend. "Say, in about an hour?"

Tarah was so hungry that she arrived at McDonalds long before John and quickly gobbled down a cheeseburger and large fries. She was drinking the last of her chocolate shake when John arrived. He waved from the counter and proceeded to order his food. Tarah sat back and felt bloated.

"Well, well! Looks like someone inhaled her food." John sat across from her in what appeared to be the quiet section of the restaurant. On the other side of the room was a group of mothers and out-of-control kids. Tarah continually shot them dirty looks.

"I was so hungry!"

"Sure you weren't partying last night?" John raised his eyebrows and watched Tarah shake her head.

"I didn't really eat much last night before I headed to Jerry's, and then I was up late talking to William," She pushed her tray aside and leaned forward. "Boy, do I have a story for *you*."

"Go ahead," John bit into a Big Mac. "You've got my undivided attention."

She proceeded to describe the last few months of her life to John, summing up everything had happened to her since their last real conversation. Tarah told him about the fiasco with Jeff, meeting William, and her own experiences singing on stage. She even confessed having a crush on Wendy's ex and her feelings of guilt over the entire situation.

"Sounds like a plot from *Melrose Place*." John gave a mischievous grin.

"What's *Melrose Place*?" Tarah was confused. "Is that a movie?"

"No, it's a nighttime soap." John stopped eating and gave her serious look. "What? I thought every woman watched that show?" Tarah shrugged and he gestured her to carry on with her story as he took another bite of his burger. "So, you saw him last night at Jerry's? Were you singing?"

"Yes." Tarah nodded. "And when I got off stage he approached me and asked if I'd consider singing for his band."

"So, he is currently singerless?"

"Exactly."

"So, are you going to do it?" John's eyes lit up. "Are you going to replace that terrible singer from Tanked?"

"Well, kind of." Tarah tilted her head. "See, William wants to completely change the band. New singer, new name, and he also wants to get another guitarist so he can play lead."

John nodded as he nibbled on a fry. "Um, makes sense. I think that's a good course of action."

"Exactly, but I'm not sure if I want to do it."

"Why not?" John pushed an erratic curl out of his face. "I actually assumed that you were going to say yes. You already like singing on a stage, this is just the next step."

"But it's not the same." Tarah shook her head and leaned in closer. "I go up and sing a couple of songs and leave. If I'm in a band, I have to be a performer. I've got to keep the audience interested, talk to them, sing a bunch of songs, you know. I can handle being the center of attention for five minutes, but when I really started to think about it, I'm not sure if I am up for an hour of entertaining an audience."

"Sure, I can understand what you're saying," John replied thoughtfully. "Entertaining is a lot more work than it actually seems, but at the same time, you're already doing it—only this would be on a slightly bigger scale. No one expects you to walk on stage and be perfect the first time."

"I'm just not comfortable with it," Tarah confessed. "What if I humiliate myself? I mean, when I used to think about being in a band, it did appeal to me. But now that the possibility is real, I'm scared."

"Okay, Tarah," John stopped eating for a moment and raised his eyebrows. "A big part of life is getting out of your comfort zone. It's good to be a little scared sometimes. You will grow more as a person if you go out and do this thing. If it isn't for you, then you can always quit down the line."

"But William's really serious about this band thing. He's determined to make it in the music industry." Tarah frowned. "I don't want to jump in with both feet and then decide to jump out in a few months. I wouldn't feel right doing that."

"Why don't you just focus on the here and now," John suggested. "You don't have to worry about six months from now. Just today. I think you should call him up and say you'll do it and don't give it another thought."

"Maybe you're right." Tarah gave a small smile. "Besides, he wants to work with just me for a week or two alone before we put the band together. He hopes to find someone for guitar by then. William really has this planned out so well, you'd think it was a business and not a band."

"Well, Tarah, you know it is sort of the same. The music industry *is* a business. You have to sell and market yourself. People make a lot of money off the industry." John took a sip of his drink. "Actually, to be planning things out so carefully already is really quite smart on his behalf."

"Oh, he is smart," Tarah agreed. "He thinks we should all just practice for awhile so we are 'tight' as he puts it." She grinned and looked down at the table. "And then go play cover songs and eventually write our own stuff. He doesn't want to rush ahead too much. Trust me, he has it all planned out. We were up all night talking about it."

"Once again, I admire his attitude and initiative."

"I know you're right about going through with this." She looked back at John, who was chewing the last of his fries. "It's just scary."

"You'll be fine; plus it isn't like you have to jump on stage tomorrow."

"True."

"I think it sounds like fun. I think you should do it," John encouraged.

"I'll try."

"Great!" he said. "Oh listen, when you guys play your first show, let me know. I'll come and take some pictures of you singing."

"Thank you," Tarah gushed. She knew that John was a very talented freelance photographer and was flattered by his offer. Although he concentrated on wedding pictures, recently he could be seen at many shows around the city photographing the musicians. He always challenged himself and Tarah realized that she had to do the same.

"It would be my pleasure," John insisted. "So, what's the deal with this William guy? Is he interested in you?"

"I don't know," Tarah confessed. She felt her face getting warm. "I'm not sure if it matters anyway; he's Wendy's ex. I'm not sure if it is appropriate for me to be chasing after him."

"Okay, first of all, most men in the Thorton and surrounding areas are Wendy's ex." John started to laugh. "Plus, isn't she with that guy? Remember from the night I saw you at the Tanked show?"

"Oh, they broke up," Tarah said. "Mind you, she's dating some other guy now. She met him at a tattoo shop."

"She works fast." John glanced at a tall blonde at the counter. "So, have you met him?"

"Not yet. I've barely seen *her* since they hooked up, let alone him."

"Some things never change." John rolled his eyes. "She's a great friend when no guys are around, but once one is in sight, Wendy is missing in action."

"True."

"So, that whole Wendy thing aside, maybe William is interested in you. You seem interested in him," John observed. "Then again, if you're in a band together, dating could make things tricky."

"I can't visualize being in a band or being with William, at least not yet."

"But both are possible," John reminded her. "I think you just have to set out on this journey and see where it takes you. You never know, you could be a rock star someday, or maybe you'll be William's girlfriend someday. Maybe both."

Tarah laughed. "Sure, John."

"You have to be optimistic, Tarah."

"I know."

"Hey, and if the band doesn't know where to practice, one of my students was telling me about a place you can rent just outside of town. I can find out more details if you wish."

"Actually, we have a place," Tarah said, and her eyes lit up. "William and his brother are house-sitting for a friend of his who is working in London for a year. This guy said we are more than welcome to practice in the basement, as long as we don't make noise too late at night, and the neighbors don't complain."

"Wow, that's even better."

"It is. It's cheaper too. Plus the entire band was living an hour away. Now, William and his brother will be at that house here in Thorton. I think the drummer is thinking of dropping out of school and moving here too."

John made a face. "He shouldn't drop out of school."

"I know, William is trying to convince him to stay in, but we'll see."

"It's nice to have dreams, but he also needs his education," John said. "I'm just glad they got rid of that horrible singer they had."

"Yeah, Brian Thomas has moved away and is looking for a new band," Tarah confirmed. "Good riddance. He was horrible. I guess he was William's roommate for a few months and it didn't go so well."

"Everything works out in the end." John smiled brightly. "I think you should be very excited. It sounds like you have some interesting possibilities lined up. You never know what the future holds, Tarah. You just have to get out there and see where it leads you."

Tarah felt hopeful when she left the restaurant that afternoon. John always knew exactly what to say. He was right. You only live once, and sometimes you have to take a chance.

When Tarah arrived home that afternoon, there was a message on her machine from her dad. He wanted her to call him. She promptly erased it and called William.

"Hello?"

"Hi, it's me." Tarah spoke in a small, childlike voice.

"Hey! How's it going today? Sorry I kept you up so late last night." He spoke apologetically. "I guess I was just hyper, thinking about all my ideas I had for this band."

"That's fine," Tarah assured him. "I made my decision."

"And?" William asked hopefully.

"I'm going to do it," Tarah confirmed. "I want to sing for your band."

CHAPTER EIGHT

▼

Tarah wasn't prepared for all the work that was involved in singing for a band. In fact, it hadn't even occurred to her that the flawless performances on stage or in music videos were a direct result of hours of planning and practice. After long days of stocking shelves and helping customers at work, Tarah was often tired enough without going to William's house to practice for the evening. But she did it.

"I never thought singing would wear me out." Tarah observed on the second night, when she and William were alone at his place. Much to her relief, Michael was stuck working evenings at his job and wasn't able to join them. Like her, William usually worked till five and had evenings off. Tarah was surprised to learn that he was a mechanic at a local dealership. He rarely revealed personal information about himself, choosing instead to discuss music. It never occurred to her that he had a "real" job.

"I went home last night and crashed. Mind you, I had a long day at work." Tarah said.

William carefully stood his guitar on the floor. His gaze was fixed on Tarah, but he remained silent. The two of them had sat in the dark, chilly basement for over three hours, and the exhaustion was showing on her face as she leaned against a nearby wall. She wore the same sweater as she did on the day they met in the coffee shop.

"I'm thinking about going back to singing lessons," she continued, attempting to ignore the awkwardness between them. William was unusually quiet that night, which made Tarah wonder if he had doubts about her singing ability. "I used to go to this lady and she was really good."

"Your voice is fine," he muttered, and looked at the ground. "I think the only issue you're having is possibly straining it. You should try to focus on singing from down here." William patted his stomach while looking back into her eyes. "Not that I was ever a lead singer, but I've always done most of the backup vocals."

Tarah nodded. She recalled the same comment being made by her singing coach and knew he was right. Still, she couldn't help but to feel uncomfortable with his quietness all night. She decided to ask him if anything was wrong.

William raised an eyebrow and a smile crossed his face. "Oh, it's nothing. I'm just tired I guess. But thanks for asking."

Tarah glanced at her watch. It was after nine o'clock. "Maybe we should wrap it up for the night?"

William nodded. "I agree. And maybe next time we can pick out specific songs that we want to do when this band finally comes together." So far, they had just played around with the acoustic versions of different songs, but nothing in particular. Tarah felt as if they were spending as much time discussing their musical preferences and ideas as actually practicing. Fortunately, so far they had the same vision for the band.

"So, you might've found a guitarist?" Tarah asked as they headed toward the stairs that lead to the main floor. "Did you talk to him yet?"

"Yeah, for a few minutes today." William spirits seemed to lift as they walked up the steps together. "I guess he's been in a few bands and I've heard he's pretty good. A guy at work knows him." They reached the top step and she noted how he towered over her. Then again, at only five foot one, she was used to people being taller than her. "So he's coming over tomorrow night to discuss things a little more. I guess we'll see from there."

"Good," Tarah replied, and walked in the direction of the living room where her coat and car keys were sitting on the couch. "What's his name?"

"Jimmy something-or-another." William began to yawn and stretched. She noticed his shirt rising briefly, revealing a hint of what Wendy referred to as the "treasure trail." He caught her watching, and she quickly looked away, grabbing her jacket off the couch.

"I see."

"So, we'll see how that goes. You can come over too if you want." William's eyes widened, but he was still expressionless. "It'd be fun."

"Okay, I will," she agreed, said good night and left.

The following evening, Tarah almost dreaded going to William's house. Clearly something was wrong, and she had to get to the bottom of it. It just wouldn't make sense to get involved with this band if he was having second thoughts about having her as a singer. She reluctantly decided to just ask him and get it over with.

However, upon arriving at William's place it was clear that she wouldn't have her chance right away. The thunderous sound of guitars met her at the front door and stopped Tarah in her tracks. It suddenly hit her; *she* was going to be in a rock band. It was no longer just a fantasy, nor was it two people hanging out and playing around with songs in a damp basement. This was really going to happen.

The music seemed to become louder and its continuous flow caused Tarah to become skeptical that they'd even know she was at the door. In fact, she had to ring the bell a few times before the guitars abruptly stopped and footsteps could be heard pounding on the stairs from the basement.

William had a huge smile on his face when he opened the door. It was clear that whatever bothered him the night before was no longer an issue. But Tarah still wanted to get everything out on the open and decided to talk to him after this other guy went home.

"I think we found our guitarist." William's eyes were lit up. "This guy's fucking amazing."

Tarah laughed as she walked in the door. It was one of the few times that she actually heard William swear. "Not just good, but *fucking* amazing. I'm impressed."

"You will be." He gestured toward the basement.

Twenty minutes later, Tarah couldn't disagree with William's analysis of the situation. Even though she was hardly an expert on guitars, it was clear that Jimmy Groome was no amateur. He played particularly difficult songs by artists like Jimi Hendrix and Eddie Van Halen among others. And he was a likeable guy, down-to-earth and friendly, but clearly serious about his music. It was just what their band needed.

"You're welcome to join the band. It's yours if you want it," William grinned from ear to ear. "I'm impressed man."

"Thanks." Jimmy nodded to William then quickly made eye contact with Tarah. "I'm in."

"Cool," she muttered, not knowing what else to say. Tarah noted that he dressed like Kurt Cobain and even wore his black hair similar to that of the grunge idol; his bright blue eyes seemed to pierce through her. He was about average height, her age, and had a collection of tattoos on his arms. Jimmy later told them that he was a bartender at a dance club, which kind of surprised Tarah. He didn't seem like the type to work in that kind of bar, but William later said it was because he was a "lady's man" and thought that was the appeal.

William and Jimmy talked shop for about another twenty minutes; Tarah attempted to put in her two cents on occasion, but mostly she just listened. They both were clearly passionate about their music and the industry as a whole, discussing everything from their favorite performers to the kind of band they wanted to create. Jimmy showed a great deal of enthusiasm over the fact that their singer was going to be a "chick" rather than a guy, insisting it put them at a great advantage musically. Tarah wasn't sure if he was being sincere, but appreciated the compliment regardless.

Eventually Jimmy announced that he had to take off for the night, and the three headed upstairs to the door. He and William shook hands and said they'd catch up again on the weekend when Michael and Eddie were available. He then turned to say good-bye to Tarah, winked at her, and slid out the door.

"We hit it lucky finding him right away," William insisted, as they left the kitchen and headed to the living room where they both sat on the couch. "I was afraid we'd have to go through a million people to find someone suitable."

"Me, too," Tarah agreed, and decided to jump right into her concerns from the previous night. There was no sense in putting it off. "Listen, are you okay with me singing still?"

"Yeah." William's eyes widened. "Don't tell me you changed your mind already?"

"No." Tarah shook her head. "I just thought that maybe you did."

"No." He looked puzzled. "Why would you say that?"

"You were really weird last night, I thought it had something to do with me,"

"No." William looked away and rubbed his eyes. He looked really tired all of a sudden. "Trust me Tarah, it had nothing at all to do with you."

"Okay."

"And I'm really sorry you felt that way." He looked completely sincere and his eyes were full of worry. "I didn't mean to give you that impression. It was just a bad day."

Tarah nodded. "Work?"

"No."

"Okay." She smiled sheepishly. "Sorry, I'm not trying to be nosey. I'm just glad it wasn't me."

"No, definitely not," William said. "In fact, I shouldn't have scheduled anything with you at all yesterday. November 15 is a bad anniversary, so I couldn't really concentrate."

Tarah assumed it was the anniversary of a bad break-up. "I'm sorry to hear that."

"Yeah, so, anyway." He cleared his throat.

Tarah suddenly didn't think he was talking about an old girlfriend at all. She bitterly thought that no man would have *that* much loyalty to make such a strong statement. In fact, she almost didn't take him very seriously, even though a nagging voice in the back of her head insisted she wasn't being fair.

She suddenly felt awkward. "Forget I mentioned anything."

"No, look, I'll just be straight with you." William seemed uncomfortable as he slowly began to explain. "My mom was diagnosed with breast cancer when I was in high school. Umm, She found a lump a year before and didn't tell any of us, just her doctor who told her not to worry because it was nothing. As it turns out, it *was* something."

Tarah felt the chills running up her spine. She already sensed where this story was going and it made her feel incredibly guilty for doubting his sincerity a few minutes earlier.

"When I was sixteen, the doctor realized it *was* cancer. By then it was too late to do anything." William spoke evenly, even though there was clear sadness in his eyes. "And she died on November 15 that same year. I know a lot of time has passed, but it's still rough. So, when I didn't seem with it yesterday, I really wasn't."

"I'm so sorry." Tarah felt a huge lump in her throat. Suddenly, the problems she had at sixteen seemed pretty minor in comparison. "That's terrible. So, how did you deal with it?" The house fell silent.

"Just kept on living." He spoke in a hushed tone and gave a slow nod. "It's all you can do. Dad brought us up the best he could, although I made his life hell for about a year afterward. I got into a lot of shit. You name it, I did drugs, drank, had a lot of very short term relationships, shall we say." His lips curved into a smile.

"Really? You?"

"Yeah, really, me. That's part of the reason why I don't do any of that stuff now." He tilted his head, keeping his eyes turned toward Tarah. "I took it all to excess and it almost did me in. I learned the hard way that doing all that shit doesn't fix anything; it just makes everything worse. And makes everyone's life around you, a personal hell."

"It couldn't have been that bad." Tarah wasn't able to picture William being the wild child he described.

"Yeah, it *was* pretty bad," he insisted. "I tried any kind of drug anyone put in front of me. I'm lucky I'm not dead in a ditch somewhere or living in a crack house. I was *really* lucky, all things considered. I drank all the time. Went to school hung over, usually high. It was amazing that I graduated, but by then I had my shit together and went to become a mechanic. I loved music, but at the time I was worried that I would get caught up in the lifestyle associated with it. Eventually, I just couldn't deny that music was what I was meant to do.

"But really, it's not unusual for teenagers to do that kind of stuff."

"I know, but my dad had enough on his plate without all this shit." William had slowly managed to turn to face Tarah as he told the story. "He had to pick me up at the hospital because I had my stomach pumped and twice at the police station. Nothing major. I had some pot one time and they ended up dropping the charges. I got in a fight another time. Still, he didn't need that shit."

"I went through women like they were nothing. I was a complete prick. But it all worked out in the end. I got my act together, and I chose a different kind of life."

Tarah was shocked. She didn't know what to say.

"So, now you know all the dirt on me," William said jokingly.

Tarah had a hard time wrapping her brain around all that information. She was still stunned when she left that night, but it quickly began to make sense. It became clear why he was such an authentic person, and she had new respect for him.

After that conversation, William seemed to warm up to her and to be much more direct about whatever was on his mind.

On the following weekend, Tarah met with the other four members of the band, and together, they decided to call themselves Fire. It actually came about after Jimmy and Eddie decided to do an impromptu punk version of the song, "Light my Fire" by the Doors. It was imaginative, creative, and after a few minutes into the song, particularly funny. For some reason, the name suited them. They all had passion and drive. But the chemistry and animosity that fueled the flame, was yet to come.

William, Tarah, and Jimmy got together regularly to practice. Eddie had decided to graduate from high school before moving to Thorton in the summer, but made a trip to the city every weekend to meet with the band. Occasionally, Michael would join them, but he was mostly working evenings and weekends. Tarah didn't mind, however, she still found William's brother creepy and was uncomfortable with him. Michael clearly disliked her, and Tarah had overheard him telling William and Jimmy that they really needed a male singer, not some "dumb bitch." She was relieved when the two band mates quickly jump to her defense.

"Are you shitting me, man?" Jimmy snapped. "She's hot and she can sing. What the fuck more do you want?"

"She's got an amazing voice," William added, "a very strong voice, and that's what we need for this band."

By mid-December, their first show was booked for January of 1993. Everyone was excited. Tarah was frightened. What if she got on stage and fucked-up or couldn't sing at all? At first she hid this fear from everyone, but finally decided to tell William. She did so three days before Christmas, when they were practicing some songs in his basement. It was a weeknight so Eddie wasn't in town, and Michael and Jimmy were both working. They were alone.

He was very understanding.

"Tarah, it's normal to be nervous. But you've been doing jams and singing with us for weeks; I think you'll be fine," he said. "You can't over think it or you'll drive yourself crazy."

"You're right." She nodded. "I just don't want to screw up. I know how much this means to everyone." Tarah sighed and added, "I know how much it means to you."

"It does, but I'm not worried." William moved his chair beside her. "You'll be great."

"I'm scared because I'm kind of a fuckup." She felt her throat get dry just thinking about it. "I seem to mess up everything. My family is a mess. Boyfriends have been a mess. My job is a nightmare. I can't even hold on to my best friend, why would this work out for me?" Tarah felt her eyes water and she turned away.

"Hey, don't say that," William insisted. "Wendy is a flake, if you want my honest opinion. She's lucky to have a good friend like you, considering she isn't a very good friend back. As for your family, as you know, we all have our issues and difficulties."

Tarah blinked back the tears and looked back into his eyes.

"Your job is just a job. It isn't forever. Most people our age aren't doing a whole lot more with their lives. Some aren't even working at all." Tarah thought of her brother when he said this remark.

"Relationships are always difficult. It's just what everyone goes through," William insisted. "It's life. You can't dwell on it. You make the life you choose. And you make decisions that work for you. And sometimes you make mistakes. But you always have to take a chance and do what feels right."

William hesitated for a moment, and it appeared that he was going to say something else. Instead, he leaned in and gently kissed her lips.

CHAPTER NINE

▼

"So, which one is Phil again?" Tarah sat on Wendy's living room couch, legs curled up beneath her, a cup of coffee in hand. The two had finally managed to get together for a catch-up session on the first weekend of January 1993, exactly a week before the band's first show. With the holiday season, Wendy's busy social life, and Tarah's regular band practices, the girls rarely had free time to spend together.

"Phil is the cute tattoo parlor guy from when I got my belly button pierced," Wendy reminded Tarah, as she plunked down on the other end of the couch with her own cup of coffee in hand. She was wearing a big sweatshirt and a pair of black leggings and appeared to be comfortable, happy, and content. "You remember him?"

"I actually didn't meet him." Tarah stumbled over the words. She couldn't help feel resentful over the fact that she was almost always cut out of her best friends life when a new man appeared. It made Tarah feel a lot less guilty about the feelings that were developing between her and William. Things had indeed changed since the last time the two girls really had time to sit down and talk. But for now, it would remain Tarah's secret.

"Oh well, it doesn't matter, he's history anyway." Wendy giggled. "We went to a party and had this huge fight. I was about to leave when I saw this other guy watching me from across the room."

Tarah faked an interest but Wendy's stories were *always* the same. What started off with "our eyes met across a room" was usually romantic history within six weeks. However, it appeared that this one was just getting underway.

"His name is Thomas," Wendy announced, and moved slightly closer to Tarah, who seemed to be guarded on the other end of the couch. "He's so cute. I mean, shaved head, sky blue eyes, and kind of has that tough look, but he's a sweetheart underneath it all."

"Hmmm," Tarah wasn't picturing that just yet, but held back on her assumptions. After all, Wendy couldn't *always* be a bad judge of character when it came to men. Maybe this one was different. "So, when did all this happen? The party, meeting Thomas thing?"

"A week and a *half* ago," Wendy answered, in the same way a children would proudly tell an adult that they're seven and a half years old. Did that half of a week really make a big difference?

"I see." Tarah put on another fake smile. "That's great."

"So, you'll meet him for sure next weekend, 'cause we're going to your show," Wendy said. "What did you say you guys named the band?"

"Fire, and there are another four bands playing that night. We're first though." Tarah didn't want to reveal that according to Michael that meant they were the band that people were least interested in. As he pointed out in a rehearsal, the *good* bands play last, and the first ones were merely there to be background music while the audience arrived. William had argued this point, of course, but to no avail.

"It's so cool, my best friend is in a band," Wendy gushed. "I've been telling everyone."

"Great." Tarah faked another smile and wondered how many people were going to show up that night. She was still very nervous.

For the rest of the week leading up to the show, the band practiced nonstop. With each passing day, Tarah found herself becoming more and more confident with the selections that William had chosen for them. He had considered various factors like what was within Tarah's vocal range, what songs made them sound solid as a band, and what he felt would cause positive audience reaction. William chose songs from the late eighties and more recent tunes so he could get a feel for what the audience enjoyed. After all, they were still not certain what their sound would be as a band.

William tried to reassure Tarah about the show. He pointed out that since they were the first ones on, chances were that the audience would be small. "Once you get the first show over with," he reminded Tarah, "you'll see that it isn't so bad; it *will* get easier."

"I hope you're right,"

"I promise."

To add to the swirling emotions Tarah was already having about the band situation, she now had to deal with her newly forming relationship with the lead guitarist.

Following their first kiss a couple of weeks earlier, William had been very upfront about his feelings for her. He admitted having a crush on Tarah, but feared that it would affect their working relationship in the band if they became romantically involved. They both agreed to take things slow and see how they materialized. Tarah, however, knew how she felt. She just wasn't ready to admit it.

The day of their first show arrived, and Tarah did her best not to worry. She had taken off the entire weekend from work so they could practice on Saturday afternoon and be prepared for the show that night. The day slid by and before she knew it, Tarah found herself at Jerry's talking to the bouncer who had once escorted her out of the bar after punching her ex-boyfriend. It felt like a million years ago. She hadn't seen Jeff since that night.

"So, you've got a band now." The bouncer grinned. "Good stuff! I hope you don't attack anyone tonight."

"I'll try my best not to." Tarah laughed. "I can't make any promises."

She was secretly thankful that he was teasing her because it helped to lighten her mood. Meanwhile, Tarah noted that her supportive best friend hadn't showed up yet. Shouldn't it have been *her* trying to make Tarah relax before the show? It made her feel even farther away from the girl with whom she was once close.

Moments before the show began, Tarah glanced around the room but didn't recognize anyone in particular. There were familiar faces, but mostly just the same barflies who frequented Jerry's on a regular basis. She was glad she hadn't told her brother or mother about the show. The last thing Tarah needed was for either of them to show up and criticize her.

And then she was being rushed on the stage.

The crowd was subdued, yet interested, as the music began. Just as they practiced, the first song Fire played was "No Rain" by Blind Melon. It was one of Tarah's favorites—and not just because of the beautiful lyrics and gentle vibe of the music. She also loved the video for the song. It featured a little girl who would become famous for dressing like a bee, dancing on stage to a group of hurtful strangers, and then seeking approval until she found like-minded people. Tarah cried the first time this video appeared on television because she knew how the child must've felt, and wondered when she'd find her own group of bees to dance with. Didn't everybody want to find the place where they belonged? A place where they fit in?

The song almost went without a hitch. Then Tarah forgot some lyrics. William warned her that this could happen and told her to just keep going as if nothing happened, which she did. Only one lone man sitting at the bar seemed to even be paying that close of attention, so she wasn't too concerned. Tarah knew that if she let that one mistake throw her off track, the rest of the night would be a disaster and she wasn't prepared to let the band sink.

It was when she started their second song, "Ain't Talking 'Bout Love" by Van Halen, that Tarah noticed John arriving at the bar. He was carrying a very expensive camera in his hand. She smiled in his direction and continued to sing, finding herself growing more comfortable. People started to flow through the doors, and she noticed by the end of that particular selection that she had drawn a small crowd. Tarah continued with songs by Nirvana, Aerosmith, and Led Zeppelin. All the while, John shot an occasional picture, and she pretended not to notice.

The final song they did was "Photograph" by Def Leppard. William had suggested this because his old band played it regularly, and he wanted to see the difference in reaction between Tanked and Fire performing the same number. Maybe it was because it was one of Tarah's favorite songs, or maybe it was because of the chemistry between her and William as they sang it together, but the atmosphere in the room appeared to change from the very first note.

Standing on stage in her black, schoolgirl skirt and tights, Doc Martens, and belly shirt, Tarah sang the song with a passion that lit up the entire room. It was then that John started to snap pictures of the band from every angle. He scrambled through the audience to get the perfect shots, while the crowd gathered closer to the stage. The room seemed to suddenly get smaller as the audience grew, most of who were suddenly very aware of the young blonde who flowed naturally across the stage. There was a hint of flirtation between her and the lead guitarist, whose voice only complimented Tarah's. There was something very different about this band. There was something that really stood out.

Tarah felt like a part of her, one that she never knew existed, was suddenly released. She hit the highest note of the song and somewhere in the room heard clapping meeting her on the stage. She turned and made eye contact with William, and between that and the intensity of the performance, when Tarah turned back to look at the audience it suddenly felt like she was having an out-of-body experience. Was this really happening to her? It was surreal, a level of existence she never knew was possible; it was the most incredible high of her life; it was a happiness that combined the best gift, the warmest smile, and the greatest love, all in one shot. And when the song stopped, and it was suddenly over, it was as if she hit the ground with a thud. But the warmth of the applause kept her going as she left the stage to get a drink. Her throat was dry and her heart was racing.

Strangers met her along the way to congratulate her on a great job, a wonderful voice, and for putting on a show to remember. Did someone actually say "a show to remember" or was she just not completely out of her dream world yet? And then John was in front of her.

"Tarah, that was incredible. That last song was phenomenal!" He grabbed both her arms tightly as if to emphasize his enthusiasm. "I took the most pictures then because you were in the zone, baby. And if you don't believe me, ask anyone in this room."

Tarah gave him a quick hug but was lost for words. There was just too much swirling around her head. She couldn't believe it was done so fast. As she thanked John, Tarah was met at the bar by a couple of older admirers who offered to buy her drinks. It was unreal. She had never had so much attention in her life. She felt like she was walking around in a dream.

Wendy finally caught up to her in the crowd and gave her a strong hug, "Oh my God! I wanted to cry when I saw you up there. You were amazing!" When Wendy finally let go of her grip, Tarah was surprised to see actual tears in her eyes.

"Thanks." She gave Wendy a warm smile back. "I'm happy you were here to see it."

"I wouldn't miss it, come on now!" She giggled, and turned around. Behind her was what Tarah observed to be a creepy looking skinhead. Was this seriously the wonderful new man in her best friend's life? He had very blue eyes as described to Tarah, but they were full of anger and hatred. Didn't Wendy see this too? He barely smirked to say hello. He was wearing, what Wendy often referred to as a wife beater and very loose jeans.

Tarah exchanged hellos and quickly found an excuse to get away from Thomas the skinhead, even if it meant leaving Wendy behind too. She wanted to find William and get his impression of the new man in her best friend's life. Her eyes searched the room and she noted that a next band was now setting up. It hadn't even occurred to her to help the guys take apart the equipment. Was she really that out of it? When she spotted William a few minutes later, she rushed over and quickly apologized.

His eyes lit up with humor when he listened to her saying how sorry she was for not helping them with everything. "Are you serious, Tarah?" He began to laugh, while the rest of the boys in the band talked amongst themselves beside him. "You were amazing and if anything, you deserved to go take a break after that. Don't worry about it."

"It felt more natural than I thought it would," she confessed. "I thought it would be awkward and uncomfortable but it wasn't."

William gave her a thoughtful smile. "It never is when it's right."

CHAPTER TEN

▼

Tarah felt like she was in a dream and didn't want to wake up. Even though the band's first show had finished a couple of hours earlier, Tarah was on a cloud and floating over the moon. It was the first time that she'd ever stood out in a room full of people. After all, how many times had she been to that same bar, only to be shoved and ignored by the majority of the clientele? No one ever seemed to realize that she existed before that night, but now Tarah had strangers approaching her and complimenting the band's performance. Men were hitting on her. Women were giving her envious stares. It didn't even feel like her life. These kinds of things just didn't happen to Tarah Kiersey.

At one point, she was alone in the ladies washroom, studying her own reflection in the mirror and wondering what had changed. She looked the same. Still had the same blonde hair, blue eyes, and lean figure as before that night. Her outfit wasn't new. She smiled the same as every other day. Nothing had changed. Tarah had even sung on a stage more than once, but yet something was different about that night. Was it because she was part of a band now? Did that mean something more?

It didn't matter. Tarah was enjoying the natural high of the night. Having a few drinks, she chatted with Wendy and reluctantly attempted to include Thomas in their conversation, but he didn't have much to say. Sitting at the end of the table, he only managed to make things more uncomfortable. If Wendy noticed, she ignored it.

"So, where did all the guys go anyway?" She sipped on a beer and gave her full attention to Tarah, which was something else very unusual about that night.

"They took their equipment home," Tarah answered, tapping her fingers on the bottle of water in her hands. Since she and William had agreed to spend time together later that night, she didn't want to have any more alcohol to drink. Especially considering that he wasn't a drinker at all. "They're coming back. Well, except for Eddie, he's a minor."

"He's a minor? And they let him play here?" Wendy seemed surprised by that information. "That's weird."

"No, they didn't mind him playing, but said he couldn't stay after that in case they got caught. It could shut the place down."

Wendy nodded and Thomas frowned at the other end of the table. He had been drinking a lot all evening and was getting quieter by the moment. At least Wendy's new boyfriend had chatted a bit earlier in the night.

"So, where are you guys going to play next?" Wendy's eyes lit up. "I can't wait to see you again."

"We don't have anything scheduled, at least not yet."

"I bet you will soon."

"I hope so."

Much to Tarah's relief, William, Michael, and Jimmy returned before the third band was finished playing their set. Jimmy headed right to the bar, while Michael followed William around like a lost puppy. In the beginning, Tarah had tried to give Michael the benefit of the doubt, but any compassion she once had for him was long gone. He turned out to be as unpleasant as he looked. In fact, it was hard to believe that the two brothers were related. William was gorgeous, caring, and thoughtful, but his brother was unattractive, mean-spirited, and an asshole. Tarah had even asked William once how he put up with his sibling and to that, he merely said, "He's family," and shrugged. She wasn't sure exactly what that meant.

"We're back, did we miss anything?" William grinned, and his eyes met with Tarah's but she quickly looked away. The last thing she wanted was for anyone at the table to know their secret.

"I was just asking when Fire is going to play again." Wendy sat up on the chair. "I *love* that name by the way, Fire! How cool is that."

William gave a polite nod. "I don't know when we're playing again, but I hope it's soon."

So did Tarah. She craved the rush of being on stage. It was very easy to see why musicians became enthralled and seduced with performing.

Jimmy joined them at the table. His eyes were automatically scanning Tarah and the bottle of water she held in her hand. "What's with the water, Kiersey? Can't handle a *real* drink?" A huge grin crossed his face, and his eyes lit up as he spoke. She was still just getting to know Jimmy, but it was clear that any kind of peer pressure he was inflicting on her was harmless and fun. "Come on, let's do some tequila shots." He gestured toward a wall full of alcohol, which was close to where they sat. "At least have a beer or *something*." Jimmy carefully took her arm in his hand and pretended to drag her to the bar. Tarah heard herself laughing as they pushed through the crowd and propped themselves up on the barstools. Jimmy ordered them each a shot of tequila. Trying to keep up with her new friend, Tarah downed the tequila and squinted in misery as she bit into a slice of lemon.

"Oh, God! That was disgusting." Tarah made a face. "I feel like puking after that."

"Oh, *come* on, don't tell me you didn't do tequila shots before?" Jimmy leaned in closer to Tarah and for a moment she felt slightly uncomfortable, but quickly realized he wasn't trying to provoke any kind of intimate contact.

"Yes, I've done every kind of shot," Tarah fired back. "But I don't have to like 'em."

"Understood, but you know what makes tequila shots taste better?"

"Chasing them with something that actually tastes good?" Tarah quipped.

"Nope, you just do a lot of them and slowly, they begin to taste better and better," Jimmy joked.

In the spirit of things, she decided to order a tequila sunrise. Both her and Jimmy joined the others back at the table and Tarah noticed that William was drinking cola. Even though he had made it clear on more than one occasion that he had no issue with people drinking around him, Tarah couldn't help but feel as if she were doing something wrong or inconsiderate. She noticed that Wendy was not at the table, but Thomas was still there. However, her best friend returned only minutes later.

"Hey, Tarah, I was in the bathroom and I saw this girl from work." Wendy spoke excitedly as she sat back down on her chair. "She saw me hanging out with you and was saying how much she loved your voice, and she also told me that you had a voice like the brunette in Heart. Isn't that cool?"

Thomas remained quiet and seemed to almost snicker into his drink; William and Jimmy exchanged looks.

"Yes." William nodded. "I honestly can see that, Tarah. You have a very strong voice."

"I'd fucking say," Jimmy threw in. "Ann Wilson can fucking sing, either of those Wilson sisters can sing, man. No fucking question there. You are *that* good, Tarah."

Michael was less impressed. "I wouldn't go that far."

And that's all he said. Tarah felt her confidence sink a little but didn't want to let on. She glared at him. Wendy was looking into her face and seemed to be reading Tarah's thoughts.

"Oh, fuck off, Michael." She turned to her right and shot the remark at him like a dart. "Don't be such a prick."

"Yeah, man, what's your fucking problem?" Jimmy was quick to join in on her defense. Tarah couldn't help but notice that William didn't say a word.

"Whatever," Michael snapped. "Live in your delusional world." He slammed his beer bottle on the table causing it to make a loud thud, spilling the liquid on Wendy's hand. Avoiding eye contact with all of them, he stood up and quickly got lost in the crowd.

Tarah didn't say anything but took a long sip of her drink. And when a waitress came around, she ordered another one. It wasn't until later when she got up to go to the ladies' room that she realized that her legs were slightly wobbly, her vision was somewhat blurred, and suddenly all Michael's words just didn't matter anymore. Nothing did. At least not until she was sitting in the stall, suddenly cut off from all the noises that were distracting her from within the bar. The echoes of music and people were still there, but for the most part she was hiding away from all the voices, other than the ones inside her own head. She was questioning all of the remarks people had made about her talent. She was wondering if Michael was right. Was she delusional? What if she were to wake up in the morning and all this was just a dream? Was it just a once-in-a-lifetime deal? Was this her fifteen minutes of fame?

Finally composing herself and stuffing her demons far inside her heart, Tarah flushed the toilet and went out to wash her hands. This time, she stared at the person in the mirror and didn't feel so confident. The girl who looked back at her was hopeless and pathetic. Her eyes were glazed over and full of anguish. There was a spark earlier in the night but it had disappeared. Maybe it had never been there in the first place?

Back to the bar she went and ordered another drink. Everything was becoming way too real for her now and Tarah just wanted to get back to the place she was only hours ago. She wanted to feel as happy and excited about life as she had after singing on stage. But how could you capture a feeling and hold it inside your heart? How could you find happiness and hold onto it forever, just as some people held on to misery for a lifetime?

Shortly after her return, Wendy and Thomas got up to leave. Flying around the table, Wendy gave Tarah a big hug and said she'd call her the next day. Thomas barely said good-bye to them, shoving both hands in his jean pockets and slouching over as he waited. Wendy cheerfully joked with everyone before heading for the door, and then she was gone.

As the night came to an end, Jimmy went to get a drink and seemed to disappear. Back at the table, William and Tarah discussed Wendy's new boyfriend.

"He may be an okay guy once you get to know him." William shrugged before drinking the last of his cola. "I know he seemed kind of like an idiot tonight, but he may be okay."

"I don't like him. I don't get a good feeling about him."

"Do you ever get a good feeling about Wendy's boyfriends?" he teased. "Seriously, though."

"I know, I don't usually like any of them," Tarah confessed, wondering if she was being too harsh. "But this guy, I don't know, I just don't get a good feeling about him—in a different way than the rest."

"Well, they say to always listen to your instincts. Let's hope you aren't right though, for her sake."

"Yeah." Tarah considered Thomas for a moment and finished her own drink. It was her sixth tequila sunrise. "I guess he probably won't be around long enough to worry about anyway." She forced a grin on her face, but her expression was otherwise sad.

"Want to get going?" William gestured toward the door. "It's getting pretty late and, ah, you're a bit drunk." He showed no judgment. "I don't want to have to hold your hair back later while you puke. Want to get something to eat?"

"What makes you think I will puke?" Tarah stood up from her chair. "I can handle it."

William laughed and pushed some hair out of her face as he rose. "Let's just say, I've held a lot of hair back for girls who also thought they could handle their alcohol."

Tarah hit him playfully on the arm, and they headed outside to his van.

"It's so cold." Tarah pulled on her jacket. A chill went up her shirt and sent shivers through her spine. She rushed to jump in the van door, pulling the jacket even closer to her body.

"Want to grab some food? A sandwich or something?" William asked, jumping in the driver's side and turning on the ignition.

"Kind of, but it's so cold, I don't want to move again till I'm home. I'll just get something there."

"I don't mind going in to get you a sandwich at Subway or whatever." He pointed to a nearby sandwich shop. "You can stay in the van and keep warm."

"Really?" Tarah was a little surprised by the offer. "Are you sure you don't mind?"

Twenty minutes later, they were sitting in Tarah's kitchen, both were eating a turkey sub. William did most of the talking, and Tarah began to yawn as she sobered up. It had been a long day.

"You look tired, I should get going soon so you can crash," William offered a few minutes later as he finished the last bite of his sandwich. "We can talk more tomorrow."

"It doesn't matter." Tarah wrapped up the rest of her sub and set it aside.

"No, you really look like you need to get to bed," He stood up and slowly headed to the door where he leaned in to kiss her; but there was something different this time. His lips were more forceful than usual, causing her to think back to the moments on stage when she looked into his eyes and felt as if they were singing only to one another. An intensity of that moment that was now erupting in her heart, and she found herself kissing William with more passion than they had ever shown to one another before. They always seemed to hold back a bit, but this time she allowed her body to just go with it. He was not shy to follow her lead, and with his hands on her back, he eased her closer to him. She heard herself moan gently, and that was the only sign he needed to turn off the lights and lead her into the bedroom.

CHAPTER ELEVEN

▼

Tarah had no idea how the music industry worked. It never occurred to her that the owner of Jerry's could have had some apprehension about allowing a new, unknown band to join his Saturday night lineup. So she was quite surprised to learn that they got in primarily because of her reputation at the jam sessions.

"The words *music* and *business* just don't seem to fit together for me," Tarah admitted to John one evening over coffee at a popular café. It was close to the end of January and the first time she'd seen her friend since the night of Fire's show. He brought along some of the photographs from that evening, and much to Tarah's delight, they were fantastic. She was quite pleased when he offered her a copy for their promotional posters.

"You'll get used to it." John wore a gray sweater that looked like it was two sizes too large for him. Not that he was very big in the first place. The lines on his face were the only sign that he was older than she was; his clothes, hair, and slim body made him look younger than his real age of thirty-five. "The music industry is a *huge* business. It's all about money. The record companies, the musicians, everyone wants their piece of the pie."

"It's just depressing," Tarah confessed. "It takes the fun out of it."

"It doesn't have to, always remember that it's a business, but don't dwell on it." John sipped his coffee and tilted his head slightly. "Just think of it this way. If your band goes on stage and does great, not only do you have local bar owners wanting you to play at their business, you also have a fan base that'll follow you around from show to show. And the more fans you have, the more you'll be in demand. Eventually you'll start playing bigger shows. It's kind of exciting really, not boring and dreary like business appears to be for you."

Tarah considered his words, and carried them with her from that night on. After their original show, there was a rumble about Fire, and eventually bar owners began to call. At first, it was mostly for smaller, weeknight shows. William and Tarah spent a great deal of money getting photocopies of posters made in order to advertise every one of their shows. However, with so many other bands out there trying to push their own music, Fire was often lost in a sea of colorful posters on college bulletin boards and at local pubs. It was also not unusual for William or Tarah to put up their posters only to find them ripped down a few days later, replaced with another local artist's advertisement. It was very discouraging.

By the end of February, Fire was becoming pretty well-known. Local bars were asking them to play weekend shows and the band was starting to see familiar faces at each of them. Much to Tarah's disdain, many of the young, female fans were there trying to get William's attention. He brushed it off as no big deal, always talking to the eager girls and attempting to be friendly, but made it clear to Tarah that he had no interest in any kind of hookup with these women.

"You have nothing to worry about," he would assure her, and she believed him. By this time, the two were spending more nights together than apart. Still, neither of them revealed their relationship to either their friends or family. In a way, Tarah felt strange keeping it a secret, and sometimes she worried that it was *he* who didn't want anyone to know that they were together. Of course, she knew it was just paranoia and insecurity that made her feel that way. He was usually the first person to consider fessing up and dealing with any backlash from Wendy, Michael, or anyone else. But Tarah wasn't ready for that. She wanted to hide in her secret world with William, because not sharing their relationship with others somehow made it more special to her.

In the first few weeks of March, the band was becoming increasingly busy with shows on most weekends. This, along with their work or school schedules, began to take a toll on them all. So in mid-March, when William's twenty-fourth birthday came around, they all decided to enjoy a weekend off to relax. The band deserved it. Since Fire had come together, they'd all worked nonstop either practicing or performing.

"I know what I want to do for my birthday," William announced a few days beforehand. He was lying in bed beside Tarah. They'd just awoken. "I want to go back home to Springdale on Sunday afternoon. Just you and me. I can show you where I grew up and the house I used to live in. You know, all that kind of corny stuff."

"I'd love to." Tarah gave him a sincere smile. She wanted nothing more than to learn everything she could about William. He was such a remarkable man, so kind and sincere. It took her a while to finally accept that he was simply just a good person, without the games or bullshit she had endured with other guys. She realized that having to grow up so fast at such a young age, made William a much more mature person than she was used to being around. Maybe even more mature than she was.

On Sunday morning, William and Tarah woke up early and slowly got ready for their drive to Springdale, which was west of Thorton. It was a small town, the same one Wendy grew up in before moving to the city to attend business school. Although Tarah had never been there, both William and Wendy's stories gave her a picture of what to expect. Or so she thought.

Arriving in Springdale, Tarah was taken by surprise. Unlike the boring, hick town that Wendy had often described, Tarah felt it was beautiful and relaxing. There wasn't much traffic and people seemed down-to-earth. William had never really said anything bad about his hometown, but he had given Tarah the impression that it was lacking in opportunities and was behind the times. However, she found it sweet, and a part of her just wanted to move away from the city life to somewhere less hectic.

"I love it here," Tarah announced as they walked along the main street sidewalk, hand in hand. "I just feel like I'm on vacation from my real life."

"I like the fact that we can be ourselves here." William gave her a sweet smile. "We don't have to hide that we're together."

"Yeah."

"Tarah?"

"Yeah?"

"I don't want to hide it anymore." He stopped in the middle of the sidewalk, and unlike in the city, people didn't push past them in a hurry. In fact, a little old lady took her time walking by the couple and gave them an encouraging smile. "I think we should tell everyone the truth about us."

"Okay." Tarah hesitated.

"I know it won't be easy with Wendy or Michael, but we just have to deal with it and move on. I don't want to lie. It's just not me." William searched her eyes and she just nodded. He was right. It *wasn't* him.

"Okay." She agreed but wasn't ready to think about how she was going to bring this up in conversation with Wendy.

"Mike isn't going to like it," William said, and they began to walk again.

"Because he doesn't like me."

"It's not that," William assured her. "I guess since mom died, he's just used to having me there. I'm the older brother and I've always been there for him."

Tarah didn't understand what one had to do with the other. Why did it matter if William was in a relationship with her?

"I think he's scared that if I get involved with someone, I won't be there for him."

Tarah wanted to protest and complain, but she remained silent. After all, it was William's brother.

"I know."

"As for Wendy, I think she'll be fine."

Tarah's best friend had recently broken up with Thomas, simply saying that the two wanted completely different things, and she left it at that. Since then, Wendy had met another guy. All Tarah knew about him was that he was divorced, his name was Brad, and he was in his early thirties. Although a part of her thought that there was a bit of an age gap between her twenty-one-year-old friend and this guy, William seemed to think that maybe it was a good thing. As he pointed out, maybe it would give Wendy more structure in her life. She needed someone mature. Tarah reluctantly agreed and admitted that she was always a little suspicious of her friend's boyfriends. But there was usually a reason for her suspicions.

Tarah and William spent the entire day together. After exploring the downtown area, they stopped for lunch in a small, but elegant café. Later they went for a drive, and William pointed out his family's home, the place he went to school, the house where Wendy grew up, and the fast food restaurant where he held his first job. The final place before they went home, however, surprised Tarah.

"Do you mind if I stop at the graveyard?" William asked, as they drove through the streets of Springdale. "I know it's kind of depressing, but I'd really like to stop by my mother's grave."

"Not at all." Tarah spoke gently. "I don't think it's depressing at all. In fact, I think it's kind of nice."

As they silently drove to the graveyard, Tarah considered how she rarely went to visit her own mother who was still living. And here William was, going to his mother's grave. It made her feel guilty. It made her feel like he was a better person than she was, but Tarah didn't verbalize her feelings.

The skies became dark along the way and by the time they arrived at the graveyard, a gentle sprinkle of rain had hit the van's windshield. Tarah was undecided whether or not to join him at his mother's tombstone. What was she suppose to do? She'd never been to anyone's grave before and had very little experience with death. In fact, no one close to her had ever died.

"Do you want to come with me?" William asked, after parking the van. "You don't have to; I know it's starting to rain."

Her first instinct was to say no, but there was something in his eyes that pleaded with her to join him. She said yes.

They walked in silence through the graveyard, hand in hand, as he led them through the tombstones. The smell of spring was in the air, and they trudged through the remainder of wet snow.

"It's right there." He pointed to her left, and she followed as he rushed ahead. She felt his hand squeezing her own and she squeezed back. They approached a small tombstone next to a fence. She read the words:

BEVERLY SUSAN STACY, 1948-1986

Tarah quickly looked away while William knelt down before his mother's final resting place. Everything around them was so quiet that she didn't even want to breathe for fear of ruining the moment. She wondered what William was thinking. How did you ever get over the death of a loved one? She naively hoped to never find out.

"Are you sure you don't want me to leave you alone?" Tarah asked nervously. She didn't even know if she was acting appropriately for a graveyard. Was she supposed to do something?

"No, that's fine." William flashed her a smile. "I should bring some flowers sometime this summer and leave them here. I don't know much about that kind of thing, but I know my aunt used to do that when mom first died. Not so much anymore."

"We'll do it this summer." Tarah leaned in and hugged him. She felt tears in her eyes but quickly blinked them away. "I feel so sad for you. To have lost your mother so young."

"It's just the way it turned out." William tried to reassure her as he slowly stood up. "It wasn't easy, but in another way, maybe it was a little easier because I was so young. I think death is more difficult when you're an adult. When you're a kid, you don't think about stuff like the things you didn't do or say, like you do when you're older."

Tarah nodded.

"I guess that's why telling people about our relationship is important to me," he said. "I don't want to ever regret anything or feel that I have to hide something. I understand why we've been hiding it, it was my idea too, but I just feel it's time to be honest. Life is just too short."

"I agree."

They left the graveyard in silence and then drove back to Thorton. Looking in the side mirror, Tarah was disappointed to leave Springdale behind. It was the escape she needed. And she'd look back to that day with happiness, especially when they both told everyone about their relationship later that week.

Wendy was a lot less dramatic about it than Tarah had expected—maybe even a little too calm. She wished them well but didn't really say much else about the entire situation.

Michael was pissed, as William later reported. He told his brother that it was never a good idea to "shit where you eat," and if the couple were to break up, their band would probably end too. Tarah hated to admit it, but he did have a point. What if they did break up? What would happen with the band? Would all this work be for nothing? Was it a good idea to work and be together at the same time? Was it a conflict of interest? It was surprising that Michael had made no personal attacks but just talked of the band. Maybe William wasn't telling her the entire story.

As for Tarah's family, she only told her mother about it during a phone conversation.

"Is he from a nice family?" she asked.

"Yes, mom," Tarah assured her; even though Michael was the only family member she had even met. William's dad wasn't at home on the day they went to Springdale.

"Does he have a job?"

"Mom, I wouldn't date a guy who didn't have a job." Tarah rolled her eyes. "He's a mechanic."

"Ah, nice." Her mother approved. "How do you know him?"

"We're in a band together."

"Yes, the band you're in." Claire Kiersey snickered. "You still doing that? Tarah you should concentrate on something more substantial than music. You're too smart for that."

"I like it."

"Well, it's a nice hobby."

"Yes, it is." Tarah didn't bother to explain to her mother that they were quickly becoming one of the more popular bands in Thorton. In fact, in recent weeks, local bars were rapidly seeking them out. They were making a name for themselves.

"So, this boyfriend of yours, am I going to meet him?" Her mother asked the dreaded question.

"Someday." Tarah smiled to herself.

There was a time when she would have been frustrated with all these invasive questions. But when she thought of how William no longer had a mother to pry into his life, she felt her own heart become light. "Someday soon, mom."

CHAPTER TWELVE

▼

"She had a little baby girl." Tarah could hear her mother's voice echoing through the hallway of the hospital, long before she could see her face. Suddenly, Claire Kiersey was rushing toward her, arms opened wide. She gave Tarah a strong hug before letting go to wipe the tears from her eyes. "A beautiful baby girl. I was in the delivery room with Sara when she went in. Oh, Tarah, you should've been here. You could've come in with us."

Tarah bit her lip. There was no way she would have gone into the delivery room, but she wasn't about to tell her mother that.

"So, what did she name the baby?" Tarah felt awkward standing under the bright lights of the hospital. All around her, medical staff and strangers wandered by, and she felt like she was stuck in a moment that would never end.

"Oh—" A tear slid down her mother's cheek, and her short hair fell flat on her head. She wore a pair of track pants and a matching jacket. "Caitlin Summer, and she took Bobby's last name for the baby. I was so relieved."

Tarah had no idea why that was relieving, but didn't want to ask. Did it matter? The two weren't married nor did they seem interested in the subject.

"Nice name," she said. She secretly thought it was kind of soap opera-like, but once again held back. It had been a long day, and Tarah wasn't interested in fighting with her mother. After working till five, she joined the band for a performance at Bluetown, a smaller bar on the city's north end.

"Oh, Tarah." Claire pulled her daughter aside to sit down on a nearby bench. "I wish you could've been there for the birth. Sara did so well. Bobby was so excited, he's in there with her now."

Tarah nodded. "I got here as soon as I could. We had a show to do. I figured she wouldn't have the baby this fast."

"A show?" Her mother's entire expression changed. Suddenly, her forehead was wrinkled and dark eyes stared at Tarah. "You were doing your band thing when your brother's baby was being born? Oh, Tarah, how could you pick that over your *own* brother?"

"Well, mom, we made a prior commitment to be there. We couldn't just, not show up." Tarah raised her eyebrows, surprised by her mother's reaction. "We had this booked for weeks, we can't cancel at the last minute. It could ruin us as a band."

"Oh, Tarah, no, don't tell me you really put that music thing ahead of your family." Her mother avoided eye contact with her. "I can't believe it. You have to get your priorities straight."

"I have." Tarah was a little taken aback by her mother's comments. Was she seriously suggesting that she drop this show, which their band was getting paid for, to see the birth of her niece? She wasn't even close to her brother or Sara. "My music is important to me, and our band is doing well. If we bail on a show, it looks bad on us."

"Well it doesn't look good on you to bail on your family," her mother lectured. "I'm very disappointed in you."

Anger rose inside of Tarah. It was one thing to not take her music seriously, quite another to try to manipulate her into feeling guilty. Why couldn't her mother understand that her band was very important to her? "Whatever," she hissed, and got up to leave, but Claire jumped up and grabbed her arm before Tarah could get away.

"Hold on, before you fly out of here, you had to come see your niece," Claire insisted. "And you're going to regret not being here for her birth when you see her."

Tarah silently followed her mother as she rambled on about how long the baby was and her birth weight. She wasn't sure what relevance that had but nodded as if she did. Her mother then reminded her that Sara had been two weeks overdue and had to be induced. Tarah didn't know anything about babies. Even as a teenager, she refused to baby sit anyone other than her own brother. Children weren't of interest to her.

When they arrived at the nursery, they stared through the glass and her mother pointed out the new addition to the family. Tarah, mindless, said the things she had always heard other women say about babies. "She's so tiny and cute. She looks like Bobby. I bet they're proud." But sadness crossed Tarah's face as she looked through the glass at the babies on the other side. It suddenly occurred to her that she had no emotional reaction to this child at all. In fact, to her, the baby looked the same as pretty much every other one in the room.

After receiving another lecture from her mom about not being there for the birth, Tarah left the hospital and went to see William at his home. She had left Bluetown as soon as their set was done and headed directly to the hospital, and she was curious how the show went over. Instinctively, she felt their performance was strong, but sometimes it was hard to read a crowd.

William opened the door. "Hey!" His face lit up when he saw her. "Come in."

Tarah automatically glanced around to make sure Michael wasn't nearby and was relieved to find that he wasn't. "Home alone?"

"Yeah, Mike went out with Jimmy to a strip bar." He ushered her into the living room, where the theme song for *Law & Order* pulled her attention toward the television.

"And you decided you'd rather watch TV over going to a strip bar?" Tarah teased as she plunked down on the couch. William sat beside her

Leaning in to give her a quick kiss, he gave her an honest smile. "Yes, I was hoping you'd stop by." He sat back on the couch. She did the same, only snuggling closer to William. "Strip clubs aren't really my thing anyway; they're a little raunchy for me."

"You really are the perfect guy, aren't you?" Tarah smiled.

"Obviously," he said with a straight face, then immediately started to laugh. "Don't get me wrong, I've been in a few strip clubs, but it's not my thing."

Tarah nodded.

"So, no baby yet?"

"Actually, there was a baby." Tarah hit the mute button on the television remote. "Apparently she had it before I arrived. Luckily, because my mom seemed to think that I was going to join them in the delivery room, which I wasn't."

"Really?" William said. "Not even for your brother's child?"

"My brother and I aren't close. And I'm just not into kids."

"Why not?" William tilted his head.

"I don't know, to be honest," Tarah admitted, and she turned to face him, with both legs curled up beneath her. "I'm just not a baby person. I don't know why not because I'm a girl and apparently we're all suppose to be baby people."

"Maybe you would be if it were your own," William suggested.

"I don't know," Tarah said. "And as for my brother, I think it's a mistake that they had a baby. They don't have jobs, and they live with her parents. How stupid is that?"

"True, it's not very responsible. But maybe this baby will make them want to do better," William suggested.

"You're such an idealist." Tarah leaned forward and gently kissed him.

"It doesn't make any sense to be any other way."

Fire continued to be busy throughout April. By the month's end, the combination of work and performing was wearing the band a little thin. Jimmy continued to play all their shows even though he had caught strep throat. Eddie was worn out because of the added demands of school as he reached closer to graduation. And Michael just became increasingly cranky and difficult to work with. Even William, who usually got along with everyone, was having heated arguments with his brother during rehearsals. As a group, they decided to not book any shows for a few weeks and take a small break. Tarah was tired but afraid that the lack of shows would make people start to forget about Fire.

"Don't worry about that," William warned. "It'll only add to the anticipation of our next show."

And he was right. When the band finally played again around mid-May at Bluetown, the bar was packed. The only low point was when a few drunken college guys attempted to boo them off the stage. Tarah felt her heart racing anxiously but continued to sing as if nothing was wrong. Eventually, the intoxicated guys were thrown out of the bar when they began to grab the ass of more than one female customer.

Unfortunately, it wouldn't be the only time the band was heckled on stage.

During a show two weeks later, they ran into a similar problem. While playing a sketchy bar that Tarah had wanted to refuse originally because it seemed like dive, they had more trouble. This time it was directed at her.

A group of guys in their early twenties were sitting at a table close to the stage when Fire began to play. At first, Tarah thought they were just drunk and rowdy when they started to yell at one another and laugh hysterically, but somewhere along the line that stopped. Instead, two of the inebriated guys screamed in her direction while the others laughed. At first, she wasn't really paying attention, but when she realized that they were tossing insults toward her, Tarah instantly felt like she was back to her first day on stage. Feeling flustered and awkward, she ended up screwing up some lyrics when singing "Dream On" by Aerosmith. Although she could tell they were insulting her, she hadn't heard what they said. But that changed.

"Hey you dirty whore, why don't you take off your clothes and really entertain us?"

And that's when she stopped singing. The band slowly did the same, and Tarah turned her attention on them.

"Do you have a problem, asshole?" she yelled out bravely, even though she felt sweat pouring out of her body. Her heart was pounding and she felt her face burning under the combination of lights and anxiety. She wanted this moment to end more than anything. Everyone was looking at her, and she felt the weight of their stares. She wanted to cry but held back.

"Yeah, fuckhead," Jimmy started to scream out toward the guys while taking his guitar off. "What's your fucking problem?"

All the guys at the table were yelling various comments to Jimmy now, and suddenly Tarah saw a beer bottle fly through the air and barely miss his head. The next thing she knew, he jumped off the stage and attacked one of the guys at the table. The rest of the band was right behind him, even William, much to Tarah's surprise, and she was left standing alone on stage. Stunned.

Some bar patrons quickly jumped to the band's defense, and before Tarah could process everything that was happening, two huge bikers along with Jimmy and Michael were throwing punches at the obnoxious guys who had heckled her. William was screaming at the guy who had called her a whore, and Eddie seemed to be shadowing him. Tarah felt someone ushering her off stage and turned to see an overweight lady in her early forties gently helping her through the crowd.

"Come on, honey, get away from all this craziness." She had long, black, curly hair and big, brown eyes that were surrounded by heavy, black eye makeup. She was almost bursting out of her low-cut top and wore three long chains around her neck. "I've been here before, dear, you want to get away from these idiots before you get hurt. A tiny little thing like you."

The stranger led her outside and proceeded to pull a cigarette from her purse. "Honey, once I was near a fight like that and got a black eye from just being at the wrong place at the wrong time. Trust me on this one; I've been around this stuff enough times."

Tarah guessed she had been around a lot in general, but she smiled at the stranger. She liked her. There was something unexpectedly motherly about her.

"Thanks," she barely whispered, and quickly cleared her throat.

"No problem, dear." The woman lit her cigarette, then extended her hand. Tarah shook it. Removing the cigarette from her mouth, the woman introduced herself. "I'm Lila."

"I'm Tarah."

"Nice to meet you, Tarah." Lila gave her a kind smile. "You have a great big voice for a little girl. Bet you hear that a lot."

Tarah laughed. "I do." She was wondering about the boys inside and hoped they were okay. "Do you think they'll call the cops?" She pointed toward the door.

"Oh no, honey, trust me, the last thing they want around here is cops."

"Good."

Lila took a long puff of her cigarette and nodded. "They'll break it up soon."

She was right. While the two women talked, Tarah saw two of the drunken guys who were heckling her being thrown out of the bar. Literally. Both landed with a huge thump on the pavement and immediately jumped up and started to run for their lives.

"Stupid little fucks," Lila said. and offered a shivering Tarah a cigarette. "Sorry, honey, forgot to ask if you wanted one." When Tarah shook her head no and smiled, Lila continued, "This is a biker bar and we don't get into anyone's business, contrary to what you may have heard. We just do our own thing and mind our own business and expect the same courtesy from others. But we don't want no dumb-ass drunk kids hanging around here, starting shit."

Tarah was a little surprised to learn that they were playing a biker bar, but did see Lila's point. "I really appreciate that they jumped in because my band may have been over their heads on this one."

"Oh, honey, that's men for you. They get their testosterone running and they instinctively want to either fight or screw. Don't mean they're good at either though," she said matter-of-fact like, and Tarah began to laugh.

"Well, one is better than nothing," Tarah countered, and Lila began to laugh with her.

Eddie came outside, and Tarah introduced him to Lila.

"Where's the rest of your band?" Lila asked, as she threw her cigarette into a depleted snow bank.

"Inside," Eddie said, as William joined them. His eyes were on Tarah.

"Are you okay?"

"I'm fine, a little cold, but fine."

He nodded and continued to watch her carefully as if he wanted to say something, but he looked apprehensive.

"You guys going to play for us some more?" Lila asked. "You're the best band we've had here in ages."

"Ah, I don't know," William said. "I just assumed we were done because of the fight."

"Nah," Lila insisted. "If anything, you'll probably have free drinks for the rest of the night. Considering you already added some excitement to this place.

Michael and Jimmy suddenly made an appearance. Jimmy's shirt was ripped, but other than that, neither looked worse for the wear.

"Man, those guys totally kicked those little fuckers' asses." Jimmy spoke excitedly, pointing at a group of bikers who were smoking nearby. "One was actually crying. Can you believe it?" He turned to Tarah. "Crying!"

Lila began to laugh and gestured for everyone to go inside.

"I believe it," Tarah said. "I just saw two of them being tossed out."

Fifteen minutes later, the band was back on stage and singing as if nothing had happened. No police arrived. No one got in trouble for starting a fight at the bar. In fact, suddenly all the bikers wanted to buy her and the rest of the band drinks, just as Lila had suggested.

After Tarah and William got back to her apartment that night, she plopped down on the chair and announced that she loved that place. "We have to play there again, everyone was so nice."

"Tarah," William gave her an angry look, "you do realize that we just played at a biker bar, right?"

"Yeah, so?"

"So?" William shook his head and for the first time, appeared to be frustrated with her. "The last thing we need to do is to be playing at a biker bar. Those guys are dangerous; you should've seen what they did to one of those kids in there. I thought they were going to break both his arms."

"They were assholes."

"They were kids," William corrected her. "Drunk kids, and regardless of how stupid they were, they shouldn't have been beaten up like that."

Tarah felt her heart sink. After everything those guys had said to her, and he was taking *their* side. She told him as much.

"Look, I know they were pricks, but I just think the bikers were a little too tough on them. I'm not trying to justify what they said to you."

Tarah sighed and looked up at the clock. It was ticking very loudly and she was a little drunk. It was three twenty in the morning.

"I don't want to fight," William said. "Come on, let's just go to bed. We can talk about it more in the morning."

But Tarah knew they wouldn't agree on this situation. William did things the "right" way, she knew a part of her enjoyed seeing those jerks get hurt. It was just one of the ways they were so different. Deep down, she knew he was right. But maybe she didn't want to be right.

When they had sex that night, William was much rougher with her than usual. At times, he was even hurting her, but she liked it. She wanted him to hurt her. There was a new intensity in their relationship that didn't stop outside the bedroom but seemed to overflow on every aspect of their lives together. He was still the same sweet guy, but they would never again be that same couple who held hands walking down the street. A crush turned to love. Disagreements turned to heated arguments. Jealousy became explosive. And the band's music became more powerful than anyone could have anticipated.

CHAPTER THIRTEEN

▼

Tarah would later say that the summer of 1993 was one of the best she ever had. Fire was very popular and showed a lot of promise. She and William were head over heels in love and planned to move in together later that fall when the person he was house sitting for returned to Thorton. Michael was happily dating some girl for most of the summer and was therefore more tolerable to work with. John was giving her a lot of great advice about the music industry and becoming a closer friend, since Wendy had almost completely disappeared from her life. Wendy's distance was probably the one dark spot that tarnished the pretty picture of her summer.

"When did this all start?" John asked Tarah one day when she expressed concern. The two had met during her lunch break at work. "Wasn't she always out of the picture when a new man came around?"

Tarah chewed on her ham sandwich and thought about it for a minute. "Yes, but not to this degree. I mean she was still in contact with me. Now, when I call her, she barely talks five minutes and says she has to go. That's if she answers at all."

"Have you tried to invite her to do something?" John was drinking coffee as usual. "Maybe she thinks that with William and the band, you're too busy for her."

"No, I don't think that's it." Tarah sat her sandwich down. "I think maybe she's mad because I'm with William. He was, after all, her ex."

"Yes, from when she was *sixteen*, Tarah. That was a long time ago and she dumped him, correct?" John reminded her.

"Yes, she did." Tarah nodded. "I understand what you're saying, but maybe she still has some feelings for him. I know she had a crush on him when we went to see his band last fall. In fact, that's the reason we went."

"Isn't that the night you met William?"

"Yes." Tarah began to eat her sandwich again. "And I realize that she ended up with some other random guy that night. I get that. But she seemed to cut me out of her life when I told her that we were together. It's one thing to think we had a date or something, but I kind of just threw this on her."

"But you did say she had another boyfriend. Have you met him?"

"No, but if she's mad at me, she may not want me to meet him."

"Tarah, I don't want to play the counselor role with you." John leaned forward. "But I have to tell you, I think this has more to do with your conscience than anything. Honestly, I think *you* feel guilty for being with her ex or from hiding it from her as long as you did. I don't think she has an issue with it."

"Then why is she not talking to me?"

He hesitated for a moment and looked away. "Tarah, I think Wendy is in some kind of controlling relationship."

"What?" Tarah began to laugh. "You can't be serious? Pretty, popular Wendy who goes through guys like they were socks? Not likely!"

"She goes through men like socks because she's really insecure." John spoke in a hushed tone. "And the fact that she's not around anymore since meeting this new man, kind of suggests it. At one time she'd at least be out with the guys she was dating, *somewhere*. But from what you've told me, you never see her anywhere: not at your work, not at the shows, nowhere. I'm not saying she's being beat up, I'm just saying that it sounds like she may be in a negative situation with this new guy. I have a bad feeling about it."

"Should I go see her?"

"Maybe you should."

Tarah still wasn't convinced that John was right. In her heart, she knew Wendy was angry with her because of William. Nothing else made sense.

Tarah did everything she could to renew the friendship. However, her phone calls were ignored and attempts to visit Wendy were a wasted effort. She was never home.

"I think she hates me," Tarah admitted to William one night. She lifelessly fell on the couch, defeated after her most recent effort with Wendy. "She isn't talking to me at all."

"Maybe there's something going on that we don't know about," William suggested, as he leaned forward to give her a quick kiss on the cheek.

"John thinks it's because she is in some kind of abusive relationship with this new guy," Tarah told him. "But I think she's not talking to me because I'm with you."

"I don't think it's because of me and you." William shrugged. "She was flirty with me at first when I saw her last fall, but that's about it. I don't know about the abusive thing though either."

It was when Tarah attempted to visit Wendy at the bank later that week, only to learn she had quit her job, that William showed some concern.

"She quit? Maybe she got another job?"

"Nope," Tarah replied. "They said she just quit."

Eventually, Tarah decided to leave yet another message on Wendy's machine expressing her concern. She tearfully confessed to John that she thought something was really wrong, but felt powerless to do anything.

"Just call once in awhile and let her know you are there for her," John suggested. "There isn't much else you can do. It's up to her now."

He had also suggested that William contact her family. Since they were both from the same small town, John said that perhaps they should be informed of her unusual behavior in case there was something seriously wrong. However, when William did so, Wendy's mom insisted everything was great. In fact, she said that her daughter had finally met the man of her dreams and was busy making wedding plans.

"She's getting married?" Tarah felt like someone punched her in the stomach when she heard the news. "I don't even know what to say. She just met this guy."

"I was shocked too, but her mother insists that she isn't acting strange at all." William put his arm around Tarah, seeing her blinking back tears. "Her mom thinks it's normal that once you "find a man," you just leave the rest of your life behind. She doesn't seem to understand that Wendy also left herself behind too."

Tarah slowly began to accept that Wendy was no longer her best friend— or her friend at all—after that day. She felt deeply hurt by the snub. It was the pain of this and other events in her life that inspired her when she was writing songs for Fire's CD that they planned to record and sell at shows. The entire band was supposed to work together on the music, but she, Jimmy, and William ended up writing all the songs. Most were high-energy rock, except one, which was about the hurt of an ended friendship. It was called "A New Life" and its lyrics expressed the sorrow of feeling dismissed by an old friend. When people later heard the song, they assumed it was about a relationship between a couple that went terribly wrong. However, a very small group of people knew the truth. One day, Tarah would learn that Wendy cried when she finally heard the song, because she knew it was about her.

Musically speaking, it was a great summer. Other than one strange incident where Prince turned his name into a symbol, it was pretty eventless in the entertainment world. Tarah and William listened to Pearl Jam, Nirvana, and a newer artist named Lenny Kravitz. Tarah became obsessed with the attractive singer and was always listening to his music, whether it was in the old tape deck of her car or a CD at home.

"Did you know that Lenny Kravitz helped Madonna write "Justify my Love?" Tarah asked William one evening over dinner. "I think I'm going to buy Madonna's *Sex* book. John told me he thinks it will be a collector's item some day."

William raised his eyebrows. "Well, her CD that went with it certainly has added to the mood on more than one occasion."

Tarah only smiled, embarrassed, and looked away. She always used to have the *Erotica* CD playing, especially when they were in bed.

As the summer came to an end, Tarah felt content with her life. She thought back to how much everything had changed in just one year. The summer before, she was almost too frightened to walk on stage to sing for a small audience at jam sessions. This summer, she was performing for hundreds of people at a time with little fear. It was still scary sometimes, but she could cope with her nerves. Partying was no longer her reason for getting through the workweek; she only drank on occasion now and only had a few drinks when she did. She felt like she was living on a completely different level. Her life was good, and she was much happier than she ever had been before—something she never would have thought possible just a year earlier.

Her relationship with William was great. Usually. But when they did fight, it was almost always on nights that the band played. Women seemed to flock to Tarah's boyfriend, even though she was often right next to him, and frequently propositioned William for sex.

The first time it happened, Tarah thought she was hearing things. It was clear they were a couple and yet this attractive *slut* was brazenly hitting on her boyfriend as if it were no big deal. She even suggested that Tarah could join in "if she wants," and William quickly turned her down and abruptly pulled Tarah away.

"I can't believe that just happened!" Tarah yelled over the music that now blared through the room, replacing their live performance a few minutes earlier. "I can't believe she did that!" A part of her wanted to tear the other girl apart, while the other side of her felt threatened.

"Don't worry about it," William insisted. "Some girls are groupies when it comes to musicians. It's the same thing with guys in sports or—"

"You have groupies now!" Tarah continued to grow increasingly upset. "Oh my God!"

"Calm down" William grasped her arm and took her into an empty corner of the bar. "It's just part of the music thing. You don't have to be famous to have groupies; some girls just think it's somehow important to be with a musician. Anyway, you have them too, so you should understand," he attempted to reason. But any so-called groupies that Tarah had were usually old or disgusting men. She didn't have guys who looked like Lenny Kravitz hanging off her. Not even close.

"It's hardly the same thing. That girl was gorgeous." *And falling out of her shirt*, Tarah recalled. Hadn't she seen William's eyes wander to the girl's cleavage? It was difficult not to look. Especially when Tarah's breast size was minimal in comparison. "How can I *not* be angry?"

"Because you know I wouldn't do anything," William said matter-of-factly. "Tarah, we've been together for months. I'm with you all the time, and it should be clear that I don't want to be with anyone else. Why would you even worry?"

Tarah didn't know how to respond. Suddenly all the music and people around her were suffocating and she just wanted to leave.

"Besides, if our band really makes it someday, this is going to be the norm. It's just the way it goes. And I can't be a prick to all these girls because they're fans, right? Doesn't mean I'm going to screw them, it just means that I have to nicely tell them no."

Tarah was silent. Suddenly she wanted nothing more than to talk to Wendy. Only another woman would understand her situation, but she didn't have any other female friends.

"I know," Tarah finally replied. "I know."

She glanced across the room to see Jimmy now talking to the same girl who had approached them. He clearly enjoyed the constant stream of women that flowed through these shows, but this woman didn't seem as impressed with him as she'd been with William.

But when Tarah caught another girl trying to hit on William a few weeks later in early September, she wasn't as understanding.

It was the night that her brother and his girlfriend decided to drop in to see Tarah sing. Much to her relief, the show had gone great, and even Bobby had to admit that the band had talent. Sara quietly agreed but didn't really say much. She was suffering from severe "baby blues," according to Tarah's mother, and Bobby was attempting to get her out of the depression. Since their daughter was born, her brother had actually found a job at a call center and was trying to better his life, just as William had once suggested. He was friendlier toward Tarah, even encouraging about her band. But as they were talking after a show that night, Bobby looked past his sister and in mid-conversation said, "Is that William with that girl?"

Tarah felt her heart racing as she turned around to catch another girl, a gorgeous brunette, grabbing William by the crotch. Without thinking twice, she flew across the room and shoved the girl on the floor. Before she had a chance to do anything, William roughly grabbed Tarah's arms and pulled her back. She felt fury as she watched the brunette slowly stand up and inform

William that he could do better. "Why would you want to be with her? If you want a real woman, come to talk to me."

Tarah tore out of William's grasp and grabbed the stranger's arm to pull her back, but this time the bar's bouncers were pushing the two girls apart. Tarah could hear her brother yelling at William; much to her surprise, he was defending her.

"Okay, enough girls." The larger of the two bouncers glared at Tarah, before escorting the stranger out of the bar. The other bouncer informed Tarah that he wouldn't kick her out *this* time, but not to let it happen again. It didn't matter. She was out the door before anyone could say another word. When she got outside, Bobby was on her heels.

"Tarah."

She turned around. Tears were streaming down her face. "I can't do this Bobby. I can't deal with this shit with other girls around him all the time. Maybe I should leave the band." She was gasping for air, and her brother quickly gave her a strong hug.

"Don't do that," Bobby insisted. "Tarah, you did great in there. I just can't believe he let that girl do that. What an ass."

He let her go, and Tarah wiped her tears away. She could see William coming out of the bar. "I'm sorry Bobby, I'll be fine. It's just one of those things."

"Tarah." William caught up to her. "I'm sorry, she just grabbed me, and the next thing I knew you were right there." He shook his head and seemed dumbstruck. "I swear I didn't even think she'd do something like that."

"Come on," Bobby jumped into the conversation. He had only met William one time before, and the two seemed to hit it off, but they weren't anymore. "She was hitting on you; she didn't just walk over and grab the goods. You gotta tell girls like that to back off, tell them that you have a *girlfriend*."

"Bobby, it's okay," Tarah said softly. "I'm fine. Thanks."

Bobby studied her face before slowly nodding and starting to walk away. "Tarah, if you need anything, I'll be inside."

"Look man, I'm really sorry about this," William apologized to Bobby. "I swear, I would never do anything to Tarah like that. Never."

"Okay." Bobby appeared skeptical and walked back toward the bar, but only after giving Tarah another long look.

"We have to talk." William ushered her toward her car. She was glad she brought it with her that night, rather than traveling with William in his van. "I don't want to do it out here."

She knew what that meant. He was dumping her. But why wouldn't he, she decided, there were lots of women who would gladly take her place. By the time she was in the car, Tarah felt numb and just wanted to disappear.

"Tarah, you can't get so jealous," William insisted. "First of all, you know I wouldn't cheat on you. And second of all, you know there will always be girls like that hanging around. It doesn't matter if I'm in a band or not, there are always other girls who want to get with a guy, even though they know he has a girlfriend. Some people are just like that. It wouldn't matter if we quit the band and moved to some hick town."

"But you know, or I thought you knew, that I'd never cheat on you." William spoke calmly while Tarah just stared into her steering wheel. She felt frozen and couldn't move. "I'm sorry about what happened back there. I swear I didn't do anything to encourage it, and your brother probably had a point, I should've gotten rid of her before she tried something like grabbing me. I certainly didn't think she'd do that. I guess I'm a little naïve."

"But we can't let stuff like this get between us, if there is going to be an us."

"If you want to break up with me, just do it!" Tarah heard herself yelling. "Go, just go! Go with that girl. Do whatever you want."

"Aren't you listening to me?" William raised his voice. "That's not what I said."

"You just said *if* there's going to be an *us*." Tarah turned to him with accusing eyes. "It's like you're threatening me."

"No, that's not it!" he snapped, and frustrated, he leaned against the back of the seat with his eyes closed. "Listen, I've got to help the guys get the stuff together, and then I can go to your place and talk about this some more. Or I can go to my house. It's up to you."

Tarah didn't say anything. She couldn't speak.

"I'll go to your apartment." And then he was gone.

She pulled out of the parking lot in a fog. Luckily, there wasn't much traffic at that time of night. She drove through the city and cried hysterically. What was she doing? She knew William wasn't lying to her, but yet she continued to push him away. What if he didn't come to see her later that night? What if he changed his mind and left with the other girl? Tarah imagined them together naked and quickly pushed the thought out of her head. Love was much harder than she thought.

But he did show up. By that time, Tarah had washed her face and put on her nightdress.

Rather than using his own key for her apartment, he rang her buzzer from downstairs. Tarah let him in.

"So." William carefully observed her. "I hope it's okay that I came over."

"Yes." Tarah bit her lip as they both stood at the door. "I'm sorry. I wasn't right to accuse you of anything. I was just so upset when I saw you with that girl. I don't know what came over me."

"I can understand that," William admitted. "I probably wouldn't have been very happy if the tables were turned."

Tarah nodded.

"But you have to learn to control your temper. It's not just about you and me, it could seriously affect our band playing at places like that again." He was referring to Devil's Eight, a popular bar that had opened up earlier that year. "We could get a bad reputation, and I know you don't want that—neither do I."

Tarah knew he was right. That was the last thing they needed now that Fire had gained popularity.

"Anyway, it's fine. The owner heard about the fight and wasn't too concerned so it's okay."

"I'm so sorry." She rushed into his arms, and tears started to run down her cheeks again. He held onto her tightly and then they kissed. But the kiss quickly turned hot and feverish, and within minutes, William and Tarah were in bed.

CHAPTER FOURTEEN

▼

"I can't believe you're really getting married," Tarah said to her brother as she sat across from him on a late September evening. What Tarah *really* couldn't believe was how much her relationship with Bobby had changed. Since March, the two siblings had slowly turned into friends. It was a nice surprise. "Did you decide on a wedding date?"

The evening sun was going down and shone through a window, gently touching Bobby's face. He no longer resembled her kid brother, but now looked like a man. His short, dark hair and warm, brown eyes greatly resembled those of their mother, and Tarah looked like their father. Unfortunately, she didn't anticipate the relationship with her dad to change, as it did with Bobby. The two spoke only a couple of times since the birth of Caitlin, but there was nothing for them to talk about other than the newest member of the family. David Kiersey had been away for so long that he barely knew his own children. Tarah had learned that their father wasn't invited to the wedding.

"We're thinking mid to late November actually," Bobby said, and shrugged. "I don't know, it's not going to be a big deal. Just a few family members, that's about it. We don't want a huge gala or anything."

"I never thought you'd get married." Tarah stood up and walked into the kitchen. Opening the fridge, she grabbed two cans of Pepsi and returned to her seat. She handed one to an appreciative Bobby. "Even to Sara, it just never seemed to be something you were even considering."

"I know, but since the baby, everything's different." Bobby stared down at his unopened can. Tarah swore she saw a hint of sadness in his eyes. "I guess in a way I'm hoping that it helps Sara get out of this depression she's been in. I don't know what to do anymore."

"Bobby," Tarah tilted her head and wrinkled her forehead, "I hope you aren't marrying her just because she's unhappy. Getting married won't make her happy."

"No, I didn't mean it that way," he insisted. "It was something we were talking about. I just hope it helps lift her spirits. Plus, now that my job is going well, we're going to get our own place at the first of next month."

"That's only two weeks away," Tarah said. "Will you have enough money?"

"Yeah, I've been doing okay at work. I don't like it, but it's going well. I keep getting extra bonuses and stuff. I've also been takin' all the overtime I can get. It's paying off; it adds up real fast."

"Good. I'm glad." Tarah was sincere in her enthusiasm. She was happy to see her brother finally getting his life together. It was ironic that the baby made Bobby so happy, while Sara so miserable. Their family doctor had prescribed some medication, but it didn't seem to be helping very much from what Tarah could tell.

"Thanks." Bobby grinned. "Hey, would you and William like to stand up for us? Sara doesn't know who to ask to be maid of honor, and I need a best man. Do you think William would like to do that for me?"

The two had come a long way since the night at Devil's Eight when Bobby jumped to her defense. Tarah had never experienced such loyalty from him and had to admit that she liked it. There was something comforting about having a brother to stand up for you when the rest of the world seemed to be caving in. Bobby and William had resolved things only a few days after the incident and were fine with one another ever since. Bobby would eventually admit not only that he approved of William, but also that he felt Tarah had made a good choice for a boyfriend.

"I don't mind being a maid of honor," Tarah said. "Just don't put me in a god-awful dress."

"Hey, we aren't going too fancy either, so don't worry about that. It's going to be very informal, with a nice, little reception afterward."

"As for William," she continued, "I'll talk to him about it later on when I see him."

William said yes that night, and the wedding plans were officially underway. Claire Kiersey spent the upcoming weeks making all the necessary arrangements, almost driving Tarah insane in the process. Her mom seemed to think that every little idea she had for the wedding should be discussed on a daily basis. Tarah didn't see what all the fuss was about, but went along with it.

Meanwhile, Fire was continuing to flourish. The band continued to work on songs for their CD. Most were a nice mix of rock, with a slight hint of grunge. All were very catchy. The band wanted to incorporate their original material slowly into Fire's shows. That way, their fan base wouldn't be thrown off track if the band were to walk on stage with completely unfamiliar material.

It appeared that Fire's goal to have a CD finished before Christmas was unlikely. William had been calling the various studios, but most were booked, much to Tarah's dismay.

"It won't be till January." William broke the news to Tarah in mid-October. "I've been trying since the end of August to get studio time. According to the guy I talked to today, a lot of bands come here from Toronto because the rates are cheaper. And a lot of people from small towns come here because they don't have access to studios."

"Fuck!" Tarah threw herself down on the couch and rubbed her eyes. "This sucks. I was hoping we'd be done before the holidays."

"I know," William replied calmly from across the room. "But it can't be helped. Plus, we are going to need help recording, mixing—"

"Oh, God!" Tarah continued to display frustration by punching the pillow next to her. "This is way too complicated."

"It's not complicated," William insisted. "There are just a lot of steps to recording a CD. Plus, we don't have enough money for everything."

"I thought we did." Tarah opened one eye and stared at him. William was now standing directly over her.

"No, we have the money for studio time. Not for the CDs."

Tarah was quickly learning more and more about the business side of music and wasn't sure if she liked it.

The band continued to be busy throughout the fall. They were now playing in other cities, including a few dates in Toronto and the surrounding area. Fire was so busy, in fact, that most of the members were cutting hours from their day jobs in order to keep up with demand. Suddenly, people were starting to see that the band was serious about becoming successful. It was not just a hobby; it was a dream.

Tarah would smile when she thought of the first show they played, almost a year earlier. They were the opening band on stage that night, unknown to the crowd. She'd been so scared—petrified in fact. Now she walked on stage with ease. And now, they were the final band to play each night. People crowded in bars to see Fire. It was unbelievable and amazing at the same time.

In early November, the band had their first taste of the press. It happened when the city's largest newspaper wrote an article about Fire. Even in that original article, written by *The Thorton Report,* they were given a taste of what was to come—and the band would sit together, for the first *and* last time, dissecting a story about Fire.

"They did say we were one of the most promising bands in the local area." William tried to put a positive spin on things, but the others didn't share his enthusiasm.

"They said the only thing that made us memorable was *her*." Michael pointed his finger at Tarah like it was a loaded gun. "That she parades around stage half naked."

"Actually, the article said 'Tarah was dressed provocatively,'" Jimmy corrected him. "And it was meant in a good way."

"Yeah, but she mentioned the fight I got into a few weeks ago." Tarah felt her face burning. Apparently, the journalist who had written the story had taken in most of Fire's recent local shows, to give a "fair and balanced review of Thorton's hottest up-and-coming band." Unfortunately, one of the nights in question was when Tarah attacked the girl who so boldly put the moves on William. "It was embarrassing enough without having it printed for the whole city to see!"

"She didn't even say what the fight was about," Eddie quietly added. "It was like she was saying that Tarah just randomly attacked this chick. It's not fair." He gave Tarah a sympathetic smile.

"People won't even care about that," William insisted. "She said a lot of good things too and announced upcoming shows. She also mentioned 'A New Life' and 'Promises.'" He referred to their original songs. "That's a good thing."

William was wrong. People *did* care about Tarah attacking a girl at one of their shows. In fact, her mother was the first person to react, but Tarah refused to talk about it. Fortunately, Bobby didn't reveal any details either. Friends, coworkers, and relatives all asked Tarah about the incident, and she found herself reliving it again and again. Eventually, she just got frustrated with the questions and became defensive.

"Why do people fucking care?" Tarah complained to John one day. "With all the positive stuff in that article, people focus on the one bad thing! I can't believe it!"

John shook his head apologetically. "Tarah, I hate to say it, but the media doesn't play fair. That's what the celebrities deal with every day—worse. Tabloids fabricate entire stories. That's how they make their money."

"But I'm not a celebrity," Tarah retorted.

"But you *are* a celebrity, Tarah," John said. "You're a *local* celebrity and that may not seem like much, but to a certain degree, you're playing the same game as the celebrities who you see on TV. Just on a smaller level."

Tarah was stunned. She even considered contacting the reporter who had written the story to tell her side, but William stopped her.

"Just let it be. Don't add fuel to the fire," he advised.

In mid-November, William went to his mother's grave on the anniversary of her death. Tarah noted that he wasn't as quiet as the previous year, but he also wasn't himself. She caught him staring absently into space, as if in deep thought. It was difficult for her to understand how his mother's death had impacted him.

About a week before Bobby's wedding, Tarah decided to stop by Rothman's photo lab on her break to buy some film for the wedding. She briefly chatted with her co-worker Linda while half-watching the printer as it sent a steady stream of pictures into their own slots and then pushed them forward, much like in an assembly line. At the end, a technician quickly flipped through each set of photographs and packaged them. Noticing another customer was behind her, Tarah slowly began to walk away. But something stopped her.

Out of the corner of her eye, she could see Wendy's face. Turning toward the printer that displayed everyone's photos as they processed, Tarah watched as her former best friend's wedding photographs shuffled in front of her eyes, one by one. She felt the tears burning beneath her lids as she witnessed Wendy standing beautifully in a white wedding gown with a man who Tarah had never met, surrounded by family and her new friends. The people in the photographs weren't even recognizable to Tarah. And as her heart raced and she rushed to a nearby bathroom, Tarah realized that one of the people she really didn't recognize was Wendy.

On the day of her brother's wedding, Tarah thought about those pictures again. As she watched Sara walk down the aisle, say her vows, and bite into her wedding cake, Tarah wondered what it would've been like to see Wendy do the same rituals. Would she have cried like she did at her brother's wedding? Would she have been Wendy's maid of honor? Would they have planned the wedding together? Each question nagged at her and made her realize how much she missed her friend. They had been through so much together, and now it was done. As if it never happened.

Throughout the ceremony, Tarah's eyes continually drifted toward William. Standing tall beside her brother, looking handsome in his tux, he was always ready to catch her gaze. She had told him the story of watching Wendy's wedding play out before her eyes and how it broke her heart. Tarah also told him about running to the deserted bathroom afterward, sitting on a stall floor, and crying for the remainder of her lunch. It was bad enough that she had not been invited to the event, but the pictures rubbed it in until she felt the burn.

At the reception, William put his arm around Tarah and whispered in her ear, "You're going to have to let it go."

"I know," she replied quietly, knowing he was referring to Wendy.

"Want to dance?" His words were gentle, and without waiting for an answer, William led her to the floor and pulled her close as "Possession" by Sarah McLachlan swept through the room. Held tight, she could feel his heart pounding against her body, and they moved so slowly that she forgot everyone else in the room. She continued to tighten her grip around him as he did with her, and as the music floated around her head, Tarah felt as if she were experiencing the most emotional moment of her life. It was stronger than any performance she'd experienced on stage. It was like being drunk, and at the same time, watching yourself in a dream that made you never want to wake up. It was beautiful and perfect. It was horrible and miserable. Tears escaped her eyes, and she didn't care who saw them. When the song ended, she felt a huge disappointment as she snapped back to reality.

Reluctantly letting go of William, she looked into his face, and Tarah knew that somewhere along the line, things had changed. It was then that she realized that love had more than one level, and she wasn't sure if they were on the same one at all.

Chapter Fifteen

▼

"It took a long time to get here." Tarah stood before the picture window in the new apartment she shared with William. Outside, large flakes of snow gently fell in the early December afternoon, while inside, the couple were evaluating each room before they started to move their stuff in. It was small, but neither of them cared. "I finally feel like I'm home. For the first time in my life."

William silently joined her at the window and put his arm around her shoulder. The friend he had house-sat for during the last year was moving back to Thorton a few days before Christmas, leaving both of the Stacy brothers looking for a new place to live. For William, it was easy. He had already decided to move in with Tarah and the two quickly found a nice and affordable apartment. However, Michael was another story.

"So, please tell me that Michael won't be sleeping in the spare room," Tarah said without making eye contact with William. There was no way she could live with his brother and they both knew it.

"Nope."

"He won't be?" She turned toward him and looked into his eye.

"Nope." He pulled her closer. "It's just you and me, babe."

"Did he find a place?" Tarah asked skeptically. A year had passed, and her feelings of distrust for William's brother had never disappeared.

"Yup, think so."

"You don't know?"

William shrugged in disinterest. "He and Eddie are getting a place, I think Jimmy too." Eddie had been renting a room since graduating from high school and moving to Thorton. Jimmy seemed to move from one girl's bed to another, living at his parent's house in between those occasions. "I think they want to rent a house so we can practice in the basement, just like what we were doing."

"You don't seem very concerned." Tarah was investigating his face. They recently had a blow-up argument when William gently suggested having Michael as a roommate. It was one of many fights, but she felt hopeful that moving in together would be what they needed to get their relationship back on track. He was a good guy, and she didn't want to lose him.

"Nope." He was staring out the window and finally looked back into her face. A spark of light shining through the glass met with his hazel eyes and she could see he was tired. They had been up packing her apartment till after two in the morning and were back up at seven in the morning to meet with their new landlord and sign the lease. "He's on his own."

"Are you sure?" Tarah continued to stare at him. She held her breath without realizing it.

William nodded. "Yes, I'm sure. You and Michael don't get along, so it would be crazy for him to live with us. Plus," he leaned over and kissed her forehead, "three's a crowd, right? It's time my brother figured things out for himself. I can't always be there to help him."

"What do you mean?"

William led her away from the window and toward the kitchen. Jumping on the countertop, he sat across from Tarah and put his hands out to gesture to her to come closer. She did. "I mean I've always looked after him, even this time. He knew a year ago when we moved in that we had to be out this month. I reminded him again in September, and yet he didn't even make an effort to find a place. He knew we were getting an apartment together. In fact, and don't get mad, but he tried to talk me out of moving in with you and moving in with him instead."

Tarah felt her face get hot and her heart start to race. She was pissed.

"Don't." William pulled her closer and slowly shook his head. His lids looked heavy, and he gave her a boyish grin. Tarah felt herself relax.

Everything seemed right with the world. Tarah and William were together in a new place. Bobby, Sara, and Caitlin also had their own apartment. Just after the wedding, her brother was promoted at the call center and began to deal only with corporate accounts. Even though he was still working in customer service, he insisted that it was an improvement over dealing with everyday customers. Plus, his boss insisted that he was headed in the right direction for further promotions. Bobby had come a long way in the last year.

Tarah was disappointed when they had to put off recording their CD in January because of lack of funds. All of the expenses from moving and Christmas caused them to fall short. It was frustrating, but William convinced her to let it go. "Things will work out in the end. We'll just get better at playing the songs, maybe even write some new ones." The band spent the rest of January playing shows throughout the province of Ontario. They rarely made any money when traveling because of gas and other expenses, but it created more attention for Fire, which would help them in the long run. They were scheduled to record their CD in March.

On the last day of January, William received news that his aunt had died of a massive heart attack, and he had to return to Springdale two days later, to attend the funeral.

"I'm so sorry." Tarah rushed over to hug him. "I can go with you. I have a shift that day, but I'll just tell them I have a funeral to go to."

"No, that's fine." William shook his head. "I'm fine. I wasn't particularly close to her, but she was my mom's only sister so I feel like I should be there for that reason. My mom would want me to be there."

"That's really nice," Tarah quietly remarked. "I think you're right. I can go though, if you want. It's not a big deal."

"No, you stay here and hold down the fort. I don't plan to stay, just go for the day."

However, an unexpected snowstorm tore through the southern Ontario on the day of the funeral, leaving William and Michael stranded in Springdale. He called Tarah with the news later that same day.

"I'll be okay," she assured him. "It's snowing really hard here too. Just stay there with your dad. Stay there until the highways are clear."

After hanging up the phone, Tarah took a long, hot bath and put on her comfy clothes. She was looking out to check on the weather once again, when the doorbell rang. A glance at the clock told her it wasn't even eight yet, so she guessed it was her brother dropping in after work. She was wrong. Jimmy was at the door. She buzzed him in.

"What are you doing out in this weather?" she asked as he shook the snow from his hair, jacket, and boots before walking into the apartment. "Should you be driving in this mess?"

"Ah, it's not that bad. Besides, I'm walking," he said, removing his boots as she closed the door behind him. "I was in the neighborhood having a few drinks and thought I'd stop by. I wanted William to check out something I just bought." He reached into the pocket of his black, leather jacket and pulled out a CD. Tarah automatically recognized it.

"Oh my God! You got *Jar of Flies*. I love Alice in Chains! I've been dying to hear it," Tarah said, and excitedly grabbed the case from his hand, staring at the CD for a minute. "William's not here, but *I'll* listen to it."

Tarah flew into the living room and Jimmy reluctantly followed her but stopped in the doorway. She put the CD in William's stereo and turned it on. Tarah's lips curved into a smile when the music began to play and she momentarily closed her eyes. "Wow." She studied the back of the case. "'Rotten Apple?' What a beautiful song. I love it."

"It's good." Jimmy spoke softly as he leaned against the doorframe. "I heard it at a friend's house and the whole CD just blew me the fuck away. It's perfection." He stared into her eyes, and his lips formed a small smile.

"I'd have to say you're right," Tarah said and stared back at him for a moment, then gestured toward the couch. "Have a seat. William would love this."

"Where is he?" Jimmy asked, as he slowly moved into the room. He seemed hesitant to sit down.

"Oh, his aunt died. He went to Springdale for the funeral. He's snowed in," Tarah hurriedly answered. "Can I start this song again? I really have to hear it from the beginning. I want to listen to the words."

"Sure," Jimmy said with a grin, his blue eyes seemed to widen. "Do whatever you need to do."

"Thanks," Tarah said as she grabbed the remote and hit repeat. Curling her legs up on the couch, she didn't speak until the song finished. "So, where were you tonight?"

"Oh, I just met a friend at a bar nearby. I stopped on the way home to buy the CD and decided to drop in here. I didn't really feel like going back to the house yet."

"I guess you don't live that far away, still I wouldn't want to be out walking tonight."

"It doesn't bother me. It's really not that bad if you're walking."

"Did you drink much?"

"Nah, just a couple of beers."

"Hmm ... I haven't had drinks in ages."

"Yeah, William's not into that, is he?" Jimmy asked, and his eyes briefly turned down toward his hands.

"No," Tarah said, and shook her head. "I'm not really into it much anymore. I used to drink plenty, but I guess that was just a phase."

"Maybe."

"My friend Wendy and I used to smoke a joint then have a few drinks before going out." Tarah had gotten over the snub by her former best friend and now chose to think only of the good times. She didn't want to dwell on the hurtful end of their friendship. "It was fun at the time, but like I said, I guess you eventually have to grow up."

"You? Smoke weed?" Jimmy said, and began to laugh. Reaching into his pocket, he pulled out a baggie that contained two joints. He held them up for her to see.

Tarah's eyes lit up. "Can we have one? I haven't had pot in ages."

"In here?" Jimmy asked, and looked around. "You want to smell up the place?"

"There's ways around that," Tarah replied. She jumped up and grabbed a collection of candles that were scattered around the room. Lighting one at a time, the misshaped collection stood in single file on the coffee table in front of the couch. She then returned to the couch, slightly closer to Jimmy. Grabbing a glass on the coffee table, she sat it between them.

"Ash tray," she replied to Jimmy's curious expression. "Light one up."

He followed her instructions and took a long, slow puff then passed it to Tarah. She anxiously inhaled and felt her whole body start to relax. "I forgot how much I missed this." Tarah almost appeared to speaking toward the joint. She took another puff and passed it back to Jimmy who was in the process of removing his jacket. They both fell silent, just listening to the CD and sharing the joint.

"So like, get this." Feeling awkward, Tarah jumped into a random story. "I was at work today, and some woman walked up to me and said I looked familiar. And like, usually when people do that it's because they recognize me from the band, right?"

Jimmy nodded; his eyes were squinting but seemed concentrated on her face.

"Not this time; guess who she said I looked like?" Tarah laughed and rolled her eyes. "Tonya Harding!"

"Hey, now, that's not such a bad thing." Jimmy insisted, while his lips spread into a mischievous grin. "She's pretty cute, so it's not really an insult."

"I suppose, I never thought about it that way," Tarah giggled.

"She is," Jimmy insisted. "I'd do her."

"You'd do anyone!" Tarah teased him.

"Not *anyone*." Jimmy laughed and took another long puff of the joint. His body seemed to relax, and he turned to face Tarah. "But you're right, I'm pretty open-minded."

"I noticed."

Jimmy pretended to give her a dirty look as he finished the joint then pulled out the baggie again. "There are some obvious differences between you and Tonya Harding," He proceeded to light up the last joint, "if you wanted someone attacked, you'd do it yourself. That's why we don't bring crowbars to our shows."

"Oh come on!" Tarah talked loudly over the music, but she clearly wasn't angry. "I've only had two fights ever, and they just happened to be when I was singing at a bar. Just a coincidence."

"There were *two*?" Jimmy took another puff and passed the joint to Tarah as his eyes swept over her face. "I only remember one."

After taking her turn, Tarah told him the story about her ex-boyfriend Jeff and his intimate encounter with a stranger at Jerry's a couple of years earlier.

Jimmy laughed so hard as she told the story that he began to choke. "Are you fucking serious? Some girl was sucking him off in the bathroom, while you were on stage singing? Wow, that's pretty *dirty*. I mean, I've done some dirty ass shit, but even I wouldn't do that." He ran his hand through his dark hair and took another puff.

"You mean in a bathroom or cheat on someone?" Tarah giggled. "You have to be more clear than that, Jimmy."

He began to laugh at her. A haze of smoke filled the room, but neither of them seemed to notice that the candles were having little effect in masking the smoke. "I don't know, I'm a little confused actually."

Tarah began to laugh harder and he joined her.

"Umm …" He thought about it for a moment. "I'd have to say, I'd never cheat on someone. And, well … the whole bathroom thing I have to plead the fifth on. I've done it in a public washroom."

"How could you cheat on anyone? You've never been in a serious relationship since I've known you," Tarah teased him.

"You've only known me a year," Jimmy calmly reminded her. "I did have a girlfriend before, believe it or not."

"Really?" Tarah moved slightly closer to him, as if to hear him more clearly. "Who was it?"

"What difference, it's no one you'd know." He slowly placed the joint between his lips.

"Why'd you break up?"

Jimmy hesitated for a minute and seemed to consider his answer. "Long story."

"Isn't it always?"

"Usually," he agreed. "It's not a big deal."

"Would you ever have another relationship, or are you having too much fun for that?" Tarah tilted her head and waited for his answer. She wondered if she looked as stoned as he did. His eyes were glazed over. There was something sexy about the way he looked at her, and Tarah wondered if that was what all the girls saw in him. Of course, he was a really cool and attractive guy too, but this was a side of him she hadn't seen before.

Jimmy shrugged and appeared bored. "It's fun for awhile, but it's a pretty shallow life. Especially when you see happy couples together and realize you don't have that."

Tarah nodded and wondered if he was lonely. She certainly had been lonely for most of her life before William, so she felt empathetic toward him.

She wondered if that was why he hooked up with all those random girls. Was it a way to escape the empty feelings when the shows ended?

"Yeah, there are advantages to being single, but it's not the same as having someone special in your life." She thought of William as she spoke. "But you always seem to be okay with it."

"Sometimes." Jimmy shrugged. "I don't really have a choice."

"Well, you kind of do," Tarah insisted. "You could date someone for more than one night. Find someone you really like."

"I have found someone I really like," Jimmy quietly insisted.

"Then ask her out," Tarah said.

"It's not that easy." Jimmy finished the joint and put it into the glass that sat between them.

"Why not?"

"She has someone."

"Oh." Tarah frowned. "Well, maybe you'll find someone else."

"Maybe," Jimmy replied, placing the cup they had used as an astray onto the table in front of them both. When he sat back, their eyes met for a long, silent moment; Tarah was deep in thought. She'd never really considered Jimmy or his life before now. Maybe there was more to him than she realized.

And then, without warning, he leaned toward her. Tarah already knew he was going to kiss her; his face was only inches away. She saw it in his eyes and felt her heart racing. They continued to stare at one another until his lips grazed hers. His breath was hot against her face when he hesitated for a moment as if unsure on whether or not to continue. Jimmy was transfixed by her eyes, and as the music continued to play behind them, she kissed him. She could taste the pot on his tongue as their mouths came together. A voice in her head questioned just what in the hell she was doing, but she didn't have an answer nor did she want to think about it.

Unlike the first time she kissed William, Jimmy's kiss started off shy and cautiously but quickly turned passionate and explosive. He moved closer to her until their legs touched, causing a shot of electricity to travel through her body. Her fingers ran over the bristles on Jimmy's face and through his hair, and his hands firmly gripped her back and pulled her body closer. Tarah knew it was necessary to stop him before things went too far, but she didn't. His hands were sliding up the back of her sweater and he was slowly moving on top of her. Jimmy's lips hadn't left hers for a moment, but it was guilt that finally made her stop him. Much to Tarah's surprise, it was more over leading Jimmy on than hurting William, which really confused her. How could she do something like this to someone who loved her so much? But staring into Jimmy's eyes as they both silently sat up on the couch, Tarah realized that William wasn't the only person who had strong feelings for her.

CHAPTER SIXTEEN

▼

"Hi." Tarah was relieved when Eddie answered the door the following afternoon. He was clearly taken aback by her visit but was friendly, if not curious. "Can I come in?"

"Sure." Eddie stood aside and watched her enter the room. "Ah, don't mind the mess."

Tarah didn't know what he was talking about until she glanced toward the kitchen. Her lips curved into a smile at the sight of an empty pizza box, a counter full of dirty dishes, and a half-full garbage bag in the middle of the floor. Typical bachelors. It was when she actually entered the room with Eddie on her heels that her smile disappeared. A brown liquid was splattered all over the opposite wall, and below it sat the remains of a rum bottle, which clearly had been smashed during a fit of anger.

"Oh my God, who did that?" Tarah felt the blood drain from her face because she already knew the answer. Michael was with William in Springdale, still attempting to dig out, and she knew Eddie wouldn't do something like this, so there was only one possible answer.

"Ah, Jimmy did." Eddie seemed apprehensive to answer. "He got home last night and was really drunk. He drank some rum that was sitting on the counter then threw the bottle across the room. And he ordered a pizza, ate about half a slice, and threw up all over the floor."

Tarah looked down but couldn't see any proof of Jimmy vomiting.

"I cleaned it up." Eddie shrugged. "It's not a big deal."

"If I was cleaning up someone's puke, I might not be as kind as you." Tarah continued to glance around. "Did he even try to help you clean it?"

"No, he actually passed out on the living room floor," Eddie said sheepishly. "By the time I cleaned up the puke, he started to come around so I helped him to his room."

"Did he say anything?" Tarah was concerned about how much Eddie knew.

"No, just that he drank a lot of tequila." Eddie shrugged. "He was way too out of it to really make sense. I don't even think he realized what was going on."

"Wow." Tarah felt her heart pounding wildly in her chest. Maybe it wasn't such a good idea to show up at Jimmy's place to talk to him. But after he stormed out of her apartment the previous night, Tarah knew she had to sort things out before William got home. She was ashamed at her own behavior but she also felt a great deal of empathy for Jimmy. She hadn't wanted to hurt him.

"Yeah, so, I'm trying to clean up before Michael gets home. He's already had it out with Jimmy more than once about leaving messes, and I don't want to be stuck in the middle of another argument," Eddie nervously explained. "I like living here and I like our band. I just want everything to stay how it is."

"Me too," Tarah quietly replied and nodded. "Do you think I can go and try to talk to Jimmy?"

"If you want." Eddie looked almost relieved. "I don't know what to say to him or what's going on."

"I'll take care of it," Tarah promised. However, her confidence teetered as she walked up the stairs that led to Jimmy's room. She wasn't all that familiar with the house, but only one door was closed. She gently knocked. Nothing.

"Jimmy?" She felt her stomach turn in fear, while her heart pounded wildly beneath her sweater. "Are you okay? It's Tarah."

Silence.

"Jimmy, I'm coming in, is that okay?" Tarah didn't want to barge into his room but was a little worried, especially in light of Eddie's story. She stalled for a moment.

From inside the room, she could hear shuffling and eventually someone moving across the floor. The door slowly opened, and Tarah could smell the distinct combination of vomit and alcohol. Jimmy barely had his eyes opened. They were bloodshot and watery. A dark beard was forming on his chin. His hair was in a complete upheaval, standing on end and in every direction. He looked to be in actual pain by even the simple act of blinking.

"What? What are you doing here?" Jimmy whispered and rubbed one of his eyes.

"We have to talk," Tarah said, and glanced behind him, fearful that another woman would be in his bed. It was empty, but the sheets were falling off the side and onto the floor. His room looked as if a tornado had flown through it. Clothes were everywhere, magazines were piled on the floor, and beer bottles were sitting on his dresser and nightstand. "But maybe this isn't a good time."

Much to her surprise, Jimmy moved aside and gestured her to come in. He was wearing the same clothes as the night before.

"Sit down." He slowly moved across the room and joined her on the bed.

"About last night—"

"Ah, you know, I can't have this conversation right now," Jimmy cut her off. He didn't look well at all, and she considered just leaving. "Can you give me like five minutes?"

Tarah nodded and watched him drag his body across the hallway into the bathroom. She heard the shower being turned on, followed by the distinct sound of vomiting. After what seemed to be more than ten minutes of continuous retching, she reluctantly approached the bathroom door and knocked.

"Jimmy, do you need anything? Are you going to be okay?" It scared her to see him this way. She felt responsible and uncomfortable. "Can I get you something? Water?"

"No." His voice sounded vulnerable from the behind the bathroom door.

Returning to his bedroom, she immediately opened a window in hopes of killing the stench. Tarah's mood was solemn as she removed her jacket, sat on his gray comforter, and waited. Eventually the vomiting stopped, and she heard the shower curtain opening and then closing again. About ten minutes later, Jimmy returned to the room, his appearance slightly improved from when she first arrived. Only a towel covered his midsection, and water dripped from his hair and ran down his chest. Jimmy caught her staring at him, and she shyly looked away. As he got closer, she noted that he looked and smelled really good. He closed the window.

"You don't look like you're up for a guest right now." Tarah stood up from the end of his bed. "I probably should leave. We can talk another time. I'll just leave your CD on the nightstand." She pulled the bright orange case from her jacket pocket. "You left it at my place."

"It's fine." Jimmy's voice was barely over a whisper. "Give me a few more minutes."

She sat back down on the bed and watched him shuffle into the bathroom with a T-shirt and jeans in his hand. Five minutes later, he walked in wearing fresh clothes. Shutting the door behind him, he walked over and sat down beside Tarah on the bed. They were very close and it made her nervous.

"What time is it?" he asked.

"One in the afternoon."

"Oh." Jimmy finally made eye contact with her and then looked away. She noticed that although he still looked like shit, there was a definite improvement from even a few minutes earlier. "So, William isn't back yet?"

"No, as far as I know they're still stuck in Springdale." Tarah remained calm even though she suspected that his remark was meant to provoke her. "Look, Jimmy, we have to talk."

"We *can*," he said. "But maybe there isn't anything else to say."

"I think there is," Tarah replied, and turned to face him. Jimmy was slumped over. "I don't want things to be weird between us."

"They won't be." His blue eyes finally looked back into hers. "You'll keep being happy with William, and I'll keep fucking every woman who walks by. There, problem solved."

Tarah searched his face but didn't know what to say. He was clearly very hurt. His remarks were meant to challenge and upset her at the same time.

"Look, can we be honest here?" Tarah asked. "You know it's not that simple."

"It *is* that simple," Jimmy said quietly. "You made your choice."

"I'm sorry," she managed.

"Sorry?" His voice carried a hint of anger. "Not as sorry as I am right about now. I knew you had a boyfriend but still put it all on the line." He stopped for a moment. "The funny part is that I went over there to see William. I didn't mean for the rest of this to happen. As soon as you said he wasn't home, I knew I should've left. But I wanted to be there with you and I'm kinda glad I stayed. You're a different person when he's not around."

"I'm not different," Tarah insisted. "He just doesn't do crap like smoke pot, so I try to not do stuff like that around him out of respect."

"But as soon as the coast was clear, you jumped at the chance," Jimmy reminded her. "What does that tell you? There's no way you would've smoked one with me if Will had been home. I guarantee it. I just need to know something." He stopped and stared into her eyes. "How can you be in love with someone who you aren't even yourself around?"

Tarah felt as if she had been hit in the stomach. Jimmy's eyes challenged hers, and she felt a huge lump form in her throat.

"That's not how it is, I told you. It's just out of respect." Tarah felt her eyes burning.

Jimmy saw that she was almost in tears, but continued, "And if you really love William, why did you kiss me back last night? You can't tell me you weren't into it, because I know you were."

Tarah felt a tear escape and trickle down her cheek. She didn't know what to say. She felt so confused and scared to face his words.

"I'm sorry," he said, as the tears continued to flow down her face. "I didn't mean to make you cry. I just had to state the obvious. I know I was high last night and had a couple of drinks, but I'm clear about what happened."

Tarah sniffed and changed the subject. "Why did you break that bottle downstairs, and where did you go last night?"

"I went to the first bar I could find and drank," he said, confirming what she had already known. "Then, I came home and was pissed off about everything. I was pissed at you for not saying what I wanted to hear. I was pissed at myself for confessing that I want to be with you. So, I got angry and smashed the bottle."

Tarah started to cry harder when she remembered his confession before leaving, and the hurt look in his eyes when she reminded him that William was her boyfriend. Looking back, it was a cold way to deal with the situation, but she was scared and hadn't known what else to say.

"I'm sorry," she whispered.

"Don't be sorry if you don't feel the same way."

The problem was that she didn't know *what* she felt. Tarah had barely slept the night before, going over the entire night in her head again and again. How did this happen? She was never a popular girl with guys before, and suddenly she had two very different men who wanted to be with her. It was very surreal and it didn't make sense. This kind of thing happened to other girls. Girls like Wendy. She stopped crying.

"I think maybe you just think you feel that way," Tarah considered. "Maybe you just care about me because we're in the same band. I mean we're always together and work closely together. Maybe you're just confused."

"Tarah, please!" he snapped at her. "Please don't tell me how I feel. I'm hardly the guy who falls for a different girl *every* week. In fact, I'm the guy who tries to fuck a different girl every *day*, so don't insult me by making it sound like this is just all in my head. I've gotten high with a lot of girls before, and I didn't tell them that I had feelings for them. True, I haven't been in a band with a girl before, but so what? Yes, we work together a lot, but we aren't attached at the hip either."

"Then how do you know?" Tarah challenged. In a way, she hoped that he'd discover that his feelings for her weren't that strong so that they could move past this and forget about it. "Why am I different from any other girl?"

"Because I just know." Jimmy shrugged. "How did *you* know when you met William that he was *the one*?"

Tarah hadn't missed the sarcasm in his voice and avoided his eyes.

"It's like," Jimmy started to explain, "… like being hit by a bus. One minute you're perfectly content with your life, and suddenly something completely unexpected just runs you down. I look forward to seeing you, and

I think of you when you aren't around. And when we're at the bar, even with all those people around, a part of me wishes it were just you and me. And even when there are other girls talking to me, I'm always very aware of exactly where you are in the room. It's almost like you're the only face I really see, the only face in the room. If that makes sense."

"No one has ever said anything like that to me before," she said, wondering if William felt that way about her as well. Jimmy had expressed how she had felt for William when they started dating. But was it still like that?

"I almost left last night when you said William wasn't home, because I knew that I wanted to be there alone with you a little too much. And I think he knows too."

"Knows what?"

"I think he knows that I'm into you." Jimmy bit his lower lip. "He'll catch me watching you sometimes and give me a dirty look. Especially when we're on stage. I just think you're brilliant on stage. I think you *are* the band. You light up the entire room."

"Oh come on!" Tarah laughed self-consciously. "I'm hardly that important."

"No, you are," Jimmy insisted. "You really are. Or at least, I think you are."

They both fell silent for a moment, and Tarah started to feel better about everything. It was just a kiss. It was over and done with. Maybe it was better to not dwell on it. Jimmy would clearly forgive her eventually, and at least he didn't hate her as she feared. And with that in mind, she turned to him to apologize for the misunderstanding. But then, he did it again.

Jimmy put his hands on each side of her face and pulled her close. She fell silent and stared into his eyes until his lips touched her own. His breath was heavy, and his tongue quickly darted into her mouth; she could taste toothpaste, and felt her body being drawn to him. He pulled her close, and she let out a small moan as he pulled her body on top of him. She could feel him hard against her stomach, and when his mouth moved to her ear, Tarah thought she was going to die. But it was just when Tarah's fingers were unbuttoning Jimmy's pants, that she heard it. Michael and William were downstairs.

CHAPTER SEVENTEEN

▼

Tarah felt relieved and guilty. Relieved that William hadn't suspected anything that day. Guilty because she had made out with another guy, for the second time, while he innocently trusted her. He assumed that she was a loyal girlfriend. And it was slowly starting to eat her up.

Things started to change. She was a little more irritable after William returned. And the crankier Tarah felt, the more understanding he was, making her feel even guiltier. Then, she slowly started to resent both guys for putting her in the middle of a difficult situation. That only lasted a few days before she realized that it was just as much her own fault. Then Tarah began to feel depressed over being so confused. What was the right thing to do?

Jimmy agreed to let her think about everything a little more before deciding how she felt. The only problem was that there were way too many things to consider. John was busy with a new girlfriend, leaving her with no one to help her out. And then her brother dropped by one afternoon when William was out, and she told him the whole story.

"Wow, my sister's in a *love* triangle!" Bobby teased and Tarah covered her face in horror. "And with two guys that you're in a band with. How much more complicated could this possibly be?"

"It's complicated enough, thank you."

"I just don't understand. You and William always seemed to be the super happy couple. I never suspected that you'd even consider anyone else."

"I never had before," Tarah said. "It never crossed my mind."

"The first time, okay, I'd blame on the weed." Bobby lay back on her couch, staring at the ceiling as if deep in thought. "But then the whole 'hanging out together while sober' thing makes me think it wasn't just the weed."

"It never crossed my mind that he was even interested in me."

"Okay, well, I actually don't agree with you there." Bobby sat up and looked into her face. "I mean you probably didn't see it. But I can't say that it surprises me that he was into you. When I think about it, it kind of makes sense. Just from the few times I've seen him around you. He has seemed very attentive toward you, or something. I can't explain it really, it just doesn't surprise me is all."

"Really?" Tarah wondered if William saw the same thing as her brother. Jimmy seemed to think so. "Jimmy is being cool about it. He said to take my time and figure out what I want. But should I be talking about this with William? Should I tell him the truth? I don't know what to do. And on top of it all, Jimmy says that I'm not myself around William. Do you think that's true?"

"Well, you're a little more subdued, I suppose. Not sure that has to do with William or not. But yeah, you are a little different now."

Tarah just nodded and didn't say a word.

The band wasn't very busy for most of February. However, they were included in a big show on the final weekend of the month at Ginger's Ale House. It consisted of local bands playing at the bar on Friday, Saturday, and Sunday nights. It was created to help people out of their winter blahs and, of course, to create business during a low point of the year.

Fire was scheduled to play during the latter part of that Saturday night, and the band was really looking forward to the show. The event was well publicized and was expected to pull in a big crowd.

Even though the band got together a lot to practice for the upcoming show, Jimmy acted completely normal around her. There was an occasional look, a glance, while they worked out band details together, but nothing that William seemed to notice. Everyone had commented on how Jimmy was much quieter in recent weeks, but no one really gave it much thought. No one, that is, but Tarah.

On the night they were scheduled to play at Ginger's Ale House, Tarah arrived at the bar early so she could meet up with Bobby and Sara for a drink. The first band was playing and a small crowd was gathered around the stage. But as she sat alone at the bar, waiting for them to arrive, she felt a hand on her shoulder and turned around to see Jimmy. Her stomach did flip-flops as he sat down beside her and proceeded to order a drink.

"Is everyone here?" Tarah asked innocently. Jimmy didn't reply. He just stared at her and slowly shook head.

"It's just you and me." His words sounded like an invitation rather than an answer.

"Oh."

He moved closer to her until his leg touched hers, sending a charge up her body. Tarah was nervous and without realizing it held her breath. "William said you were coming here early to meet your brother, so I thought I'd come here even earlier, so I could see *you*."

"Do you want to sit at a booth?" Tarah felt too exposed as she sat at the bar. She had too much to say.

"Sure."

They found one at the back of the room. *Just like a couple having a secret affair*, she thought to herself as she sat down. He slid dangerously close to her, and Tarah felt flustered and confused.

"So, I think I want to leave the band," she began, and he looked genuinely surprised.

"No." Jimmy shook his head. "If you enjoy doing this, then don't leave the band."

"I might have to," Tarah said. "I can't do this anymore. Ever since William came home from Springdale, everything's been weird. And at first, I thought it was because he somehow knew or suspected that something happened between us. But he had no reason to, and after awhile, I began to realize that it wasn't just my own paranoia."

"What do you mean?"

"I mean it's not just because of you and I fooling around or my conscience. Things with William just don't feel right. I really had hoped our relationship would improve when we moved in together, but it hasn't." Tarah felt a sense of loss even saying the words. It didn't matter that Jimmy was standing on the sidelines waiting for her, she still felt like a failure. What if she misjudged everything with both of these guys? What if she was simply just physically attracted to Jimmy? Maybe they didn't have anything beyond that.

Then again, she and William had always argued and it seemed to be about the same things: his brother's animosity toward her and the constant attention of other girls toward him. It wasn't that he did anything wrong by talking to the women at the shows, but somehow Tarah always felt threatened by it. When she'd bring up her concerns to William, he would merely tell her she was insecure. She shared this information with Jimmy.

"Well, he's right to a point about the girls," Jimmy agreed. "But there are ways to set things straight about that with them. Like, remember the time that chick grabbed his crotch after a show?" Tarah made a face and nodded. "She was talking to me afterward, and she didn't say he encouraged her, but she kind of suggested that he was being ... I don't know, just ..."

"Just tell me the truth please, Jimmy," Tarah said. "I want to know."

"I don't want you to think I'm saying shit about William to sway your attention more in my direction," Jimmy said honestly. "But the reason why I get so pissed when you talk about William like he's a saint, is because I think he likes that attention. I don't think he'd ever cheat on you, but I think he may be a little flirty or something. At least that's the impression that girl gave me." He shrugged. "I mean, I was up for anything with anyone at the time, and she certainly didn't grab my dick in the middle of the bar."

Tarah thought about what he said and nodded.

"And I'm not trying to cause shit or whatever, I want you to do what you want to do."

Jimmy slid his hand under the table and placed it on her leg while moving closer to her, causing an electrical shock to go up her spine. There was no doubt that she was very attracted to him. "But I'm not going to lie. There's nothing I want to do more right now than—"

"Hey." Tarah felt flustered to see her brother and his wife standing at the table. Jimmy didn't skip a beat but slowly edged away and said he had to see if the rest of the band had shown up yet. Bobby and Sara sat down with her.

"Well!" Bobby grinned. "What was all that about?"

"Don't ask," Tarah replied.

"Hmm …" Bobby teased. "Okay. But if he had his hand any farther up your leg, this could've quickly turned into a completely different kind of club."

Tarah couldn't help but to laugh, in spite of it all.

Fire went on stage to perform at eleven thirty that night, and the show went off without a hitch. The crowd was enthusiastic and excited. Tarah had pushed all her fears and concerns out of her mind and concentrated on the audience. There was something different about that night. She could feel it growing with each song. And when she sang "A New Life," she replaced all the sadness about her broken friendship with Wendy and filled it with the hope of what was to come in the future. Her future.

The show ended with explosive applause, and Tarah felt light as she left the stage and headed across the room to find her brother. Before she made it there, however, a man in his late thirties approached her. He was of medium build and height, wore a black leather jacket, a Metallica T-shirt, and jeans. Although she hadn't noticed him in the audience that night, he was very familiar.

"Hi, great performance out there tonight," the stranger gave her a perfect smile and extended his hand. "Peter Sampson, I'm the A&R guy with FUTA Records."

Tarah's smile faded from her face. She was stunned. This couldn't really be happening to her. FUTA. "What?"

Peter Sampson just laughed and repeated himself. "You've probably heard of us. FUTA stands for Future United Together Artists. I was wondering if you and the rest of Fire would have a few minutes to talk to me about your band and, of course, your music."

"Sure." Tarah finally managed to smile. They were a division of a major record label. She felt her heart racing. Taking a deep breath, Tarah managed to calm herself and said she'd find the rest of the band.

An hour later, the five of them and Mr. Sampson sat together in an all-night café. It wasn't the classiest place in the world, but no one really noticed.

"Listen, kids, I've been following Fire for quite some time now, and I have to say, there is just something about your band that stands out," he began slowly. Peter had bought everyone at the table a beverage, but only Jimmy touched his. Jimmy also made a point of sitting on the other side of Tarah, his thigh glued to hers.

"Really?" Eddie appeared flustered by the entire situation. "Like, how long?"

"Well, Eddie, since last year." He sipped his coffee and appeared completely at ease, even though the five people he sat with were clearly in shock. "What we like to do at FUTA Records is to follow a band over a period of time, check out their shows, evaluate their dedication, consistency, their music of course, and decide whether or not the specific band is what we are looking for. And kids, I'd have to say that right about now, you are."

The table went dead silent. Peter clearly was used to this and just continued to talk.

"I know it's a bit of a shock, but I'm assuming that discussing your future with a record company is probably something you've all thought about, one time or another." He seemed completely comfortable as he spoke, as if the six of them had been friends for years. "But I'd like to get together with you again early next week to talk about things a little more—if you'd like?"

When Peter concluded their short meeting and left the café, the band was still completely stunned.

"I feel like I'm dreaming," Eddie said. His face was red and he looked like he was going to hyperventilate. Then again, Tarah considered, Eddie was the youngest of all of them. He had just barely turned nineteen and was about to be handed something most people work for all their lives and never achieve.

"Well, we'll talk to him and check things out," Jimmy said casually, as if nothing really fazed him. Tarah gave him a quick glance and he grabbed her leg under the table.

"I can't believe it." William shook his head. "This is fantastic. Do you guys know what this means? Our hard work has finally paid off."

"Well, let's not jump the gun," Michael insisted. "We don't know what kind of deal this guy is offering. It could be the shits."

"Who gives a fuck, man?" Jimmy countered. "What do we have to lose? You work in a crummy restaurant, I work in a bar, Tarah works at Rothman's, and Eddie is flipping burgers for a living. William is the only person here who has a *real* job, so like I said, what do we have to fucking lose?"

"Well, Mike does have a point," William agreed, and Jimmy kicked Tarah under the table. Their eyes met and Jimmy raised his eyebrow skeptically. "He might try to screw us over, so we should do some research on everything."

"Oh whatever!" Jimmy snapped. "I'm going home. Tarah, can you give me a drive?"

The three other people at the table all turned to Tarah, who seemed as shocked as the rest of them by Jimmy's boldness. "Okay," she said. "I want to go home and call my brother anyway. He was dying to find out what this guy was going to say to us."

She rose from the table and tried to act casual as they left the diner. William said he'd see her later and continued to talk to Michael and Eddie, giving her the impression that he hadn't suspected anything was out of sorts.

Once they got outside, Tarah pulled her keys from her pocket. "Oh my God, I can't believe you just, like, told me to drive you home."

"Hey, I didn't order you, I *asked* you, or did you want to hear any more of that bullshit?"

"No," she admitted. "I think you're right, we *don't* have anything to lose."

"Exactly."

They both climbed into her car, and she backed out of the parking space and headed onto the road.

"It is really cool though." Jimmy spoke up as she drove in the direction of his house. "But you know what would make it really fucking cool?"

"What?" Tarah concentrated on the road.

"If you spent the night with me."

"Jimmy!" Tarah couldn't help but to laugh. "And what? Call William and say I got snowed in there?" She gestured toward the cloudless sky.

"Sure, whatever." He joined in with her laughter. "He'll probably be at the diner all night analyzing this whole record deal thing anyway. Breaking it down, writing the pros and cons."

"He's not that bad," Tarah giggled.

"Close," Jimmy replied. "Very close. I think I could have fucked you right there at the table and he would've noticed. He's got tunnel vision."

"I highly doubt he would miss that. As it is, my brother saw you grab my leg under the table."

"Yeah, your brother saw, but your boyfriend didn't notice that I had my hand on your leg, right beside him. '*Hello?*'"

"Were you doing that on purpose?" Tarah challenged.

"Maybe, just a little bit." Jimmy gave her a seductive grin. "Baby, it's time to get this show on the road."

CHAPTER EIGHTEEN

▼

After the band's initial conversation with Peter Sampson, Tarah felt as though she were living in a whirlwind. They were constantly being ushered from one meeting to another, with little time in between to absorb all of the new information. Did they want to sign with FUTA Records? What kind of CD would Fire release? What kind of image did they want to project? Who would produce their music? Did they want a manager? When would the CD be released? How would they stand out against all of the other acts already in the industry? Tarah felt bombarded with questions, and she wasn't really sure of any of the answers.

Initially, the entire band was elated. Finally, all of their hard work had paid off. They could quit their jobs and start music careers. Hopes of fame and fortune suddenly were within their grasps as they all set out on a new adventure. It was the kind of thing that most people could only dream of—and suddenly, Fire was living it.

Peter warned that there was still a lot of work ahead of them. As soon as the contract was signed, they'd have to hit the studio and record a CD. And although the band had already written quite a few songs, there was no guarantee that they'd make it onto the finished product. FUTA had the final word on what would and wouldn't be put on their first CD.

He had also warned them to be sure to create their own style of music and not to copy any of the mainstream artists who were on the radio. "One of the problems I seem to get is that I'll discover a new band and once they're signed, they try to be the next Nirvana or whoever. And it doesn't work. It's not original." Peter sat with the band in his Toronto office. It was the second week of March and one of the coldest days of '94. "I mean there's only one Kurt Cobain. Just like there's only one Madonna."

"I don't see us doing that," William assured Peter.

"Perfect. I like your style *and* your music. With the proper producer, it will be great." Peter's gray eyes shone. Tarah thought that he was a very attractive man, but it didn't look as if he had aged well. "I also like you guys because you're a rock band. I predicted six months ago that the grunge phase is going to come to an end and I stand by that. I won't sign 'em anymore. I think people are going to want something else in the future."

"Really?" Jimmy grinned. "I don't know man, do you really think grunge is on its way out? Doesn't feel that way."

"Trust me, it's on its way. Every kind of music has a phase. Disco, hair metal bands, it's all in phases." Peter sat back in his chair. "People like something new. And with the time and money that goes into a CD, I'd prefer to not take a chance. But I don't see that as a problem with you guys. Write some really catchy and memorable music. That's what will make a real impression. Write more songs, see what the best of the best is, and take it from there. Write them from your heart. Write them with an audience in mind. Who's your fan base? Who will relate to your music?"

"How do you know that?" Eddie asked in a quiet voice. "Do you judge it by who is at your shows?"

"To a point." Peter nodded and yawned. "I'd have to say your audience is people your own age. It's something to keep in mind when you're writing. What do people your age like to hear? What kind of things matter to them? For example, if I'm writing a country song for a woman in her fifties, it's probably going to have a completely different feel than a rock song directed at a twenty-year-old man."

"What do you mean?" Michael asked abruptly. "I think everything we write about is stuff that matters to everyone."

"Not necessarily." Peter didn't appear to notice Michael's attitude. "People in their twenties tend to like songs about sex, drugs, partying, love, money, and fame. Remember, a lot of twenty-year-olds love the fantasy of becoming famous, so they see themselves in their favorite bands."

"So, Tarah." Peter directed his attention at her. "You aren't saying much today. What do you think?"

"I'm just wondering what happens next."

"After you guys sign the contract, if you choose to do so, then you set a date to start recording. We'll have some photo shoots for the band, figure out when you're CD will be launched, and work on the marketing details—stuff like interviews, that kind of thing. We'll have to make a music video, too. Not to mention that once the CD is out, we start thinking of the second video, more interviews, and touring. You're going to be so busy that you won't see time go by."

It sounded intense.

Tarah met with John a couple of days later, and they finally caught up. She told him about the FUTA deal. Although she had broken the news to him on the day after first meeting Peter Sampson, Tarah hadn't seen her friend in weeks.

"So, it sounds like everything is coming together nicely," John remarked after hearing the entire story. The two of them sat in his kitchen on a Saturday evening. He had just made a large pot of coffee and insisted they'd probably go through the entire thing before the conversation was finished. "Are you excited?"

"Try nervous as fuck." Tarah grinned. "I mean, we're all quitting our jobs once we sign the contract on Monday. We have to because there is so much to do—plus, the label doesn't want our time and energy going to anything else. So regardless of the advance we'll get, it's kind of scary."

"I can imagine. Do you have any money saved?"

"Not really," Tarah admitted. "I think we'll be fine though. It's just stressful, you know? It's exciting, but at the same time, I've been feeling kind of down lately. It doesn't make sense."

"Well, even though you hate your job and are glad to leave, and even though this is something you want—" John began, and stopped to consider his words for a moment. "It's a big change in your life. It will literally change every aspect of your life within a short period of time. Not to mention that you're leaving a lot behind. Maybe you hated Rothman's, but you might find leaving there can still be emotional. It's like ending a bad relationship, you might want out but it's still not any easier to do."

Hearing the word *relationship* made Tarah cringe a bit, wondering what John would say when she revealed the whole William/Jimmy situation. But she pushed that aside for the time being. She wanted to ease into that subject. What would John think of her when he heard?

"What did your family say when you told them about it?" John poured himself another cup of coffee then sat down. "They must've been shocked."

"My brother was actually at the show on the night this Peter guy approached the band. So, he was pretty excited." Tarah thought that Bobby was possibly more excited than anyone in Fire about the news. "Mom was shocked and just warned me not to sign anything without reading it, that kind of thing. I still don't think she realizes how huge all this is."

"She will."

"Everyone at work is either really excited for me or almost resentful, which is strange." Tarah thought of the day that she gave her boss the news and told her she'd be finished at Rothman's within weeks. Although the woman appeared delighted at the time, Tarah soon heard nasty rumors behind her back. "I can't help but wonder what Wendy would think if she were around."

"Hopefully she'd be happy for you," John said thoughtfully. "Tarah, I have to admit that I think I saw Wendy at the grocery store one day. I had to look twice though, because she didn't look like herself."

"Really?" Tarah felt her heart beating rapidly. "What do you mean?"

"She looked like she wasn't well." John spoke gently. "I don't know if anything is wrong, but Wendy appears to have lost weight and she was kind of pale. I was thinking of going by to say hello, but then she seemed to disappear. I may be wrong; maybe it wasn't her."

"John, do you think maybe she is sick?" Tarah wondered. "Maybe she didn't want me to know? Maybe that's why she's avoiding me."

"Tarah, we can only speculate."

The topic then turned to his relationship. John talked at great lengths about his new girlfriend. Apparently, he had met Elizabeth at the bookstore where she worked and, after much consideration, decided to ask her out. They had been together ever since.

"She is such a great person." John went on to describe her as beautiful and caring. It was clear that he was quite smitten, and Tarah suspected that he only had time for an old friend that night because Elizabeth had a family gathering to attend. "We're thinking of going on a trip this summer to Rome. I'm actually thinking of proposing."

"Wow!" Tarah was shocked. "But you just met her."

"It's true, I did. But sometimes you just know it's the right person."

"How do you know?" Tarah listened carefully. "How do you know when it's the one?"

"How?" John raised his eyebrows. "Ah, I'd have to say it just hits you like a bus. It's not subtle by any means. There's no wondering involved. You know, I'm sure it's like when you met William."

Tarah frowned.

"No bus?"

"I don't remember a bus," Tarah muttered.

"Oh, I know we haven't talked in awhile, but you and William just moved in together. Don't tell me things aren't going well?"

"They're going." Tarah took a deep breath and proceeded to tell him the entire story about Jimmy. She avoided his eyes for the most part, thinking that John would be ashamed of her behavior. After all, he'd always been the one who encouraged her to do the right thing.

"Wow, speaking of buses!" John began to laugh. "I feel like I was just hit by another one. When the hell did all this happen?"

"Not long ago, like in the last month." Tarah spoke quietly. "It's such a mess. And now with this record deal, I'm scared that it will cause tension within the band, regardless of what I choose."

"Well, first of all," John said, "it will cause tension, but you guys will have to weather it out. And, second of all, what do you mean 'regardless of what you choose?'"

"I haven't decided yet who I—"

"Oh no, honey," John interjected. "You already know who you want to be with, you just haven't put your cards on the table. It's clearly Jimmy."

Tarah froze.

"Tarah, if you wanted to continue a relationship with William, you'd avoid Jimmy like the plague. But you aren't. How many times have you two kissed or made out lately? Compare that to how many times you've been intimate with William lately. If there were no consequences—no band, none of that—who would you be with right now?"

"But can't I care about both of them?" Tarah stumbled across the words but knew he was right. Since her original encounter with Jimmy, she had only had sex with William twice and her heart wasn't into it.

"Tarah, I'm your friend, and I can tell you it's really clear who you want to be with. I can tell and I think Jimmy can too; that's why he's continuing to persist. I don't think he'd bother if he thought this was a dead end. I also think that you've been so confused because William is a good guy. It's not like he's mean to you, so it's harder to break up with him. You know he'll be really hurt. But that is not as hurt as he'll be if he finds you lip-locked with Jimmy someday. So, you have to be straight with him."

"I can't tell him about Jimmy."

John thought for a moment. "I can see why you've been putting off making a move; this is an iffy situation. I think you have to end it with William for sure. I don't think you should tell him that you and Jimmy are ready to jump one another the first chance you get, but I think you have to be honest with him that it's not working out for you. Ease into the Jimmy thing."

Tarah felt a huge weight off her shoulders. "Thanks John, I really needed that."

"That's quite a secret to be carrying around."

"You don't think I'm a horrible person?"

"No, Tarah, you aren't a horrible person." John shook his head. "I think you were caught up with William when Jimmy arrived on the scene, that you just didn't notice any kind of spark until you finally had time alone with him."

"What if I'm wrong?"

"I think you've probably given this enough thought that you aren't wrong. It isn't like you were impulsive and broke up with William after first kissing Jimmy. I'm sure you've went over this a million times in your mind. And who knows, maybe it's a bus this time, right?"

Tarah smiled.

She felt light and free as she left John's place and returned home. But that feeling quickly disappeared as soon as Tarah walked in the door. William was waiting for her and said they needed to talk. Assuming that it was with regard to the band, Tarah went into the living room and plopped on the couch. William joined her.

Sitting on the edge of the sofa, his eyes were on the ground, and suddenly Tarah had a sense of dread fill her body. Her heart began to race, and her throat went dry. And then he calmly uttered the words she had been waiting to hear.

"Tarah, I know." The words rang loudly through a silent room.

She held her breath. Tears were forming in her eyes and suddenly the room was blurry. She felt small and shameful under his gaze.

"I knew something was wrong," he said. "But I didn't know what until I talked to Michael tonight. You know, as much as you two seem to hate one another, my own brother was reluctant to tell me that he saw Jimmy grabbing your leg under the table on the night we met with Peter. He said he hadn't wanted to get involved."

Tarah felt hot tears running down her face and she sobbed loudly. She tried to speak, attempting to explain her side, but William cut her off.

"No Tarah, I don't want to hear it." He was stern but not as angry as she would've expected. "I talked to Jimmy about all this too, because if he was being an ass, I wanted to know. At first, he denied everything. Then I told him what Michael saw and he couldn't lie about it. He told me everything. He told me that he always made the moves, that you hadn't done anything wrong. He was very honest with me. I even asked him if he was just trying to add you to a list of girls he used up and threw away; he said no."

Tarah didn't know what to say. She felt shaken to the core.

"Tarah, I would've rather heard all this from you, not Jimmy." William was somber rather than angry, and it made her feel even worse. "Why couldn't you talk to me about this?"

Tarah sniffed. "I'm sorry."

William was silent for a few minutes before saying anything further. "I really don't understand what happened here, but if someone can sway you away that easily, then clearly our relationship isn't strong enough. I love you, but I want to be with someone who only wants to be with me and has no doubts at all."

Tarah nodded silently. He had every right to feel that way.

"Mike might move into the spare room here, and I thought maybe it would be best if you moved out. You could have his old room at the house if you want it, at least for now."

Tarah nodded.

"And as far as the band is concerned, I hope we can all get along well enough to make a go at FUTA."

"Yes," Tarah barely whispered. "I know it doesn't mean a thing, but I'm sorry."

William didn't say anything as she rose from the couch and went into the bedroom they shared. With tears running down her face, she packed a bag full of clothes and returned to the living room.

"You don't have to go tonight," William assured her with a pained expression on his face. "I'm not kicking you out, Tarah."

"No, I think it's right," she sobbed. "I'll be back to get the rest of my stuff tomorrow." And with that, Tarah grabbed her car keys and left the apartment she had once thought would bring them closer together. She never would have guessed this ending to their relationship.

Tarah rushed through the hallways of the apartment building with tears falling off her chin. By the time she made it to the staircase, she had to brace herself against the wall because her body felt weak. Taking a deep breath, she slowly headed down the staircase, careful to not fall, as tears blinded her vision. She felt so ashamed and angry with herself for what she had done to William. He hadn't deserved it. Tarah felt like she would always hate herself as much as she did in that moment.

By the time she found her way to the door that would lead her outside and to her car, Tarah felt her head spinning, and a pain rang through her chest. It was a panic attack. She hadn't had one in years, not since her parents' divorce, but the pain was very real and Tarah took long, calming breaths. She just had to get through this for a few more minutes until the drive to Jimmy's house. She just had to push out the look in William's eyes and the way he quickly and efficiently ended their relationship.

Her hand curved around the doorknob and she turned it. Outside, the cold air sent a shiver through her spine as she exited the building. Tarah jumped back when she saw a figure sitting on the step. It was Jimmy.

Without saying a word, she dropped her suitcase. He stood up and wrapped his arms around her. She couldn't stop crying. And William watched them from the upstairs window.

CHAPTER NINETEEN

▼

Jimmy drove them to his house that night. Neither said a word since leaving the apartment building where he had carefully placed her luggage in the backseat of her Sunbird and ushered Tarah into the passenger side. They both knew that she was in no condition to drive. She was too upset.

Her tears may have stopped before arriving at Jimmy's place, but the sharp pain that rang through her head remained. She welcomed nothing as much as a glass of water to quench her thirst or a wet cloth to wash her face—and maybe a magical cure that made her forget the last hour of her life, if that were possible.

"Is Michael here?" Tarah could barely manage a whisper as they drove in the driveway. "I can't face him right now."

"I'm sorry, Tarah, I don't know," Jimmy replied in a soft voice. Since meeting her outside the apartment, she had seen a side of him she had never seen before. He was caring and nurturing. She felt sure he would've done anything to make her happy at that very moment. "Do you want me to go in and check?" His eyes were hopeful.

"No, that's fine," Tarah said. They both got out of her car, and Jimmy grabbed her luggage. She followed him up the steps and through the door. There didn't appear to be anyone in the house. She asked for a glass of water and he got it for her.

"Want to go to my room?" Jimmy turned to her and a grin slowly crossed his face. "I mean, not in *that* way. I'm not that much of an ass. I'll sleep on the couch." There was a moment of shyness before he added the kicker. "Take advantage, it may be the only time I ever ask you to my room and don't try to fuck you."

Tarah couldn't help but laugh. "I'm not kicking you out of your room. I'll just crash on the floor; it's fine as long as I don't have to deal with anyone else but you."

"No, the room is all yours. I'll sleep on the couch. The last thing we need is Michael reporting the sleeping arrangements to William. Plus, you need your time alone."

He gave her a gentle smile and started up the stairway that was nearby. She quietly followed. Before entering his room, Tarah stopped in the bathroom to run water over her face. Her makeup was smeared and she looked pathetic. She quickly washed and returned to the hallway.

"I cleaned it up a bit," Jimmy said, and ushered Tarah into his room and placed her suitcase on the floor. She noted that it was much cleaner than it had been on her last visit. There was nothing on the floor, the bed was made, and the window was open. He must have noticed her looking around, because he quickly commented on it. "After William talked to me, I knew he was going to confront you. So, I decided that I'd clean up here, just in case you had to leave. I figured it would be a pretty nasty scene at your place, and if you had nowhere to go, well ... you always had here."

"Thanks." Tarah stood awkwardly and looked around the room. "Is that why you were waiting for me outside my building tonight?" Her voice was hoarse.

"Yeah," he said bashfully. "Not to seem stalker-like, but I just felt really bad that I couldn't get to you before William did. I didn't know where to find you. He really flew into me, so I can imagine what he was like with you. So, when I saw your car at your building tonight, I stuck around for a bit, just in case you needed me."

"It wasn't that bad," Tarah admitted. She sat down on his bed and Jimmy did the same. "I wish he had been *more* angry with me. I'd feel less guilty that way." She spoke slowly. "William was just ... I don't know, really hurt and disappointed. He said that he and I obviously didn't have much of a relationship if I could be so easily swayed and that he would've rather heard it all from me, not you."

"I tried to tell him that there was nothing going on," Jimmy insisted. "I swear, Tarah, I even told him that it was all me and that you hadn't done a thing wrong, but he seemed to already have his mind made up that you wanted me as much as I wanted you."

"I know." Tarah nodded and wondered to herself if William somehow knew more than he was letting on. Had Eddie said something? Not that it mattered at that point. "The ironic part was that I had a long talk with a friend tonight, and he pointed out that it was clear that I wanted to be with you, otherwise I would've avoided you like the plaque. I guess he was right."

Tarah spoke slowly as she looked into Jimmy's eyes. "And I was planning to talk to William tonight when I went home, but he beat me to the punch."

"Really?" Jimmy looked genuinely surprised. "I just assumed you were so upset tonight because you *didn't* want to break up with William."

"No, I did." Tarah hesitated. "Just not like that. I should've been the one to tell him." She took a deep breath and continued, "he didn't deserve that."

"It's not your fault; I'm the one who started this," Jimmy reminded her.

"But I didn't stop it." Her eyes met his. "If I was really loyal to William, I would've stopped it right there. But I didn't want to. I should've told him, he deserved that; but at the time, it didn't seem like any decision was the right one."

"You can't help how you feel," Jimmy countered. "And it doesn't make you a horrible person."

"Then why do I feel like a piece of shit right now?" Tarah laughed in spite of herself.

"You feel guilty and that's normal. I feel guilty too, Tarah. But I'm not going to lie about how I feel. If I hadn't acted on it on that night at your apartment, it just would've been another time. Come on, we're in a band together. We're signing a contract on Monday, which means we'll be working together *all* the time." Jimmy ran his hand through his dark hair. "I'm sorry it happened this way, I *really* am. But you have to let it go."

"I feel awful." Tarah felt tears burning her lids. "He's a good person and he's never did anything bad to me. I don't want him to hate me."

Jimmy moved closer Tarah. "Just give it a few days and then talk to him. Let things calm down." He leaned in and kissed her on the cheek. She quickly turned her head and their lips met. Tarah felt so broken that she just wanted to be with Jimmy for the night, but just as their kiss became so feverish that she could hear him gasp, he moved away, and she heard him whisper, "Not like this, Tarah."

Feeling defeated, she shrank back.

"You need to get some sleep," Jimmy gently insisted. He started toward the door.

"Could you stay, just for a bit?" Tarah asked, as she lay on the bed on top of the sheets. "Just till I fall asleep?"

"Okay." Jimmy nodded and closed the door before joining her on the bed. Lying behind her, he reached over to hold her hand, which she gratefully took.

But she couldn't sleep. Tarah just stared at the clock on the nightstand. At six in the morning she was still awake. She glanced behind her to see Jimmy sleeping peacefully. She once again closed her eyes. The next thing she knew, a loud banging noise woke her. Startled, she glanced at the clock. It was now noon. Turning, she noted that Jimmy was not with her. The bedroom door was closed, and she slowly rose to look out the window.

Outside, she saw William's van and she froze. Should she go talk to him? Just as Tarah was about to rush out of the room, it hit her. William was probably there to move his brother out. But when she returned to the window, Tarah discovered that both of the Stacy brothers were hauling a mattress into the house. It was from her old bed, the one that used to sit in the spare room of their apartment. He wasn't moving Michael. He was moving *her.*

Collapsing to the floor, Tarah felt another pain hit her like a knife in the chest. She couldn't even cry. She just sat there and tried to calm down. He was moving her *in?* A day hadn't even passed since they broke up, and he was disposing of her stuff as if she were never a part of his life at all.

The sound of footsteps running up and down the stairs eventually stopped, and Tarah could hear William's van starting from the driveway. Jimmy returned to his room to find Tarah curled up in bed. He gave her a sweet smile. "Good afternoon, sleepyhead!"

She smiled back at him as he leaned over to kiss her forehead. "So, good news. William just moved most of your stuff here, and he's moving Mike's crap over, then bringing the rest of your stuff back here."

Tarah gave him a sad smile.

"What? You didn't want to come here?" Jimmy looked confused. "If you want to move somewhere else, it's fine. At least you don't have to worry about going back there for anything."

Tarah sat up on the bed. "I just feel like ... I don't know," she stumbled. "I just feel like he is getting rid of my stuff and me as quickly as possible. Last night, our breakup was short, sweet, and to the point, and now he's moving my stuff, not even a day later."

"Okay, I'm a little confused. Did you *want* to go back there to pack your own stuff?" Jimmy awkwardly stuffed his hands into the pockets of his jeans. He was wearing all black as usual. "I don't understand."

"It's not that," Tarah assured him. She certainly had dreaded the very idea of going back and gathering her possessions while William silently sat in another room. "It's as I said, I just feel like he was not exactly hesitating to get rid of me. What did he do, stay up last night packing my stuff just so he didn't have to see anything that reminded him of me?"

"Tarah, it's nothing personal against you," Jimmy insisted. "I think it's just that Mike wanted to move in, so William thought he'd just pack up your stuff *for* you and move it here until you decide what you want to do. I mean, he had to pick up Mike's belongings anyway, right? It wasn't malicious in any way."

"Yeah." Tarah covered her face trying to hide her embarrassment. He *was* right; that was exactly how William would look at things. "Do you think I should try to talk to him when he comes back?"

"No," Jimmy quickly replied. "This wouldn't be the time. He was barely pleasant with me. Especially when he realized you were in *my* room." Sitting down beside her, Jimmy laughed. "It's not funny, but it kind of is. I tried to explain that you slept in here because you were upset and I was here, but there was nothing going on. The more I tried to explain, the worse it sounded. I just kept digging myself deeper and deeper into a hole and finally just got out of their way."

"Oh great," Tarah groaned. "We still have to work with him." She glanced up to see Eddie standing in the doorway.

"Hey, guys, sorry to interrupt." He looked hesitant. "I was wondering if Michael's moving out, can I have his old room, or do you want it Tarah? I just thought ..." He drifted off.

"That I'm going to be in here with Jimmy?" Tarah finished the sentence for him. "I really didn't think that far."

"Yeah, Eddie, you might want to grab Mike's old room. It's farther down the hallway." Jimmy returned his attention to Tarah. "When we moved in, Mike said he didn't want to hear me fucking every night, so he made Ed take the room beside mine. And if you're beside ... well, you know."

"Is that okay with you, Tarah?" Eddie looked relieved.

"Sure." Tarah smiled and watched him disappear.

"Poor guy." Jimmy gave her a seductive smile. "Single and having to hear me screwing in the next room. That's got to hurt."

"How considerate of you," Tarah said sardonically.

Although she attempted to lift her spirits for the remainder of the weekend, Tarah found it difficult to push herself to unpack and set up a new bedroom. Everything was just happening way too fast for her. She spent Sunday evening on the phone. First, she called John and her brother to tell both about her sudden breakup and move. Neither were surprised and both offered to help her out if she needed anything. Then, Tarah called her mother.

"What?" Her mother was stunned. "I thought you were happy with William. Such a nice young man, why did you break up with him?" Tarah bit her lip and opened her mouth to explain, when her mother continued. "And why are you living with this group of men at a house? Why didn't you come home?"

"Mom, it's complicated. It just wasn't working out." Tarah decided that it wasn't necessary to share the details. She just wanted to get this conversation over with. "And I'm living with two of the guys in my band. Eddie and

Jimmy." Her mother had met both when attending a couple of shows the previous year.

"Eddie seemed like a quiet young man, but I don't know about that Jimmy." Her mother sniffed. "Struck me as a slimy character. Tarah, I don't think you should be living in a house with two men anyway. Men are men; you don't want to wake up one night and find one of them drunk and trying to get in your bed."

Tarah couldn't help but laugh. *Oh, if she only knew!*

"Mom, I'm fine here." She ended the conversation and went downstairs. Jimmy and Eddie were watching television.

"Hey," Jimmy called out. "Did you get all those awful calls over with?"

"Yeah, everyone knows." Tarah nodded as she sat on the couch between both guys. "Mom's wants me to move home so she can torture me in person and on a daily basis. Oh, and she thinks that Eddie is a sweetheart and you're 'slimy.'" She watched Jimmy start to laugh.

"Good judge of character," he quipped.

"Then she warned me that one of you would probably get drunk some night and try to crawl into my bed."

"I like how your mom thinks," Jimmy teased her, and Eddie just laughed.

On Monday morning, Eddie, Jimmy, and Tarah piled in her car and headed to Toronto. Michael and William were to meet them at Peter Sampson's office that morning to sign the contract. As they drove, Jimmy excitedly talked about what they were about to embark on. "It will change our lives," he insisted.

Tarah dreaded seeing William. She knew it had to happen, but hated the circumstances. This would be one of the most important days of her life, and she'd always associate it with their breakup. As it turned out, it wasn't as bad as she'd expected. In fact, she and William were civil to one another but there was clearly tension in the room.

Peter welcomed them all and sat them down in the boardroom to sign their recording contract. FUTA's lawyer, Bob Jameson, discussed each section of the contract and how it applied to them. Basically, the company was lending them money to give them a start. There were some things that FUTA would pay for, such as their hotel rooms when they were recording their CD in Toronto, Fire's first video, and some odds and ends, such as the current legal fees. However, the list of what the band would have to pay back seemed endless, such as production and marketing fees. Also, they were expected to push their music in every way possible. It didn't matter if it meant giving an interview or creating a scandal, the bottom line is that Fire had to bring attention to themselves and as quickly as possible.

"We found a producer for you, his name is Rick McClure and he's very good," Peter assured them, and then went on to name some popular bands he was associated with. Jimmy nodded and said he knew someone who worked with the producer and that he had heard good things about him. Tarah noted that Michael glared across the table at Jimmy, who sat beside her.

"He's excellent," Peter assured them. "We want you guys starting off on the right foot. But it's like I said, in the end, it's all up to you. This break is what you make of it. Your goal is to be commercially successful. Now, we'll be in touch to discuss other details as things move forward. My suggestion is to get your songs together, and get in and out of the studio as quickly possible. If you can get out of the studio in a week, it will cut down on your production costs, and we'll be willing to throw in a bonus for each of you."

"Wow, that's pretty cool," William spoke up. "But, can we do it in under a week?"

"Well, it's happened before," Peter assured him. "Rick is a great producer, and if you're ready, I think it's very possible." He gave them an assuring smile. "You know what, kids, the faster you can get out there and get a fan base, the better. And once you get that fan base, you always have to concentrate on building it and striking the iron while it's hot. It means, get the CDs out, and keep everyone interested."

And then the meeting was over. The band agreed to meet the next day at the house to pick out the songs they wanted. William barely talked to or acknowledged Tarah, and she accepted that she couldn't hope for much more, considering the circumstances.

They all went home, and no one read their copy of the contract.

Tarah was surprised to learn that her father had left a message at the house while they were out. He congratulated her on the band's success and encouraged her to call him soon. She assumed her mother had given him the new phone number.

That night, she and Jimmy talked about how strange it felt to sign a contract that would change their lives and yet have the day move forward just like any other.

"I always thought it'd be different somehow," Tarah admitted. "I don't know how, it just feels like another day."

"It is another day. But a good one." Jimmy sat on the bed, facing Tarah. He leaned against the headboard. The room was dark except for the light from a small lamp on the nightstand. "Are you feeling better?"

"Yeah, I'm getting there," Tarah admitted. "Thanks."

"For what, creating complete chaos in your life?" He grinned.

"Yes." Tarah leaned in and quickly kissed him. She thought it strange that now that there was nothing keeping them from getting together, that they didn't. But she didn't mind.

"Can I ask you a question?" she asked. Tarah watched him give her a small nod as he stared in her eyes. "How many women have you been with?"

"Oh God!" Jimmy let out a quick laugh and covered his eyes, pushing his black hair out of his face. "Baby, you don't wanna know."

"Really?" Tarah wasn't sure how she felt about that.

"Why? It's just a number. It's not exactly something to be proud of." Jimmy's lids were heavy, causing him to look seductive and inviting. "I don't have any diseases, and I'm not telling you."

"Well, wouldn't you want to know how many guys I slept with?"

"No." Jimmy shook his head, suddenly more alert. "I don't. I really don't. It's irrelevant; it's got nothing to do with you and me."

"But what if—"

"No, I don't," he cut her off. "I don't care how many guys you did or didn't sleep with. If you were a virgin or slept with some women, *then* I'd want to know. But otherwise, I really don't want to know, babe." His face lit up in a smile.

Tarah laughed, but accepted that. "Can I ask you something else though? Why did you do it? I mean, why didn't you have relationships?"

"Oh, I had a relationship once—that was enough," Jimmy admitted.

"But you said you wanted to be with me."

"I do." Jimmy nodded. "But you're the only woman I've ever really respected."

"Wow, really?" Tarah was a little surprised.

"Yeah,"

"Why don't you respect other women?"

Jimmy seemed hesitant for a moment. "It's a long story. I guess it started when I was a kid, I was kind of fat, and girls were always total bitches to me."

Tarah was stunned. Jimmy was hardly overweight; in fact, he had a lean body and was known to lift weights in the basement.

"Yeah, I know, I'm not now." He sighed. "When I was a kid, I was. And other kids were pretty mean about it. Girls especially. I remember there was this one girl I really liked, and I decided to ask her out. She totally made a huge spectacle of it. It was the school joke for a while because she was really pretty and I was the loser. Her name was Suzanne Bordon."

Tarah gave him an empathetic smile. "I didn't exactly have that problem in school, but I was really skinny. I mean, skinnier than I am now." She glanced down at her small figure. "Kids made fun of me for it and said I was anorexic."

"See, you kind of know what I mean," Jimmy said. "Anyway, while I was still fat, I ended up dating a really nice girl named Sally. I was seventeen and she was the first girl I slept with. While we were still together, I started to lose weight. I was going to the gym, and my dad even hired a trainer. Sally moved away for college and dumped me, right about the same time that I started to really tone up. Then, suddenly all the girls were like chasing after me—all the girls who used to humiliate me."

"It was kind of weird. I liked the attention, but I was still a little resentful of all the teasing and the hell they put me through." He shrugged. "So anyway, I dated this one girl and we basically didn't do much more than have sex all the time, because she was a little older and more experienced. Then we split up and guess who suddenly is interested in me? Suzanne Bordon."

"Oh my God!" Tarah laughed. "She had nerve."

"Oh she *did*," Jimmy agreed. "So, I went out with her on a date and the whole time I'm thinking, *What the fuck, she wouldn't give me the time of day before.* So, I fucked her and dumped her the same night."

Tarah was stunned but then started to laugh.

"Then, I fucked most of her friends and dumped them too. Of course, 'cause women are nuts, they all chased after me, even though I treated them like dirt." Jimmy reached over and grabbed Tarah's hand. "So, I guess I just kept screwing them all behind each other's backs, and that's how my reputation as a dog started."

"It's kind of funny even though it's mean."

"It *is*, and kind of sad at the same time," Jimmy said. "It amazes me the shit women will put up with when it comes to men. You know, it's crazy. The meaner I was to them, the more they wanted it. When I was fat and nice, they hated me. Meanwhile, I had been playing guitar for years and joined a band, and then I started to work at a bar; both putting me in the position to meet a lot of women. I think the rest is pretty self-explanatory. The numbers just kept rising."

"Women always go nuts for any guy in a band. And well, the bar thing was clearly easy access."

"Actually, working in a bar gave me a big reality check on women." Jimmy shook his head. "The bigger scumbag at a bar, the most fucking pussy he gets. Trust me. I've seen it. Another reason why I didn't respect women."

"What did you think when you first met me?" Tarah asked. "Did you think I was like those girls?"

"No, I genuinely liked you. You seemed really cool and held your own with the band. I always wanted to talk to you but you were usually with Will."

"But you were always kind of flirty with me, right?"

"Well, yeah," Jimmy laughed. "I said, I didn't think you were a dirty skank, I didn't say that I didn't want to nail you."

Tarah laughed. "Thank you."

"For wanting to nail you?" Jimmy continued to laugh.

"No, thank you for everything," Tarah said, squeezing his hand. "For making me laugh so much when I didn't really want to, and for everything else."

"For upsetting your life?"

"I think it's a good upset."

CHAPTER TWENTY

▼

"Of course not." Colin Whitfield spoke bluntly to the band. The short, pudgier middle-aged man was wearing a pair of glasses that looked too small for his face. His office was almost like a home away from home; Colin had a couch on one side of the room, a bar on the other, and even a small bathroom in the right-hand corner. There were two unusual paintings on each side of the large window behind him.

It was a week after signing a contract with FUTA, and the five had gathered in the office of a well-known entertainment lawyer to discuss their options. As it turns out, they didn't have any. "They definitely aren't going to suggest that you bring a lawyer along when you sign. FUTA has *way* too much to gain by *not* having someone representing your interests. In fact, I just hope when I read this contract that you guys aren't getting completely screwed. It wouldn't be the first time."

Colin sat forward in his chair and tapped the document sitting on his desk. It was much thicker than Tarah would've thought a record contract would be, but apparently that was no excuse for not taking the time to read it. However, even when she'd tried, Tarah wasn't even sure if she understood it. Now, as she sat before Colin Whitfield, she felt her stomach tying in knots as she waited for the other shoe to fall.

"But if it's a bad contract, we can fight it right?" William spoke on behalf of the band. "Since we didn't have a lawyer present."

"No, in fact a judge would question not only *why* you didn't have a lawyer that day, but also why you neglected to read it and negotiate."

"But we were given the impression that their lawyer was there on *our* behalf," William calmly spoke, appearing much more relaxed than the rest of the band. "The guy we were dealing with even said that we wouldn't be charged for the lawyer fees."

"Of course not." Colin gave a short laugh. "It's because he wasn't your lawyer in the first place. But don't feel bad, record companies aren't known for their integrity." Colin fingered through the contract. "Now, I'm going to glance over this quickly and let you know what I think. I'll give it a more thorough reading later on and get back to you on the specific details; however I've seen enough of these over the years that I can pretty much pinpoint the key areas and then let you all be on your way."

Tarah gave him a small smile when he looked her way. She felt genuinely stupid after having Colin point out the obvious. Glancing toward Jimmy on her right, she noted that he had a look of disinterest on his face. Eddie was on her left appearing tense and nervous. Beside him was Michael, who turned quickly to glare at her; William sat at the end and, to her surprise, made actual eye contact with her for the first time since their breakup. It was just a quick look, but Tarah sensed no hostility from him, and it somehow made her feel better.

"First of all," Colin spoke up, and Tarah averted her attention back to the man behind the desk. "I see you won't be getting a huge percentage off the CD sales, but I've seen worse. You'll get more actually from selling band merchandise."

"Band merchandise?" William asked.

"Oh, you know." Colin waved his hand in the air. "T-shirts, that kind of thing. Anything with your name on it."

William nodded, and Colin went back to the contract.

"Looks like they're going to support you decently while you are on your tour, but you'll be paying for the majority of the expenses. I was afraid they'd really screw you over there, because tours are expensive." Colin continued to glance through the pages, and Tarah could feel her heart pounding. "They really want you to market the band every chance you get, and they plan to pay some on the original advertising. Also, they'll pay for the CD launch, which is nice."

"There is an exclusivity clause here that indicates that FUTA doesn't want you to play for another label during the time you are signed with them. You can, however, be a guest on someone else's label, if it's acknowledged it in their credits that you're with FUTA. That's pretty much the norm. It'll say something like 'courtesy of FUTA records' with your name."

"Looks like they plan to really push you on the radio side of things, a real plus." Colin continued to scan the pages on his desk. "They want to have a lot of 'final says' on things. I don't know if I like that. For example, final say on the songs you'll be choosing for the CD, on the cover art of the CD, that kind of thing. They'll probably haul in some image consultant and wardrobe person to tell you all how you should look too." Colin sounded bitter as he scratched his head and wrinkled his nose. "Hmm, this one's interesting." His eyes ran back and forth over the paper, building up the anticipation before announcing his discovery.

"Looks like FUTA wants to keep you around for five CDs, which is good. I was a bit worried they may have tied you down for years in this contract. Never a good thing but this is the really interesting part." He pointed at the document and looked directly at Tarah. "Looks like *you* could've had your own lawyer and hammered out a deal with these guys because they clearly want you around. In fact, Tarah, it says here you have to stay with the band for three years as part of this contract. I don't see that very often, so they clearly want to ensure that you stick around. It suggests that they consider you to be the key person in the band."

He went on to read the contract, but Tarah felt all eyes on her. She didn't even have to look around to see who'd have the questionable expressions or the angry glare. Without turning her head, Tarah's eyes slowly turned toward Jimmy, who genuinely looked excited for her.

"So," William spoke up. "If she were to say, quit, what does that do to our contract?"

"Let's just say," Colin grinned at Tarah, then quickly looked back at William. "You really want to keep on her good side."

Later that same week, Fire found a manager for their band. Her name was Maggie Eriksson and, just like Colin Whitfield, she was located in Toronto.

Maggie was young, attractive, and very businesslike. Unlike Colin, she didn't address the band in casual tones, but spoke to them as clients. She was professional and direct.

"First of all, I would've preferred that you had found a lawyer before signing the contract," Maggie said, repeating what the entire band had heard from everyone in the last week and a half. "However, from the sounds of it, Mr. Whitfield doesn't seem to feel you did too badly on the deal, so that *is* a plus."

"He just said that he could've done better for us." Eddie had continued to wear his worried expression since the day they first spoke with Peter Sampson.

"To be honest, he probably could have, but then again, most lawyers *will* tell you that they could've got you a better deal, regardless. You have to remember that he was trying to win you over as a client," Maggie pointed out, and then jumped to another topic. "So you're currently recording a CD?"

"We start on Monday," Tarah replied, and Maggie slowly nodded.

"And they want you to finish it in a week." Maggie wrinkled her forehead. "I understand that they're probably throwing money or some type of deal at you in order to keep production costs down, however when all is said and done, it's your reputation that's on the line. I wouldn't spend six months making this CD, however you do want to make sure that the finished product best represents the band." Maggie sat up very straight in her chair and displayed complete confidence. She didn't have a dark hair out of place or a chip on her nail polish. Everything was perfect.

"I think I want you to go in and work on the CD and not worry about anything. FUTA is going to be down your throat every chance they get, trying to push you to the top before you have five minutes to think straight; that's all they care about. I'm not going to lie to you, in their eyes you are *just* a product they want to sell." Maggie cleared her throat and turned her attention toward Tarah. "Not to seem cruel, but that's how this industry works."

"Now, as I said, I'd like to see you go into the studio and make the absolute best CD possible so that we have a great product to work with." Maggie's pale brown eyes flickered from one of their faces to the next. "Meanwhile, I'm going to find a good photographer to set you up with a press kit and photos for the CD. I'm going to have someone come in to talk to you about your personal style as a band, what image you want to project if any. We'll cover all the bases to make you the best you all can be."

"We'll work together with FUTA to come up with a CD launch party and see what we can do tour-wise," she continued. "I'd like to have you be an opening act for another band to give you experience touring throughout the country and the opportunity to build a fan base here before we launch you in other countries."

Tarah felt like her head was swimming. It didn't matter who they talked to, it was just another list of what they had to do. It was overwhelming.

Glancing at Tarah, Maggie seemed to note her expression and make a comment specifically toward her. "Don't worry, you don't have to think about all this today. Just focus on the CD. I'm the one who worries about the details; that's what you pay me for."

As it turned out, the manager and lawyer were going to be paid extremely well, which made Tarah wonder if they were getting in over their heads.

"What if we don't succeed?" Tarah asked her brother over the phone later that night. "We still owe all this money to the record company."

"I think you'll be fine," Bobby reassured her, while Caitlin cried in the background. "It sounds like this lady has it all under control. I mean, that's why you're hiring all these people. They're there to take care of you. In fact, maybe you should schedule a meeting with your manager sometime as a one-on-one to discuss your concerns. Sounds like she knows what she's talking about."

"I already have one," Tarah replied. "She wants to meet with each of us individually to go over details in the future. My meeting is at the end of the month."

"Just don't stress about it till then," Bobby insisted. "It'll all work out in the end."

Caitlin's cries seemed to get louder, and Bobby excused himself to check on her. Apparently Sara wasn't feeling well and had gone to bed. Although Tarah had no idea how she could sleep with that noise in the same apartment.

Hanging up the phone, she noted the rare silence in her own house. Usually the television or music was echoing throughout the rooms, either that or one of the boys would be practicing in the basement. Eddie had a date earlier in the evening, but Jimmy was never too far away.

Exhausted, Tarah climbed up the stairs to her room. Although she and Jimmy were dating, she was kind of thankful that they weren't sharing a bed. In fact, much to her surprise, he hadn't really made any kind of move on her as of yet. They kissed and talked, but things never really got out of hand like they used to when she was still with William. Jimmy, she noticed, had come on really strong in the beginning, but seemed to mellow out after she had moved in. Not in a bad way. In fact, the more she unraveled him, the more she liked Jimmy. Underneath it all, there was a calm side of him that he rarely displayed to anyone else.

As she walked by his room, she saw him sitting on the bed with his guitar in hand. Looking up he sighed, "I'm just not happy with the beginning of "Swim on my Beach." I don't like how William wants to start it. Man, it just doesn't sound right."

"Maybe you need a break from it," Tarah suggested. "I don't know about you, but I can't concentrate on anything after the last week. I feel like way too much is going on at once."

Jimmy listened, his head tilted slightly. He gave her a small smile and set down his guitar. "I know you're still stressing about Colin's comment on how you're *the* person in the band, but don't worry about it. I think it's great."

"I think you're the only person who feels that way." Tarah walked in his doorway.

"Well, that's too fucking bad." Jimmy stood up and approached her. "It is what it is. I don't feel threatened if you're the most popular person in the band or whatever. Who cares?"

"Michael. Possibly William. Eddie looked surprised too." Tarah felt as if her entire body was being weighed down by that one comment, and she wasn't sure why.

"Don't let it get to you." Jimmy leaned in and kissed her. "I hate to tell you this, but once the band takes off, you'll hear some really bad comments about you, me, all of us, so take advantage of the nice ones. This will seem minor someday. And you know what, I don't think you should be uncomfortable with it. Fuck, there are singers out there who would cut off their right arm if they could have that kind of power. Don't take it for granted. It's a card you might have to play someday."

And with that, he leaned in and kissed her again. This time, her arms curled around his neck while his hand carefully touched her back and pulled her body closer to him. Automatically, his mouth hungrily enclosed hers, and his breathing became labored. She felt him become hard against her, and Tarah gasped for air. Jimmy stopped kissing her and leaned his forehead against the top of her head. Through the dark strands of hair that fell over his face, Jimmy's eyes stared straight into Tarah's and for a moment, it felt like she had stopped breathing.

Without saying a word he leaned forward and pushed his door closed. She was mesmerized as she watched Jimmy removing his T-shirt, then jeans and socks. Wearing only a pair of navy boxers, he stepped forward with an engaging grin on his face. Running his fingers over Tarah's chin, he simply said, "This would work a lot better if you took yours off too."

Feeling embarrassed, she looked away from him and laughed. But he had already gone to work, unbuttoning her sweater and letting it drop to the floor. She started to unbutton her jeans and soon they joined her knitted material on the floor to form a small pile. Wearing only a thong and bra, she stepped away from her clothes and into Jimmy's arms. His mouth instantly covered hers, and his hands ran down her back and over her butt, where he pulled her body closer to him.

As he carefully moved her onto his bed, Tarah thought about something her brother had said earlier that night. Everything always *did* work out in the end.

Chapter Twenty-One

▼

"I just feel like I'm never going to get it right," Tarah complained to Jimmy. The couple was on a lunch break, walking out of the Toronto studio on a warm April afternoon. It was about to be the third twelve-hour day of working with Rick McClure, and the entire band was exhausted. The popular producer was demanding, settling for nothing less than perfection. "I don't feel as if I'm able to give him what he wants."

"Yeah, but the guy's demanding because he wants us to put our best into the CD. It's not because he's a fucking prick," Jimmy reminded her, and reached for her hand and gave it a squeeze. "Come on, I'll buy you Subway."

Tarah smiled and followed him inside the nearby sandwich shop. Ten minutes later, they were sitting beside a window and eating their food. "Jimmy, do you think Rick thinks I suck?"

Jimmy mouthed the word *no* and shook his head. "He's just pushing ya because he knows you can do better. Trust me, I used to take professional singing lessons."

"You did what?" Tarah sat down her sandwich. "*You* took singing lessons. You never told me that."

"Yup, back in my fat days I had a vocal coach because my parents wanted to get me involved in stuff." Jimmy calmly chewed his food. "Plus, they'd do just about anything to keep me from hiding in my room all the time."

"I'm sure it's because you had talent," Tarah reassured him, as she bit into her sandwich. "I don't think it was *just* to get you outta your room."

"I don't know." Jimmy didn't seem convinced. "I was the fat kid, so I didn't feel very sociable, and obviously I wasn't playing any kind of sports. They didn't have much else to work with other than music. I already was playing guitar, so they decided to try vocal lessons, and it turned out I was pretty good."

"See, it wasn't just to get you out of your room," Tarah repeated, and took the last bite of her sub. "They saw your potential."

"Yeah." Jimmy rolled his eyes. "They saw my potential to become a chronic masturbator if I didn't get out of my room once in awhile."

Tarah started to laugh and choked on her food. But Jimmy didn't miss a beat.

"That's all I did back then, Tarah. Played guitar or with myself all day."

"I can't believe you're seriously telling me this." Tarah finally regained her composure, glancing around to see if anyone overheard their conversation; but the customers at the nearby tables were not paying attention to them. "So, you're saying …"

"All summer when I was like fourteen and fifteen, yeah, that's all I did." Jimmy acted very matter-of-fact about it, but he was clearly enjoying Tarah's reaction to his story. "So, on my sixteenth summer, my parents made me take singing lessons then I started working out. But it's like they say, 'practice makes perfect.'"

"I really hope you're talking about the music thing." Tarah took a quick drink of her water.

Jimmy shrugged. "Yeah, that too."

"Hey, guys." Tarah heard a voice and turned around to see Eddie approaching them. "I walked by and saw you in the window."

"Hi." Tarah slid over and Eddie sat beside her.

"So, what's up?"

"I was just telling Tarah my story about why I took singing lessons," Jimmy said, and yawned.

"Oh man, you didn't tell her *everything* did you?" Eddie was wide eyed. "I mean, the same story you told me like a few weeks ago?"

"Yeah." Jimmy nodded and looked bored. He returned his attention to Tarah. "I was telling Eddie that since we weren't officially 'together' at that time, that I hadn't jerked off that much since—"

"Okay." Tarah put her hand up. "I get the picture, Jimmy." He raised his eyebrows while smiling at her, and she felt her face grow hot. Things certainly had changed since that particular conversation between him and Eddie.

Jimmy gave her an evil grin and continued, "*Anyway,* I actually used to sing for my last band. And play lead guitar. So, after 'taking the long road' version of this story, my point is that I took singing lessons for a year, and you're singing is great. There's nothing wrong with it. Guys like Rick just push you because they know you have the potential to do better, and they want that to come across on the CD."

"It's true, Tarah." Eddie nodded. "I even heard him say that he wants to get the best out of us all."

"But I find he pushes me more."

"Yeah, but you have to remember, the label thinks you're the VIP of the band," Jimmy teased her. "They want to make you a star."

Tarah sighed. "Not everyone agrees on that point." She knew he was only teasing her, but she was growing tired of the extra tension in the band since their meeting with Colin Whitfield. Already, Michael had managed to make several snide remarks regarding the portion of the contract that insisted she stay with the band for three years.

"I think it's cool, Tarah," Eddie piped up, and seemed to read her thoughts. "Don't listen to Michael. He's an asshole."

"We're all in agreement there," Jimmy said, pushing some hair from his face. "I wish we'd gotten rid of him before the contract, man. He's going to be impossible to work with. Even now, with the CD, he's annoying the fuck out of me."

"At least he's not living with us anymore," Eddie said.

"We used to plot his death for fun," Jimmy joked. "But William would've had a fucking heart attack if we ever suggested that Mike leave. In fact, we *did* suggest it once and he insisted we needed him." He paused. "I don't know what the fuck for, bass players are a dime a dozen."

"That's what I thought too," Eddie added. "Everyone else gets along." He suddenly turned to Tarah. "I mean, well, kind of."

Tarah gave a small smile and stared down at her hands. Since their breakup, she and William managed to be civil toward each other. In fact, it surprised her to see that William didn't seem to have any issue with Jimmy, but just her. Not that she wanted the two of them to clash, but she didn't want him to hate her forever.

"It's fine, Eddie. It's to be expected, right?"

But it did bother her. Tarah had considered contacting William on more than one occasion to clear the air. After all, they all had to work together and the last thing they needed to do was fight all the time. It would be long three years if they did, because clearly Tarah couldn't easily get out of the contract before that time if she wasn't happy.

So when the band was taking a break later that day, Tarah decided to talk to William. Jimmy had disappeared and Michael had gone outside for a cigarette with Rick. She nervously decided to use that as her opener.

"I didn't realize Mike smoked." she said as she approached William. He was reading something in the newspaper and didn't respond to her at first. Tarah glanced across the room at Eddie, who was watching them closely, and he gave her a sympathetic smile. But William eventually replied.

"Huh?"

"I said I didn't realize your brother smoked." This time she felt a little hostility creep in her voice. Was he going to punish her every day? "What's with that?" She sat down beside him.

"I dunno. He quit smoking a long time ago and recently started again." William answered her question, but she still received a chilly reception. "I think he's stressed about everything with the contract."

"I think we all are." Tarah cleared her throat. It had been a long day and she was afraid of losing her voice before the end of the week. "Listen William, I don't want you to hate me. We all have to work together now, and regardless of what you might think, I never meant to hurt you. I swear I didn't."

William nodded. "I realize that, Tarah, but it was out of nowhere. I didn't even know anything was wrong; then I suddenly learn that Jimmy is hitting on you?"

Tarah nodded slowly. How could she reply to that? It was true. "You're right. I should've said something. I should've told you sooner. But I was confused." She hesitated for a moment and prayed Jimmy or the others didn't return to the room. "You were the perfect guy, and I didn't want to hurt you. But at the same time, we just seemed to argue so much."

"I know." He surprised her with his reaction. "We did, and then had make-up sex."

"It wasn't always like that," Tarah reminded him. "But yes, it did happen."

"Look, I'm going to be honest with you about something." William spoke in a hushed tone. "I automatically regretted breaking up with you that night. And you know, I almost went downstairs and told you that I wanted you to stay. But then I looked out the window, and there's Jimmy, already waiting for you."

Tarah felt her stomach turn. No wonder he hated her.

"And then I realized that things were how they should be. Even now, I still feel that way. We would've just gone upstairs, had make-up sex again, and everything would be tense again the next day. It just … it was time. I'm not going to pretend that I love the fact that you're with Jimmy, of all people. The guy who probably screwed half the women in this city, especially considering that he told us guys a lot of the nasty details whenever you weren't around." Tarah felt that remark hit harder than it should have. She knew Jimmy's past and shouldn't have been surprised.

"Not to say he's a horrible person, I don't think he is," William continued. "I like the guy, I always have, but I just wish it had been someone else. Someone I didn't know. Someone I didn't have to work with."

Tarah nodded. "I understand."

Jimmy returned right at that moment and proceeded to sit down with them and start talking. It made Tarah feel even more uncomfortable. It was just basic chitchat about their songs and the band, but it was awkward. She hoped it wouldn't always feel that way.

By Friday of that same week, the CD was almost done. The band only worked till noon that day. Rick insisted that they take it easy on the weekend and be prepared to finish early the following week. He also complimented Fire on being "very professional, easy to work with and respectful." Rick also suggested that Tarah relax her voice on the weekend, because it had become very strained. "No wild partying!" he insisted.

Tarah certainly had no energy to do much of anything at that point and even dreaded her meeting with Maggie that afternoon. Throughout the week, their manager had met with individual members of the band over lunch to discuss their career goals. Now it was Tarah's turn.

According to Jimmy, it wasn't a big deal. "You basically get a free lunch and tell her where you want the band to go. That's it."

With that in mind, Tarah met Maggie at a chain restaurant located close to the studio. She spotted the band's new manager right away. Tarah quickly joined her.

"Hello, Tarah." Maggie gestured at her to sit down. She wore a dark blue blazer and a matching skirt. A white blouse underneath seemed to bring out her eyes. Just as during their original meeting, her makeup and hair were flawless. "Nice to see you, Tarah. How did your studio time go? The boys were all reporting good things when I met them throughout the week."

"Great." Tarah's voice was clearly strained, and she coughed immediately after speaking.

"*Eww*, that doesn't sound too good," Maggie remarked, showing signs of sympathy in her face. "I suppose they've been wearing you down all week. I heard the band had long days at the studio."

Tarah simply nodded.

"That's too much. I can understand for the instrumental part of the recording, but I don't think it was necessary to drain your voice that much." Maggie shook her head. "I know you didn't sing the entire time, but I'm sure you still did more than should've been expected to."

"I suppose," Tarah barely whispered.

"Don't worry, I won't make you talk too much. In fact, I'll do most of the talking." Maggie sipped her coffee and a waitress approached them. Tarah ordered a tea and a Caesar salad. Maggie shook her head no and explained she had already eaten. "I had a rather large breakfast this morning during a meeting."

Tarah nodded.

"So Tarah, I want to thank you again for meeting with me today. I understand that you must be tired at this point. I just wanted to go over a few details about the future of the band."

Tarah sipped on her tea; it seemed to soothe to her throat. She didn't much care for the bitter taste, but simply enjoyed the warmth of the drink.

"First of all, I wanted to say that I reviewed the band's contract this week and found it quite interesting. And as we already discussed, FUTA clearly considers you the key member of Fire."

"Yeah." Tarah rolled her eyes. "I don't understand what that's about, but it's pissing off some people."

"I can imagine it would." Maggie grinned and took a sip of her coffee. "But that isn't unusual in a band, in fact, more times than not, the singer receives the majority of attention, and it causes some friction between members. There are some legendary examples of that kind of thing in some of the biggest rock bands. It's not uncommon. But to a point, it's a threat to the other members. What if you want to walk? Where does that leave them?"

"I have to stay three years." Tarah cleared her throat again.

"You should've asked for some honey in that tea." Maggie glanced down at the cup. "And yes, I know about the three years. The label is probably hoping that the band becomes successful, and when it's at its peak, you will quit and go solo."

"Wouldn't they want the band to stay together?"

"Sure, but it's hardly realistic. How many bands stay together, with their original members, past a few years? Really, think about it."

"Well, some do."

"Some, but not many."

Tarah nodded. She was right on that one.

"Regardless, we have to focus on the here and now. This is the thing, Tarah, as your manager, you always have to be completely honest with me." Maggie leaned forward on the table. "Now, that doesn't mean the world has to know the truth about your life, but I do, so that I can at least get rid of the vultures when they start circling. I have to ask you something that isn't any of my business, but it's in your best interest that I know."

Tarah sipped her tea. "I don't understand."

"Tarah, what is going on with all of you?" Maggie leaned forward and spoke quietly. "There's like a really weird tension within the band. I noticed it from day one, and as I talk to each of the members, just judging from their attitudes about one another, it's clear that something's going on with you guys."

Tarah sighed and quickly told Maggie the story about her, William, and Jimmy. She explained how she and Michael hadn't gotten along before the breakup with William. Now it was just impossible.

"Wow, that's quite a dynamic." Maggie smiled. "Love triangles are fun in soap operas, but not in the real world—let alone within a band. That would explain the tension I felt during that first meeting."

Both women smiled.

"Well, thank you for sharing that with me. It makes my job easier when I know my clients better." Maggie finished her coffee, while Tarah pushed a crouton around her plate. "When I think about it now, it's clear that Fire is the most appropriate name for your band after all."

Tarah agreed. There definitely had been lots of that between her and William, and now between her and Jimmy. Not to mention the hatred she felt toward Michael, and probably the anger both the Stacy brothers felt toward her and Jimmy. It was a strange situation. Why couldn't things been simpler? But deep down, Tarah felt like things were about to get a lot more complicated.

CHAPTER TWENTY-TWO

▼

"Oh, baby, I'm so glad that our CD is done!" Jimmy remarked, collapsing on the hotel bed where Tarah quickly joined him. With his arm around her, they slowly kissed, and she laid her head on his chest. The rest of the band had returned to Thorton after leaving the studio earlier in the afternoon, but Tarah and Jimmy had decided to stay in Toronto and have a few drinks with Rick McClure after they finished recording. The producer told them animated stories about bands he had previously worked with, and all in all, the three had a good time.

"I know," Tarah said, and closed her eyes. "I'm glad everyone was happy with it. FUTA, Rick, all of us." She could feel his chest rising and falling beneath her hand, and his fingers brushed over her arm. "I just can't even think about next week."

"They have a lot planned for us," Jimmy agreed. "Photo shoots and meeting with Peter and the director to talk about our first single. Maggie also mentioned something about planning the CD launch and some media stuff. I'm thinking we'd all be smart to just move to Toronto. This is where we're doing most of our work."

"I like where we're at right now," Tarah said, opening her eyes. "I know it's not the greatest house ever, but it's comfortable."

"I'm pretty comfortable where I am right now too." Jimmy rolled on his side and brought his mouth down hard against Tarah's, abruptly ending their conversation.

The following morning, the couple checked out of the hotel and headed back to Thorton. Tarah drove on the 401, while Jimmy anxiously played with the radio.

"There's this guy ... I can't remember what station it is ..." Jimmy continued to flip the dial around. "But he does this cool talk show in the morning, where people call in and comment on a current topic. It's usually about celebrities and their most recent controversies. The other day he was talking about how Madonna went all mental on Letterman."

"What are you talking about?"

"You didn't hear?" Jimmy continued to play around with the radio. "She went on Letterman and said 'fuck' a whole bunch of times and gave him her dirty underwear or something. I didn't actually see it, but people were pretty pissed the next day. She wouldn't get off the stage, and I guess she was super rude."

"Really?" Tarah could hear the surprise in her own voice.

"Yeah, I mean, I know she's your idol," Jimmy said, slanting his eyes in her direction. "But that was a little fucked-up, even for me. I can't believe you didn't hear about it."

"No." Tarah shook her head. "I can't—"

"Oh, found it!" Jimmy sat back in his seat. "What were you saying?"

But before Tarah could answer, the DJ announced something that shocked them both. Kurt Cobain was dead. He had committed suicide, and his body had been found on the previous day. The DJ went on to talk about Nirvana's history, the details of the case, and the public reaction.

Glancing toward Jimmy, Tarah didn't even know what to say. Kurt Cobain had been *his* idol. He looked completely shocked by the news and remained silent. His eyes were downcast, and suddenly it was as if his entire spirit had deflated. She felt helpless and didn't know how to respond.

"I'm sorry, Jimmy. I wish there was something I could do or say."

He shook his head slowly and took a deep breath. "There's nothing you can do or say." His voice had no emotion. "He's dead."

Tarah continued to drive, eyes forward, and listen to the DJ as various fans of Cobain called the live show and talked about how the musician had inspired their lives. Some cried. Others blamed Courtney Love for his death. One girl was angry with the singer for committing suicide, insisting his actions would only cause others to do the same. One fan compared Cobain to Morrison and Hendrix, saying that all the greats died young. Other people just talked about his body of work and how it reflected a generation. The DJ declared that grunge died on the same day as Nirvana's singer.

Jimmy didn't say anything for the remainder of the drive home, and Tarah grew increasingly worried. She eventually turned off the radio and tried to discuss the death with him, but he wasn't talking. It surprised her to see Jimmy that way, and she decided perhaps things would improve once they arrived back to Thorton, but they didn't. He went to bed as soon as they got home. Eventually Tarah did the same, curling in beside him and holding his hand as he had done with her the night she and William had broken up. She didn't know what else to do.

The next morning she woke to find his side of the bed empty. Glancing at the clock, she saw it wasn't even seven o'clock. With fear in her heart, she jumped out of bed and searched the house for him. For a split second, Tarah worried that the devoted fan had decided to follow in his idol's footsteps and hurt himself. Jimmy had never showed any signs of depression before, other than the day after confessing his feelings for her, but what if there was something wrong and she didn't know? Finally, after looking through the entire house, Tarah found Jimmy. He was in the basement sitting on a chair, playing Nirvana songs on his guitar. He stopped when he saw Tarah walk down the stairs.

"I woke up and you weren't there," she said in a quiet voice. "I was worried."

"I'm fine." Jimmy set down his guitar and looked at her. His eyes were full of sadness, but unlike the night before, she now saw some life in them. "I'm sorry for not saying much yesterday, I guess I was just so shocked by the news. It's weird, because it wasn't like I knew the guy."

"It's still upsetting." Tarah approached him. "It's still a life."

"I just don't know." Jimmy shook his head. "A part of me doesn't believe he committed suicide, but another part isn't surprised at all."

"Last night, before I went to bed, I saw on television that maybe Kurt Cobain felt like he sold out and couldn't deal with it." Tarah spoke quietly and felt a chill go up her spine. The thought of someone so close to her own age dying was hard to accept. "But they also said he was doing a lot of drugs."

Jimmy considered her words for a few minutes. "Tarah, do you think we're selling out?"

She shook her head no.

"But when Fire makes it, can we make sure we never get to the place where the business makes us hate our own lives or ourselves?" Jimmy asked. "I want you to promise me that if you ever feel like we're going in the wrong direction, that you pull me the fuck out of it all."

"But how will I know?" Tarah wrinkled her forehead.

"It'll be the day when you feel that it just isn't worth it anymore." Jimmy paused. "It'll be the day when the business has taken over our lives and our music. I guess it'll be the day when we feel like we have no integrity left."

Tarah nodded. "I will. That's if we ever become successful. And even if we do, who's to say we'll have that problem."

"I think we'll be a success, I'm just not sure how successful," Jimmy insisted. "But there always comes a point where celebrities lose their way. I mean, a few days ago it was Madonna. Did she have to go on Letterman and be rude and obnoxious to him? No, of course not. But she did. There seems to be a certain level of fame where celebrities lose their perspective, and I don't want to do that."

"Do you think Kurt Cobain lost his perspective?"

"I don't know," Jimmy said. "I really don't. A part of it was the drugs. Drugs really fuck up people and how they think. But at the same time, maybe he did lose his perspective. Maybe he just had to focus on the music and not worry about anything else. I don't know, Tarah.

On the following Monday, Maggie called them to say that FUTA had decided on "Swim on my Beach" as the band's first single.

"So, Tarah, I'd like to have the band meet with me later in the week to discuss the details."

"Sure," Tarah agreed, on everyone's behalf.

"Perfect," Maggie said, sounding very upbeat and encouraging. "Of course, we can't make any promises about how the song will be accepted once it's out there, but FUTA has definite plans to push this single as much as possible with the radio stations, which will help. We also have a few other ideas, but I'll discuss that when we meet this week."

Tarah found Eddie in the kitchen cooking a steak and told him what Maggie had said. He thanked her. She then went on to find Jimmy. He was in the room that they now shared, lying in bed and watching television. Tarah repeated the same information to him.

"Cool. Guess what?" Jimmy said. "I'm completely naked under this blanket. Want to come join me?"

Tarah smiled and was just about to reply when the doorbell rang.

"Who the hell is that? No one ever comes to visit us." She headed downstairs. In the weeks that she'd been in the house, only the other band members and her brother had dropped in. Tarah was in for a big surprise. Her mother was at the door.

"Tarah, you're never home when I'm trying to find you." Claire Kiersey pushed past her into the house. "I tried to call earlier and the line was tied up, as usual." Tarah knew Eddie was on the phone with the girl he had been seeing recently, but felt no need to share this information.

"I don't know what to tell you mom." Tarah spoke nervously. "Three people, one phone line?"

"Anyway, it doesn't matter, Tarah. I had to talk to you about a couple of things that are important, and I'd rather do it face to face." She glanced into their kitchen to see Eddie cooking his steak. He merely waved to Tarah's mom, who said a polite hello, before she boldly headed into the living room.

"This place isn't bad. A lot cleaner than I had expected." She opened her coat and glanced around. "Aren't you going to show me around, Tarah?"

"Ah, mom, can you just tell me what's going on first?" She made up a quick excuse, knowing Jimmy was stark naked upstairs. "You have me kind of worried now that you said you had stuff to talk to me about. What's wrong?"

"I realize that, Tarah, but I'd like to see where you live."

Just then, she saw Jimmy on his way downstairs. Luckily, he had clothes on. He exchanged amused smiles with Tarah and said hi to Claire before going into the kitchen with Eddie. "Where's my fucking dinner, Eddie?" he joked, but Tarah's mother didn't look amused.

"How can you live with him?" Claire made a face and pointed toward the stairs. "Just up here?"

Without waiting for an answer, Tarah's mother rushed up the stairs. Her daughter followed.

Peaking into the bathroom, Claire gave her nod of approval. "It's cleaner than I thought. You never know when you have young men living in your home, what the bathrooms will look like."

She then peaked into Tarah's room. "Very tidy." She stopped in front of Jimmy's bedroom and titled her head. "Does this belong to that Jimmy guy or Eddie?"

"Jimmy."

Her mother walked into the room and pushed a pair of Tarah's thongs that were on the floor, with her shoe. "For the love of God! Do the girls go through here so fast that they can't even get fully dressed before leaving?"

Tarah was too stunned to answer. But it was when she heard Jimmy coming up the stairs behind her that she froze. This couldn't be good, she decided. Her mother was in his room inspecting it, pissed off and Jimmy was about to be confronted with it.

"Hey?" He looked from Tarah to her mother.

Claire left Jimmy's room with a look of disdain on her face. "Sorry, thought that was my daughter's room, but apparently not." She walked past Tarah's room and down the hall, where she pretended to be impressed with a picture hung on the wall while glancing inside the Eddie's door. Jimmy looked like he was going to laugh and stepped back into his room. He picked up the thong that Claire had just inspected and pretended to lick it. In order to smother her own laughter, Tarah had to turn away from her mother who was headed back in her direction.

"Let's go back to the living room," she suggested. However, just as Tarah arrived at the top of the stairs, almost home free, her mother suddenly stopped in her tracks.

Tarah glanced toward Jimmy, who was now sitting on his bed inspecting one of his guitars and ignoring Claire Kiersey. But her mother was taking a long look past Jimmy, and it suddenly occurred to Tarah what was going on. It wasn't that Jimmy had a few of her belongings in the room, it was the fact that he had *most* of her stuff scattered everywhere. Her clothes, candles, books, and even Tarah's alarm clock sat on the nightstand.

"Tarah, are you *sharing* this room with him?" Claire pointed toward Jimmy, who looked up from his guitar with a deer-in-headlights expression on his face. His eyes met with Tarah's, something that her mother hadn't missed.

"That's what is going on here? You broke up with William to live with him, didn't you?" Claire had a combination of hurt and anger in her face. "Tarah, what are you doing?"

"Mom, it's not like that." She slowly walked back to the entrance of Jimmy's room.

Her mother shook her head. "Tarah, you sound just like your father when he left me for another woman." The comment was harsh and abrupt. "I thought you were better than that."

"It's not the same thing, mom," Tarah said quietly.

"And now look at your father," her mother continued, and much to Tarah's surprise, she had tears in her eyes. "He's alone and has cancer."

Tarah stopped in her tracks. Her father had *cancer*? She opened her mouth to say something but couldn't.

"He's been trying to call and tell you for weeks, but you never call back." Her mother wiped a stray tear from her eye. "You barely are in touch with your family at all. Your brother is having marital problems and is dealing with work *and* a baby all the time, since Sara doesn't seem to want to deal with her responsibilities. But you don't know these things because you are clearly living a very separate life from the rest of us. I'm your mother, and I didn't even know that you were shacked up with this guy."

"His name is Jimmy." Tarah felt blood rush to her face. "And I've been busy, very busy, recording a CD. I'm sorry I didn't know about my father, but you've talked to me within the last few weeks, and if you knew, you didn't tell me. Bobby *has* talked to me and hasn't told me about his problems, so I didn't know he had any."

"Your father has cancer," her mother repeated. "He's very sick. I didn't feel it was my place to tell you."

Tarah burst into tears and covered her face. She felt someone's hand on her arm and thought it was her mother's until she heard Jimmy speak.

"Look, you may not like me and that's fine. But you know what? Don't do this." Jimmy gently ushered Tarah toward the bedroom. "Don't attack her."

There was silence for a few minutes, and Tarah sat on the edge of the bed.

"I'm sorry, Tarah," she heard her mother say, and then she was gone.

"That wasn't right." Jimmy comforted her. "She shouldn't have told you like that. I'm sure it's just because she's upset herself, but it's not right."

"I know." Tarah wiped away her tears. "She is right though, if I was in touch with my dad, I would've known he was sick. He's called here, and I just never call him back."

"So you'll go see him," Jimmy encouraged. "I'll go with you if you need me to."

"It's fine," Tarah sniffed. "I'll be fine. Did she leave?"

"Yeah," Jimmy said. "I heard the door close downstairs. I think she was really out of line to talk to you that way."

"That's just how she talks to me."

"Well when you love someone, you don't purposely try to make them feel bad," Jimmy insisted.

"I know."

"I mean," Jimmy seemed to be lost in thought for a moment before continuing, "I would never say something to purposely hurt you." He looked into Tarah's eyes. "And I love you."

Tarah felt as if the world had suddenly stopped and was waiting for her response. "I love you, too."

CHAPTER TWENTY-THREE

▼

"I'm done with crying," Tarah announced the next morning. She was lying in bed beside Jimmy, who barely had his eyes opened. It was six in the morning. And although the two had talked openly about their love the previous night, Tarah awoke the next morning thinking instead about her mother and their horrible argument the previous night. "I'm finished. I'm tired of being an emotional basket case. All I've done for the last few years is cry. I cried when Jeff cheated on me, when I should've been angry. I've cried all the times that random girls were hitting on William, when I should've been questioning what was really going on. I cried when Wendy abruptly ditched me from her life, and last night I cried over this crap with my mother. I feel like I just resort to crying all the time, and I hate that about myself. I need to grow up."

"I think it's a pretty natural thing to do in all those circumstances," Jimmy muttered, and pulled her close. "You're allowed."

"It is, but it's not. I have to be stronger. Especially now that my father is sick." Tarah faced him in the bed they shared. "Mom had no right to talk to me like that last night. You're right about that. I'm starting to see why my dad *did* leave her."

"There's always so much more to these things, Tarah. Don't take sides. In a way, it's like the situation with William, you, and me. We all have our side of things, and in a way, we're all right, and in a way, we're all wrong. And really, it's none of your business what happened between your parents, and your mom shouldn't have dragged you into it; although I'm assuming from how she talked yesterday, that she always has."

Tarah nodded. "She did. She used to bad mouth him to us all the time. Then she fell into a big depression. I was left looking after the house, my brother, everything. In a way, I became *her* parent, rather than the other way around."

"That's not right," Jimmy said with a yawn.

"No. I was angry that I took on all this extra shit, and I guess I blamed my father ever since. If he hadn't left us, then I wouldn't have been in that situation. And after awhile, he just was around less and less."

Jimmy nodded. "Are you going to talk to him?"

"Yes, as soon as I can."

Although David Kiersey seemed taken aback by both Tarah's call and her suggestion that they spend some time together, he happily accepted the invitation. Tarah said she'd drop in that same evening. It felt strange talking to her father, not to mention making plans with him, but it was time. She had to grow up and face the things she had worked so hard to avoid.

She rang the doorbell at her dad's place at six o'clock. He buzzed her in without even checking to see who was there. And when the elevator opened on his floor, the first thing she saw was her father standing in his doorway, waiting for her.

"Tarah, please come in." David Kiersey smiled at his daughter. She stepped inside and saw that his apartment was nice but very plain. Her father was never interested in decorating and had settled for the basic essentials of a television, a couch, and a coffee table. Glancing into the kitchen, Tarah noted that it was the same. The cupboard was clear of any kind of clutter. A single letter sat on the table with his handwriting on the envelope. She sat down on the couch.

"Dad, mom was over last night and we had a fight." Tarah decided to jump right into the topic at hand, rather than making up small talk. She stared down at her hands while thinking about her mother's harsh words. "Did she tell you?"

"Yes," David softly replied, and joined his daughter on the couch. His dark blond hair was cut short, and his blue eyes were hidden behind a pair of glasses. He was always clean-shaven and wore a simple blue sweater and pair of loose jeans. Tarah wondered if the pants were baggy because he had lost weight or if that was just the style he chose to wear. She automatically felt guilty for not knowing the answer. "I was a little upset with her for saying anything about me having cancer. I wanted to tell you that myself."

"I know," Tarah insisted. "But in all fairness, it wasn't like I was ever around *for* you to tell me. Mind you, she could've done so in a more considerate way."

"I understand your mother was upset because of your living conditions," he said in a matter-of-fact way, with no judgment in his voice—something Tarah wasn't sure if she deserved, considering how much judgment she had made toward him over the years. "I don't agree with how she handled it, but I'm not surprised."

They shared a smile. "She told me I was just like you because I left one guy for another, just like you left her for another woman."

"That was a long time ago, Tarah," her father reminded her. "And our situations were completely different. You didn't have a family at home when you left."

"I know, but in her eyes there is no difference. She liked my last boyfriend, and she doesn't like Jimmy, so she thinks he's the enemy. And she doesn't even know the entire story." Tarah turned toward her father. "Kind of like I didn't know the whole story when you left us. I didn't have a right to hold that against you for all these years, and until mom said those terrible things to me last night, I hadn't considered that sometimes life is more complicated than it may seem."

"That, you're right about," David Kiersey agreed. "In my case, I'll be honest with you, your mother and I married too young. And in some ways, maybe that's what makes her nervous about these relationships you've been involved in. I know it concerned her when your brother was married so young, and now, according to her, they're having issues in their marriage. I think she's scared you'll jump the gun and make the same kind of mistakes that we did."

"I don't plan to get married right now."

"It's something you should only do when you are ready, regardless of your age. In my case, it wasn't a good idea because we didn't know ourselves and grew apart. Not everyone does. It was never about you and your brother, but unfortunately she got you both in the middle. It wasn't fair of her to do that."

Tarah smiled and thought about Jimmy's words on the subject. "That's what my boyfriend said, he said it was none of my business what happened between the two of you, and mom shouldn't have made Bobby and I take sides."

"He's right about not taking sides, but then again, you and Bobby are part of the family so you deserved more of an explanation."

"Mom went over the deep end," Tarah said, and found that she was finally starting to relax. She sat back on the couch. "I guess I saw that and held it against you too."

"I'm sorry that happened," her father replied, and hesitated. "I'm sorry about a lot of things, but I hope we can put all that behind us now and focus on the future."

Tarah nodded and paused for a moment. "Mom told me you had cancer and I was so upset, I didn't even think to ask for any details." She was scared to ask about her father's health. In fact, although she had been circling the topic, Tarah feared making that final landing. Cancer was a scary word.

"I have prostate cancer," David Kiersey replied. "I have to go for surgery in two weeks to have my prostate removed."

Tarah didn't know what to say.

"We caught it just in time; the doctor said he doesn't foresee any problems, but they want to remove it right away and then do some more test. Maybe chemo."

"That's scary," Tarah said, and thought about how William's mother died of cancer. What if her father did too?

"It is, but it was caught early. It's the best possible time to find out and have the procedure done," Tarah's father assured her. "But let's not talk about that, let's talk about *you*. I want to hear about this recording contract. It sounds fantastic."

Tarah was apprehensive about skipping over the topic of cancer so quickly, but decided that maybe it made her father more comfortable, so she told him about the band and the contract they just signed. He was very excited to hear the details and even admitted to seeing the band play live a few times.

"Really?" Tarah was surprised to learn this information. "I don't remember ever seeing you at any of the shows."

"I usually hung back in the crowd," he admitted. "I wasn't sure if you wanted me there, so I tried to keep out of sight. You were incredible every time I saw you sing; I was really quite amazed by your talent. I was very proud."

"Thanks," Tarah said, and smiled bashfully. "I appreciate it."

It felt strange to be having a real conversation with her father. But it also felt good. It seemed that in some small way, their relationship was starting to mend. Tarah spent time with him until he started to yawn, then she left and went to her brother's apartment. There, she hoped to catch up on what was going on in his life.

She was relieved to find him at home. However, he wasn't in the best of moods when Tarah arrived. Apparently Caitlin was sick again, and Sara was at her parent's place, leaving him home alone to care for the child.

"It wouldn't be so bad," Bobby insisted over a loud baby screams coming from the next room. "But I just got home from work, and she practically ran out the door. The baby was crying and she didn't care, she just left."

"Can I do anything to help?" Tarah felt helpless. She didn't know the first thing about babies.

"No, it's fine." Bobby appeared frazzled. "Maybe we will get together later this week. I'll stop by after work or something."

And then Tarah left.

The rest of the week was busy. The band was being pulled in every direction. If they weren't speaking with a photographer or video director, then the members of Fire were in meetings with either Maggie or Peter. On one occasion, both their manager and FUTA's A&R guy gathered the band in the room to discuss the CD cover. It was one thing after another, but slowly, progress was being made. Dates were being set, and a timeline was formed. Maggie was suggesting that the CD launch party be held on May 24, which ironically was Jimmy's birthday.

"We'll start making plans for that when we meet again," Maggie insisted. "Until that time, if anyone has any ideas, let me know, and we'll see what we can all come up with. I want to check out a few of the better establishments here in Toronto, and then we'll go from there."

That same week, a photographer spent an afternoon taking pictures of the band in various locations. Tarah quickly saw why celebrities always appeared perfect in photos. A whole group of people followed them everywhere, making sure their hair, makeup, and clothing were just right. One stylist actually ripped a bigger hole in Jimmy's jeans before the photographer even had a chance to pick up his camera, insisting it was more "visually appealing." Lights were arranged in specific patterns to best profile the band, and a computer program would remove any flaws in the final images.

The video was in the planning stage of production. Since the song "Swim on my Beach" was chosen, the director insisted that they actually go to a beach in the southern states to do the shoot. They had already decided that only a section of the video would be shot at that location, but so far, it seemed that it mostly involved Tarah doing the scenes that were meant to come across as seductive. Of course, the lyrics of the song had strong sexual overtones, so no one was surprised by idea. They just all went with the flow.

The CD would simply be called Fire. The label still wasn't sure what they wanted on the cover. Did they want a photo of the band or something else? It was one of many details in the air.

Tarah was quickly beginning to see why Jimmy had suggested that they move to Toronto, since it seemed that they spent the majority of their time there. However, the entire band was tied into a lease; William had one at the apartment they had once shared, and the rest of the band had one at the house.

"Maybe it'll be better to move in December," Jimmy suggested. "By then we'll have a clearer idea where the band is going."

"Hopefully," Tarah replied.

As the month moved forward, Tarah was talking to her father more than she had in years. There were some strained conversations with her mother, but they were few and far between. Even though her brother was busy with his family and job, he did manage to drop by Tarah's house one evening after work.

"You look exhausted," Tarah remarked, as soon as he walked in the door. She noted the dark circles under his eyes. "Come, sit down."

"I can't stay long." He went into the living room and collapsed on the couch. Jimmy and Eddie were in the basement working on a song. Tarah could hear them talking loudly over the sound of drums and guitar. This was the norm at their house, but she had to wonder if it bothered her brother. If it did, he didn't let on.

"Tarah, I think I'm going to have to get a divorce," Bobby admitted a few minutes into their conversation. Tarah thought about the day her brother broke the news that he was getting married. So much had changed since that time. "Sara is not happy, and I just don't feel like I know her anymore. She barely has time or interest for Caitlin, and we fight all the time. I think I'm going to take the baby and move home with mom. Sara can do whatever she wants." Unlike Tarah, Bobby didn't have a lease tying him down.

"Really? She doesn't even want to be around her own baby?"

"I think she's still in a depression. I'm not sure, but it's getting to be too much for me to handle. She's not even trying to help herself, and I'm nervous that she isn't even looking after the baby when I'm not there."

"I hope you're wrong."

"I hope I am too." Bobby spoke frankly. "We already discussed separating at the end of the month."

"I'm sorry Bobby."

He shook his head. "It's fine. Tarah, at this point, I'm not upset to be ending the marriage. I don't have time to even think about it, and to be honest, I'm tired of going home to a house full of misery. It's time to cut my losses."

They continued to talk about her brother's plan of action, and just as he was about to leave, Bobby asked about the tense relationship between Tarah and their mother. She quickly told him her version.

"Wow, so she told you dad had cancer like that?" He frowned. "Jesus. Did you talk to him?"

"Yes." Tarah told him what their father had to say, and he nodded.

"That's what he told me too."

"Do you think he's going to be okay?"

"I really hope so. We've missed so much time with him," Bobby replied, and then he left.

CHAPTER TWENTY-FOUR

▼

"Well, it looks as if everything is in the works," Maggie announced to the room, which included the five members of Fire and Peter Sampson. They were all sitting in her office taking care of last minute details. "As you know, the video for "Swim on my Beach" is set for later next week. Also, I've found a bar for the launch party. I have it reserved for May 24, as we originally discussed."

"Okay, so first of all, we have to talk about the video," Peter jumped in excitedly. "Now, as you know, we're flying to the states and shooting some footage, then coming back to finish it locally. We're only scheduled for two days, so hopefully everything can be done in that timeframe. Then the footage goes into post production, and hopefully sooner rather than later, we'll see the end result."

"But what do we do in the video?" Eddie had lines of worry on his face. "I've never done anything like this before."

"Don't worry about it," Peter insisted, giving Eddie a relaxed smile. "That's not your problem, that's up to Dylan Banks, he's your director. Just do what he says, and don't worry about it."

Eddie nodded and appeared a little more at ease.

"Dylan's great," Maggie joined in. "I've had other clients who have worked with him, and he's a pro. He's done lots of music videos and knows the drill. So just relax and have fun; he'll take care of you."

Tarah shared Eddie's concerns and wondered what exactly Dylan was going to make *her* do in a video that was meant to be provocative. Maggie already had someone help her select the wardrobe for the shoot: two summer dresses that were stylish and cute, as well as a pair of really short shorts and an equally small tank top. Apparently, the guy's wardrobe was not as much of a concern.

"Now, as for the party," Maggie glanced at Peter for a second. "I've booked it at a new bar called Cocaine, it's a *great* place. It's located in the entertainment district, and I've been talking to the owner and it looks like the launch party is officially in the planning stage."

"We're launching our CD at a bar called *Cocaine?*" William said, with a look of skepticism in his eyes. "Won't that somehow give the wrong impression about what kind of band we are?"

"Oh no," Maggie insisted. "Believe it or not, it's just named after the owner's favorite song."

"The Eric Clapton song?" Peter asked, then laughed. "Isn't that about doing cocaine?"

"No," Jimmy spoke up. "It's an anti-drug song."

"Really?" both Peter and Tarah asked at the same time.

Jimmy shrugged. "That's what I read. I dunno."

"Anyway, it's a terrific place. You guys should go and check it out sometime," Maggie insisted with an enthusiastic smile on her face. "I'll keep you posted. We haven't nailed down all the details yet."

"Oh and we're gonna have some more photos taken on the days you shoot the video," Peter added. He was looking down at some notes he had scribbled on a notebook. "And it'll be an early day—we'll be meeting at FUTA at five in the morning to catch a plane for the beach shoot. We want to make the most of the day."

"Isn't just Tarah doing the beach shots?" Michael asked, with a hint of frustration in his voice. "Why do we all have to go?"

"Actually, there will be shots of everyone." Peter answered his question with a great deal of patience. "And yes, most of them are of Tarah, but not exclusively."

"Hey, it's spring, and you have an opportunity to go to a warm beach," Maggie said, with a grin on her face. "Take advantage of it."

"One more thing," Peter cut in. "I'm going to arrange some interviews with local journalists before the CD is released. And I want to make sure the band gets some radio exposure too. I've got some connections in radio here, and many of them have sister stations in other locations, so that will give the band a huge boost—along with the video, that is. I think we're on the right track."

"And by connections," Maggie grinned, "he means that FUTA is paying them quite well to push your song." Peter smiled and said nothing.

"Really?" Eddie asked. "I didn't think radio stations worked that way."

"Well, money talks," Maggie insisted. "It does make the world go around."

"I guess it's not love anymore?" Jimmy joked.

"Not in this business." Peter gave his perfect smile. "It's all about the money."

"Oh and I wrote something yesterday," Maggie jumped in again. "When you do your CD launch, an announcer will come out to introduce you … obviously. And I think I know what we should ask him to say."

Picking up a piece of paper from her desk, Maggie's eyes glanced over it quickly, and then she looked up at the band. In an almost seductive manner, she slowly said the words that would follow the band for years to come. "First there was a match … then, there was a spark … and now, there's Fire!"

Tarah felt a chill go up her spine. She realized it hit pretty close to home for her on a personal level, not to mention a professional one. Her eyes met with Jimmy's, and she found herself staring at him. Quickly breaking away, Tarah looked back at Maggie and nodded.

"I like it." William was the first to speak. "It's catchy."

"I don't, it's corny," Michael complained. Maggie looked slightly irritated. "We need something better than that."

"Well, of course, it will be more expressive than how I just read it off the paper," Maggie insisted and stood up, suddenly appearing very stern. "I plan to have the announcer yell out the last part of it, and then have the band start playing from there."

"I like it," Tarah spoke up, if for no other reason than to dispute Michael's opinion. "I think it's neat."

"Me too," Jimmy chimed in. "That's cool. Maybe you should read it, Maggie. I think you did great just now when you read it."

Tarah smiled, sensing that Jimmy was going a little overboard with his compliments, more to irritate Michael than to flatter Maggie.

"Yeah, that would be kind of cool," Eddie added.

"We should look at all our options." William quickly defended his brother.

"Nah, Maggie made it sound sexy," Jimmy countered. His tone was so innocent that it probably made everyone suspicious. "We need sexy."

"Well, I *do* thank you, Jimmy." Maggie seemed humored and relaxed once again. "I think it'd be in your best interest to have someone a little more charismatic on stage before you, not me. But I appreciate your input." She turned her attention back to Tarah, and they shared a smile.

With all the good things that were coming her way, Tarah wanted to feel the joy associated with dreams coming true. However, she was finding it increasingly difficult with all the recently added stress in her life. Not only was she nervous about the video shoot and everything related to her career, Tarah was now greatly concerned about her father's health, as well as her brother's upcoming divorce.

"That's pretty sad, when you think about it," Jimmy said to Tarah, later that same night. They were sitting on the back step of their house, smoking a joint. It was late in the evening, and the sun had long disappeared in the April skies. There was a chill in the air after a spring rainfall earlier that day. "Your brother just got married last fall, and he's already getting a divorce?"

"Yeah, but he got married for the wrong reasons." Tarah said in a quiet voice. "I think he wanted to make her happy because she was always so depressed. Plus, when they had the baby, he wanted to do the right thing."

"How old is the baby?"

"One."

"Wow, and her parents were already married and divorced?"

"Yup."

"Well, at least she probably won't remember it," Jimmy said, referring to Caitlin, as his eyes stared down at backyard. The two fell silent.

"You never talk about your family." Tarah often wondered why he seemed to avoid the topic, especially when he was very open about everything else. "I feel like I never stop talking about mine. I take it since they haven't been around the house that you aren't close?"

"Not really," Jimmy replied, and took two quick puffs of the remainder of the joint, then threw it beside his foot. His shoe ground it into the step. "I used to live with my parents before I moved here, but it was just sort of my home base."

"I remember William saying that once. He said you basically bed-hopped and went to your parents in between."

Jimmy raised his eyebrows, and a small smile broke out on his face. "He said that, did he?"

"Is it true?"

"No," Jimmy said, and laughed. "I wasn't exactly famous for spending the night at many girl's places after I had sex with them. I actually crashed at *his* house a few times, but he was always at your place, so he didn't probably know. I even crashed at Eddie's place some too—slept on his floor, or should I say, passed out on his floor."

"Really?"

"Yup, I stayed at other friend's places too. Guys I was in bands with before Fire and shit like that."

"Did you avoid going to your parents for a reason?"

Jimmy shrugged and avoided eye contact. "Not really. They're okay, but they weren't exactly happy about my lifestyle choice by any means."

"The sleeping around?"

"The sleeping around, working in a bar, drinking, partying all the time. Pick one. And I understand," Jimmy said, leaning forward slightly. "They just felt that paying for stuff like getting my ass in shape and giving me music lessons were supposed to make my life better. But instead, I ended up not going to college and working at a bar. I drank a lot, did drugs, and slept around. Not exactly what they had dreamed up for me."

"I see their point."

"So can I," he said, and nodded. "I just wasn't interested in getting a real job or going to school. And I guess being fat and teased for so long, I had a lot of steam to blow off. And I love music, I can't imagine doing anything else."

"I bet their proud now," Tarah said. "Now that you have the contract."

"Yes." He nodded in agreement. "They were on vacation when that happened, so I actually just told mom the other day when she called to remind me about my sister's wedding. She was pretty pumped about it, and I'm assuming she told dad once he got home from work."

"Your sister's wedding?" Tarah asked. She knew he had an older sister named Jillian, who was a hygienist. But that was about it. "I didn't know your sister was getting married."

"I knew she was engaged, but she was engaged like for like *years*," Jimmy replied. He was leaning over slightly and looking into Tarah's face. "I didn't think she was actually going to get married. Most people who are engaged for a long time never really intend on it, I don't think."

"So when's the wedding?"

"What's the date today?"

"April 21."

"Really?" Jimmy thought for a moment. "Then Saturday. She's getting married on April 23."

"You're shitting me," Tarah said, suddenly feeling anxious. "You do realize that you're going to have to get a tux or something, right?" She started to laugh.

"I'm so baked right now, Tarah. I don't want to think." He covered his face and laughed with her. "Mom got me something to wear so I wouldn't fuck it up. I have to go to her house tomorrow and make sure it's not hideous. But I'm not part of the wedding party, so it's all good. I just have to show up."

Tarah continued to laugh. "You better make sure, it *is* in only two days, right?"

"I will tomorrow."

The next day, Jimmy went to his parent's place then returned home with an armful of clothing. It not only consisted of a suit, but other stuff that he hadn't bothered to pick up since his move in December.

"Mom had a suit for me and it fits, so it's cool," Jimmy said, collapsing on the couch. "I don't want to wear it, because I'm sure I'll look like an idiot. She's already mad because I asked if I could wear my sneakers."

"Probably not," Tarah said.

"Oh, yeah, are you coming with me?" Jimmy asked casually. "It's kind of a big deal I guess."

Tarah's eyes flew wide open. "Jimmy, I don't have a dress. It's *tomorrow.*"

"Maybe my mom can find *you* something to wear too." He grinned. "Just wear anything. You always look great."

"It's a wedding, I can't wear just *anything*. Plus, I don't want to meet your family for the first time and look like a bum."

"Hey, my mom is just excited that I'm actually in a real relationship. You could come to the wedding wearing pretty much anything and she wouldn't care."

"You told your mom about me?" Tarah said, suddenly feeling that not having a dress wasn't such a big deal after all.

"Of *course* I told my mother about you." Jimmy looked into her eyes with a shy smile. "And she can't wait to meet you."

Tarah managed to find a flattering blue dress in her closet that was simple, yet appropriate for a wedding. She wanted to make a good impression on his family and felt nervous about meeting them, especially at such an important event. Jimmy didn't seem to think it was such a big deal, but he was much more laid back than Tarah.

On that Saturday, Jimmy took his car to the church. Tarah had given her Sunbird to Bobby after learning about the record contract. She didn't really need it anymore, and he was pretty down and out after the breakup, not to mention vehicle less. Tarah even promised to buy him a new one after her career took off.

"By the way, thanks for coming to the wedding with me." Jimmy flashed her a smile as they drove along. Tarah felt like she was going to be sick, she was so nervous. "You look really pretty."

"Thanks. You look great too." Her eyes scanned him once again. She couldn't get over how different he looked with a suit, tie, and with his hair pulled back in a ponytail. Jimmy was always very handsome, but there was an air of sophistication to him that Tarah hadn't expected. Not that he was at all comfortable in his wedding attire, which was obvious by the way he kept pulling at his collar until red marks appeared around his neck.

As soon as they walked in the church door, a tiny woman who had the same eyes as Jimmy, rushed up to them with an explosive smile on her face. She stopped to study Tarah. "Jimmy, is this the girl? Oh, she's so pretty!"

Her frail hand reached out to the object of her attention and she introduced herself. "I'm Jim's mom, Annette."

"Hi, Annette, I'm Tarah." She smiled and shook hands with the tiny woman. Even though she wore heels, Annette was shorter than Tarah. "It's nice to meet you."

"You too, dear." Annette then rushed over to give her son a hug. Tarah smiled when she saw how gentle and sweet he was with his mother. Regardless of how casually he spoke of his family, it was clear that he loved his mom.

Annette happily ushered them both into the church and to their seats, which were right next to both her and Jimmy's father. Tarah noted that her boyfriend's black hair and perfect smile were both attributes that he adopted from his dad. Annette introduced Tarah to her husband, and he enthusiastically shook her hand, with a surprised expression on his face.

Jimmy reached for Tarah's hand, and she leaned close to his ear and whispered, "I can't believe that you're in a church and haven't been hit by lightening yet."

Jimmy laughed. "No, but we're not out of the woods yet, baby."

The wedding was simple, but nice. Jimmy's sister was beautiful in a strapless white gown, but her expression was serious. Tarah thought wedding days were supposed to be happy, but the bride appeared to be fulfilling an obligation rather than being happily in love. Tarah thought it was strange, but decided it was possible that the bride was just nervous.

After the wedding was finished, family gathered for photos, and Tarah stood aside. Even though Jimmy was very uncomfortable in his suit, he managed a perfect smile and actually looked happier than the bride. Tarah brought this up while they were driving to the reception. She didn't understand why Jillian looked so miserable on her wedding day.

Jimmy took a deep breath. "My sister's just like that, wound up really tight. She wants the perfect wedding, the perfect life, the perfect job, but Jill's so stressed all the time, that she never enjoys anything. It's pretty sad, but she's always been the overachiever."

"Really?"

"Yeah, she always puts way too much pressure on herself." Jimmy had concern in his eyes as he spoke. "When she was like sixteen, Jill actually had a really serious eating disorder."

"Oh wow." Tarah frowned.

"Yeah, she was in the hospital. It took a long time and family counseling to get her back together again."

"Anorexia?"

"Yeah, it was bad too. It was scary, man. I hate it when girls don't eat to be toothpick thin. It's so weird." He shook his head. "She was into modeling and stuff back then. I mean, she wasn't like Cindy Crawford famous, but she was doing some stuff in Toronto, and she was passing out all the time. We still worry about her if she starts losing weight."

"So you all did counseling because of it?" Tarah suddenly realized that it was bizarre that his sister was starving herself as a kid, while he was overweight. She had a strange feeling about that.

"Yeah, it was a family issue that started it all."

"Okay." Tarah watched his expression change. He looked upset and turned quiet, like the day he found out about Kurt Cobain's death.

"I'm sorry, I didn't mean to pry." Tarah sincerely felt bad. She wasn't trying to ruin his day.

"It's fine, just something I don't want to talk about right now."

"That's fine." Tarah nodded and purposely changed the topic. "I felt weird being at that wedding today. The last one I went to was my brother's and it was with William. It's kind of ironic since both of those relationships are over."

Jimmy smiled, but still seemed a bit upset. "This one's going to be different. I mean, my sister will drive that poor fucker up the wall and they'll probably break up, but we get along good, right?"

"We do." Tarah exchanged smiles with him.

"You know, considering we live, work, and *are* together all the time, we get along really well," Jimmy thought out loud. "We don't fight."

"True."

The wedding reception turned out to be fun, and even Jillian seemed to lighten up in spirit. Jimmy introduced Tarah to his sister, who in turn, gave her a hug. "I hope to get to know you better." She seemed sincere.

"I'm telling you," Jimmy loosened his tie as they walked around the room. "My family is so stunned that I'm actually in a serious relationship that they don't even know how to react around you. My mom loves you though, that's for sure." Tarah felt her face get hot. "The whole time we had our pictures done, she kept saying how nice you seemed, how pretty you were, and how much she liked you."

Tarah smiled and didn't know what to say at first. "I guess that's a far cry from my mother's reaction toward you."

"Yeah, well my mother also didn't come into our house and find a thong on my bedroom floor."

"True."

"Speaking of thongs," Jimmy put his arm around Tarah and pulled her close. "Have you ever done it in a wedding reception bathroom?"

CHAPTER TWENTY-FIVE

▼

"It's not what I thought it'd be," Tarah admitted to Jimmy during a break for the shoot of "Swim on my Beach." They were located in Myrtle Beach, South Carolina, and although Tarah felt the scenery was beautiful, she barely had time to enjoy it. Since their arrival, she'd been rushed through hair, makeup, and wardrobe, before being pulled aside by Dylan Banks to discuss details of the video. The director was much younger than Tarah had expected, yet more knowledgeable about his profession than others she would meet later in her career.

"The shoot?" Jimmy sat next to her on the sand. She wore one of the dresses that had been picked for the video; he was overdressed in jeans and both a short and long sleeved t-shirt. In fact, the entire band was dressed in their normal spring clothing when leaving the Toronto Pearson Airport early that morning, and now they regretted it. The temperature had been thirty-five degrees Fahrenheit in Toronto that morning, while it was eighty degrees in Myrtle Beach.

"Yes, but don't get me wrong," Tarah was quick to backtrack; she pushed her sunglasses closer to her face and watched her own reflection in the pair that Jimmy was wearing. "It isn't like I had a clue really, I just didn't realize how precise the director would be about where I stood or how I leaned. Weird stuff like that. It just feels strange." So far, Dylan had focused the majority of his attention on Tarah as she lip-synched the song while doing the typical vamping that most women did in music videos. Dylan would often rush up to her just before cameras began rolling to make subtle changes, whether it be moving Tarah's hair to cascade over her face or lifting her dress to show a little more leg. At first, she felt really uncomfortable with the scenes, but eventually she relaxed and went with the flow. It also helped that the rest of the band left the set to have a late breakfast—all except for Jimmy. He chose instead to watch how things were put together behind the scenes and occasionally ask questions, just as he had during the process of making their CD.

"I know, but this guy is a photographer. So he has a vision in mind when he does all this stuff," Jimmy reminded her. "He's very meticulous. Besides, all the stuff Dylan had you do was actually really hot. This is going to be a great video."

They shot long into the day. Fortunately, around four o'clock, someone brought food to the set. Neither Tarah nor Jimmy had eaten a thing that day and were looking forward to the table full of food. However, just as Tarah was about to take her second helping, the video director took her aside and reminded her that she was about to shoot the scene that required the short shorts and snug tank top. "You don't want to be bloated and have to suck in your stomach," he reminded her. "Trust me, I know. I've worked with a lot of models in my time, and the last thing you want is to get cramps in your stomach from sucking it in all day."

Tarah smiled and glanced around to make sure Jimmy wasn't around to hear this conversation. Noting that her boyfriend was discussing something with a cameraman, she felt more at ease as she threw the rest of her food away. Dylan was right of course, but Jimmy was not likely to understand his point, especially considering the food issues Jillian had through her teenage years.

It was well into the evening when the shooting finally ended. The band was rushed to the airport to head home. Tarah drifted into a deep sleep, only to awaken when it was time to switch planes. They were both so exhausted after reaching their Toronto hotel room that night, that both Tarah and Jimmy immediately passed out.

A wake-up call alerted them a couple of hours later. Tarah resisted the urge to cry; she was just so exhausted that it was unimaginable to her that the band had to shoot more footage for the video that day. It was ironic to her that so many artists made their lifestyle look glamorous and stress-free in videos and interviews, when in fact their own schedule always rushed Fire into one thing after another. When she expressed her feelings to Jimmy, who was overtired and frustrated, he merely pointed out that a lot of people were working a great dealer harder at much more difficult jobs.

"It's not like you're out there doing hard, physical labor for minimum wage." His eyes were bloodshot, and he had not shaven in two days. "Come on, Tarah, we work hard again today, then we don't do fuck all for the next couple of days."

Or so he thought. After shooting for most of that day, the band was instructed to meet with Peter Sampson early the next morning. By that time, the entire band was edgy and apathetic. Even William, who tended to remain positive in most situations, looked ragged and annoyed.

"I know you guys are exhausted after the last couple of days of working on the video." Peter appeared refreshed and rested, something that Tarah resented. "But I heard from Dylan that we got some terrific footage, and he's very excited about putting this video together."

No one said anything.

"Furthermore," Peter continued. "I'm not sure if you're aware of this, but your video was given a slightly larger budget than most newcomers to the business would receive. We've been having quite a few meetings behind the scenes, and a lot of people here at FUTA feel very confident that Fire is going to very successful, so we enjoy putting more money toward your success."

"Now, I have some great news," Peter went on, and opened a drawer of his desk. He removed five small cardboard boxes. "Your CDs are in!"

Suddenly, everyone was very alert. Each member of the band was handed a cardboard package, each contained ten CDs to be distributed to friends and family. Tarah just stared at the cover, stunned. She looked like a completely different person in the picture. Although, the photograph made them all appear attractive, there was a touch of perfection to each of them. Even Michael looked slightly more pleasant and handsome than in person. It made Tarah wonder what the finished music video would look like.

The band left the office shortly afterward, each much more enthusiastic than when they first arrived. Suddenly, the FUTA deal seemed more real than it had before. It was really happening. Although they were overtired, Jimmy insisted that he and Tarah drop off CDs to each of their families on their way home, and she agreed.

Their first stop was to see Tarah's mother and brother, but neither were home. Tarah had a spare key and crept into her childhood home, placed two CDs on the kitchen table, and left a note explaining why she'd dropped in. She couldn't wait to see what their reaction would be.

Next, she wanted to go see her father. He was in the hospital, having had his surgery a couple of days before they were set to shoot their video. However, once arriving there, she realized that visiting hours hadn't started yet. A young nurse suggested that she leave the CD on her father's nightstand, but Tarah insisted that she wanted to go back and see him later that night.

Outside, the April air was warm and refreshing. Maybe she didn't need sleep after all, Tarah decided. She and Jimmy had already stopped for coffee, and it seemed to be waking her up—or maybe it was the high of success.

Their next stop was at the dental office where Jimmy's sister worked.

Jillian was standing alone behind the main reception desk, studying a file when they arrived. She glanced up and her eyes widened at the site of her brother. "Jimmy? What are you doing here?" A smile curved her lips and she appeared much more at ease than at her wedding only a couple of weeks earlier. She then turned her attention toward Tarah. "It's nice to see you again." Then back at Jimmy. "What's going on? You look horrible." She began to laugh.

"We've been shooting a video for like … two, three, forever. Anyway, I wanted to stop by quickly and drop off something for you." He handed her the CD. "We just got 'em this morning."

Jillian ran her hand over the CD, and her eyes lit up. "Wow, this is fantastic. I can't wait to hear it." She studied the cover and then looked back at her brother. "I'm so proud of you, Jimmy! This is great. Honey, you so deserve this after … everything." There were tears in her eyes.

Tarah felt her own smile fall from her lips. Everything? What did that mean?

"Thanks," Jimmy said bashfully. "We better go, so you can get back to work."

"Okay." Jillian held the CD in front of her chest and hugged it close. This vision was stuck in Tarah's head as he reached for her hand and led her out of the dental office. She wanted to know what his sister was referring to, but knew it just wasn't the time to ask. *Honey, you so deserve this after … everything.*

The next stop was at his parent's house. His dad was at work, but Jimmy's mom was home. She also appeared alarmed by his appearance.

"Jimmy!" She grabbed his arm and pulled him into the door. "Come in. Tarah, how nice to see you dear." Annette hugged both Tarah and Jimmy. "I was just having some coffee, want some?"

"No, that's fine," Jimmy replied. "We're actually pretty tired. Um, we just stopped in to give you this." He handed her the CD.

"Jim, it's your tape you were making," his mother exclaimed.

"CD, mom."

"Oh, sorry, dear." She shook her head and the curls that surrounded her face wobbled around. "A CD then. What a nice picture of you, Jimmy." Then she looked up quickly. "And you too, Tarah, you look beautiful. My, I can't wait to listen to this later."

"You'll have to give it a listen, and tell me what you think." He smiled and she patted his arm.

"You know I'm going to love it because you were a part of it."

"Thanks."

"Are you sure you won't have some coffee?" She looked hopefully between Tarah and Jimmy.

"No, mom we *are* beat." Jimmy shook his head. "We've barely slept with this video we've been making. Long days."

"You both look tired, maybe you shouldn't be driving, Jimmy. Do you two want to take a nap upstairs?" She asked in an innocent manner, but Jimmy's eyes were suggesting otherwise.

"No, that's fine, thanks," Tarah answered. After Jimmy's mom hugged them both and they were outside, Tarah grabbed his arm and said what had crossed her mind while in the house. "It's pretty bad when I can read your thoughts. I know what you were thinking when she suggested we take a nap."

"We've never done it in my childhood bed." He grinned. "She never would've suspected. Trust me."

When they arrived home, Tarah was about to pass out when Jimmy insisted she open her eyes. Her vision was blurry and she couldn't focus on what was in his hand.

"What is it?" she muttered, and he held a pill in front of her face. "What's that?" She rubbed her eyes.

"Something to keep you awake, so we can party."

"What?" Tarah sat up. "What do you mean?" She examined the white pill in his hand.

"It's speed."

"Where did you get speed?"

"I had it here."

"You have speed. You *take* speed?" Tarah was surprised.

"Not often, but I've taken it before," he admitted. "Come on, Tarah, we have to celebrate! We just finished a music video, and today we got our actual CD in our hands. We can't just sleep now."

"Sure we can, then party tomorrow."

"No, it won't feel the same tomorrow." He leaned in and kissed her gently. "Come on, do it for me? Please. We'll have some drinks, get all fucked-up, and then crash tonight. It'll be fun."

Tarah looked at the pill. She took it, and he did the same.

The rest of the day was about them partying. After reapplying her makeup and changing, Tarah suddenly felt like she didn't need to sleep at all. The world was going in slow motion, while she went full speed ahead. Her heart raced and she had to get up and go, somewhere, anywhere. And Jimmy was right with her.

It was just after lunch, and without eating, they went to the bar closest to their house. Ironically, Jimmy would later confess it was the same place where he'd gotten wasted on the night of their first kiss. The same night her life took a sudden turn. Tarah found her eyes wandering the bar, wondering where he might have sat, what he drank that night, and what it would've been like to be a fly on the wall. Then she started drinking.

They did tequila shots. Jimmy chased his with beer, while she drank rum and Coke. Music by Soundgarden and Stone Temple Pilots filled the room, and the drinks just kept coming. One after another, Tarah barely had time to finish one, and she had two more sitting in front of her. She had no concept of time. It didn't matter. People dropped by the table to talk to them. Some were friends of Jimmy's, other's recognized them from being in a band, and still others simply heard the news that they were recently signed by FUTA. In fact, Jimmy told everyone who came nearby. People were buying them shots, and Tarah would later learn that someone gave Jimmy some more pills. She just didn't know what they were. He didn't take them.

By the time they left that evening, Tarah could barely walk. She kept falling down and Jimmy laughed at her. Then she started to cry, and he picked her up and carried her the rest of the way home. She passed out on the way there. Tarah opened her eyes again to see Jimmy climbing into bed beside her, wearing only his boxers. She still had her clothes on.

"I don't feel good." Tarah felt her stomach churning. "I think I'm gonna be sick."

Jimmy jumped up and grabbed a nearby garbage can just in time for Tarah to lean over it and puke. She felt him pulling her hair back; the vomiting never seemed to stop. Tarah felt tears burning in her eyes and she prayed for it to end. And finally it did.

Jimmy was still holding the garbage can, now half-full of vomit, in one hand, while holding her long, blond hair in the other. She felt a cold sweat throughout her body and decided that she'd never drink again.

"Are you okay?" Jimmy whispered. She nodded and he took the garbage can into the bathroom. Tarah heard the toilet flush then water running. Eventually she got up and joined him. He was rinsing out the tub. Jimmy gave her a worried look.

"Are you going to be sick again?"

"No." She turned to the sink and ran cold water over her face; it seemed to sober her up immediately. Reaching under the sink, she pulled out some Listerine and rinsed out her mouth. Jimmy gently touched her back as he slid out of the room. Tarah used the bathroom and returned to their bed.

"I feel so stupid." She curled up beside him.

"Don't." He ran his hand over her arm. "You drank a lot for someone as small as you. I'm sorry I kept giving you drinks. I really—"

Tarah suddenly jetted out of the bed and to the bathroom. She was sick again. Unfortunately, it happened twice more that night. Both times she had been asleep and awoke suddenly, only to make it to the bathroom just in time. Jimmy continued to look after her. Finally, around dawn of the next day, she fell into a peaceful sleep.

CHAPTER TWENTY-SIX

▼

"I realize that he has to be hooked up to all those machines, but it doesn't make it any easier to see," Tarah admitted, as they walked across the hospital parking lot after visiting her father. It was two days after her drinking excursion with Jimmy, and she still didn't feel back to her old self. Her headache was long gone, and she had eaten something earlier that day, but emotionally, Tarah felt like a basket case. "I don't understand, because I saw him on the day of his surgery too, and it didn't hit me quite like this."

"It's been a weird week," Jimmy said. Unlike Tarah, he was back to himself the day after their night out. The lack of sleep along with the drinking and speed didn't seem to faze him at all. "So, what did your dad say when he saw our CD?"

A smile stole away some of her original gloominess. "He loved it." Tarah looked up at Jimmy who nodded. "He can't wait to listen to it. It's pretty cool. I just wish he was well enough to come to the launch party."

"Speaking of the launch party," Jimmy said as they arrived at his car and they both got in. "It's a good thing we're practicing again tonight. It's been ages since we've actually played together, and the release party is coming up soon; it's only a few days away. I almost forget what it feels like to be on a stage for fuck sake, we've been so tied up with this other stuff."

"It's all important stuff though," Tarah pointed out as they drove through the parking lot. "We had to make the CD, obviously, and everything else is all part of promotions. It's a necessary evil."

"You sound like Maggie now," Jimmy said, turning down his window to pay for their parking, and leaving it down as they drove onto the street. "I know it's all important in its own way, but it won't help much if we suck ass at the launch."

Tarah nodded. Maggie was scheduled to meet them just before the official launch to go over the band's itinerary. "I can't believe that she's actually going to hire someone to help coach us for interviews. Why can't we just say what we're thinking?"

"I don't think it's for that reason. It's just sort of to teach us how to make the best of the interviews and to not like, offend anyone. I dunno."

"At least we won't look stupid during interviews," Tarah sighed.

"But you know what? It's really just starting," Jimmy reminded her. "We're just sailing down the runway now; wait till we get into the air."

William and Michael showed up at the house around seven that evening. The five of them jumped right into practice mode and finished a couple of hours later, agreeing to meet more that week. However, before the Stacy brothers left, the band sat around and talked about the CD launch party. Everyone was encouraged about the future except for Michael.

"We could do all this shit for nothing." He was quick to jump in with his opinion. "And if we suck, FUTA could tear up the contract and send us packing."

"We didn't get signed because we suck," Jimmy said defensively. "FUTA isn't investing a ton of money in us because they think we'll fail."

"It's always a possibility." William jumped to his brother's defense. "He's right, a lot of people flop, but not everybody. We'll just have to make sure we're one of the ones who succeed."

"I think we will," Eddie said hopefully.

"Well, everyone's going to have to keep their shit together then." Michael looked directly at Tarah. "We can't cancel practices because anyone is too hung over or fucked-up to attend them."

Tarah frowned, knowing that he was referring to a practice they had recently missed because she was too sick. She was just about to say something when Jimmy jumped to her defense.

"Oh, fuck off, Mike! So what? We were celebrating and it got a little out of hand, who gives a fuck?"

"That's the thing with you Jimmy, *everything* always gets out of hand." Michael's voice rose. "The drinking, the drugs, the women, you've always been out of control. How do we know that you're not going to fuck us over this time too? You and this one," he abruptly pointed at Tarah, "break up someday, where does that leave all of us? You may have calmed down a bit now, but as soon as you and Tarah hit the rocks, you'll be back on the skank circuit, partying it up and bringing the band down."

Tarah felt the hairs rising on the back of her neck, and she felt helpless as Jimmy charged toward Michael. Fortunately, William intercepted before a fight broke out.

"What is wrong with you guys?" William snapped at both Jimmy and Michael. "We have a once in a lifetime opportunity to do something we all love, and that should be our focus here. Not petty crap."

His attention then turned toward Michael. "As for Jimmy, we've never had an issue with him before. We missed one practice, so what? We met tonight instead. No big deal."

Both Michael and Jimmy seemed to be backing off at this point, but William continued to talk. "I think we've all had some kind of issue with one another at some point." Tarah noticed that his eyes glanced at her as he spoke, and she looked away. "But we're going to be together from now on and we're going to have to learn to get along. This is a big opportunity, and I don't think anyone wants to miss out on it."

Enough said. Michael muttered something about having a smoke and headed upstairs. Eddie seemed a little nervous and uncomfortable and disappeared immediately. Jimmy continued to show signs of frustration in his face and without a word, left the basement, leaving Tarah alone with William.

"Why is your brother like that?" Tarah said, feeling her own heart racing even though she wasn't involved in the conflict. "Why does he do that?"

"Provoke people?" William asked. Now that everyone else was out of the room, it was clear he was as tense about the dispute as everyone else. "I don't know, Tarah. He's just like that. Always has been. I try to give him the benefit of the doubt."

"He's so negative."

"I know, I try to make him see things differently, but I guess it doesn't always work." William shook his head.

"It's just depressing," Tarah said. "And I know it's my fault practice was cancelled. I was hung over, but I've had a lot on my mind lately. With my dad being sick and all."

"How is your dad?" William turned his attention toward Tarah. His eyes were full of compassion and a confidence that Jimmy didn't always possess. "I know you mentioned that he had cancer. And you *know* that I can certainly relate to having a sick parent."

"He's doing well." Tarah nodded. "It's really hard for me to go see him hooked up to a hundred different machines. I was there earlier today and it was awful."

"It's normal to feel that way." William continued to watch her. "Cancer is an ugly disease, it just takes away from people so much. Sometimes it feels as if your entire family has it, not just the person who is actually sick."

Tarah nodded sadly. He definitely understood. "How did you deal with it when your mom was sick?"

William took a deep breath. "It wasn't easy. You know that; we've talked about it. Mind you, my mom was a lot worse off than your dad. By the time I found out, it was too late to do anything." He slowly stood up and moved the chair aside. Tarah did the same. It was time she went back upstairs. There was something changing in the room, and she knew it was time to end the conversation. "But I think he'll be fine," William continued. "And as awful as it sounds, at least being sick brought him back into your life."

Tarah knew he was right. "I just wish it wasn't like that."

"I know."

"I'm scared that one day he'll tell me that the cancer has spread." Tarah started to walk toward the stairs and then stopped and turned toward William. "It's always a possibility."

"You can't think about that," William insisted. "It's a long time before he'll be completely out of the woods, even in the best scenarios. You just have to take it one day at a time."

Much to her surprise, William leaned in and gave her a hug. Tarah had forgotten how good it felt to be in his arms, but there was something very different now. It was comforting but she no longer felt an attraction to him. And she didn't think he felt one for her either.

Then they went up the stairs and William left. Tarah found Eddie in the living room watching television.

"Where's Jimmy?"

"I think he went upstairs," Eddie replied. "I wish Michael would stop being a dick."

"Me too," Tarah said before heading to her room. She found Jimmy there, sitting on the bed. He was clearly still upset.

"Don't listen to Michael," Tarah said as she approached the bed. "Forget what he said."

Jimmy ignored her for a minute. She had never seen him so angry. "I can forget about Michael," he sharply replied. "If *you* can forget about William."

"What's that suppose to mean?"

"It means I saw you hugging William in the basement." Jimmy's eyes were dark, and Tarah felt her heart pounding with such force that she feared an anxiety attack.

"It wasn't like that Jimmy," she assured him. "We were just talking about my dad being sick and he hugged me. He knows what it's like since his mother died of cancer."

His eyes were glued to her face as he listened. She saw Jimmy's face relax slightly. "Are you sure? I don't think I've got to remind you what was going on with us, when you were still together with him."

His words hit Tarah hard. "It didn't stop *you* either." She spoke evenly. "I didn't make the first move."

"You didn't stop it either."

"So now you're going to hold *that* against me?" Tarah challenged, and she felt her heart racing even faster. "At the time, I don't recall you having a problem with doing anything with me behind William's back. So, now it's suddenly an issue? You automatically assume the worst of me? Who's to say you won't go back to how you were, sleeping with all those girls?"

Jimmy jumped up from the bed. "Who's to say I won't?" he snapped and flew out of the room and down the stairs. The front door slammed.

Tarah was stunned. She closed the door and sat on the bed. Was he trying to say that he was going to cheat on her? Is that why he left? She felt hot tears burning her eyelids. Tarah blinked and they rapidly started to fall down her face. What was she thinking? That a guy who was once involved only in casual relationships would permanently change for her? Maybe the thrill of being in a relationship had worn off for him. Maybe seeing her sick and having to take care of her two nights earlier brought him back to reality. Maybe seeing William hugging her was the final straw.

Tarah lay in his bed and quietly sobbed for what felt like hours. Closing her eyes, she could smell his cologne on the sheets, and Tarah wondered where he was right then. And what he was doing. Eventually she was so swept up in misery that she grew exhausted and fell to sleep. She later awoke to a dark room and glanced at the clock. It was eleven thirty and he wasn't home yet.

Deciding that maybe it wouldn't be a great idea if she was in Jimmy's room when he finally arrived home, Tarah slowly rose from the bed and wandered into the next room. Her room. The one she hadn't occupied since first moving into the house. She climbed under the covers and stared at the wall. Alert to every little sound, wondering when or if Jimmy would come home, Tarah began to cry again. She wanted so much to talk to someone, to have assurance from a friend, but decided against it. John would be sleeping, and who else was there? Maybe her brother, but considering he now resided with their mother; Tarah was apprehensive about calling him up.

Instead, she turned and twisted and finally fell to sleep. In her dreams, she saw Jimmy having sex with another woman, and she started to cry. Tarah suddenly awoke with tears in her eyes and wondered what time it was; then she realized that someone had a hand on her shoulder. Jimmy.

"What are you doing?" His voice was gentle. She could smell alcohol on him. He was sitting on the edge of her bed. "Why are you crying? What are you doing in here?"

Tarah quickly used her sleeve to wipe her eyes and sat up. She could smell pot on his breath. Jimmy's eyes were fixated on her, and he leaned forward to kiss her, but Tarah turned away.

"Where were you?" She felt her voice catch in her throat. "What time is it?"

"I was out and now I'm back," he replied. "It's three in the morning; why are you crying?"

Tarah was stunned. Didn't he realize what was going on? They had just fought, and he left for hours, coming home smelling like alcohol and pot. She thought of how he once said that when he had sex with a girl, he rarely stayed the night, and wondered if that was the case this time too.

"I had a bad dream," she finally replied.

"What did you dream?" His voice was a whisper. His hand was now on her arm.

"I had a dream you had were having sex with another girl," she answered honestly.

"Tarah." His eyes continued to stare into hers and his face was only inches away. She could feel his hot breath on her face. "I didn't have sex with anyone tonight. I promise you that."

"Where were you then?"

"I was at the bar, drinking. Alone. Thinking." He looked away for a long minute and didn't say anything. "I called my sister, and she came and got me."

"At three in the morning?" Tarah was skeptical.

"No, at like ten or eleven." He looked back into her face. "I was at her house talking to her about stuff. She just dropped me off. If you don't believe me, call her. Actually, you don't even have to do that, I asked her to call you tomorrow."

"I don't understand." Tarah shook his head. "You barely talk to your family ever and suddenly you spend hours with your sister."

"It's not that we don't get along." Jimmy shrugged out of his leather jacket and threw it on the floor. "Some stuff happened when we were kids." He stopped and his hand reached for hers and the entire room was still. He didn't talk for a long moment. "It just, it's hard to be around my family because it brings a whole bunch of stuff back that I don't want to think about, and ironically that's why I was with my sister tonight. She's the only person who understands."

"Okay," Tarah said, and tried to be patient. "I'm still confused."

"That's because I'm not making a whole lot of sense." Jimmy squeezed her hand and smiled. "I was upset when I left here tonight because of the William thing. I had no right to fly off the handle; I was already pissed off when Mike said all that crap to me, and then to see Will hug you, just pushed me over the edge. I knew there was nothing going on."

"Then why did you get so mad?"

"I honestly don't know," Jimmy said. "I guess because I don't have a lot of experience with this kind of stuff. I've never lived with a girl, and I never felt this way about anyone. It's pretty scary sometimes. This is new for me. But I'm sorry for saying the things I said. I know you'd never cheat on me, and I promise, I'd never cheat on you either." He slurred his words a bit but looked genuine.

She nodded. It did make sense. He continued.

"And anyway, I was talking to my sister about some stuff tonight, and she thinks I have to be upfront with you." He squeezed her hand and fell silent. "Never mind, I can't do this." Jimmy shook his head. "Come on, let's just go to bed." He stood up and pulled on her hand. Tarah started to stand and suddenly stopped.

"No wait," she said in a quiet voice, and he turned back to face her. His eyes showed signs of vulnerability. Tarah had never seen him this way before and wondered what was going on. "Please tell me. You're starting to worry me."

Jimmy let out a long sigh and looked at the floor. The moonlight shone in the room and seemed to directly touch his face as he moved back to the bed and sat beside her. "I never planned to talk about any of this with anyone again, other than my sister," he began. "And I wasn't going to get into it with you either, but Jill thinks I should."

"Okay." Tarah put her arm around Jimmy's shoulder and leaned her head against it. "Please tell me."

He took a deep breath and hesitated. "Remember how I told you that my sister had an eating disorder?" Tarah nodded. "Well, when she was in the hospital, Jill had to go through a lot of counseling." He stopped and turned to face Tarah. "My sister was raped when she was twelve. Brutally raped."

"Oh my God!" Tarah gasped. "That's horrible!"

"And I saw it," Jimmy confessed solemnly. "I was ten years old and was so scared, I turned and ran away. I didn't get her help. I didn't even really understand what was going on."

"I feel so awful for both of you." Tarah felt a tear slide down her face, which she quickly wiped away. "That's horrible."

"Don't worry about me. It was Jill that really suffered." Jimmy's eyes were downcast. "We talked about it back then, and she made me promise to not tell anyone, so I didn't. The guy who raped her was a friend of the family, and Jill had a crush on him. So when he raped her, Jill automatically thought she had provoked it somehow. The fucking asshole." Jimmy hesitated for a moment, shook his head, and returned his gaze to Tarah's face. "She still isn't right. The anorexia is an ongoing thing that started after the attack, even though my family wants to pretend she's better. As for me, I dealt with it by shoving food in my face and getting fat."

"It wasn't until the counseling at the hospital that the truth came out," Jimmy added as he moved closer to Tarah. "That's when my parents got me into counseling and ironically, it was the psychiatrist who encouraged them to get me involved in stuff; I loved music, so they bought me a guitar."

"And then I had singing lessons and that's why my parents got me a personal trainer down the line. The psychiatrist told them that I used food as a crutch. That's why my family gets so angry when I drink or smoke pot or whatever. They think I've just moved on to another way to escape dealing with stuff. And that's why I avoid my family."

Tarah was silent, but her brain was working a mile a minute. It made so much sense. Suddenly it all fit together. Tarah felt closer to him now that he revealed something so personal to her. Not knowing what to say, she pulled him close and hugged him for a long time. Neither of them said a word.

Finally, she let him go and he cleared his throat.

"So, that's my secret." He tried to smile, but it didn't work. "That's why my parents and sister love you so much. They really thought I was permanently damaged, and I'd never be able to have a real relationship. They think that's why I used to be a player. I just didn't want to be close to anyone. And well, what I told you about not respecting women too, I just don't want you to think that what Michael said tonight was true. If we fight like we did tonight, or even break up, I'm not going to be necessarily out doing the same thing. And I wouldn't cheat on you."

"I believe you," Tarah whispered. "Thank you for telling me the truth. I'm so sorry it happened to you, and I'm really sorry about what Jillian went through. It breaks my heart to hear that story."

"Well, we survived. We talked a lot about that tonight," Jimmy admitted. "And she felt strongly that I should tell you everything. She said if I didn't, it was just going to control me. Not to say I'd tell the world, she wouldn't either, but there are some people I guess you need to share these things with and you're one of them. Maybe you'll be the only person who will ever know why I'm such a fucked-up person."

Tarah leaned forward and gave him a quick kiss. "In a way, I think that makes me love you even more."

CHAPTER TWENTY-SEVEN

▼

"That movie sent chills up my spine," Tarah said as she and Jimmy left the theater. After a great deal of coaxing from Eddie, the couple had finally gone to see *The Crow,* and it was clear that neither of them regretted it. "The fact that he died while the movie was being shot just makes it so much more intense. I *loved* it."

"He didn't just die while the movie was being made," Jimmy reminded her as they moved through the crowd and into the parking lot. "Brandon Lee died on set during taping. That's pretty fucked-up."

"I know, it's so sad. The poor guy," Tarah commented as they found the car and climbed inside. "It was so good. Even the music was cool. I *love* that song by The Cure. I want to get the soundtrack."

"I've never heard a song by The Cure that I didn't like." Jimmy started the car and was silent for a long moment then his voice quietly added, "That movie hit a lot closer to home from me than I expected."

Tarah didn't even have to ask. She knew Jimmy was referring to horrific rape scene of Eric Draven's fiancée, Shelly Webster. Tarah had found that part too upsetting to watch and automatically turned to see Jimmy's reaction. It seemed that within seconds, her boyfriend's response to the movie went from that of a casual viewer to someone who was would have gladly jumped right into the film. His eyes were glued to the screen, and he appeared completely absorbed in every second of the movie. They had been holding hands, and she felt his entire body become tense; for a moment she began to fear that he'd want to leave. Tarah confessed this to Jimmy as they drove home.

"No, I didn't want to leave. It's just like I said, it hit a little too close to home for me," he repeated, and sighed. "I just love the fact that they showed a victim taking back his power. Unfortunately, that doesn't usually happen."

Tarah nodded, and they both fell silent for the rest of the drive home.

The couple had become closer since that emotional night when Jimmy revealed his dark family secret. She found herself wondering about the ten-year-old boy who happened upon his older sister being victimized. How had it changed him? But the really interesting thing about Jimmy's confession was how it changed the way Tarah saw him. Although they rarely argued, in cases where his comments or actions seemed harsh or irritating, she'd think of the scared child he once was, and back away from the argument. Suddenly, the small things didn't seem like such a big deal. She had come a long way since the time she was in a relationship with William.

The CD launch was getting closer, and Fire was preparing to meet with journalists to discuss their CD in the days leading up to the party. Before that happened, the band gathered together with a group of exec's from FUTA to view their first video. Tarah was excited and a little nervous.

As it turned out, she had a reason to feel both emotions. The video for "Swim on my Beach" put the entire band in its best light, capturing each member's personality and strength. The video was done with a lot of class, yet showed a very provocative side of Tarah, which was something she had anticipated but felt awkward watching, especially in a room mostly full of strangers. It was one thing to act a certain way on stage when you were caught up in the moment, quite another to see it before your eyes. Over all, everyone appeared to be happy with the end result. That was, until the members of Fire got outside and away from everyone at FUTA. That's when things took a bad turn.

"Dylan really came through for us," William commented, just as they walked out of the building. "I can't wait to turn on the television someday and see our video. Or even turn on the radio and hear our song. I just hope that we catch on." He looked ahead and smiled.

"That's gonna be *crazy* man!" Jimmy put on his sunglasses and chatted with William about the various aspects of the video that he liked. Tarah and Eddie fell behind and discussed a new girl in the drummer's life, and Michael lit up a cigarette and seemed to avoid everyone. For a few minutes, as the warm sun touched down on the five of them, it appeared that all was right with the band. And then, just before they reached their vehicles, Michael butted out his cigarette and spoke up. Tarah wasn't sure what William and Jimmy had said to provoke him, but clearly she was once again the center of a battle.

"You mean *Tarah's* scenes on the beach?" Michael's harsh tone automatically caused the rest of the band to stop their conversations and turn their attention to the band's bassist. Everyone stopped walking. "'Cause the video *I* just saw only showed one second of the rest of us on the beach, the rest was of Tarah. In fact, most of the video was of Tarah."

"That's not true." William surprised her by taking a stand against his brother. "It was pretty balanced. Sure, she was probably featured a little more than the rest of us, but I don't think that's such a stretch considering she's the singer."

Tarah was a little stunned by Michael's comment and worried that he was right. Ever since learning of the section of their contract stating that she had to stay in the band for three years, Tarah was self-conscious of her role with Fire. She wanted to be on equal ground with everyone else, but feared the four guys didn't see it that way.

"Oh, who gives a fuck?" Jimmy complained. "Our band is signed, we've got a video coming out, and have a CD release party soon. Isn't this what we want? Or do you want to go back in there and dispute the fact that you *think* Tarah got more attention than the rest of us to Peter? Give it a rest man!"

With that, William and Jimmy began to walk again and talk, while Tarah was stuck behind with Michael. Eddie seemed uninterested in joining the conversation.

"Those two can say whatever they want," Michael said as he glanced toward his brother and Jimmy. "But unlike them, I haven't had you suck *my* dick, so I'm under no obligation to kiss your ass."

"What the fuck, man?" Jimmy turned around as soon as he heard the degrading comment. Both Eddie and Tarah distanced themselves from Michael, as soon as they saw Jimmy flying back in their general direction. This time William wasn't able to intercept an attack. Tarah was stunned as she watched an enraged Jimmy punch Michael in the face. Just as William caught up with them and went to pull Jimmy back, two large men flew out of the FUTA building and quickly put an end to a fight. The next thing they knew, the entire band was back in Peter's office. Tarah felt like they were children being hauled into the principal's office.

"Look kids, I don't know what is going on with all of you," he was stern but yet friendly at the same time. "But you can't start fights in our parking lot. Hold off on your fighting until there are cameras around at least," he joked. Or Tarah thought he was joking.

"It won't happen again," Jimmy insisted. "Can we go?"

"Sure," Peter said, and Jimmy was already standing up from his chair. "But keep it off FUTA property in the future."

"No problem," Jimmy insisted, and started for the door. Tarah stood up to catch up with him and shot a glare toward Michael. However, it did give her some comfort seeing the bruise forming just below his eye.

Once outside, everyone was relatively quiet. Jimmy continued to walk ahead of everyone. William looked as if were on the verge of saying something and eventually did. "You guys, we may not always agree with one another, but we have to try to keep it together for the band's sake. We can't keep arguing and fighting."

"What?" Jimmy turned his head, but kept walking. "Are you for fucking real, man? Didn't you *hear* what he said about Tarah? It's very disrespectful and insulting."

"I agree." William shot his brother a dirty look. "But that's the point; we've got to have some respect for one another if this is going to work out. We don't have to be the best of friends, just get along."

Of course, the speech had to be directed toward Michael because the rest of the band did get along. Tarah didn't bother saying anything. Jimmy continued to walk ahead until he reached his car. Eddie and Tarah got in, and Michael sat in the passenger side of William's van.

"Honestly though, guys, do you think I was in the video more than anyone else?" Tarah asked them once they were on the 401 on the way back to Thorton.

"No," Eddie answered quickly.

"But who cares if you were?" Jimmy shrugged. "It's not a big deal. It wasn't like we were stuck in the background or not in the video. It's just Mike trying to start something as usual."

Tarah silently nodded.

The band spent the next day doing interviews. The first one was with an entertainment reporter for *The Thorton Report*, followed by others with local newspapers, television, and finally radio stations. It seemed their music was received warmly wherever they went. The only exception was a Toronto paper that reviewed the CD and said it was "An amateur's attempt at best," and also that Fire had a lot of work to do before becoming anything more than a one-hit wonder. Everyone in the band took it with a grain of salt, and Maggie reminded them that any publicity was better than none at all.

"It doesn't matter who you are," she insisted. "Someone is going to criticize you. Look at it this way: out of all of those interviews and reviews you had recently, you only had *one* bad comment. I've seen the vultures in the media rip apart some of my clients. It's not unheard of in the industry. Practice putting on your thick skin now because it's not going to get any easier."

Of all the members of Fire, Tarah was the one who accepted critical words and didn't care. They just rolled off her back.

The band decided to practice on the one free evening they all had before the CD launch. No one mentioned the fight that had broke out in the FUTA parking lot, and things remained relatively calm between the band's members. Jimmy and Michael were civil, but generally avoided one another. Everyone was getting excited for the big night and hoped that it pushed the band in the right direction.

With only two days left until the CD launch, Tarah wasn't feeling well. At first, Jimmy suggested that she had mono, but Tarah insisted that it was merely being overtired and stressed. What she didn't tell him was that her period was five days late and that a pregnancy test was sitting on the bottom of her purse. And although she didn't want to face the fact that she could be pregnant, Tarah knew it was something she couldn't put off any longer.

But just as she was about to bite the bullet and take the test on the afternoon before the launch party, Jimmy rushed in the room.

"Our song is on the radio!" Tarah pushed her fears aside and followed Jimmy downstairs, then outside. He had apparently been cleaning the car and had a local radio station on when their song came flowing through the speakers.

"Oh my God!" Tarah put a hand over her mouth. "They're really playing it!"

"And that's not all," Jimmy insisted. "They even said we were 'a hot new band,' which is pretty cool. This is just the beginning, babe." He leaned forward and gave her a quick kiss. Then pulling the keys from the ignition, Jimmy announced that it was time to celebrate and the car could wait.

"We got to find Eddie. Is he home?" Jimmy asked.

"No, he's out."

"Okay, we've got to call Will then."

Tarah watched him rush inside and slowly followed him. Jimmy was already on the phone. At the same time, he was opening a bottle of Captain Morgan and making a drink for both of them. Tarah wasn't sure how she was going to get around this one. If she was pregnant, drinking definitely wasn't a possibility.

Just then, she remembered her test sitting upstairs in their room. Had she taken it out of the bag? She was about to go upstairs and hide it when Eddie arrived home, and she rushed to the entrance to tell him about their song being on the radio.

"No way!" Eddie's eyes lit up. "Oh my God, Tarah. That's great. I wonder if they'll be playing it all the time now?"

"Who knows how many times they've already played it and we just didn't know," she suggested. "It's so exciting."

Jimmy was off the phone and walking toward them. She noticed the drinks were still on the kitchen counter. "Did she tell you man? Come on, we're just about to have some drinks." He rushed back in the kitchen with Eddie in tow. All she could think about was going to hide that test.

"Jimmy, I'm not feeling well—"

Eddie and Jimmy were involved in a discussion about the song being on the radio, so Tarah thought it was the opportunity she needed to rush upstairs to hide the test. She made a dash up to their room and grabbed the white bag. Slowly, she slipped the blue box out and stared at it. If she was pregnant, did that mean the end of her career before she even started? It wasn't like the band was yet established and she could work around it—not even close. Then she thought about the field day Michael would have with the information.

Downstairs, Jimmy and Eddie were talking and laughing. Tarah sat on the bed and considered for a moment how lucky men were not to have pregnancy fears. She wondered how it could have happened when she loyally took her pill daily, but then it hit her. What about the night she had went drinking and was so sick? She had taken her pill around noon that day then threw up that night, what if the pill hadn't had time to work?

Tarah felt her heart begin to race. Sitting the test down, she felt the room begin to turn black, and her temperature seemed to instantly rise. Feeling like she was about to pass out, Tarah leaned forward and felt a huge thump as she fell on the floor. Pain rang out through her arm, and she could hear the clunk of footsteps flying up the stairs.

"Tarah?" She could hear fear in Jimmy's voice as he leaned over her. "Are you okay?" His hands were tightly gripped on both her arms, and she felt the room start to become clearer, while her body turned ice cold at the same time. She blinked and looked up to see both Eddie and Jimmy by her side. Feeling slight embarrassed, Tarah slowly started to sit up.

"What happened?" Jimmy was wide-eye and still holding on to her arms. Eddie volunteered to get her a glass of water and rushed out of the room. "Are you okay? Want me to take you to the hospital?"

"No," Tarah insisted. "I'm fine. It's nothing."

"Are you sure?" He sat on the floor beside her. "You're white as a ghost."

Footsteps rushed up the stairs, and then Eddie handed her a glass of water. She noticed him glancing toward the bed and look away quickly. That's when Tarah realized that the pregnancy test was in full view. She assumed that was the reason Eddie left shortly afterward, saying he'd be downstairs if they needed him. She sipped on the water and wondered how to get out of this awkward situation.

It was after Eddie left that Jimmy helped her off the floor, and Tarah felt her stomach sinking, knowing that he was about to see the blue box sitting on their bed. And then it suddenly caught his eye.

"Tarah." He picked up the test and held it in his hand. "Are you pregnant?"

"I don't know," she barely whispered. "I'm late."

"Why didn't you tell me?" He seemed concerned as he tilted his head.

"I was scared." Tarah cleared her throat. "Scared that I might be, and scared you'd be angry."

"You make it sound like I'm some kind of raging bull." He gave her a nervous smile, and Tarah shook her head no.

"But the timing? Right now, when our band is starting to take off." She blinked back the tears and took a deep breath. "Plus we haven't been together that long. It's hardly an ideal time to have a baby."

"I agree," he nodded. "Do you know for sure? I mean is this the first test you bought?"

"Yeah." She sounded very child-like when answering. "I'm scared to find out."

Jimmy nodded. "That makes two of us, but you'll have to do it sooner or later." His words were gentle. "Maybe you should do it now and then if you are, we'll figure out something."

Tarah took the test from his hand and silently went into the bathroom. Once the door was closed, she felt tears burning through her eyelids and sliding down her face. Fearing the worst, she cursed the timing and reluctantly took the test out of the box. She followed the instructions.

Minutes later, Tarah was relieved to find out it was negative. Flushing the toilet, she washed her hands and face, then returned to the bedroom. Jimmy was sitting on the bed and appeared as nervous as she had felt only seconds earlier.

"It was negative." She spoke evenly. "No baby."

"Really?" He sighed a breath of relief and walked over and hugged her. "There is only one problem then. How come you passed out? That's not normal, Tarah."

"It's fine." She let go of him. Climbing on the bed, she lay down and watched him close the bedroom door. "I think it's just more panic attacks. I used to pass out as a kid too. It was never anything."

"You've been under a lot of stress." Jimmy walked over to the bed and seemed almost apprehensive to touch her. "With the band stuff and your dad. But maybe you should get checked out."

"I will."

"Tarah," Jimmy started, and hesitated. "I don't want you to take this the wrong way." He sat down beside her on the bed. "But are you eating okay?"

"Yes."

"I don't want you to think I'm trying to project something on you because of my sister's eating disorders. So don't think that," Jimmy insisted. He was clearly hesitant to say anything. "But you just don't eat much. Maybe it's just because of stress, but I've noticed it lately."

"Really?" Tarah started to close her eyes. "I don't know what you're talking about. I'm eating lots."

But she was lying.

CHAPTER TWENTY-EIGHT

▼

Tarah reluctantly went to her doctor the following morning. She had tried to convince Jimmy that it was a waste of time, especially considering the CD launch was that night and she wanted to practice, but he was very insistent.

"So?" Jimmy asked when she arrived home a couple hours later. He was still in bed and just waking up as she walked into their room. "What did he say?"

"Not much." Tarah quickly removed her shoes and climbed under the covers with him. "Since I didn't have breakfast, he wanted me to get some blood tests done and that's about it. He doesn't think I'm pregnant but just really stressed." And underweight. But she didn't bother to mention that fact.

"Good." He pulled her close to his naked body. She could feel his hot breath on her face and Tarah sunk into his arms. She felt comfort in knowing how much he worried about her. "He's probably right. It's just stress."

She quickly fell back to sleep.

Tarah later awoke to an empty bed and automatically jumped up to look for Jimmy. Running through the house like a mad woman, she finally found him in the basement. With a guitar by his chair, he was leaning over a notebook and appeared to be deep in concentration.

"Happy birthday!" Tarah exclaimed as she ran down the stairs. "Oh my God! I forgot it was your birthday this morning. I feel like such an ass!"

An amused smile crossed his face. "Thanks. You can give me my present later." He seductively raised one eyebrow.

"What are you doing?" Tarah walked closer to him.

Tapping his pen on the notebook, he sat back in his chair. "I'm just working on a song. I couldn't get back to sleep this morning and came down here to play around with some ideas."

"Really?" Tarah went over and sat on his lap and quickly kissed his lips. "Can I see?"

"Sure, but remember that I'm just playing around with it now." He turned the notebook toward her.

"That's okay, I understand," Tarah said, sliding one arm around his neck. Her eyes scanned the paper, and she smiled. The lyrics were very personal and clearly about their relationship. "These are beautiful."

"Do you think so?" He pulled her close. "They're pretty rough and—"

The phone rang and Jimmy took a deep breath. "That's probably my mom to wish me a happy birthday."

"Okay." Tarah reluctantly got off his lap and followed him upstairs.

It wasn't his mother on the phone. It was Maggie Eriksson, who wanted to give them last minute details about that night. Jimmy reported the details of their conversation after getting off the phone, which included meeting their manager before the party. It was going to be a hectic and stressful day.

William and Michael dropped by the house late that afternoon to gather their stuff. An hour later, the band was in two separate vehicles on the 401. The plan was to drop off their equipment at Cocaine and then go to their hotel to get ready. The band was scheduled to return to the bar at seven to meet with both the owner and Maggie.

Tarah, however, was a mess. Nervous and anxious, she rushed around the hotel room and attempted to put an outfit together but to no avail. It didn't seem to matter what clothes she put on or what Tarah tried to do with her hair, nothing seemed to look right. Finally, she collapsed on the bed in frustration and started to cry. And on top of everything else, her stomach was tied in knots.

Jimmy, who wore black jeans and a T-shirt, insisted he was as ready as he could be and volunteered to go to a nearby pharmacy to get something to ease her nausea. Shrugging helplessly, he admitted to not knowing what else to do.

Tarah sat on the edge of the bed and looked into his eyes. Right away, she could sense his nervousness and found some comfort in the fact that she wasn't alone in her fears. Giving him a small smile, she slowly nodded. "Actually that would be great, if you don't mind." She spoke quietly and watched him shake his head no. "I'll try to sort myself out."

"Okay," he started to the door. "Do you need anything else?" Jimmy's voice was very soft and gentle. "Something to eat?"

"No, thanks." She took a deep breath. "I'll be fine."

But as soon as he left, Tarah felt her heart racing when she tried to figure out how to get herself together on time. Then someone knocked at the door. It was Maggie.

"Tarah?" She looked the tiny woman over head to toe. "You're not ready yet?"

"I can't seem to do anything right, Maggie." She watched the band's manager walk in the room and close the door behind her. "I'm so nervous."

Maggie, as usual, was as cool as cucumber. She wore the same attire as usual, which was a blazer, matching mid-length skirt, and designer shoes. "Okay, first of all take a deep breath." Tarah did so and watched Maggie dig through her purse. She pulled out a small container.

"What's that?" Tarah asked curiously, while simultaneously holding her stomach.

"Something to get your back on track," Maggie insisted. "Coke."

"Are you serious?" Tarah jumped back slightly. "I don't think that's a good idea. I can't be all fucked-up when I go on stage."

"Trust me, Tarah." Maggie was calm. "It won't mess you up; just do a little, and it'll take the edge off." When Tarah didn't reply, her manager continued, "Do you seriously think I want you to do anything to affect your performance tonight? It's not going to be much of a show if you're too nervous to sing. Or even get dressed for that matter." Maggie gave a friendly smile and gestured toward Tarah's robe. "Just think about it."

Tarah considered everything she said for a moment. She certainly wasn't going to get it together on her own. "I've never done cocaine before," Tarah admitted, feeling slightly shy. "And I don't know what to do with my hair or anything; I feel like I'm losing it."

"Okay." Maggie put her arm around Tarah and led her into the bathroom. "We'll take care of that. I'll pick out something for you to wear." Her light brown eyes danced around. "I'll help you with your hair and makeup. It'll be perfect, I *promise*."

Tarah nodded. She certainly had nothing to lose at that point. She felt completely consumed by fear and anxiety. Standing back, Tarah was wringing her hands as Maggie opened the container on the bathroom counter, made two short lines of white power, and used a small straw to inhale it. Rubbing her perfect nose, Maggie's eyes were watering as she gestured Tarah to do the same. She did it and made a face.

"I don't like the taste. I need a drink of water," Tarah insisted.

"Nope, what you need to do is get ready," Maggie replied, and disappeared into the next room; Tarah studied herself in the mirror. Her eyes were all messed up, but Maggie had been right, she felt fantastic. Suddenly her concerns about the upcoming show were irrelevant. Everything felt wonderful and perfect. She smiled at her own reflection.

"Here." Maggie was back in the bathroom, holding a red tank top that tied up the front, a short black shirt, and matching tights. "Put these on. Do you have a pair of shoes too?" Tarah nodded and pointed toward the next room where a pair of long, black boots with platform heels sat. "Perfect!" Maggie said, and pushed the clothing in Tarah's arms and shut the door.

Fifteen minutes later, Tarah was dressed, her makeup was on, and Maggie was doing the finishing touches on her hair. She looked great and hadn't a worry in the world. That was when Jimmy got home.

"Hey." He looked surprised to see Maggie. "What's up?"

"What's up is," Maggie said, combing out Tarah's hair, "we're going to the party in style. A limo will be picking us up in about fifteen minutes.

"Really?" Tarah turned around. "I didn't know that."

"Well, that's what I was here to tell you but we got a bit sidetracked when you weren't ready yet." A small smile crossed Maggie's lips. "Surprise!"

"Wow." Jimmy walked into the bathroom with a bottle of Tums in his hand. "The pharmacist said—"

Then he stopped. Looking into Tarah's face, he glanced toward Maggie, then back at his girlfriend. "What are you on?"

Tarah's mouth fell open, but she was speechless; Maggie quickly intercepted.

"We did a line of coke to help get her mind off things," she answered in a tone that suggested it wasn't a big deal.

"Really?" Jimmy didn't look excited over the news. In fact, he looked annoyed. "Tarah, you don't want to get messed up in coke."

"I, ah—"

"Don't worry about it, Jimmy," Maggie insisted. "She didn't do much. She'll be fine."

Jimmy looked skeptical, but didn't say anything. Tarah felt her heart sink. He was clearly disappointed in her.

The band gathered together in the hotel lobby shortly after six thirty and made their way outside. Their limo was waiting. William commented on how everything was starting to feel surreal, as Tarah calmly noted all the people on the sidewalk who were stopping, attempting to catch a glance of who was getting inside the luxurious vehicle. She felt like she was floating.

The rest of the evening seemed to fly by. They arrived at Cocaine and were ushered in the front doors like celebrities. Although huge signs outside the bar were advertising the band's CD release party that night, Tarah still couldn't shake the feeling that no one really cared. They were too new to have established much of a fan base other than the ones who followed them around from bar to bar. It surprised her how indifferent she felt about everything now. No worries or fears.

They were introduced to the bar's owner and were shown around the establishment. It was huge and modern. The stage was quite large and some people were already there, setting up their equipment for them. There was also a lower level to the bar where people could sit and talk in small groups or play pool. Usually a DJ was in this section, but not that night. Overall, Tarah liked it, but she'd been in so many bars and clubs since joining the band, that she rarely saw any major difference from one place to another. They were all dark, dreary, and made guests feel like they were entering an escape from their everyday lives.

The doors were opened at seven thirty and the band was scheduled to perform at eight. Until then, they gathered in a backroom and had a meeting with Peter Sampson and Maggie. Both talked about what that night meant to the band, discussed the possibility of opening for an established act in the near future, and explained how important it was to network.

"After the show is done, get out there and talk to people," Maggie insisted. "Potential or current fans, and people from the record company and local radio stations—there will be media here, and also friends, family, anyone else you invited."

"This is your night to give your career a huge kick start," Peter reminded them. "Take advantage of it."

Before long, they were waiting as a DJ from a local radio station announced them. He briefly mentioned their CD and first single, and then went on to repeat the lines Maggie had wrote weeks earlier. She was right, Tarah noted, it did sound much different with the right announcer.

"First there was a match, then there was a spark, and now there's FIRE!" The final word was their cue for the band to start playing one of their loudest songs from the CD. Tarah was stunned to see the entire bar was packed. Just as Maggie had suggested, she felt completely at ease once she started to sing. Tarah missed performing, and it seemed like ages since she was on a stage. There was electricity in the room that no one could've anticipated; it reminded her of the first time she sang at Jerry's with the band. She had long forgotten the fear but would always remember the euphoria of singing that night. This one was a hundred times better.

The show went incredibly well. The band seemed united with the same goal, which was to leave the audience wanting more. Judging by the crowd's reaction, she was pretty confident that they'd succeed. She concentrated on every word and put on the best performance possible. Glancing through the audience, Tarah recognized that her brother was there, and eventually saw John and a woman she assumed was Elizabeth. There were other familiar faces—either people she recognized from FUTA or a few fans from their pre-contract days—and others who were clearly media.

When they finally finished playing, the audience gave an enthusiastic ovation. Tarah felt very emotional for some reason and forced herself to calm down as she left the stage. She grabbed a bottle of water, but what she really wanted was alcohol.

"Tarah!" She heard her name and turned around to find John and a slender, young, blonde woman. "That was fantastic!"

"Thank you." Tarah smiled and accepted John's hug. "Tarah, this is Elizabeth."

"Hi." Elizabeth gave her a shy smile. "Nice to meet you. Your band was wonderful."

"Thank you. I appreciate it."

The three continued to talk for a few minutes until Maggie came along and whisked her away. "There are some people from the radio stations who I want you to introduce you to."

The rest of the night consisted of meeting people. Tarah spent most of the evening talking to strangers who were quick to introduce themselves, while the rest of the band disappeared within the large establishment. She wondered where Jimmy was and felt her heart sinking an hour later when she found him talking to another woman. The familiar sense of jealousy crawled in her heart, just like all the times she had dealt with the same emotion when she was dating William. Maybe nothing had really changed after all.

Before she could catch up with him, however, someone pulled her in another direction. Tarah felt like she was faking a smile for the rest of the night as she continued to move her way around the room, always half looking for Jimmy. Eventually, she came across her brother who quickly gave her hug.

"God, you are a hard woman to track down!" He smiled. "Mom was going to come but said she'd baby sit, so I could come instead."

"Thanks." Tarah finally felt like she could be herself. "What did you think of the show?"

"Loved it!" His eyes sparkled. "I think everyone was really impressed, Tarah. You're on the right track."

"Have you seen Jimmy?"

"I did for a few minutes." Her brother had briefly met Jimmy on two other occasions. "I talked to William too. He was with some model-looking girl. I don't know where Jimmy went. I'm sure he isn't too far away."

Tarah smiled, and the two said their good-byes, as her brother had to return to Thorton that same night.

Tarah eventually found Jimmy. He was with the same girl from earlier that night, Jillian, and his mom. She put on a fake smile and went over to see them.

"Well, hello!" Jimmy's mom rushed right up to her and gave Tarah a strong hug. "What a wonderful singer you are, dear."

"Thanks," she said as the tiny woman moved away from her and gave her a mischievous wink.

Jillian was right behind her, giving Tarah a long hug. "You looked beautiful on the stage." When she let go of Tarah, she quickly added. "Mom and I unfortunately have to take off and get back to Thorton, but you and I *must* get together sometime for lunch or coffee. Sound good?"

"Absolutely."

She then turned to give her brother a hug; Tarah wondered who the girl was who was standing with them. She was very pale with black hair and green eyes. *Very beautiful*, Tarah thought bitterly.

After Jimmy's family left, he finally introduced the girl as a fan named Andrea. Tarah gave the girl a questionable look and introduced herself. Andrea clearly wasn't impressed with Tarah, but said a quick hello back. Just as Tarah was about to ask Jimmy why he was hanging out with this girl all night, Maggie came along and hooked her arm around her waist.

"Come on, Tarah, we have to go for a walk." She pulled her away.

"Maggie, I really can't go too far," Tarah muttered. "That 'fan' of ours has been hanging out with Jimmy since early in the evening. I've gotta find out what her deal is."

"Oh, I *know* she's been hanging around him," Maggie muttered. "I saw it too and want to talk to you about her."

"Where are we going anyway?" Tarah asked as they headed behind the stage area.

"We're going to have some 'girl talk.'" Maggie ushered her into a small, private bathroom that was marked Staff Only and closed the door. It was clean, large, and looked very elegant for a public restroom. It also had some chairs, a porn magazine, and a condom dispenser. "Now, this room is only for a few selected people." Maggie dug in her purse and pulled out the cocaine once again. "I've got a plan that will not only keep your boyfriend on the straight and narrow, but it'll keep that *fan* out of the way."

"I don't understand." Tarah suddenly felt very unsophisticated. She watched Maggie make more lines, this time on a mirror that just happened to be on the vanity stand, and inhale more coke. She then passed the straw to Tarah who reluctantly did the same. After the excitement of being on stage, followed by the many other emotions that followed her throughout the night, she just needed something to take the edge off.

"Okay, that girl," Maggie pointed her finger toward the wall, "has been on his ass all night." She spoke evenly as she carefully put the container of coke back in her purse. "You've got to learn how to deal with groupies *now*, or you'll going to have a lot of trouble ahead. Jimmy is a really attractive guy, and you've got to let the skanks out there know he's yours."

Tarah was completely taken aback by Maggie's words. She hadn't guessed her to be anything but utterly professional until that night. Now the band's manager was giving her clear instructions on how to deal with Jimmy and Andrea. And the scary part was that it sounded like it would work.

"I'll do it." Tarah's eyes were sparkling as she briskly walked toward the door with Maggie on her heels. Once they were back in the crowd, they quickly spotted Jimmy with Andrea trying to cozy up to him. He didn't look very comfortable and appeared relieved when Tarah returned.

"Hey, there you are." He smiled and gave her a quick kiss. Out of the corner of Tarah's eye, she noticed Maggie giving an approving nod then introduce herself to Andrea. Meanwhile, if Jimmy noticed that she was high, he didn't comment.

"This girl is following me around," he muttered. "I'm trying to be nice, but it's kinda getting on my nerves."

Tarah gave him a seductive smile. "It's okay Jimmy, she's allowed to have a crush. Don't worry about it."

"Hey Tarah," Maggie called out. "We're going to the bar to get a drink, would you like to join us?"

"I'll be right back Jimmy." She gave him a quick kiss. "I have a birthday surprise for you when I get back."

"I won't move." He grabbed her ass, and then watched the three girls walk away.

Except they didn't go for a drink, but instead Maggie escorted both of them to the same private bathroom. The same one they'd just snorted coke in.

"Where are we going?" Andrea looked confused and clearly was a little drunk. Maggie smiled and shoved the brunette into the bathroom. Tarah followed and shut the door.

"What the *fuck* do you think you're doing with *my* boyfriend?" Tarah suddenly felt herself turning into another person.

"I thought he was single," Andrea insisted. "He seemed to be into me and—"

Tarah used all her strength to shove the girl against the wall. "You keep the fuck away from him, or I will make you fucking pay! Got it?"

Then Tarah calmly walked to the door and opened it. Maggie was waiting on the other side. Andrea slipped past them both in tears.

"Problem solved." Maggie spoke confidently. "Now, I've got some people to attend to, you go find Jimmy."

After getting a drink, Tarah found her boyfriend talking to Eddie. The three of them went to the bar to do a shot together, and then their drummer disappeared.

"So, where's my surprise?" Jimmy slid his arm around her.

"Follow me." Tarah sat down her empty glass and reached for Jimmy's hand. Together, they went to the private bathroom that it seemed no one else knew about, and she locked the door. Gently easing him against the same wall that she had just shoved Andrea against, Tarah pushed her own body against his and began to kiss Jimmy with an intensity that quickly left him gasping for air. Her hand was slowly traveling down his chest.

"I think I like where this is going," Jimmy muttered when Tarah finally released his mouth, and her hand unbuttoned his jeans. Tarah's lips roughly met with his again, while her hand reached into his boxers.

She finally ended the kiss. "I think you will too," Tarah replied, as her head slowly traveled down his body.

CHAPTER TWENTY-NINE

▼

The party ended around six the following morning. Tarah and Jimmy didn't get back to the hotel and into bed till almost seven thirty. The sound of a ringing phone was what finally woke them at three that afternoon.

"Hello," Tarah reluctantly answered, while she watched Jimmy open and then close his eyes. She felt like absolute shit.

"Good morning, Tarah!" Maggie exclaimed from the other end of the line. She had a hint of laugher in her voice. "How are you doing today?"

"I don't feel so good." Tarah was a little irritated by her manager's teasing. "Last night was crazy." Her mind quickly skimmed over the events, and she finally smiled. "It went well though, didn't it?"

"It went *exceptionally* well, Tarah, that's why I called you. I've been hearing nothing but praise about the band since I got to my office today. Peter Sampson called me and he was extremely impressed with you guys. He said everyone was professional and *exceeded* his expectations. Very high praise! Also there are a few articles in local papers detailing the event, which also gives us great exposure."

"Wow, that's great." Tarah began to wake up and automatically crave a hot cup of coffee.

"So, did you have any more problems with that Andrea chick? I'm assuming not." Maggie let out a small laugh. "She didn't stick around for long after you gave her a piece of your mind."

"I still can't believe, I ah …" She glanced toward Jimmy and wasn't sure if he was asleep or not, so didn't finish that sentence. "It was totally not in character."

"I take it Jimmy is awake?" Maggie said. "Don't worry, I understand it isn't in character for you, but you know what, it had to be done. Trust me, Tarah, these groupies are like leeches. You don't want to encourage them to stick around for long. Plus, if word gets around that you aren't to be messed with, it might scare some of them off."

"It isn't the first time I have had that concern." Tarah continued to glance toward Jimmy. "In some respect or another." She thought back to her relationships with Jeff, then William. There always seemed to be another girl attempting to push her aside, as if she weren't worthy of her boyfriend at the time.

"Well, you get that regardless of whether you are in a band or not," Maggie quickly reminded her. "But when you're in a band, especially one that is about to be as successful as yours, the problem can increase. But don't think it doesn't go both ways; you're the center of the band and will have your own collection of obsessed fans soon enough."

"I can't picture that," Tarah said. "I just don't see it."

"Start seeing it," Maggie insisted. "Because it's going to happen."

After their conversation ended, Tarah decided to jump in the shower and get dressed. Jimmy was still in bed and slowly opened his eyes as she grabbed her purse and was about to head for the door.

"Just gonna leave me, are you?" he muttered, but there was clearly humor in his voice. "Whatcha doin'?"

"I'm going to get some coffee for us."

"C'mere."

Tarah followed his instructions and watched him slowly sit up revealing the Celtic tattoo on his left arm. He rubbed his eyes as she approached. His hair was standing on end indicating the rough night he'd just experienced. A small beard was forming on his face and she thought how sexy it looked. Jimmy's eyes met with hers as she stood beside the bed purse in hand, and he smiled.

"So, we have to talk about a couple of things."

Tarah felt her stomach turning. This couldn't be good. She frowned. "What?"

"About last night."

"Okay." She was hesitant to hear what Jimmy had to say.

"Okay, well sit down." He patted the bed and she followed his instruction. "First of all, I'm not trying to tell you what to do, but I'm not crazy about the coke thing."

"I know."

"I've done it, it's not the biggest deal ever, but I just don't want to see you get too messed up in that shit." His blue eyes shone as he spoke. "It's just bad shit to get into. There's like two guys in my last band that got into it hardcore and it totally fucked the band. We could've gone far, but one of the guys got arrested for possession and the other went to rehab." He shook his head.

"Anyway, not to suggest that I'm *just* worried about the band here, because I love you and don't want to see you go down that road. It's not pretty. I just never thought I'd see you do that shit."

Tarah nodded and she felt her heart sink. "I never thought I'd do it either."

"And that's basically my point," Jimmy remarked. "There's really easy access to all that stuff in the music business and more so now that we're signed. It's common knowledge. That's why you've got to think on your feet. If you ever want to do it again, just promise me that we'll at least do it together. I know it sounds stupid, but I'd feel a little better about it that way."

"Okay." She spoke apprehensively.

"Good. Now, the second thing I want to talk to you about is that girl from last night." Tarah felt her stomach sinking again. Did he know about her threatening Andrea?

"Okay," she said reluctantly.

"Now, she was like following me around," Jimmy explained. "I just didn't want you to think I was like William when you were together or even the guy you dated before that, what's his name?"

"Jeff."

"Exactly," Jimmy replied. "I didn't do anything with her, I made it clear that you were my girlfriend, and she still followed me around. I didn't want to be too prick since it was our launch party and they all seemed to want us to be on our best behavior."

"I understand."

"Do you?" Jimmy's eyes searched her face. "I really hope so, because I don't want you to ever think I'd cheat on you."

"I didn't," Tarah insisted.

"Good, well I tried to get rid of her a couple of times but she just didn't get a hint," Jimmy said and started to cough. "I even went for a piss and she waited outside the washroom for me. Surprised she didn't follow me in."

Tarah began to laugh.

"I'm serious," he said. "Oh, and speaking of bathrooms, I really liked my birthday gift." Jimmy raised his eyebrows slightly, and Tarah felt a smile creep on her face. "Thank you."

"You're welcome."

Fire met in the hotel lobby the following morning to review what Maggie had mapped out for the band. Three interviews were scheduled, followed by another photo shoot, and a final meeting with their manager later in the afternoon. It was through one interview with a national women's magazine that Tarah realized how large of an impact the CD release party actually had on people in the industry. The interviewer spoke enthusiastically on the huge success of the gathering, and how Fire was anticipated to become "the band to watch" during the summer of '94.

They all met with Maggie later that same day and she had news. "You guys will be touring with Confusion 45 this summer."

Tarah knew the band, but really wasn't a fan of their music. Nevertheless, it was an opportunity, and that was all that mattered.

"Cool." Jimmy was the first to respond. He was sipping on his coffee and didn't appear to have a care in the world. "I don't get them but whatever, man, it's a chance to get out there." Tarah noticed that he echoed her own thoughts on the subject.

"Exactly." William remained positive, but beside him, Michael was scowling in silence; Eddie didn't respond one way or another. "They're well-regarded though. Where are we going to be touring?"

"Well, no specific dates or cities have been announced yet," Maggie replied confidently. "However, it looks like across Canada for sure, possibly getting into the states. Their popularity has increased a great deal since one of their songs was featured on that … show? I can't think of what it's called, but it's one of those dramas that are really popular and I couldn't possibly find the time to watch."

Tarah shared a smile with her. "So when do we find out more details?"

"Not sure, as soon as they come in I'll certainly let you all know. All I know for a fact is that they were considering several bands to tour with but chose Fire. Of course, they're under the same label as you, so that may have helped out."

Maggie went on to talk about the single, "Swim on my Beach."

"The song is doing very well. FUTA is apparently pushing to get it lots of airplay. There's a station here in Toronto that plays it *all* the time." She stopped and seemed to note the surprise on everyone's faces. "Which I'm assuming you didn't know? Oh yes, I'll have to give FUTA credit for a job well done there."

"Wow," Jimmy exclaimed, and got up to locate a garbage can to throw away his empty coffee cup.

"The video is getting a lot of airplay as well, and before the tour, we'll have to get another video out there. In the meantime, I've had some requests for Fire to play around the city here in Toronto. I realize it's not as glamorous as touring across the country with a big act like Confusion 45, but it's great exposure."

"And it's work," Jimmy added. "We owe the record company an obscene amount of money right now, so we're in no position to say no to anyone."

"I wouldn't worry about that right now," Maggie replied. "Trust me, when you start making money, FUTA will be the first person to take their cut." She gave him a humored grin.

"And you'll be the second," Michael remarked. Tarah wanted nothing more than to respond to his rude comment, but remained quiet. Maggie didn't look particularly offended by the remark, nor did she respond.

Everyone headed back to Thorton later that day after making plans to meet for a rehearsal later in the week.

The next morning, Jimmy announced that he wanted to spend the afternoon completing the song he had started on the morning of their CD launch party. He also suggested to Tarah that they start to write some songs together before the tour started that summer.

"If we're busy touring, we mightn't have a lot of opportunities to really sit down and work on some good stuff. So, it makes sense if we get started now."

"Agreed," Tarah said. She was getting ready for her lunch date with Jimmy's sister, while he still lay in bed. "Maybe Eddie can either help us too, or at least, let us know what he thinks of whatever we come up with."

"Sounds good." Jimmy sat up in the bed as Tarah applied her makeup in the mirror across the room. "William said he and Michael are going to work on some stuff, but what he probably really meant is that *he* is going to work on some songs. I somehow can't see Mike writing a song."

"He claims he has before."

"Sure, whatever." Jimmy watched Tarah and fell silent for a moment. "So, listen, I guess that Will met someone on the night of the party."

Tarah quickly stopped putting on her mascara and saw Jimmy watching her reaction in the mirror. It wasn't that she hadn't expected or wanted that day to come, but it still felt weird to know that someone she once loved was seeing someone else. Not that she had a right to make any judgments. "Really?"

"Are you okay with that?"

"Of course I'm okay with it," Tarah said, turning around to make eye contact with Jimmy. "It's just weird to hear about. Not that I don't want him to be with another girl, it's just going to be uncomfortable to be around."

"He got over it when it was us" Jimmy pointed out fairly. "If anyone had the right to be uncomfortable, it was Will after we hooked up. Especially since we were living in the same house. Granted, nothing was going on really at first, but I'm assumed he thought we were in bed five minutes after you left him that night."

"I know," Tarah said, and went back to applying her mascara. "Who is she?"

"Some model." It was then that Tarah recalled her brother remarking on seeing William with a "model-like" girl on the night of the party, but at the time she was so wrapped up with finding Jimmy that she hadn't really paid attention. "Her name is Lindsay. I saw her, she's hot and all, but really skinny."

"How skinny?"

"Like 100 lbs skinny."

"I'm 100 lbs."

"Yeah, but you're also five foot nothing," Jimmy said with a smile. "She's like five nine, about my height. That's way too skinny."

Tarah acted very nonchalant about the news but her mind was going in several different directions. After all, most people wouldn't like the idea of their ex-boyfriends going out with models. Not that it should've mattered, but it still bothered her even though she had no right to feel that way.

Jillian picked her up just before noon, and they headed to a trendy, downtown café. Tarah thought it was clean and quiet, two qualities that she loved in any food establishment. Jillian chose a table at the back of the room, and Tarah promptly sat across from her. Although Jimmy's sister always put her at ease and was very friendly, Tarah was a little nervous to be having lunch with her. After all, their meetings were usually short and didn't require any amount of conversation.

They ended up talking about Jillian's work at the dental clinic, about the band, and the recent party to officially release Fire's CD. Then the topic of Jimmy came up. Tarah was intrigued, but didn't know how much she should discuss with his sister.

However, that wasn't a problem. Jillian kept the conversation pretty light, mostly talking about her younger brother growing up and how proud she was of him.

"I'll say he's quite enamored with you." Jillian smiled and Tarah noticed a sparkled in her eyes, similar to the one Jimmy had when he laughed. It was one of the few traits they shared. Even their personalities couldn't have been more different. "The poor guy was so upset that night that I picked him up at the bar."

Tarah silently nodded. She hated to even think about it. Tarah had been in such agony that night, fearful that he wouldn't come home at all.

"I took him to my place, hoping he'd sober up." She shook her head. "I don't like it when he drinks like that, it's pretty scary because he sometimes sinks into a depression." Tarah silently nodded, thinking back to the snowy night when he first admitted his feelings for her. "But we had a long talk then I dropped him off at home."

"I'm glad everything turned out okay," Tarah confessed. "I was a little worried that night too."

Jillian leaned forward on the table and tilted her head. Her eyes were full of compassion and caring, but Tarah sensed that she wanted to say something more about the subject.

"What did Jimmy tell you about when we were kids?" Jillian asked curiously. Tarah hesitated to say anything at all, unsure of if she was betraying a confidence. Sure, Jimmy's sister had insisted that he tell her about their family's horrible tragedy, but how much information was Tarah really suppose to know?

"He just told me that …" Her voice trailed off, and Tarah was relieved when Jillian jumped in.

"He told you about the rape?" Jillian's voice was low.

"Yes." Tarah gave a sympathetic smile. "He did, and I'm sorry you had to go through that."

"Thanks." Jillian gave a sad smile. "Did Jimmy tell you that he saw it?"

"Yes."

"And how it affected him?"

"Yes," Tarah said automatically, but then backtracked when noticing the expression on Jillian's face. She appeared skeptical. "I think?"

Jillian sat back in her seat and took a deep breath. "He probably said he just ate a lot and got into music, or something like that?"

"Yes, wasn't that true?" Tarah felt her heard pounding rapidly and didn't like where their conversation seemed to be going.

"It is," Jillian assured her. "But there's more." There were lines of worry on her forehead, and Jimmy's sister seemed to struggle with the decision of whether or not to say something. "I don't want to betray him in any way, but I worry about Jimmy. I worry a lot more than he realizes. And I know you're there for him, if he ever needs anyone." She looked down at the table and then at Tarah again. Pushing a strand of blonde, wavy hair behind her ear, Tarah noticed that the café seemed quieter for a moment. The song "Release" by Pearl Jam flowed through the room, and she waited for Jimmy's sister to speak. The longer the silence went on, the more nervous Tarah felt.

"The day it happened, I had returned home early from school. Both mom and dad worked back then, so I was home alone. I guess the guy …" she hesitated for a moment, "his name was Doug, but that doesn't really matter. Anyway, he must've followed me home or something because the next thing I knew he was at the door. Of course, I had a huge crush on him, so let him in and to make a long story short, he forced himself on me."

Tarah shook her head sadly. She didn't even know what to say. It felt like no words would be of comfort after such a horrific tragedy.

"The only reason why I knew Jimmy was there, was because he screamed when he saw Doug holding me down and heard me crying."

Tarah could picture what Jillian described and she was stunned. How could either of them have lived through that day and ever feel safe again? It broke her heart for both of them.

"He ran out of the room, which is good because Doug might have hurt him. Who knows?" Jillian licked her lips and seemed to be pacing herself. "So by the time my parents got home, I had scrubbed myself raw in the shower, locked the doors, and cried. Jimmy stayed away for a long time and mom thought he was just at a friend's house. When he finally came home, I grabbed him and hauled him upstairs and begged him to never tell what he saw."

"Was he upset?"

"He was confused. He didn't really want to talk about it," Jillian replied. "He shut right down. But I fooled myself into believing that we both got over it. Like we even knew the first thing about recovering from something so traumatic. I always thought I was okay, that I just had a minor fixation on my weight. I thought Jimmy was fine too. He seemed fine. A little anti-social but fine."

"About the same time I started to model was when I started to not eat very much. I got a lot of compliments for being so thin and photographers told me that I'd get more work if I stayed tiny. So I did."

"I had crushes on men in the industry, and I'm ashamed to say that I hooked up with a photographer who was twice my age when I was fifteen. There were others after that who took advantage of me; I guess they could sense that I was pretty messed up and like vultures, they preyed on it."

"Anyway, I started to hate myself and eat less. It was a downward spiral" Jillian calmly continued. "Meanwhile, Jimmy was going through a hell of his own, and I didn't even know. After the rape, it started with nightmares. He was always having nightmares about the rape. Of course, as Jimmy got older, the more he understood what had happened, the more it upset him. Then he started to eat a lot. He gained weight, kids started to pick on him in school. He didn't have any friends. I didn't realize how bad it was because I was so wrapped up in myself."

A tear formed in the corner of Jillian's eye, and she wiped it away. There was so much pain in her voice now, and Tarah feared for what was coming next. She felt her eyelids burning but did her best to remain strong.

"He must've felt so alone. And no one really thought about it because he was a good kid, a quiet kid, and he didn't seem unhappy." Jillian stopped as a waitress dropped by the table to fill their coffee cups. After the girl left, Jillian leaned forward and gently delivered the words that had been haunting the room since they arrived. The room seemed to become colder, and Tarah's palms began to sweat.

"I don't know what Jimmy told you, but the reason why all this stuff with the rape came out was because he tried to hurt himself."

Tarah felt her chest become tight and for a moment, she couldn't breathe.

"Jimmy tried to commit suicide when he was thirteen."

CHAPTER THIRTY

▼

"Wow," John replied in a calm voice after Tarah told him the whole story about Jimmy and his sister. "That's absolutely horrible."

"I know." She sniffed. Tarah went to visit with John shortly after her coffee date with Jillian and now sat in his living room. "I'm just glad Jimmy wasn't home when Jillian dropped me off. I know if I had seen his face, I would've started to cry just thinking about how he once …" But the words caught in her throat. She couldn't even say it. "Why didn't he tell me?" The tears began to overflow again.

"Probably for a lot of reasons," John insisted, and handed her a box of Kleenex. "I'm guessing he didn't want you to feel sorry for him or maybe he was trying to protect you. Often people who attempt suicide feel like they spend the rest of their lives under a watchful eye, almost like their friends and family expect them to try again. But you have to remember, Tarah, he was just a kid, and he was carrying a huge secret around. No one had ever talked to him about it other than to tell him *not* to talk about it. And he was only twelve or thirteen when he attempted suicide. That's not an easy age no matter who you are, let alone to have this horrific memory in the back of your mind."

"I know." Tarah sighed and looked around John's apartment. She was glad that his girlfriend wasn't there when she had arrived. This situation was much too personal to share with someone she had only just met. "I understand why he felt that way, I really do. And I know that he probably wouldn't ever do that again, but what if he did?"

"Tarah, you said yourself that he had counseling as a child. I'd be more worried if you said he *didn't* have any form of psychiatric help."

"And, over all, it sounds like Jimmy is pretty well-adjusted," John reminded her. "And from my few times of meeting him, he seems to be full of life. I wouldn't worry about it. It's nice to know where he's coming from though; it's something to keep tucked away but don't dwell on it."

"Everything makes more sense now," Tarah thought out loud as she slouched over. "It's probably why his family worries so much about him drinking and partying. I guess they probably see that, and his old player attitude toward women, as acting out or something."

"And he may have been acting out, but not necessarily toward his sister's attack," John added. "After all, he was in his late teens, right? I'm assuming that because he's in his early 20s now. He could've just been blowing off steam like everyone else in that age group."

Tarah smiled. "True. He told me once that women treated him like shit when he was overweight, so he basically was a dog because he didn't respect them."

"Very possible." John nodded. "Considering how mean they probably were when he was overweight, that doesn't surprise me. A lot of people go a little crazy when they first shed weight. It's like they are discovering a new person underneath all of it."

"Until recently, he always seemed to avoid his family."

"Probably because he wasn't proud of his life," John said thoughtfully. "Then he had this successful band, a steady girlfriend, things he knew they would respect him for."

Tarah was silent for a few minutes. "I still don't know how I'll be able to look at him the same way now that I know about the suicide attempt." She rushed to clarify herself. "Not to say that I'll look down at him, I just mean that I'm scared that every time I look into his eyes I'll think of that and want to cry."

"Why would you cry?" John asked calmly, leaning forward with a cup of coffee in hand. "Sure it was horrible that he felt that low about his life at one time, but he survived and apparently came out stronger. It's unfortunate that it had to get to that point, obviously, but my guess is that it wasn't so much a suicide attempt as if was a cry for help. He probably knew someone would find him after he took the pills."

"That still makes me feel for him."

"And to a point," John said, "you should. But in a productive way, by simply making yourself accessible to him. That way he can tell you on his own time *or* tell you if he ever feels that low again."

Tarah took John's words very seriously and felt much better after talking to him about Jimmy. They then shifted gears, and John told her about the upcoming trip he and Elizabeth planned for the summer. They'd decided to go to Rome for two weeks in July. After a busy year at the high school where

John worked, he was much in need of a nice holiday. He was really looking forward to it.

She left John's place shortly afterward and was happy to find Jimmy at home when she returned.

"Hey, babe." She saw him looking out from the kitchen, where he was making a sandwich. He stopped to watch her walking toward him. "You're just getting home now?" As Tarah moved in his direction, she saw him through different eyes but prayed to keep strong. She promised Jillian she would not say anything. "Did Jill drag you off to the mall?" He grinned, and she thought of how much she loved him.

"No, no mall." Tarah sighed. "I went to see John for a bit. I never see him anymore and wanted to find out the news. I guess he and his girlfriend are going to Italy this summer. I'm so jealous!"

"We'll go too, someday," Jimmy assured her. "Maybe if everything works out with the band, we'll tour the world."

"I hope you're right." Tarah moved closer to Jimmy and wrapped her arms around his neck, tightly hugging him. His arms enclosed her waist. "I missed you today." She thought of all the horrible things he had experienced and continued to hug him close, forcing tears from entering her eyes.

"Wow, it's only been a few hours, Tarah." He hugged her back. "You're getting a little *clingy*, I might have to dump you," Jimmy teased.

Tarah began to laugh. "Okay, if that's what you gotta do." She slowly let go of him and looked in his eyes. He looked slightly suspicious of her impromptu hug so she quickly covered things up. "I was talking to John today about how happy he is with Elizabeth, and I just started talking about how happy I was with *you*." Tarah then considered throwing something else in. "And your sister told me how sad you were on the night we were fighting. She said you were scared that we were through after that night."

His face softened and the suspicion in his eyes disappeared. "I was. I thought I totally fucked-up everything."

"Me too," Tarah confessed. "The whole time you were gone, I thought you hated me. I felt so heartbroken."

"I could never hate you." Jimmy gave her a quick kiss. "I feel horrible about the rotten things I said to you that night though. I was way out of line."

"We both were," Tarah assured him. "It's in the past now. Let's forget it."

"Agreed."

Maggie scheduled a meeting with the band a few days later to discuss the upcoming tour with Confusion 45.

"So, I was on the phone all morning, and it looks like everything is set for this summer." Maggie put on a pair of reading glasses and glanced over a piece of paper on her desk. "First of all, I've got the band booked at a couple of locations in the greater Toronto area." Looking up from the paper she was reading from, Maggie quickly added, "We're talking larger bars of course, this is including another date at Cocaine. The manager was very impressed with your performance last time and insistent that you come back!"

Noting general approval from the band, Maggie continued. "So after that, you'll be starting a tour with Confusion 45 on June 21. They set some dates here in Ontario and then plan to go east, followed by the western part of the country. Essentially, you'll be on tour during the summer at larger venues. But we're talking smaller stadiums, not anything like the SkyDome. Places that play under seven thousand. Of course, most of them probably won't be filled. But they're talking about having another band join the tour as well, so that will help."

Tarah felt her mouth drop opened. *Under seven thousand people?* How was she supposed to jump from playing bars to stadiums? Sure, Fire was merely an opening act for a more successful band. It wasn't as if they were filling up those places on their own merit, but even thinking about playing to that kind of audience made her heart pound furiously. From the corner of her eye, she saw Jimmy watching her reaction.

"Now, before the tour, I want you all to be as prepared as possible." Maggie searched each of their faces. "Your performance *must* be 100 percent, remember that most of the people who go to Confusion 45's show will not be very familiar with Fire. Your job is to get their attention. That's your main focus during this tour. I know that sounds pretty ... *intense,* but keep in mind that a lot of bands really get a boost opening for a more recognized band." She gave them a quick nod and looked down at her papers again. Shuffling them around, Maggie continued.

"Now before that, I have you scheduled to do some interviews at some radio stations in the city—including the one I mentioned that was playing your song regularly. I left a message for Peter to call me regarding your next single. I personally like "A New Life" simply because it's much slower and softer than "Swim on my Beach." It gives things balance. Again, I'll discuss that with Peter sometime soon."

"I think that's about it." Maggie scanned over the sheet of paper. "Oh." She looked directly at Tarah. "A couple of things I wanted to mention to you. First of all, take extra care of your voice before the tour starts. Try to avoid germs as much as possible. I don't have to tell you that, of course, but it's more important now because of the fact that Confusion 45 is taking a chance with a relatively new band on the scene. We just want to make sure everything is perfect. Also, I'm going to look into FUTA giving you an advance on wardrobe for the tour. Now, not saying the clothing picked out by the boys is less significant," she grinned and scanned over the guys' faces.

"Trust me, Maggie," Jimmy quickly spoke up. "I don't think any of the guys here will be too upset if you *don't* make us go shopping for new clothes."

Everyone but Michael laughed; he just rolled his eyes.

"Okay good to know!" Maggie smiled. "So Tarah, what we're going to do is try to get a wardrobe allowance and have someone come in to help you pick out some outfits for the tour. It's simply because you're the singer, and therefore most people's eyes will be focused on you when the band plays, so I feel that it wouldn't hurt to get you some really cool outfits. I loved what you wore the night of the party, so more stuff within that line. Because you're so tiny, it'll be very easy to find workable clothing for you."

Tarah smiled, her brain was still stuck back in the *under seven thousand people* portion of the conversation.

It wasn't until the meeting was over and Tarah got in the car with Jimmy and Eddie that she panicked.

"How am I going to sing in front of that many people?" Tarah fidgeted in her seat. "Does that scare you guys like it scares me?"

"A little bit," Eddie softly replied. "But then again, I'm in the back where no one really notices me."

"I'm not," Jimmy said as he drove through traffic. "Don't think about it or you'll mess yourself up. Believe me, you'll be fine."

"I don't know. I'm not sure if I'll be fine," Tarah responded.

"You said that on the night of the party and you were fine," he replied, then glanced over at Tarah, and she wondered if he remembered *why* she had gotten through the night with such ease. The coke. "I don't think you'll have anything to worry about. First of all, I can't see these places being packed solid. It's just Confusion 45, after all. Also, as scary as it might sound, this is what we signed up for with the contract. To play huge audiences, that's the difference between playing for fun and playing for real."

"I know." Tarah was getting frustrated. "I'm not saying I won't do it, I just meant it's really scary when you're the one singing in front of that many people."

"I realize that, Tarah." Jimmy spoke gently. "But what you have to remember is that you've been scared before, but you always land on your feet."

Tarah shared a smile with him and considered his words. Jimmy was right of course, it was too soon to dwell on it, and things usually worked out fine in the end.

By the time they arrived home, Tarah was complaining of a headache and went to take a nap. She woke to a dark room and would have been content to go back to sleep, but something stopped her.

It was a noise coming from downstairs. At first, Tarah thought it was the television, but quickly recognized a girl's voice screaming at the top of her lungs. Suddenly wide-awake, she heard rustling on the other side of the bed and realized that Jimmy had been asleep beside her. Turning to look at the clock, he announced it was three in the morning.

"What the fuck is that noise?" He rose from the bed only wearing his boxers. Grabbing a T-shirt as he left the room, Tarah sat up and waited.

Regardless of the fact that their bedroom door was now open, the reason the girl was crying downstairs was still not clear. At first Tarah was concerned that perhaps the person in question was someone from Jimmy's past, but after hearing Eddie's name thrown around a few times, it was clear that she was infatuated with the band's drummer.

"Look." Jimmy's voice spoke up. "If you guys want to fight, that's fine. But can you at least keep it down? My girlfriend and I are trying to sleep upstairs."

The girl said something in response to Jimmy's comment, but was crying far too hard for Tarah to make out the words.

Tarah heard Jimmy sigh loudly. "Look, this is none of my business. It's up to you guys to find out for sure and then make a decision. But screaming and fighting about it now, in the middle of the night, just isn't going to resolve anything."

The house fell silent.

"Sorry," Eddie finally spoke. His voice was clearly full of defeat. "I'm sorry about the noise."

Tarah could hear Jimmy walking back upstairs. He returned to their room and shut the door behind him.

"What was that about?" Tarah asked. "Who's that girl? Was it Eddie's girlfriend?"

"I'm not sure if it's a girlfriend or what the deal is but she only looks to be fourteen or fifteen," Jimmy replied as he climbed back into bed. "But you aren't going to believe what she just told me."

"What?" Tarah said, as his warm body got close to hers. "She's mad 'cause he dumped her?"

"Nope," Jimmy whispered. "She's down there saying she's pregnant with his kid. They were fighting because he wants her to get rid of it."

"What?" Tarah's eyes flew open. "You're shitting me."

"No." Jimmy gave a short laugh. "Hey, I was fucking shocked. I didn't know what to say. I didn't really want to get involved but, yeah, he wasn't denying it."

"Eddie's such a sweetheart," Tarah said as she snuggled up to Jimmy. "I hope she isn't just saying it's his to take advantage of him."

"I don't know, Tarah. It's probably best we don't get involved."

"It's ironic really," Tarah whispered, while Jimmy started to kiss her face. "Eddie, the quietest of all of us, of the band, the house, the people we know—he may be the one to have a baby."

Jimmy slowly shook his head. "It's crazy, isn't it?" His lips gently pressed against her, and their thoughts were quickly dissolved.

CHAPTER THIRTY-ONE

▼

Fire returned to the stage of Cocaine on the first weekend of June. They once again played for a large crowd. But there was something different. For the first time, Tarah felt like she was singing for an audience of *fans* rather than a group of barflies or random people who just happened to be out on the same night. It was as if *they* were the main event of the evening. The audience was enthused. There was unmistakable excitement in the air, and when the band played their final song of the night, "Swim on my Beach," Tarah was surprised to see people in the crowd who were singing along. It was clear that the wind had shifted direction, and so had their futures. She knew that her life was about to start spinning, and it'd be up to her to make sure she didn't lose control.

After leaving the stage, Tarah noticed that people were approaching the band throughout the night. Some wanted pictures to be taken with them, and a few even requested autographs. At first, it was a little embarrassing to Tarah, especially considering that they really weren't famous by any stretch of the imagination. Sure, they had a recording contract, but so did a lot of other people who weren't in the mainstream media. However, as one guy pointed out to Tarah, it was a great time to approach their band since they were still relatively unknown and therefore *still* approachable.

"Later on," he added, "when you've become famous, chances are that everyday fans like me won't be able to get anywhere near you with security and your entourage."

Tarah laughed hysterically at the notion. "Oh, I don't think you'll have to worry about that happening." The idea seemed ludicrous to her.

"Hey, you never know," Jimmy pointed out minutes later when she repeated the stranger's comment. "Who's to say he isn't right?"

"Oh, come on, Jimmy! Are you serious?"

"Hey, you gotta dream big sometimes." He draped his arm over her shoulder and continued to look down at her face as they headed toward the bar. But then Tarah suddenly stopped, and Jimmy looked up to see what made her stall. Eddie and a girl were right in front of them.

"That's the screamer!" Jimmy managed to casually whisper in Tarah's ear just before they walked over.

"Hey." Eddie seemed self-conscious in front of the two people who were not only his roommates, but also friends. "Um, Tarah, Jimmy, this is Brooke." He seemed anxious and uncomfortable, and Tarah noted that the girl was very subdued and didn't look happy. However, she managed to put on a small smile when she shook hands with Eddie's band mates.

She was a pretty girl, Tarah considered, but her brown eyes had dark circles under them, and it almost appeared that she had been crying. Brooke's hair was stringy and lifeless, and her face was quite pale. Tarah could clearly see that she was younger than Eddie. Scanning the young woman quickly, she failed to see any baby bump.

After some awkward conversation, Brooke and Eddie said they were taking off for the night and left. Tarah and Jimmy exchanged glances.

"Wow, they don't look happy at all," Tarah remarked as they made it to the bar. "What do you think is going on?"

"I don't ask questions." Jimmy shrugged and quickly ordered them both a drink from the bartender. "But he did mention the other day that she wants to keep the kid. I tried to tell him that it may not be his at all, but he seems to believe her."

"It's very possible. We don't know much about her." Tarah smiled when Jimmy handed her a drink. "Are they together now?"

"He didn't really say." Jimmy led her toward a corner where there was less of a crowd. "I'm afraid she's trying to manipulate him."

"Really? I hope not."

"Me too, but let's face it, Eddie is pretty impressionable. He doesn't seem to have a lot of experience with girls, and to be honest, it sounds like they weren't very serious in the first place. Now he's going to be stuck with a baby to look after."

"How pregnant is she supposed to be?"

"I don't know," Jimmy admitted. "Listen, I'm kinda tired. Do you want to take off after we finish our drink?"

"Sure." Tarah nodded. "I think that's the first time you ever wanted to bail from a party early."

"And to go to bed and *sleep* at that," Jimmy joked, and the two walked along laughing, almost running into William and the girl who Tarah quickly assumed was Lindsey.

"Hey." Jimmy was suddenly wide-eyed.

"Hi, guys." William appeared a little uncomfortable as he scanned the faces of Jimmy and Tarah. "Lindsey, this is Jimmy and Tarah from the band. Guys this is Lindsey." He almost appeared hostile while doing introductions, but a slight grin appeared on his lips.

Tarah faked a smile toward the girl, just as she assumed Lindsey faked one back at her. With the combination of height and heels, she was barely shorter than William, and her blue eyes gave Tarah a quick once over. Jimmy hadn't exaggerated when he commented on the girl's weight, but Lindsay carried her thinness like a trophy that she held proudly in the air. She was very tanned, with long, honey blonde hair that was perfectly styled. Her nails were freshly manicured and made Tarah's own hands look pathetic in comparison. Over all, Lindsay was pretty typical of what every guy wanted, or so Tarah thought. She was the perfect accessory.

The boys had a quick conversation, and Tarah was surprised when William broke eye contact with Jimmy just long enough, to scan her own face. She wasn't sure if it was because of that or not, but Jimmy reached out to grab onto her hand as he continued to speak to William. It was very strange, and Tarah quickly finished her drink while in their company. And then it was over.

"Man, that was weird," Tarah commented, as they walked out of the bar. "First there was the super uncomfortable situation with Eddie and Brooke, then we come upon William and his new girlfriend."

"You mean, Barbie and Ken?" Jimmy turned to her with his infectious smile. "The funny part is that I don't think either of those girls actually talk. Neither of them said a word to us, other than maybe hi. Weird."

"That's true," Tarah agreed, as they climbed into his car. She was also starting to feel tired and could barely keep awake as they drove back to Thorton. Her brain kept drifting back to meeting Lindsay, and remembering how William seemed to monitor her reaction to the entire situation. It made her very unsettled.

Back at home, Tarah rushed to get ready for bed where Jimmy was waiting for her. As she turned off the light and moved close to him, she noticed his eyes were wide opened and watching her.

"Tarah, can I ask you a question?"

"Sure."

"And you have to be honest with me."

"I'm always honest with you," Tarah said, and gave him a concerned look and moved closer to the warmth of his body. "What's going on?"

"I don't want you to think that I'm jealous or anything, but do you still have any feelings for William?"

Tarah felt like she was hit with a bucket of ice. "What? No, Jimmy, no. Why would you say that?"

"I don't know," he admitted, and pulled Tarah a little closer to him. She could feel his hot breath against her face. "I just worry about that sometimes. I feel guilty sometimes for what I did, I basically was out to steal his girlfriend and I did it. Maybe I manipulated your feelings? Maybe if I hadn't been so pushy, you would still be with him?"

"Don't do that." Tarah ran her hand over his naked arm. "Don't play the 'what if' game. William and I had problems, and I know that eventually we would've split up. I don't regret my decision."

"What about tonight when you saw him with the other girl?" Jimmy tilted his head and looked through the dark into her eyes. His voice was gentle and relaxed. "Did that bother you at all?"

"It was strange. It felt weird, but I wasn't jealous." Tarah explained herself carefully. "I don't know if she's the most personable girl in the world, so that was kind of awkward. But I don't want to be with William, I want to be with you. I love you."

"But you used to love him," Jimmy whispered, as if to challenge her and Tarah was surprised by the insecurity that had snuck into his voice.

"I did," Tarah admitted, and noted how depressed Jimmy looked. "But I love *you* now. And it's not the same as it was with him. It didn't always feel good with him. There were so many times I felt like he was trying to be a father to me, like I was incapable of looking after myself. And I don't like feeling that way. I never feel that way with you. It's just always good. We work well together, we laugh, we have fun, and we don't fight. Do you know how often William and I fought? Plus, I just never felt like I was number one with him. Never. Or if I was number one, there was always a good chance I'd be thrown back in second place if Michael had a tantrum."

"You're definitely number one with me." Jimmy spoke honestly and ran his hand up and down her back. "Everyone else in this world can go to hell as far as I'm concerned."

"Don't say that, you've got your family."

"I know. And I don't mean that to be disrespectful toward them," Jimmy insisted. "But if they were to ever to turn against you, I promise you that I'd still put you first. You've changed my life." He hesitated for a moment. "You might've even saved it."

The last comment really hit Tarah hard. She thought back to the conversation she had with Jillian about Jimmy's past and wondered if he'd ever hurt himself again. "Don't say that. I didn't make that much of an impact. If I wasn't around, you'd be fine," she whispered.

"No, I wouldn't." Jimmy looked to be drifting off as he spoke. "My life was going nowhere and fast. You've made it worth living."

And with that, he closed his eyes and fell to sleep. Meanwhile, Tarah lay beside him, wide-awake.

The next morning, Maggie called Tarah to remind her about meeting a fashion consultant later that same day. "It's going to be fun!" the manager insisted. "Sandy will find all sorts of cool things for you to wear on the tour. She knows her stuff."

Maggie was right. Tarah met with Sandy, and over coffee they discussed the kind of clothes that she found appealing. The fashion consultant made some recommendations. The young woman was only a few years older than Tarah, so she knew what the latest trends were, but yet she had been trained in the field and so knew what clothes complimented specific body shapes and complexions.

Afterward, they went shopping at malls and boutiques, finding outfits, shoes, boots—everything. Tarah was stunned by the amount of money Sandy was putting on a credit card that she'd later learn was provided by FUTA. After the shopping was complete, they sat down for dinner and discussed her hair and makeup. By the end of the day, Tarah felt like she'd spent time with a friend all day rather than someone hired to dress her.

When she arrived home, Jimmy went outside to help unload the car and was stunned. "That's a lot of fucking clothes!" He began to laugh and grabbed a bunch of bags with one hand, while steadying shoeboxes in the other.

"That's nothing. You should see the price tags on them," Tarah commented, as she removed the last of the purchases from the car and shut the trunk. "Insane."

"Nice though." He waited for her to rush ahead and open the door to let him in the house. "I'm sure it will be added to the band's tab. So for God sake, don't let Michael know!"

"He'd be so mad." Tarah watched Jimmy crossing the entranceway. "Like he needs another reason to resent me."

"So, any more shopping trips planned?" Jimmy followed her upstairs to their room, where they both dropped everything on the floor. "Or is this it?"

"This is it," Tarah sang out. "But I'm going to the hairdresser and makeup artist in a few days to see what they can do for me."

"Why, you look fine." Jimmy looked skeptical.

"It's just for a trim. They might throw in some funky color too, not sure." Tarah pushed back her long, blond hair and shrugged. "The makeup artist will give me a 'distinct look' according to Sandy, whatever that means."

"Who's Sandy?"

"The fashion consultant I was with today," Tarah replied, and looked down at all the bags and shoe boxes on the floor. "It was fun. I miss having female friends to do stuff like shop with."

"I could go shopping with you, but I doubt that I'd be much fun," Jimmy said with a grin. "Unless we were lingerie shopping, that is."

"We did that today too." Tarah glanced at one of the bags. "Just for bras that will make me look a little less flat-chested."

"She actually told you to do that?" Jimmy appeared apprehensive.

"No, but she's right, the clothes do look better if you've got more of an hourglass figure."

"Whatever." Jimmy shrugged. "Next they'll be telling you to get a boob job."

"Well, actually it was brought up." Tarah seemed hesitant.

"Oh, come on!" Jimmy said, raising his eyebrows. "Don't tell me you're going to go under the knife for FUTA. I mean, seriously."

"No, I didn't say I was going to," Tarah replied. "But it's would not be completely unheard of if I did."

Jimmy shook his head. "I don't get it. I like you how you look. But anyway, show me some of your outfits, princess." He sat on the bed. "Better yet, model them for me."

"Okay." Tarah excitedly pulled clothes out of the bags and sat them on the bed, trying to pick out matching outfits. She saw Jimmy glancing at the tags and sighing loudly.

"Tarah, these clothes are like size one and zeros." He was holding a skirt in his hand.

"Yeah," she said. "So?"

"So, that's kinda small, don't you think?" Jimmy set down the clothing he'd been looking at and fixated his gaze on Tarah. "I mean, I don't know much about girl's sizes but a zero seems really fucking small."

"It's just the way they're made," Tarah assured him. "It's not a big deal."

He didn't look convinced. She ignored his reaction and grabbed an outfit and headed for the door. "I want to surprise you, so I'm gonna go next door then come back and model for you."

"You do what you got to do." Jimmy forced a smile while glancing down at another tag, which was hanging out of a brightly colored shopping bag that sat at his feet. "I'll be here waiting."

Later that evening, Tarah was making Hamburger Helper when the doorbell rang. Jimmy, who was in the process of finding clean plates, took off to answer it. A minute later, she turned to see him walking in the kitchen with her brother.

"Bobby! I didn't know it was you at the door," Tarah said with a huge grin on her face. "How's it going?" She rarely saw her brother now that he was living back home with their mother. Between Caitlin and his job, Bobby barely had time for anything or anyone.

"It's going," he replied, and sat down on a chair. "I was just talking to Jimmy about the show you guys did for the CD release. It was crazy. Wish I could've stayed later than I did, it looked like a good party.

"It was pretty cool, that's for sure." Jimmy sat on an empty chair. "There will be other parties though."

"Yeah." Bobby shrugged. Tarah noted that he looked very tired but didn't say anything. "So, dad was saying you're going to tour with some other band? He couldn't remember what they were called though."

"Confusion 45," Tarah replied. "Not my favorite, but they're really popular so it's kind of cool they wanted us as an opening act."

"That's wild." Bobby shook his head. "I can't believe my sister is going to be a rock star."

"Well, maybe," she said and began to laugh. "Let's not get ahead of ourselves."

"She has no clue how big of a deal all this is," Jimmy said to Bobby with a huge grin on his face. "Sure, we could still fail, but all signs aren't pointing to that."

Tarah put a cover over the cooking food and leaned against the counter. "It isn't that I don't have a clue what's going on." She hesitated for a moment. "I just can't visualize us being famous. It's so surreal and strange. And how do you know when you've made it, anyway?"

"When you sign with a label?" Bobby shrugged, and a smile slowly crept on his face.

"Ah, when your songs are on the radio, when you join a tour that takes place in stadiums, you know, that kind of thing," Jimmy rattled on. "Not to say that we're household names or anything, but it has to start somewhere."

"Whatever." Tarah rolled her eyes and stirred the food again. "Anyway, Bobby, what's going on with you?"

"Not much," Bobby sighed. "Just work, mom, baby. That's about it."

"Is Sara ever around at all?" Tarah asked.

"Nope." Bobby shook his head. "She cut off all ties. I'm actually talking to my lawyer soon to see if I can get sole custody. She hasn't even come to see Caitlin since we split up."

"Sara is the mother, I'm assuming?" Jimmy asked, and Bobby nodded. "Wow, that's pretty cold."

"Ah, she's been in some kind of depression for ages now," Bobby replied.

"Has she ever *not* been in a depression?" Tarah said, and frowned.

"True," Bobby said. "But I've got to figure out something to get out of that house and away from mom, or *I'm* going to be in a depression. She's really driving me insane. But it's going to be tough with day care and everything, that's the problem."

"Oh God, you must feel trapped." Tarah couldn't even think of moving home again. "I couldn't do it."

"You do what you've got to do," Bobby said. "By the way, mom's pissed because you never go see her."

"She doesn't come to see me either."

"Do you seriously think she would after the last time?" Jimmy reminded her. "Your mother was horrified."

"I don't know the details," Bobby confessed, and turned toward Jimmy and apologetically added, "But I know mom doesn't like you very much."

"That's not fair," Tarah whined as she checked the food again. "She didn't even talk to him. It's just because she was mad that I broke up with William."

"That, and she found a thong on our bedroom floor," Jimmy piped up. "That didn't go over well."

"Oh God!" Bobby shook his head and laughed. "I would've loved to see her reaction. She's so uptight about that kind of thing."

"It wasn't pretty." Tarah joined in with them and started to laugh. "I can't believe she hasn't let that go yet."

"When was that?"

"When I first moved in."

"I don't know why she wanted you to be with William," Bobby said, and yawned. "You guys fought all the time. God, remember the time that girl grabbed his crotch after a show." He turned toward Jimmy. "I was talking to Tarah and over her shoulder I see William talking to this chick and it looked kind of strange. The girl was like being too friendly. Anyway, I commented on that to Tarah and just when she started to turn around, there was the girl grabbing him."

"Yeah, I was standing at the bar and saw the whole thing, including Tarah fucking losing it." Jimmy stretched his legs out.

"Well it pissed me off cause he acted as if he was the innocent victim." Bobby shook his head. "And I'm like, it's my fucking *sister* man, you don't pull this shit. But then Tarah and him seemed to be okay so—"

The phone rang.

"Just sec." Tarah rushed into the next room. "Watch the food, Jimmy."

They continued to talk while she hurried to answer the phone. It was John. They discussed his upcoming trip at the end of the month, and Tarah finally excused herself, saying that her brother was visiting. Hanging up, she could hear Bobby and Jimmy's voices more clearly as she returned to the kitchen.

"But I'd never tell her that …" Jimmy was saying, and Tarah stopped in her tracks.

"It doesn't surprise me," her brother was replying. "Glad she got away from him."

Tarah took a deep breath and entered the room. Her brother was standing up.

"Hey, where are you going?"

"I gotta jet. It's been a long day." Bobby slowly passed her to head toward the door. "I just had to get away from mom for a bit."

"Glad you did." Tarah gave him a sincere smile and watched him leave.

Returning to the kitchen, she saw Jimmy turning the food off. "It's ready." Then he saw the look on Tarah's face. "What?"

"Jimmy, I overheard you guys talking," Tarah said quietly. "You said you'd never tell me something?"

Jimmy looked hesitant to reply and studied her face. "Tarah, just forget about it."

"No, I can't forget about it," she said, and moved directly in front of him. "Please tell me."

Jimmy took a deep breath and bit his bottom lip. "I was just telling your brother that the night William had that girl grab him at the bar … I saw him kissing her earlier that same night."

Tarah was stunned. "Why didn't you tell me this before?"

"I knew it would hurt you." Jimmy stared into her eyes. "That's why I once kind of hinted around to you that he may have encouraged it a bit. I didn't want to tell you what I saw because I was afraid that you'd think I was just making it up. After all, it was still during the time where you weren't 100 percent sure if you wanted to be with me or him."

"I'm not saying that anything else happened or that he ever cheated on you." Jimmy clarified. "I just know what I saw. And it was a pretty intense kiss. And I guess that's one of the reasons why I probably didn't really have a conscience at the time about trying to get with you."

"But you said the other night you felt guilty for trying to take me away from him," Tarah reminded him.

"It wasn't the right thing to do. But at the time, I didn't care. I wanted to be with you, and I didn't think he deserved to have you," Jimmy confessed. "But now, I always wonder to myself if you'd be with me now if I hadn't butted into your relationship with William. And a part of me sometimes wonders if you still love him."

"I don't love him," Tarah said with tears burning in her eyes due to a combination of humiliation and frustration. Humiliated that William pulled the wool over her eyes. Frustrated because Jimmy couldn't seem to believe that he was the man she loved. "I only love you. But now, I feel like a fool because he did this right under my nose."

"Please don't cry." Jimmy pulled her close and wrapped his arms around her. There was a long silence. "I'm sorry I didn't tell you."

"I just can't believe he was doing that behind my back, then getting mad at me when I got upset." She sniffed. "It makes me so angry."

"Just let it go, Tarah."

"I wonder what else he did behind my back."

"Nothing that I'm aware of." Jimmy pulled her closer.

"Promise me you'll never do that to me?"

"I promise."

CHAPTER THIRTY-TWO

▼

"Oh my God!" Tarah said in a hushed voice as she covered her mouth and slowly closed her eyes. Having rushed into the living room to speak to Jimmy, she found herself abruptly stopping in her tracks. A news story reporting the brutal murders of Nicole Brown Simpson and her friend Ron Goldman filled the television screen, with photos of the crime site casually displayed for the viewer. "That's horrible! That poor woman."

"I know." Jimmy appeared very solemn. "They think O. J. Simpson did it. What a fucking sick bastard."

Tarah felt frozen to the floor, her eyes staring toward the television, her body not moving an inch. A 911 call that Nicole Simpson had previously made was being played, the words displayed on the screen for the viewer to read while the frightened women's words filled the room. Tarah felt shaken by the emotion in victim's voice. It disturbed her that that same person was now dead.

Tarah continued to follow the story for the upcoming days, even watching a bizarre police chase that involved Simpson and a white Ford Bronco, a few days later. Curled up with Jimmy in bed, the couple commented on how tragic and horrible the double homicide must have been for those close to the victims. Jimmy was repulsed by the idea of a man ever being physically violent toward a woman, let alone murdering her, while Tarah was full of despair and anger. She knew that the band would someday have to write a song about domestic violence.

On the days leading up to the tour, both Maggie and Peter had meetings with Fire to discuss everything from last minute details to a general timeline describing the band's summer. Everything was planned out for them. A new video would be shot in July, this time for the song "A New Life," and other things such as interviews, photo sessions, and opportunities to meet their fans would be squeezed in between dates. Everything would center on the tour, and although the Canadian side of things was all scheduled, there were hints of some US dates in the latter part of August.

"If that happens," Maggie pointed out two days before the tour was to begin, "you'll have ample opportunity to introduce yourself to an American audience and hopefully get some radio play in the states. It's generally a little more difficult to get noticed in the US, but I think Fire is capable of doing it sooner or later. And of course, we'd all prefer that it be sooner rather than later."

The entire band was hyped about finally playing before audiences that ran in thousands, but Tarah was secretly still fearful of the possibility. She was so nervous on the days leading up to the June 21 show that she was barely eating and, on two occasions, was vomiting. Jimmy was quite concerned about her health and insisted that she get some food in her stomach.

"I'm just worried about you," he said one night when Tarah barely ate three mouthfuls of rice over their nighttime meal. "You aren't very big to begin with, and now you're barely touching your food. I don't want you to get sick, and come on, look at what happened to Jill. I don't want to see someone else in my life end up in a hospital bed because she doesn't want to eat."

"It's not that I don't want to eat." Tarah heard herself snapping at him, something that she hadn't really done before. "I just can't. I can't even think about food. It's not like I'm starving myself on purpose. Once the tour starts, I'll get back into my normal eating habits."

Jimmy leaned against the kitchen counter and took a deep breath. His blue eyes were watching Tarah carefully as she pushed the white pieces of rice around on her plate. "I'm not trying to be a prick by saying all this, you know that don't you? Come on, you know how sick my sister was when we were kids. When I don't see you eat, I can't help it, that's what I think of."

Tarah shrugged. "I just don't want food right now. I'm so nervous about the tour. This is big. What if I fuck it up? What if I get on that stage and I can't sing or I make the band look bad? I feel like all the pressure is on me."

"It's not though," Jimmy said, and walked over to the table and sat down beside her. "It's on all of us. We *all* are feeling a pressure. We either get it from Maggie or the record company or ourselves for that matter. We all know how big this is, and we're *all* in it together."

"But I'm the one out there," Tarah said, her head leaning against the wall beside her. "I know, we all are out there, but I'm the one front and center. I can ruin everything."

"Which is what you thought when we did the CD launch, but you did great," Jimmy once again reminded her. "You're really your own worst critic.

Maybe even your own worst enemy for that matter. You can't worry about all this stuff; just take it as it comes. You'll be fine. We'll all be okay."

The members of Fire didn't have the opportunity to meet anyone from Confusion 45 until June 20, the day before the tour began. Peter had the two bands get together in his office to meet and take care of last minute details. Tarah found that the four members who made up the band were friendly, down-to-earth, and pretty normal considering they were celebrities. In fact, they were the polar opposites of Fire in that they all seemed to get along relatively well, respect one another, and were generally a great deal alike. Looking at her own band, Tarah felt that there couldn't possibly have been a more diverse group of people. Eddie was the quiet one, while Jimmy was vocal. William was positive, while Michael was negative. And she was the girl.

The two bands finished their brief meeting and made plans to join up early the next day before their first show in outskirts of Toronto. "It's at a smaller stadium," Tommy, the lead singer from Confusion 45, informed them. "Which is kind of a good way to start a tour. Gives you a chance to ease into things, especially if you haven't played in a while like us." The tall, lanky singer informed them that his band had just finished working on their new album, which had taken them a few months.

"A few months?" Jimmy spoke up as they walked toward the elevator. "They wanted us to push our CD out in the shortest time possible. Peter wanted it out in like a week, but it took us a bit longer."

"That's FUTA for you," Tommy said, as they filled up the elevator, and Tarah noted some bitterness in his voice. "They'll push and push ya to get everything done as soon as possible. The more albums you can put out, and the faster, the more they like you. They want to make money off your ass and as soon as possible."

Tarah found her eyes wandering to the always-positive William, who appeared to be taking this news all in stride. Jimmy simply nodded and listened attentively, while Michael frowned, and Eddie appeared to be lost in his own thoughts. It didn't surprise anyone that FUTA was aggressive.

"That's what they're all about," Tommy continued. It appeared that he was the spokesman for the rest of Confusion 45 because everyone else was silently listening to his words. "The more money you make, the more they want you to make. If that means some bad publicity along the way, so be it."

Tarah considered a scandalous story about Confusion 45 only a couple of years earlier. It involved the band's drummer being accused of having sex with a minor after one of their shows. Now that she was starting to learn the industry, it occurred to Tarah that maybe the reports weren't as balanced as they then appeared. The little bit of experience she'd already endured with media had taught her that sometimes things were much more complicated than how they were presented.

"So, we should try to avoid starting any shit then?" William asked, his eyes glancing toward Jimmy. "You know, so they don't have anything to work with for bad publicity."

"They don't need anything real, that's the problem," Tommy answered just as the elevator door opened and the two bands ejected. A couple of young fans caught sight of Confusion 45 and quickly rushed up to Tommy and the others for an autograph. After they left, the two bands continued to talk.

"So, they just make stuff up?" William asked. "Is that what you're suggesting?"

"It's not so much about making stuff up," Tommy explained. "It is about exaggerating the truth. You just gotta keep in mind that they're here to market *you*. They invested a lot of money in your band, so they want to make sure they get their money's worth."

"I see." William nodded.

"Long story short," Tommy began, grinning as the two bands started to part ways. "FUTA doesn't really stand for Future United Together Artists it stands for Fuck you Up The Ass, 'cause when all's said and done, that's what they wanna do." The singer gave them a big smile, slid on a pair of sunglasses, and walked away behind the rest of his band. "See you all in the morning."

"That doesn't sound very encouraging," William remarked after they left. "But I guess it's normal that they want to push the band." He shrugged. "And I guess we don't know all the details of their situation. It only makes sense that they're going to try to get the band's name out there; you can't argue with that."

"Doesn't mean we want to be dragged through a scandal like they had," Jimmy added, sliding both hands in his pockets. Looking bashful, he glanced around the building. "It does make you wonder though how many of these celebrity shit stories are made up by their publicist or something, just to get some attention in the media."

"I think we're fine," William insisted. Michael gave him a skeptical look, and Eddie still appeared to be a million miles away. "We aren't exactly doing anything too crazy and wild." His eyes stopped on Jimmy, then Tarah. "At least, I hope not."

"Yeah, William," Jimmy voice jumped in with a hint of sarcasm mixed in with humor. "We have huge, wild parties at our house every night, with lots of drugs and group sex. Come on, man."

"Hey, I wasn't suggesting a thing," William spoke sternly, and turned toward the exit. "Now, I've got to run. I'm meeting Lindsey for lunch."

Tarah watched Jimmy turn back to her and roll his eyes, while William walked away with Michael in tow. "For fuck sake, why does he automatically assume that we're going to be the center of any so-called scandal anyway? *He's* the one dating the anorexic, snotty, model bitch. You just know those are the ones who have all the skeletons in their closets."

"Hey, at least he doesn't have some girl he just met pregnant." Eddie surprised them both by adding in his two cents. He seemed to be more critical of himself than anyone else was. "Guys, I don't know what I'm going to do."

"What does she want to do?" Tarah asked, and gestured for them to head toward the same exit that William and Michael had just used. The three of them began to walk. "Does she want to have the baby?"

"Yeah." Eddie nodded and sighed. "I know it's my responsibility, but I feel like for once in my life everything was going the way I wanted, then suddenly this mess falls right in my lap."

"Well, man, it doesn't have to ruin your life," Jimmy reminded him, as they reached the exit and walked out into the warm, June sun. "I mean, throw some money at her every month, and visit the kid once in awhile. You don't have to marry the girl or stay with her."

"I feel like I should." Eddie walked slouched over to the car. "She keeps telling me that she thought I really cared about her and stuff, that she was nothing more than a one night stand, that I used her and then threw her away. Plus she's so young, she's only seventeen." He stopped for a moment and glanced at Tarah, then Jimmy. "I swear, I didn't purposely set out to hurt her. We were just drinking and having fun, then we hooked up like twice and now look at the mess I'm in."

"I feel for you, man." Jimmy nodded. "It seriously could happen to anyone. She doesn't want to have an abortion either? I'm surprised she even wants the kid."

"She said she doesn't believe in abortion," Eddie answered, and the three climbed in Jimmy's car. "I can't argue with that."

"I don't think I'd want a kid in that situation." Tarah threw in her opinion as she fastened her seatbelt and watched Jimmy turn the ignition. "Because it seems kind of, I don't know, a bad situation to start a kid's life off in. I mean, look at my brother. He got married to Sara because she had a baby, and they're going through a divorce now. They weren't even married a year. So now their daughter has parents who aren't even together or talking."

"Not that your brother's ex is even seeing her kid," Jimmy reminded her. "That's even more of a mess."

"Well, I couldn't do that." Eddie suddenly seemed very self-assured. "I couldn't just forget my kid like that. But at the same time, I don't really want a relationship with Brooke. She's kind of clingy and stuff. I guess she's just not right for me."

"I don't know, man." Jimmy tapped on the steering wheel. "Personally, I'd make sure it's your kid. I mean she might see you as a meal ticket. A guy who just signed a record contract, she probably assumes you're either are or are going to be loaded someday. You just never know, there are some crazy chicks out there."

"Crazy *people*," Tarah corrected him. "It isn't just women."

"You know what I mean," Jimmy said, his eyes seeming to avoid Tarah's. "There are some girls who use a baby to keep a guy in their life. I just don't want to see Eddie go through that if he doesn't have to."

"I agree." Tarah nodded.

"I don't know, the last time I even suggested that it might not be mine," Eddie said, his cheeks turning red. "She got really angry with me and started screaming. It actually was the night we were at the house fighting, when you came downstairs, Jimmy."

"No shit?" Jimmy made a face. "Well, at least you have a few months to think about it."

"I know," Eddie muttered, and then remained quiet for the rest of the way home.

That night in bed, Jimmy brought up the topic to Tarah. "I really think this girl is trying to manipulate him." He gently ran his finger over her face in the dark. Both were wide-awake even though it was after two o'clock, thinking about the upcoming tour. Their bags were packed, and they were ready to go. "I have a bad feeling that he's going to try to do the 'right' thing and end up fucking-up his life."

"I hope not, but I think you're right," Tarah agreed. "But it's like you said before, maybe we shouldn't get involved. After all, he's probably not going to listen to us anyway."

"At least our tour starts tomorrow." Jimmy slowly started to close his eyes. "When we're out rocking the country, maybe it'll take his mind off of all this mess. Or maybe it will give him a different perspective all together."

"I hope so," Tarah said. "It's going to be a crazy summer."

CHAPTER THIRTY-THREE

▼

"I think that was one of the most incredible experiences of my life." Tarah admitted to Jimmy after Fire did their first stadium show. She had surprised herself that morning when she awoke feeling no fear at all. In fact, Tarah had pushed the upcoming show completely out of her mind until moments before they went on stage. Even then, she forced herself to focus on nothing more than the performance. She had no other choice but to do it, so Tarah decided to just not think about it. As it turned out, it was the perfect solution to her problem.

"Didn't I tell you?" The couple sat backstage in a small dressing room and shared a joint. Jimmy gave her a satisfied smile as he tilted his head and stared into her face. "I knew that once you were out there and felt the reaction from such a big crowd that you'd feel very differently about it. The audience tonight was pretty fucking wired, so we just fed off one another. It was just what I've always dreamed of."

"It was pretty cool, wasn't it?" Tarah finished off the joint and stomped it out with her boot. "I wasn't sure what they'd think of us, since we obviously weren't the main band they came to see, but everyone was really cool. I'm starting to think that we're more popular than I originally thought."

"Told you so," Jimmy teased. "You've gotta admit, it's pretty cool playing for a larger audience. I knew that once you did it, you'd never want to go back."

"You talk like you've done this before," Tarah said

"Nope." Jimmy shook his head. "But anytime you go to a big show, you can feel something different in the air. It's like magic."

"It's amazing to be on stage and feel the excitement of the room," Tarah said thoughtfully. "It just fills you up. I felt that way, to a degree, the first time Fire played a show together. It was really incredible, but tonight just takes that completely off the radar. I really think I'm going to enjoy touring this summer."

"We have lots of dates ahead of us," Jimmy said, taking out a pack of gum from his pocket and offering some to Tarah. She accepted. "It makes you want to fly offstage at the end of the night and start writing new songs. It's crazy."

"It is," Tarah said with a smile on her face. She secretly was proud of herself for facing and overcoming her fears. It was the first time that she really felt encouraged , to make their band everything it could be. Before that day, she felt more like she was just following the leader rather than striving for anything bigger or better. Tarah never had specific plans or goals, but seemed to follow mindlessly what the rest of the band said or did. Now, she felt like an official member of Fire.

The band continued to increase in popularity as the tour moved forward. Their fan base also increased, and Fire's first single regularly played on the radio. Tommy told them not only did FUTA pay off radio stations to play their artists' songs, but also that the company was known to bribe DJs to start hype over a new band. He told Jimmy and Tarah that there was a rumor that the label had once signed a well-known teenage singer only to exploit her.

"Man, they had that girl all cracked out on drugs and everything," Tommy informed Jimmy and Tarah one night over a few drinks. The remaining members of Confusion 45 and Fire didn't join them. "Fuck, she was a drug experimenter at first, but rumor has it they had some of her inner circle get her into coke and pills. It was a shitty deal; the kid was in rehab all the time, and eventually FUTA dropped her."

"Why would they want her taking drugs?" Tarah asked. "Wouldn't they want her to have her shit together?"

"Controversy, to make her more rebellious in the media," Tommy replied, and took another drink of Corona. "Fuck, they love that 'cause it brings more attention to their artist, which is great in such a competitive industry. Plus, it made her less inhibited. Of course, once they started to lose money, they ditched her. Now her career is over."

Tarah and Jimmy exchanged looks.

"That's how the industry goes." Tommy spoke to them honestly. "It's all money, money, money."

In mid-July, both bands took a few days off before continuing their tour into western Canada. Fire was scheduled to shoot their video for "A New Life." Unlike "Swim on my Beach," this production promised to be more modest, mainly being shot in a studio and in a couple other locations around Toronto. The entire process was simpler this time, and unlike with their first video, the band had a better understanding of what was expected of them.

They also knew how important a good video was to maintain and increase their status in the industry. Although Tarah found it to be slightly boring compared to their first one, the fans disagreed. It received more airplay and attention than Fire's original single.

The bands reunited and continued their tour during the latter part of July. There was a distinct difference between the east and west coast audiences, something Tarah noticed right away. Unlike in the first half of their tour, Fire was quickly increasing in popularity. CD sales went up, and so did the sales of their merchandise. Fans were as anxious to see the newest band in the music circuit play as they were their more advanced touring partners. By the time their Canadian tour ended, Confusion 45 already had some American dates planned, which would keep the two bands on the road for the upcoming weeks.

But success had its negative side too.. As Fire grew in popularity, so did the media attention. Various entertainment shows and articles not only discussed the talent of the band, but also their sex appeal. William and Jimmy lured in many female fans, and Tarah captured the attention of many male admirers. Not only did this kind of recognition make them all slightly uncomfortable, it also created more resentment with Michael, who insisted their popularity only took attention away from the band and it's music.

The day finally came when an entertainment show reported that not only was William dating a popular model, but also that he had had a relationship with Tarah in the band's earlier days. And as the story began to unfold, it was reported by other "sources" that Jimmy was now Tarah's boyfriend. Although some fans loved this idea, others resented Tarah for having had the romantic attention of both of the band's most sought-after males. When details came out that she had actually left William for Jimmy, some more zealous fans accused her of being a slut, among other things. The remarks were hurtful to her, and Tarah couldn't believe that people had so much emotional attachment to two men they hadn't even met and really knew nothing about outside of their music and interviews. It quickly became clear to Tarah that women in the industry were often treated much more harshly than their male counterparts—and with a different set of rules all together. It would become a reality that she just couldn't escape.

But more was to come. As the media dug deeper into their personal lives, they began to find more controversy. Apparently a "source" from FUTA reported seeing Jimmy and Michael getting into a fight on their property earlier that year, stating that there was a great deal of tension within Fire. They also reported that Tarah wasn't a stranger to fights either, having had "regular" disputes during the time they played the bar scene, before being signed by FUTA.

"I only had two fights ever," Tarah complained, when Maggie reported this particular news story to her. "One was before I was even in a band, and the other was when I was still with William."

"Well, apparently that's enough to make you a serial fighter," Maggie joked, then quickly became serious. "Don't worry about it; the whole thing will blow over. They always exaggerate things in the media. Your band is new and they are just looking for new blood to talk about. That's how they get their ratings. No one wants to hear good news stories about celebrities, just bad ones."

Tarah wasn't so sure that they fit into the category of celebrity, but agreed with Maggie. Little did she know that the worst was yet to come. Apparently hearing the stories about Fire and Tarah's terrible temper on television was enough to bring out all the exhibitionists. That included Jimmy's groupie from their CD launch at Cocaine.

The young brunette spoke innocently about going to Fire's CD release party, only to be attacked by a very jealous Tarah Kiersey. Andrea, the woman in question, claimed that she was merely asking for Jimmy's autograph when Tarah hauled her aside and attacked her. The interviewee than went to say that she was threatened and quickly left the premises. "I don't really think I had had a choice at that point," she added.

Tarah learned this information through a phone call from Maggie, when the band was on the road in a northeastern state. "You better discuss this with Jimmy before he finds out," the band's manager recommended. "It's about to become publicly known if it isn't already. I was approached about making a comment. I said there was no truth to it at all."

"Thanks" Tarah said, and sighed loudly. "I feel like *I'm* the one being attacked right about now." After she hung up the phone in their hotel room, Tarah reluctantly admitted the entire story to Jimmy. He remained quiet, showing no emotion as she spoke.

It made her nervous.

"It sounds like she got her fifteen minutes of fame," he finally said. "That's clearly what she wanted."

Thinking that maybe he thought it was a fictional account of the night, Tarah felt the need to be honest with him. "It did happen though. I *did* attack her."

Jimmy began to laugh. "Oh, well, *that*, I have no doubt about. It's such a typical 'Tarah' thing to do, but you do know it wasn't necessary. I wasn't going to do anything with that chick."

"I know, but I was just so pissed off at the time," Tarah said as she thought back to that night. "Although, I'm pretty pissed right about now too."

"Don't let it get to you. You must realize that they have to find something to make a story. We're new on the scene, and they're going to dig up all the dirt on us they can find. That's just how it goes. It's not right, but it happens."

Tarah knew he was right, but from that day on, she became very defensive with the media. She refused to comment on any of the stories wrote about her, figuring it would simply just add fuel to the fire. Knowing that their band was only a small part of the music industry, Tarah often wondered how major celebrities dealt with it.

One person who took the reports very seriously however, was Tarah's mother. After the story about Andrea was public knowledge, Claire Kiersey wasted no time contacting her daughter to comment.

"Tarah, why would you get into a fight? I didn't raise you to be like that. It gives a really bad impression of you." She sounded irritated over the phone. "You can't go around starting fights just because another girl looks at your boyfriend. Besides, if he's any kind of boyfriend, it won't matter anyway."

"Mom, Jimmy is great." Tarah couldn't hide the irritation in her voice. "He would never cheat on me, if that's what you're suggesting. It's more complicated than it sounds on television, and I just don't want to talk about it."

"I think you should get a hold of that reporter who did the story and straighten her out. I actually considered calling her myself and—"

"Mom! For God's sake,." Tarah snapped. "Don't call the reporter. Don't talk to reporters about me at all. They'll just twist the story around to make me look bad."

"Well, it's a bit too late, a reporter stopped by yesterday afternoon to talk to me about you, and I did."

Tarah was furious. Her eyes bulged out, and she felt her heart racing. This wouldn't be a good thing. "What the hell did you say?"

"The truth," her mother insisted. "I answered their questions about William and Jimmy, about how you got started with the music, that kind of thing."

"And you told them what?"

"I told them the truth." Her mother stuck by her original comment. "I told them that William was a nice young man and that I wasn't so sure about Jimmy, which I'm not. I told them that you always had a short fuse, and I thought that stemmed from your father leaving us when you were a kid—" Tarah pulled the phone away from her ear and Jimmy looked up from the magazine he was reading on the other side of the hotel room. Then he watched Tarah hang up on her mother.

"What was all that about?" Jimmy eyes widened. "Wasn't that your mother?"

"My mother talked to a reporter." Tarah sat on the edge of the bed, slumped over and appearing completely defeated. "She actually *openly* talked about my relationship with you and William."

Jimmy's mouth fell open. "Are you for real? They tried to talk to my entire family, but no one would budge. I can't believe she'd do that to you."

"That's my mother," Tarah insisted. "It's all about her. I knew they tried to talk to Bobby and he wouldn't. They didn't track down my dad, but he wouldn't either. Only my mother."

"Oh man, that sucks." Jimmy moved over beside her on the bed and gently put his arm around her. "I take it that she didn't have anything good to say about me."

"I don't think so." Tarah took a deep breath. "I should call Maggie and tell her.."

When the story finally made the news, Jimmy's mother was the most upset of anyone. She was in tears when talking to her son a few days later, horrified that Tarah's mother would say such things about him. Jimmy managed to calm her down and insisted it didn't really matter what Tarah's mother thought of him.

"She doesn't have to like me," Jimmy replied quietly into the phone. "It's not going to change how I feel about her daughter."

Tarah was embarrassed by her mother's interview with a well-known journalist. She felt betrayed and hurt.

The tour continued throughout the states during the fall and finally ended in mid-November. Tarah and Jimmy started to look for a place in Toronto, while Eddie decided to move in with his increasingly pregnant girlfriend. Michael and William were also talking about moving to Toronto since it was more central, but didn't really discuss any details with Jimmy or Tarah. It seemed that other than when they were working together, the band members pretty much led their own separate lives. Sometimes Tarah would hear tidbits about William and Lindsey on the news, but it was never anything he shared with the rest of the band. It was all pretty strange, and it surprised Tarah that they all were so disconnected from one another. It hadn't always been that way.

Life went on. Tarah helped her brother move away from their mother's house and into his own apartment. He didn't really need much financial help, but the assistance Bobby did receive was graciously accepted. Tarah tried to spend time with Jillian whenever possible and after the tour ended, she finally learnt about her friend John's summer. He cheerfully announced his engagement to Elizabeth. Everyone was so happy. Everything seemed great. But Tarah was about to receive a phone call that would break her heart.

CHAPTER THIRTY-FOUR

▼

The move from Thorton to Toronto was a bittersweet one for Tarah. Although she was looking forward to sharing a luxurious apartment with Jimmy in one of the city's more prestigious neighborhoods, she couldn't help but shed a few tears for the house left behind. It represented an important period of her life, and one that she'd never forget.

It was after the truck was loaded and ready on moving day, that Tarah made one last emotional walk through the house. It was supposedly to double-check on things, but it was really to say good-bye to the home that made her feel secure and safe in every possible way. Each room reminded her of an event, a day, or a moment of the past year, and she found tears sliding down her face as she relived them once again.

Upstairs, she glanced in on the spare room, the bedroom that originally was to be hers. Tarah automatically recalled that horrible night when she lay there for hours, fearing that her relationship with Jimmy was over. It was that same night when he revealed a part of himself that had been so carefully hidden for most of his life. The excruciating experience of wondering when or if he'd come home, followed by the relief and emotional confessions that followed, made the entire night seem like a turning point in their relationship. It was the difference between two kids playing house and the maturity of real love and commitment.

She moved on to the bedroom where Jimmy had comforted her after the breakup with William, the room they shared their most intimate moments and conversations, the place where she began to fall for him. Returning to the hallway, Tarah thought of the awful fight she had with Claire Kiersey the previous spring. The day that she saw the bitter and selfish side of her mother changed the course of their relationship, but it helped to mend the one she had with her father. It had been bittersweet, indeed.

Walking down the stairs, Tarah wasn't able to look back, and she used her sleeve to wipe tears from her face. Who ever thought that this house she had taken for granted for the past nine months would be so hard to leave?

Glancing in the living room, Tarah thought of the many conversations that had taken place between her, Jimmy, Eddie, and any other guests who dropped by. Eddie had already moved out a few days earlier and in with Brooke. He had gathered his stuff quickly and left without saying good-bye. If Tarah had thought for a moment that he was happy about his new living arrangements or the baby due in January, perhaps she would've been excited for him. But she knew that he took this new family on as a cross to bear, rather than a blessing. He wasn't the same sweet kid he'd once been, rather now was cold and indifferent. Tarah missed the old Eddie and, in a way, felt she was saying good-bye to the teenager with hope in his eyes, as she left the room.

Walking into the kitchen, Tarah looked directly at the wall where she had once discovered the remains of a broken liquor bottle. It had been the day after Jimmy first confessed his feelings for her and had gone out on a drinking rampage. How naive she had been to think that her attraction to Jimmy could've been swept under the rug, merely because it was more convenient to remain loyal to William. There were some things in this world that could not be denied, no matter how hard you tried.

And finally she thought of William. It was one year earlier that they had moved in together. How long had that lasted? Now he was moving in with Lindsay, something that was reported in entertainment magazines and gossip sections of the newspapers. After all, he was in a band with rising popularity, and Lindsey was a well-known model who had done everything from fashion shows in Paris to the cover of *Vogue*. Michael had recently made the cruel remark to Tarah that his brother was finally "moving up in the world" when it came to girlfriends. Ignoring his rude opinion, she had simply walked out of the room.

Maybe he deserved it though, Tarah considered. After the horrible way she had ended their relationship, perhaps he deserved to have a perfect model girlfriend. If there was such a thing as karma, perhaps he had found what he deserved. She hoped he was happy, but would never forgive herself for the horrible way they'd ended their relationship. Work had forced a mutual agreement to move past bad memories, but somehow, Tarah knew it would follow her for the rest of her life.

Taking a deep breath, she finally walked out of the house and gently closed the door. Jimmy was waiting for her outside, wearing dark sunglasses and holding a cup of coffee in his hand. "The moving truck left a few minutes ago. Are you ready to go?"

Silently Tarah put on her sunglasses and nodded.

A week later, after the couple was officially moved into their new home and had time to rest, Jimmy suggested that they come up with some song ideas. The band had decided to work on their next CD after the holidays, as their third single was released from their debut CD. Fire's popularity was growing faster than Tarah would've expected only a few months before, keeping FUTA very happy and making the members of the band financially comfortable. CDs were selling, their songs were playing constantly on the radio, fan bases were increasing, and everything seemed to be going well.

A couple of weeks before Christmas things changed. Tarah was at home making a list of last minute items she needed to pick up for the holidays, when the phone rang. She was surprised to find a clearly upset William on the line.

"I just got a call from Wendy's mother." He seemed to hesitate and Tarah feared the worst. "Tarah, she's in the hospital."

"Oh my God!" Tarah felt her heart racing. "Is she okay? What happened?"

"She was beaten up really bad."

Tarah took a deep breath. "Someone beat her up?"

"Yes." William cleared his throat. "Her husband."

Jimmy wasn't home, so William agreed to pick her up on his way to the Thorton hospital. When she got into his car, it was clear they were both visibly shaken by the news. Tarah was relieved that his girlfriend wasn't with them. It just wasn't the time or the place to deal with her.

"So, how bad was it?" Tarah finally asked after driving in silence for several minutes. "Do you know?"

William raised his eyebrows and gave her a look of compassion. "Tarah, it was pretty bad." She silently nodded. "Her mother admitted to me that it wasn't the first time he's done this either."

Tarah thought back to a conversation she had with John a year before, when he had predicted this very situation. How had he known? At the time, Tarah pushed the possibility to the back of her mind. After all, Wendy had chosen to push everyone from her life. It wasn't as if they had the opportunity to see signs indicating problems.

After finally arriving at the hospital, Tarah felt numb. Later, she wouldn't remember walking through the doors or going in the elevator to the correct floor, it was all a blur. But she would remember seeing Wendy's mother crying in the waiting room, and William attempting to comfort her. That's the first proof she had that this situation was very serious. The second one was when Tarah actually walked into Wendy's room.

She barely recognized the woman who had once been her best friend. Her face was so badly bruised that it took Tarah's breath away. Wendy's left arm was in a cast, and Band-Aids were on her opposite hand. Red marks around her neck made it apparent that someone had tried to strangle her, and Wendy's lifeless eyes were unfamiliar to Tarah. She could only remember the girl who was full of excitement and happiness. It was like looking at a stranger. Someone she didn't know.

"You came," Wendy whispered, and slowly reached her hand out toward Tarah. There were tears in both their eyes, and Tarah felt too stunned to even talk. She walked over to her friend and gently touched her hand. It was cold and fragile. She'd lost weight. "I'm so glad you came to see me."

"Of course." Tarah cleared her throat as her eyes scanned the many injuries that covered Wendy's body. She wanted to say something more, but when Tarah opened her mouth, nothing came out.

"I'm sorry, Tarah." Tears continued to run down Wendy's face, over the bruises and down her chin as she continued a strong grip on Tarah's fingers. "I'm sorry that we lost contact. It's just so hard to explain how it happened. I don't even know myself to be honest. But please forgive me."

"I already have," Tarah said quietly, and watched Wendy continue to stare at her. She moved her head slightly, but it was clear that the patient was in a great deal of pain. "Is it true? Did your husband do this to you?"

Wendy's eyes quickly looked away, and her hand slid away from Tarah's. "Yes, he did." Her voice was childlike. "It's not the first time he's done it. But it's the worst one."

"Why did you stay with him if he was doing this to you?" Tarah asked the obvious question, but she already knew the answer. It was tenth grade Family Ed class all over again. Abused women stayed because they lacked self-confidence and believed they were doing something wrong to bring on the attacks. But yet, she had to hear the words come from Wendy's mouth.

"I loved him," she slowly answered. "Because I thought it was me who made him so angry. I'd never had great experiences with boyfriends before, and here was this guy who loved me unconditionally, who promised he'd never leave. I just thought that I'd take the good with the bad and eventually he'd change. He had a lot of stress because of his divorce and ex-wife so it only made sense that Brad lost his temper from time to time. I didn't think he meant to do it. And whenever I'd want to leave, he'd always be so sweet and beg me to stay, promising he wouldn't do it again. But he always did."

"I just can't believe that you were in an abusive relationship," Tarah confessed, and slowly sat down on a nearby chair. The sun was shining through the window on the opposite side of the room and touching Wendy's face, making her bruises even more apparent. "I never would've thought you'd be someone who'd have a guy hit you." As soon as she said the words, Tarah realized how stupid that remark sounded. How could you seriously pick out the 'type' of woman who would be abused? It wasn't that simple.

"I never did either." Wendy gave her a small smile. "I really didn't think he'd ever hit me. There was no reason to think he ever would. Everything was normal at first. I guess, looking back, he was a bit controlling with me sometime, but I didn't think that was because he was an abusive person. I just thought it was because he loved me so much. I really thought I had hit the jackpot."

Tarah slowly nodded. It made sense. Wendy had always been someone who wanted desperately to be loved, that's why her relationships were many and frequent. It had been her goal to find someone to be in her life permanently and maybe her vulnerability was something this Brad guy preyed on. Tarah's mind quickly flashed to the wedding photos she viewed on her lunch hour at Rothman's the previous year, but she couldn't recall the man Wendy had married. His face was a blur in her mind.

"Some jackpot," Wendy sighed. "I guess I was way off."

"You made a mistake." Tarah attempted to comfort her. "Now you can move on."

"I will," Wendy said in a child-like voice. "I promise you that." Her eyes met Tarah's, and she attempted a small smile. "I won't ever go back."

"Good." Tarah felt only slightly relieved. "What are you planning to do once you get out of here?"

"I'm going to my mother's in Springdale," Wendy replied. "I promised her I'd go home so I could heal and try to get my life back in order again." Another tear slid down Wendy's face, and Tarah felt her heart go out to her. "I don't even know where I'm going to start."

"Don't worry about that now," Tarah assured her. "Just one thing at a time. One day at a time. Right now you have to get stronger and the rest will work itself out."

"I know," Wendy agreed. "It will."

A knock on the door interrupted them. William slowly entered the room and his eyes scanned Wendy carefully, but there were no tears. In fact, Tarah could see the anger in his face, and it reminded her of the night they had broken up. Standing up, she promised Wendy she would come back to see her and left so that William could visit with her in private. Walking out the door, she quickly went into the ladies' washroom and threw some cold water on her face. How far both she and Wendy had come from their partying days, but yet they were still miles apart. She wondered briefly what William was saying to her at that moment, then pushed the thought from her mind and left the bathroom.

Tarah purposely avoided Wendy's mother in the waiting area, unable to comprehend how someone that close couldn't have seen the signs. She preferred to be alone with her thoughts. Finally, William walked out of the hospital room. After going to talk to Wendy's mother again briefly, he met Tarah down the hallway and they silently headed toward the exit. It felt weird being with him, she thought. It was like being with a stranger. But then again, hadn't she felt the same way with Wendy?

Outside, Tarah felt the bright light hit her eyes before she could realize what was going on. Suddenly her silent thoughts were traded in for the abrupt attack of the media. Although she had previous experiences with television reporter and journalist, never before had she felt completely bombarded by reporters. *"William, is it true that you were just visiting with an ex-girlfriend? Was she in an abusive relationship? How did you feel seeing her today?"* Glaring at the one reporter who seemed to be the most ambitious, he roughly grabbed Tarah's arm and pulled her through the crowd. She ignored their questions and felt like she was about to hyperventilate. *"Tarah, is true that your friendship with this woman ended when you started to date her boyfriend? Has she forgiven you for that betrayal? Are you and William back together?"* And the questions followed until they were both safely in William's car where Tarah finally could breathe again.

"Oh my God!" Tarah pulled on her sunglasses, as the vultures hovered outside. The media attention was clearly directed mostly at him, since he was dating a famous model. "I can't deal with this today! Not after what I just saw."

William was silent and finally managed to get away from the reporters and out of the hospital parking lot. They were both quiet.

"Nothing's sacred," William finally commented. "No one's life means anything to those people. If you're a celebrity, suddenly you aren't a real person anymore. You don't have privacy."

"But isn't that what we signed up for?" Tarah gently reminded him. "I mean, do we have a right to complain?"

"I realize that we are putting ourselves out there. But I didn't sign up for *this*." William gripped the steering wheel in frustration. "I do understand, don't get me wrong. But that was a hospital. And we were there because someone we know was badly hurt. Shouldn't there be a line drawn somewhere in the sand? Shouldn't there be some limits to where our private lives end and our public lives start?"

"I wish there were," Tarah answered. "But we both know that those days are long gone for us. Fame comes with a price."

Neither said another word until William arrived at Tarah's place in Toronto.

"Do you think she'll go back?" Tarah asked him before getting out of his car. His eyes met with hers, and at first he didn't answer. Were they thinking the same thing?

"I hope not," he finally said, and his fingers once again gripped the steering wheel.

"Me too," Tarah said, and got out of the car.

Jimmy was home when she returned. She'd left him a note briefly explaining the situation, but quickly blurted out everything after walking in the door.

"I'm really sorry for your friend." Jimmy gently put his arm around her. "I really didn't know her, but I'm still really sorry to hear what happened. You have to be some kind of loser to beat up a woman." Tarah found herself thinking about to the Nicole Simpson murder that was reported on television earlier that year. "I hope she's okay."

"Thanks." She felt his arm pull her into a strong hug.

"Do you think she'll leave him?"

"I don't know," Tarah answered honestly. "I hope so."

"So was William upset?" Jimmy asked after finally letting go of Tarah.

"Yes, he was angry, I could tell," Tarah answered. "And then when the television cameras and all those people were outside, it just pissed him off more."

Jimmy nodded. "It's definitely not the time or place. And you know it was pretty bad if Will got mad, because he rarely gets angry."

"I know," Tarah agreed. "Believe me, I know."

Five days later, Wendy was released from the hospital and went to her mother's home in Springdale to recuperate. She had made one phone call to Tarah, telling her that she planned to go to Toronto to visit over the holiday season, so that they could catch up on old times. The two women talked on the phone for over an hour, about the past, the present, a new future. But Tarah felt a tugging in her heart when their conversation ended. Where she should've felt relief and happiness, she instead felt reluctance and a strange awkwardness in the air. After hanging up the phone, Tarah sat in silence for about ten minutes and glanced around the room. There was something very unsettling about their conversation but she couldn't figure out what. She almost picked up the phone and called Wendy back, but quickly realized how ridiculous that would appear.

Two days before Christmas, Tarah received the shocking news. Wendy's ex had gone to Springdale to beg her to go back to him. When she said no, he pulled out a gun and killed her, and then turned the gun on himself.

CHAPTER THIRTY-FIVE

▼

"I still can't believe it happened." Tarah said to her boyfriend as she pulled the gray blanket tighter around her body. With no makeup and wearing a pair of red, flannel panamas, she was curled in a fetal position on the king-sized bed that she and Jimmy shared in their new apartment. Tarah hadn't even combed her hair in two days. Not since Wendy's funeral. "It doesn't seem like it's real for some reason. I just talked to her a few days before it happened. I keep expecting for the phone to ring and to hear Wendy's voice again." Tarah's eyes began to water and quickly overflowed to run down her face. "She was planning to come here and visit me. Just like old times."

"Tarah." Jimmy knelt down beside the bed and looked into her eyes. His hand gently wiped away the flow of tears that were falling nonstop since she learned the news. "Baby, I wish I could do something, *anything* to make this easier for you, but I just don't know what to do or say anymore."

"It's okay." Tarah sniffed. "It's fine."

"No, it's not fine, Tarah." He leaned in closer to her and took a deep breath. "I'm really worried about you. I know it's perfectly normal to mourn your friend, especially in the horrible circumstances that she died, but I'm worried about what this is doing to *you*. It's been almost a week and you haven't stopped crying. I know I'm not an expert on mourning, it just seems like you need to try to live again. Even just a little bit."

"I know." Tarah sniffed. "I just can't stop thinking about him walking into that room and shooting her. She must have been so scared. And then I think about the fact that her casket was closed because her face was unrecognizable." A new flood of tears exploded from her eyes causing Jimmy to jump immediately onto the bed, and pull her body up into a sitting position. Wrapping his arms around Tarah, he silently held her as tight as he could until her sobbing finally stopped. After a few minutes of silence, he gently told her what was on his mind.

"Tarah, I think we should go on with the New Year's Eve show." He was referring to a special performance that had been scheduled at one of the more popular bars in Toronto, weeks earlier. Jimmy waited for her to reply, but when she didn't, he continued, "I know it'll be hard to do, but I really think being on stage again will do you a world of good. I'm scared that you aren't going to make it out of this dark place if you don't push yourself." Releasing his grip, he looked into her eyes. They were red and swollen, and her face was pale with pink blotches. "I wouldn't suggest it if I didn't think it was the right thing to do."

"I don't know if I can." Tarah spoke honestly. "I don't know if I can ever get out there again."

"Tarah, come on," Jimmy said, as he ran his fingers up and down her back, hoping to provide some sort of comfort to her. "You don't mean that. I love you and I'm not going to let you stop your entire life because of Wendy's death. She wouldn't want you to do that and you know it."

"I do," Tarah said, and looked down. Clearing her throat, she slowly nodded. "Wendy would want me to go on and do the show. I know she would. She even talked of being there to watch that night. It's just going to be so hard."

"I know, but you have to do it," Jimmy whispered. "You can't let this tragedy take over your life." He hesitated for a moment before continuing with what had been on his mind since the murder. "Tarah, don't be mad at me for saying this, but you always said that after your father left, your mother fell into a depression and didn't even want to leave the house. I just keep thinking of you telling me that story, and I'm kind of scared that you'll do the same thing. It's normal to mourn, but there has to be a point where you continue your life again. Even though it's difficult."

"You're right." Tarah sniffed and nodded. "I know you're right. I have to do this show. I have to do it for Wendy."

Jimmy broke the news to the rest of the band that the show for that particular night, would go on. Everyone was relieved especially William, who called Tarah that same afternoon to discuss Wendy, her funeral, and the upcoming performance.

"Tarah, I know it may seem soon to jump back on stage." William spoke gently through the phone lines. "But I really think it's the right thing to do. I truly believe Wendy would want you to get right back into it. And believe me, I've known Wendy longer than you, and I know how difficult all of this has been. A part of me doesn't want to do anything on New Year's Eve either, but deep down I know that we have to. I think it's important that we do that show."

"I agree," Tarah said in little more than a whisper. "I was thinking we should dedicate the show or a song to her. Something in her memory."

"Actually, I wanted to talk to you about that." William seemed hesitant to go on. "Listen, there's a song that I'd really like us to do for her that night. I'd like us to do "Home Sweet Home," because every time I hear it, I always think of Wendy. It was her favorite song when we were dating in high school, and it's a song we've done before, so the band is familiar with it. I just feel like it's appropriate." Tarah felt tears gathering in the corner of her eyes and she tried to blink them back and listen to his words. "And it'd mean a lot to me too if you were to agree to sing it. We can leave it till the end of the night even, just so it's not too emotional for you."

"Okay," Tarah said, and cleared her throat. "That would be fine."

"If something happens that you really can't do it when the time comes, just let us know, and we'll end the show with something else."

"Okay," she repeated, and took a deep breath. "Will do."

Tarah felt herself become stronger over the next couple of days, then even stronger on the morning of the concert. However later that same day, she was secretly nervous about the upcoming show. As much as Tarah wanted to get back on stage to commemorate her friend, she wasn't sure if her heart was in it. But she did it anyway.

From the moment Tarah walked on stage, she felt uplifted by the entire crowd. There was an energy in the room that she had never experienced before; it was almost as if everyone in that audience was giving her strength, just so she could get through the show. It filled her body with warmth and love and it radiated through Tarah's performance. She watched people in the audience as they sang to her songs, shared laughter with friends, and kissed their significant others, and she found her own heart fill with love. Life was short, and you had to live as big as you could, for the time you had.

In a way, Tarah didn't want the show to end. The stage was an escape from the realities of her life, and she wasn't ready to face them again. If only it could go on forever, but it couldn't.

And then it was time for the night's final song. The hit by Motley Crue would be familiar to all their fans. But even before she started to sing, Tarah knew it'd be one of the hardest moments of her life. She took a deep breath and stared into the audience.

"This last song is dedicated to my friend, Wendy." Tarah said in a brave voice, even though she felt like a knife was digging into her heart. She could hear Michael, Eddie, and Jimmy departing the stage, leaving her alone with William. They had decided earlier that day to do an acoustic version of "Home

Sweet Home," just the two of them. It seemed appropriate in some ways, and yet Tarah feared it would be much too intense.

Taking another deep breath, she turned her head and quickly glanced toward William. She momentarily wondered if her own eyes reflected the sorrow in his, and she quickly looked away, fighting the tears. He started to play and Tarah closed her eyes and began to sing. At first, the melody seemed to drift through her soul, creating a calming effect throughout her body. But then she began to envision Wendy's face as she sang the words, and by the time she was halfway through the song, Tarah was unable to control her tears.

She sang perfectly, while tears slid down her face, and from the side of the stage, Jimmy watched nervously. In the audience, fans were singing along, and many were also reflecting her sadness. It had been no secret in the media that Tarah's close friend had been brutally murdered during the holidays, however she was unaware that her personal nightmare had been front-page news the day after Wendy's death. She could almost sense people in the audience who related to her intense sadness, thinking of their own personal tragedies. It was the first time Tarah realized how music connected everyone. It reached out from one heart to another, to places no one else could even see, and touched people in ways nothing else ever could.

Throughout the performance, William was continually glancing toward Tarah with a worried expression on his face. When the song finally ended, she waved and said good night over the enthusiastic cheers from the audience, as she calmly walked off stage. She felt her breathing increase as if she'd just finished a race. Jimmy and William crowded around her asking if she was okay, but Tarah couldn't answer. Their voices were echoing through her head, and she felt her body leaning against a wall, and then sliding down to the floor. She trembled as her emotions that were mildly sustained through the performance suddenly caught up and broke through like a hurricane. She didn't talk and was gasping for air; an intense pain shot through her chest, and Tarah wondered if she was having a heart attack. She could hear the panic in their voices, but couldn't understand what William and Jimmy were saying. Suddenly, as she gasped for air between her sobs, Tarah felt her body being lifted off the floor.

Closing her eyes, Tarah felt cold air touching her face as her body was moved rapidly outside and into a car. She opened her eyes again to see Jimmy hovering over her, as the pains in her chest seemed to worsen by the minute. Confused at first, Tarah realized that William was driving frantically through traffic; her breaths became shorter and her lungs were heavier. The tears seemed to stop at the realization that she was having a hard time breathing at all anymore, and she calmly gave into it, accepting that maybe she was about to die right there on New Year's Eve.

Then forced air filled her lungs and the shock jolted Tarah. Where did it come from? Her eyes opened and she realized that both William and Jimmy were hovering over her still. Then once again, she felt her body being lifted in the air. Although she continued to have some difficulty breathing, Tarah saw bright lights and people rushing all around her; her body was suddenly on a hard surface and being rushed away from Jimmy and William. A sharp object dug into her arm and Tarah jumped, realizing it was a needle. An older woman with short, red hair and a worried expression was looking into her face. She was in a hospital room.

"We had to give you a needle to calm you down, Tarah." She spoke slowly, and there was something in her tone that was soothing. "The young man outside said you have panic attacks, and I believe that's what's happening right now. We had to calm you down immediately."

The words were barely out of the nurse's mouth when Tarah felt her body begin to relax. Breathing was no longer a struggle, and she silently thanked God that she hadn't died on the way to the hospital. Looking around the room, Tarah suddenly felt a little embarrassed by her condition. She slowly sat up on the bed. The nurse shook her head.

"Now, just sit back for a few minutes. You just had a very bad attack. I'd advise you to lay back and take it easy."

Tarah did as she was instructed and began to yawn.

The nurse nodded. "The medication will make you drowsy, which you need right now." She headed toward the door. "Just stay still for a few more minutes. Did you want either of the young men to come in?"

"Yeah, sure, both of them are fine." Tarah pushed a strand of hair out of her face and sniffed. She yawned again.

William walked in the room alone. His eyes were full of concern as he quickly scanned Tarah's face. "Are you okay? Fuck, I'm so sorry I made you sing that song. Tarah, if I knew, I swear I never would've asked you." His voice carried a hint of emotion as he moved closer. "I'm really sorry."

"It's okay." Tarah put up her hand up as she continued to fight her drowsiness. "I wanted to do it, so please don't apologize. We had no way of knowing that it would upset me this much, I didn't even think it would."

"I know but…" William sighed loudly and pushed a strand of hair out of his face and his eyes were solemn. "Tarah, you have no idea how scared Jimmy and I were. We thought we were going to lose you at one point, your face turned blue—"

"Oh my God, Tarah," Jimmy exploded into the room and rushed to her bedside. His hand firmly grasped her wrist. "Please tell me your fucking okay."

"I'm fine," Tarah said quietly. "They gave me a needle to relax me, it's kind of making me tired."

The two young men exchanged looks, but it was Jimmy that blurted it out. "Tarah, we thought you were going to die. You stopped fucking breathing, I've never been so scared in life." His blue eyes darted through her in a combination of caring and genuine fear. "I thought you were going to die." He repeated, and then a calmer William gently touched Jimmy's arm, as if to encourage him to relax.

"Tarah," William began to slowly speak. "It was pretty serious. You really should talk to someone about these attacks. It was … it was *really* scary seeing you that way."

Jimmy nodded, and suddenly he looked as wiped out as Tarah felt. William suggested that he take them both home.

"Do we need to do anything else here?" William asked, as Jimmy helped Tarah off the bed.

"No, man, everything is taken care of." Jimmy was visibly upset as they silently left the hospital.

Tarah fell to sleep on the way home and only awoke when William stopped in the front of their building. Before she and Jimmy unloaded from the car, he once again apologized to Tarah. "You clearly weren't ready tonight, and I shouldn't have asked."

"It's fine," Tarah insisted. "I wanted to do it. Please don't worry about it."

And with that, she and Jimmy got out of his car and headed into the building. Once inside their apartment, Tarah collapsed on the bed. "I'm so tired. I just want to sleep. I don't care about my makeup, my clothes, nothing."

She watched Jimmy as he sat on the side of the bed and leaned forward. "Jimmy, are you okay?" Tarah sat up at the same time he turned toward her, and although he tried to hide the fact that a few stray tears were falling down his face, she saw it. "Jimmy, I'm fine." She wrapped her arms around him and he turned and pulled her closer to him.

"I'm sorry, Tarah, I don't want to seem like some fucking pussy," he whispered. "But you really scared me tonight. I *really* thought you were going to die in front of my eyes. I mean, Tarah, you stopped breathing."

Although she opened her mouth to say something, suddenly nothing seemed to be sufficient. "I'm sorry I scared you."

"No, please don't apologize," Jimmy said, and closed his eyes for a moment. "That's all we've all been doing. William apologizes for making you sing that song. I apologize for even making you do the concert in the first place, and now you're apologizing for worrying us. It's done; it isn't anyone's fault that any of this happened. You have panic attacks and this was just a really bad one. I just hope that it never happens again."

"It never did before," Tarah assured him. "Not like this."

"I hope it never does again."

"I have to learn how to calm myself. I tend to get caught up in the attack which is the worst thing anyone can do." She sniffed.

"Then, that's what you'll have to do," Jimmy said, kissing her on the side of the face. "I just thank God William was there."

"Yeah, you certainly weren't in any condition to drive." Tarah rested her head on his shoulder.

"Well, that too." Jimmy seemed reluctant to continue. "Tarah, I feel like a complete fucking idiot. When you stopped breathing tonight, I didn't even know what to do. William did though, and he gave you mouth-to-mouth."

Tarah was stunned by the news.

"William saved your life. And I sat there like an idiot and watched you stop breathing." He looked away from her. "I could never live with myself if anything had happened to you."

Tarah could hear the hurt in his voice and quickly pulled him even closer to her. "But I'm fine so don't worry about it. You were just scared. You would've figured out what to do if you had to."

When their eyes met, she knew he wasn't convinced.

"Remember what you said earlier?" she whispered. "None of this is anyone's fault. We're not going to play the 'what if' game. Let's just be thankful that everything's okay now."

"Okay." Jimmy's eyes softened and a smile slowly curved on his lips. "You're right."

"I know I'm right." Tarah felt unable to fight off the tiredness any longer. "I have to go to sleep because I'm going to pass out anytime."

"Okay." Jimmy turned toward her. "Just one more thing though."

"What?"

"Happy New Year, Tarah." He leaned in and gave her a slow, lingering kiss that sent chills up her spine. There was a clear reluctance on his part, almost like the first time they had ever kissed, and he felt unsure about showing her any affection at all. His hot breath warmed her face when he stopped, and for a long moment, they just stared into each other's eyes.

CHAPTER THIRTY-SIX

▼

"My life has changed so much since this time last year," Tarah said to John Duffy on a January afternoon in 1995. He was sitting across from her on a plush loveseat in her apartment. Although he claimed his visit to Toronto was merely to check out her new home, both of them knew that John was also quite concerned for her well-being since Wendy's death, followed by Tarah's bad panic attack on New Year's Eve. "I don't even feel that I'm the same person I was this time last year."

"That doesn't surprise me," John said, before taking another sip of his coffee. "Tarah, you were with William this time last year, working at Rothman's, and only doing music on the side. It's pretty safe to say that 1994 was full of extreme highs and lows."

Tarah nodded and let the year play back in her mind. She watched everything from her breakup with William, to falling in love with Jimmy, and of course, signing a recording contract with FUTA. And still, the most shocking event of her year was the day she received the phone call from William, telling her that Wendy was dead. The words had echoed through her mind on that December morning but she had refused to allow them to connect. After denying the tragedy for about five minutes, trying to justify to William why it wasn't true, Tarah had finally broke down and accepted the horrible reality. Wendy was gone.

"But you always pay for your good fortune," Tarah said bitterly as she set down her own coffee cup on a nearby table and frowned. "I got Jimmy in my life but in order to do that, I had to really hurt William. I got the record contract, but I lost Wendy. In fact," Tarah shook her head. "I actually lost her twice. The first time she cut me out of her life and then because she was killed. Is this how life is always going to be, John? Do we always have to pay for the wonderful moments with awful ones? Is that what life is really about?"

"No," John said, and gave her a sympathetic smile. "One has nothing to do with the other. I promise you that. You weren't paying for the wonderful moments in your life by having awful ones. You got a recording contract and are becoming successful because you worked really hard. So did the entire band." He paused and Tarah considered how the tragedy of Wendy's death and her emotional performance on New Year's Eve had actually helped to increase Fire's popularity. It was a bittersweet victory.

"As for Jimmy, you didn't even see that one coming." John spoke with calmness in his voice. "And when it did, you learned that your relationship with William had many flaws. It was just a matter of time before you both would have called it quits. It's unfortunate, but someone always gets hurt when a relationship ends, but you wouldn't have done him a favor by staying if your heart wasn't in it."

"I know," Tarah reluctantly admitted. "I do regret how things happened though." She fell silent.

"Tarah, how have you been since Wendy's death?" John broached the subject carefully. "I mean, how are you *really?*"

"I wasn't doing well at all until after our show on New Year's." Tarah avoided his eyes as she spoke, glancing down at her hands. "But the panic attack really brought me back to life, ironically. I guess I had to hit rock bottom before I could climb up again. I still miss her though. I still think about her a lot and wonder why this had to happen to her. I don't think I'll ever understand."

"That's normal," John said. "It's going to take time to mourn her, but chances are you'll never fully understand why this had to happen. But I'm glad you're doing better."

"I am," Tarah assured him. "I know I worried everyone after that panic attack. I scared Jimmy so much that he's practically walking on eggshells around me now. Meanwhile, a part of me just wants to get out of here and live again. Not take anything for granted. I've even been working on a song about domestic abuse. I'm going to call it 'Wendy's Song.'"

John slowly nodded. "That's a wonderful thing to do, Tarah. I'm sure that song will touch a lot of people, and it's a wonderful way to keep her memory alive."

"I hope so."

In the latter part of the month, Fire had been asked to join a tour that was already in progress, making them the third band on board. Although nothing was confirmed, Maggie heard a rumor that they'd been asked in an attempt to increase slumping ticket sales.

"Of course, they'll never confirm this rumor," Maggie told the band a few days before they went back on the road. "If we knew it for a fact, they know we could demand more money for getting their balls out of a sling. As it stands now, it's only a rumor, but I nevertheless suspect it's true."

"Could we really make that much of a difference?" William asked skeptically. "I know we've increased our fan base, but is that enough to save this tour?"

"I think you'll be pleasantly surprised," Maggie informed him. And she was right. Some of the stops on the tour sold out before the bands made it to their area. In fact, in the short period of time that Fire was on the scene, they'd managed to capture a great deal of fans. Even though it was what they'd always worked for, Tarah was still surprised when someone approached her for an autograph or asked to have her picture taken with them.

Even more than that, Tarah was overwhelmed by the amount of correspondence she received after Wendy's death was made public. People wrote emotional and compassionate letters expressing their own sorrows in similar circumstances, some who had been abused women themselves told their stories and it filled Tarah's heart. It gave her even more inspiration to write a song dedicated to her late friend, something she and Jimmy had worked on closely together. Although it was the most difficult song that Tarah had ever done, in the end it helped her to work through her grief. When it was finished and presented to the other three band members, it was generally agreed that the song was beautiful, powerful, and sent a strong message out to those who listened. It would definitely be on their next CD.

The band already had the studio booked for a week after their tour was to end. Jimmy and Tarah wrote a few songs, and William joined in on the majority of the CD. Eddie and Michael were simply not interested in writing, other than to add extra ideas once the majority of the work was done. Although Tarah often found it frustrating that not everyone in Fire participated one hundred percent, Jimmy convinced her it was probably for the best.

"If Michael were here, do you really think we'd get anything accomplished?" he asked one afternoon. "I mean, really?"

Tarah quickly agreed that William's brother probably would hinder the process more than anything. As for Eddie, on the third week of January he became a father to a little boy who he and Brooke called Zak. It was clear from the start that both parents were much too young and inexperienced to take on the duty they had been presented with. Tarah tried to give them the benefit of the doubt by suggesting that perhaps time and patience was all that was need. Jimmy was skeptical.

"I don't know, Tarah," he said after seeing the new parents together with the baby boy. "I don't think they have any fucking clue which end is up with that kid."

"I think her mom is going to stay with Brooke and Eddie to help them out," Tarah said thoughtfully. "We'd probably be no better at it."

"No, it's not that." Jimmy wrinkled his forehead. "Eddie seems impatient and Brooke just seemed too out of it. I don't think they should be bringing up a kid but then again, what do I know?"

Tarah's father continued to feel better and ended up taking on the role of the band's accountant. The doctor's had been monitoring his health since being released from the hospital the previous year and so far, reports were coming back clear. It didn't look like the cancer had spread.

Tarah and her mother continued to have a strained relationship, although Claire Kiersey had made more attempts to patch things up with her daughter after Wendy's death. And even though Tarah insisted that she hadn't had any panic attacks since New Year's Eve, her mother continued to insist that a doctor examine her and she should start taking pills to relieve some of her anxiety. This wasn't a possibility for Tarah.

"I don't want to live my life doped up," she told her mother on numerous occasions. "I need to deal with life as it is and not have to rely on a pill to get me through stress. Now that I signed a record contract, my entire life is stress. I just have to learn to deal with it better."

Of course Tarah's mom loved the fact that it was William, not Jimmy, who had given her daughter CPR on the night that she had stopped breathing while on the way to the hospital. "William is such a lovely young man and I owe him everything for saving you." And although she didn't say it, there was an unspoken slight against Jimmy for not jumping in to save his girlfriend that night. Tarah certainly didn't place any blame on Jimmy and understood that he was just shocked and scared. She, herself, probably wouldn't have reacted any better if the tables had been turned. But Tarah certainly would never tell Jimmy of Claire's attitude toward the subject, knowing the he already felt bad enough on his own.

Ever since the night of Tarah's bad panic attack, Jimmy was concerned about upsetting her. Eventually she made him realize that she wasn't made of glass and would be fine. But although he was being overly cautious toward her health, Tarah seemed to do the complete opposite. While they were on tour, she had partied a little harder than usual and occasionally experimented with drugs. On one occasion, Tarah tried Ecstasy, something that had gained great popularity in nightclubs. Jimmy was furious when he found out and made her promise not to tamper with such a dangerous drug again.

"You could get hooked to that shit and fuck up your whole life," he fumed on the night in question. Her buzz quickly disappeared. "I don't care if you smoke a little pot, fuck I do that, but when you start getting into this other shit it's a whole other game." She decided it was the last time she'd experiment with this drug. And in the future, she tried to stick with occasionally using coke, but even that was rare.

Another surprising event on the latest tour was Eddie's sudden promiscuous behavior. The same kid that was once shy and unassuming suddenly had adopted Jimmy's former playboy behavior. Even though Eddie had a girlfriend and baby at home, he was hardly secretive about the fact that he cheated on her every chance he got. And now that the band was growing in popularity, there were many opportunities. The fans automatically were drawn to his sweet, reserved manner and found him charming and approachable. Plus, with Jimmy committed to Tarah and Lindsey constantly on William's arm, it was clear that the fans weren't going to make any headway with the more alluring members of the band. Michael didn't get quite as much attention, but it was clear his poor attitude and nasty disposition didn't turn fans off either. He also had his share of groupies.

"If you had told me at one time that I *wouldn't* be the player in this band and Eddie would be," Jimmy began, laughing one night after their show, as he and Tarah watched their drummer leave with a girl on each arm. "I wouldn't have believed you."

"Do you ever regret not being like that anymore?" Tarah was curious. After all, they'd been together for about a year at that point and she often wondered if he grew tired of her. "Do you ever wish you had your freedom now that we are touring and there are tons of pretty girls around?"

"Babe, you make it sound like I'm locked in a fucking cage." Jimmy began to laugh as they walked toward the exit. "I'm with you because I want to be."

"Don't you miss hooking up with these other girls?" Tarah asked, showing no judgment. "Don't you think about it sometimes?"

"Tarah, come on." He grew frustrated with her questions as they headed outside into the cool evening air. "If I say yes, you'll be mad. If I say no, you won't believe me. I'm happy with the way things are with us, end of story."

Tarah realized that it wasn't a fair question and that it probably came out sounding more like an accusation and so changed the topic. The last thing she wanted to do was start a fight.

When the tour ended in the first week of April, the band went into the studio to record some new material. They took a month to record it. This time, Jimmy was shadowing the band's producer, eagerly learning all the steps in the recording process. His ultimate goal was to learn the recording aspect of the business and to produce other bands.

FUTA was impressed with the sales of their first CD and were quite confident that their second attempt would be much more successful. Tarah felt that the material for their new CD was much stronger and had a heavier edge that would appeal to fans. And everyone agreed that the first single would be "Wendy's Song." Tarah assumed that although the band's reasons were pure, that FUTA probably saw it as cash grab, knowing the publicity she had received after Wendy's murder and her own panic attack. Regardless, she knew that the song sent out an important message about domestic violence and would be considered a tribute to a slain woman's life.

Once the CD was finished, the band made a touching video for its first single and then took a month break before getting back on the road. This time they would be playing with a popular Canadian band that was doing a full North American tour, which was anticipated to last for at least six months. The time was just a rough estimate since all dates weren't confirmed, but either way, the members of Fire were feeling hopeful about their futures and looking forward to everything 1995 had to bring.

Jimmy had suggested to Tarah that they take advantage of their time off and book a trip to Italy. It was something they had talked about many times since John had gone, and it seemed like the perfect opportunity to take off for a week or two. However, these plans were put on hold when Jimmy became ill three days before their vacation began. At first Tarah thought he just had a bad flu, but when he suddenly was doubled over in pain, she insisted Jimmy go to the hospital. He had appendicitis.

The doctor wasted no time getting Jimmy into an operating room, fearful that his appendix would burst. Tarah immediately called his family to let them know of his condition, and before long, Jillian and Jimmy's mother were sitting in the waiting room with her. Although the doctor had already assured Tarah that everything would be okay, a part of her was still scared that something would go wrong during surgery. But it didn't and Jimmy was fine.

The night before Jimmy's return home, Tarah rushed to the grocery store to pick up all his favorite foods and treats. She then went back to the apartment to clean up and get everything ready for his return. The doctor felt very confident that the patient would make a quick recovery because of his age and overall health. However, this news didn't make up for the fact that Jimmy had missed out on his trip to Italy. Tarah was surprised to see him brooding over the fact that they hadn't been able to follow through with their original plan, something she reassured him didn't matter to her.

"I just want you to be healthy," Tarah had insisted. "I don't care about Italy. We'll just go another time."

"I know but I was really looking forward to it," Jimmy frowned. "It was a big deal to me."

"It's fine, Jimmy. Really, don't worry about it."

Recalling this conversation as Tarah made up their bed with fresh sheets, she glanced at their suitcases in the corner of the room. They were both so excited about the vacation that they packed right away, but now the luggage would be a symbol of disappointment to Jimmy. Without a second thought, she quickly went to work and started to unpack the bags. However, Jimmy's were so messy, Tarah decided to just empty them out then neatly fold all his clothes. It was when everything was sitting before her on the floor that something caught her eye. She stared at the object for a few minutes before even attempting to pick it up.

Slowly, Tarah reached for the small box that sat in the midst of all the mess. Her hand shook as she slowly opened it, and tears flooded Tarah's eyes. Inside was a beautiful, sparking, diamond ring.

CHAPTER THIRTY-SEVEN

▼

It was a chilly May afternoon when Jimmy was released from the hospital. A dark cloud loomed overhead indicating that a rainstorm was about to move in, as the couple slowly walked into their apartment building. Tarah glanced at Jimmy and considered how the weather was a good reflection on his recent mood. For some reason, her boyfriend couldn't accept the fact that everybody got sick from time to time, and that he was no different from every other human being. Also, he continually complained about missing out on their trip to Italy. At least now, she knew why.

Tarah felt like a pot that was about to boil over since finding the piece of jewelry. She was excited about the prospect of having the beautiful diamond to represent their commitment. It was clearly an engagement ring, and although Tarah was hardly an expert on jewelry, she did know that it was very expensive. While a part of her felt awful for Jimmy, knowing that he must have feared that she'd find it when he was ill, another side of Tarah was over the moon. She was already living her dream, and being married to Jimmy would make everything perfect.

But she couldn't say a thing. Although the thought had flashed through her mind to fess up and tell him about discovering the diamond in his suitcase, she quickly decided that would be a horrible idea. He already felt bad enough about being the reason that they had to cancel their trip, without feeling like he missed out on surprising Tarah with the ring. No, she would remain silent and never tell him her secret.

Once in their apartment, Jimmy announced the he wanted to take a nap. A gust of cold air met them both as they entered the dark bedroom together, and Tarah realized that she must have left the window open that morning. The long, flowing curtains were flapping furiously in the wind and she quickly rushed across the room to shut it. "Sorry about that." She turned to smile at him and noted that his eyes were on the suitcases across the room. He was wondering if she had unpacked and discovered the ring. Looking satisfied to see them still full and awaiting a trip, he gave her a small, sad smile and stiffly sat on the bed.

"Do you need anything?" Tarah asked, as she headed for the door. He shook his head no. "Okay, well, I'll just be there if you *do* need anything." She pointed toward the living room.

"Thanks." He lay on top of the covers, and she gently closed the door behind her. Only a few minutes later, as she read a book in the living room, Tarah heard him shuffling around in the next room. Smiling to herself, she assumed he was checking for the ring, and Tarah wondered when he'd finally give her the beautiful gift. She was so excited just imaging the moment that she was unable to concentrate on her book and quickly set it aside.

Tarah jumped when the phone rang quickly taking her away from a wonderful daydream. She rushed to answer it.

"Hi, Tarah." It was Jillian. "How's my baby brother doing today? Is he home yet?"

"Yes, actually we just got back," Tarah replied, playing with the phone cord. "He's taking a nap."

"Oh, good, then he's doing okay?"

"Yes, he's fine. A little depressed I think, but fine."

"Yeah, Jimmy doesn't make a good patient." Jillian laughed. "Not that he ever did."

"That doesn't surprise me." Tarah felt light-hearted as the two continued to talk. Eventually Jillian suggested that they meet for lunch the next afternoon. "I haven't been to Toronto in ages. I figured I'd make a day of it: visit Jimmy and then we could go for lunch afterward. He could come with us if he was feeling up to it."

"You can ask," Tarah suggested. "But I kind of doubt it."

The next afternoon Jillian dropped in to see a slightly more pleasant Jimmy, and then the two young women walked to a nearby café. "This is fun," Tarah announced on the way. "I feel like between the touring, Wendy's death, and Jimmy being sick, I haven't had a chance just to do something relaxing."

"I suppose when you're on tour, things are pretty insane." Jillian pulled on her Chanel sunglasses as the two women walked along. The sun was shining that day, and Tarah couldn't help but noticed that Jillian was slightly thinner than the last time the two had seen one another, which was only a few days earlier when Jimmy was omitted to the hospital. Was it just her imagination?

"It *is* insane, but it's fun. For the most part."

"I bet."

The two sat outside at a popular café for lunch and talked about everything from fashion to careers. With Tarah's busy schedule, they really hadn't had an opportunity to catch up in weeks. Since their first meeting the previous year, she really liked Jimmy's sister. Jillian was such a fragile and sweet girl once she had gotten to know her. There was a sense of vulnerability about her that sometimes worried Tarah. It was as if any little thing could push her over the edge. So, it surprised Tarah when Jillian admitted that her husband wanted them to have a baby.

"Really?" Tarah stopped her fork midway to her mouth. A piece of lettuce fell back on her plate. "You're having a baby?"

"Well, Rob talks a lot about having a baby." She spoke of the idea half-heartedly while using her fork to play with the contents on her plate. Tarah couldn't help but noticed that she had barely eaten a thing. "I'm just not sure if I'm really ready for that."

Tarah gave her a soft smile and thought that was probably putting it mildly. How was a woman who clearly still had food issues go from being extremely skinny to going through nine months of gaining weight? Although she didn't say it, Tarah didn't feel it would be a good idea. At least, it wouldn't be yet.

"So what are you going to do?" Tarah tilted her head and smiled. "Maybe you should wait till you're more sure."

"Rob says I'll never be completely sure. It's just something you have to do without over thinking it and everything will work out." She gave a little laugh. "He's excited about the idea though, so I'm really thinking about it. He could be right."

Tarah really didn't have a good feeling about that idea and later reported her feelings back to Jimmy. He was sitting in the living room watching television, and she noticed that the color was starting to return in his face. Jimmy's mood had improved greatly since the day before, much to Tarah's relief.

"It's not really any of our business, Tarah." He shrugged. "I don't personally think Jill is ready to have a baby either, but who knows? Maybe that'll help her to get her eating issues under control. Maybe having a baby will take her attention away from herself and change her perspective."

As it turned out, Jillian wasn't ready to have a baby. Three days later, she ended up in the hospital after passing out at work. The doctor said she was dangerously underweight and would have to stay in until they could be certain she would stop starving herself. Jimmy was devastated.

"How can she do this again, Tarah? I don't understand," he complained after they left the hospital and jumped on the 401 to return to Toronto. It had been a really difficult day. Jimmy's father was there, silently sitting in the waiting room while his mother continually cried. Annette Groome admitted to her son that she feared having to bury her daughter, if things didn't improve. Jimmy didn't even know how to respond to this comment, so instead he gave his mother a tight hug.

"I don't either," Tarah said, but yet she herself had remained a size zero since first dating Jimmy. "I wish I knew the answer, baby."

"Me too." Jimmy was once again in a dark mood, not that Tarah blamed him. It was a difficult and heart-wrenching situation to be in. "I just thought that now that she's married and had all that counseling, somehow things would be better. But I guess neither really solves all your problems."

The comment referring to marriage grabbed Tarah's attention and reminded her of the diamond sitting somewhere in their apartment. She had checked the previous day when Jimmy was in the shower, and he had removed it from the suitcase. Searching frantically, Tarah finally decided that maybe it was better to leave well enough alone. He'd give her the diamond when things calmed down a bit.

"I think she needs more counseling," Tarah said. "As for marriage, that probably has no affect, one way or another."

"I don't know, I guess I think sometimes that marriage makes everything better." He pushed his sunglasses back farther on his face. "Maybe not, maybe it makes things worse."

And it was then that Tarah felt her heart become heavy. Was he having second thoughts about giving her the ring? After all, maybe this turn of events made him a skeptic when it came to marriage. What if he changed his mind? She wasn't even supposed to know about the ring in the first place, so it wasn't like she could say anything now. Tarah slid her own sunglasses on, wanting to hide the sadness in her eyes. She remained silent for the rest of the way home.

As the month dragged on, Jimmy no longer talked about their trip to Italy. In fact, on the spur of the moment, he decided to go back to Thorton for a few days to be with his family. Tarah certainly didn't blame him, but felt a little left out when he didn't invite her to join. In fact, he suggested that she stay in Toronto to attend the meeting with Peter Sampson the next day. They were going to get copies of their new CD, which was titled *Another Day in the Sun* in reference to their stardom.

"Just call Will, I'm sure he'll pick you up for the meeting." Jimmy spoke casually as he was walking out the door. "He won't mind."

Tarah nodded. Jimmy waved at her and left. No good-bye kiss.

Pushing back her sadness, she picked up the phone and called William to ensure her drive for the next day. As if things weren't bad enough, Lindsey answered. She was curt with Tarah and abruptly gave the phone to William. Tarah quickly explained the situation.

"Sure, no problem, Tarah. I'll see you in the morning."

After a night of not sleeping, Tarah reluctantly got up and prepared for the meeting. It felt strange not having Jimmy beside her in the morning, and Tarah wondered to herself if she'd have to start getting used to it. His attitude toward her hadn't been the best in recent days, especially since Jillian became ill. Maybe he was not only having second thoughts on marriage, but *her* as well. Tarah forced herself to not think about it anymore and get ready for the meeting.

William was chatty when he picked her up, and she responded to most of his conversation with a yawn or a smile. The meeting went well, Peter talked about the next tour and their new CD. He was clearly very optimistic about the band's future and rattled on about his projections for the upcoming months. Tarah sat in silence. On the way home, William asked her if anything was wrong.

"No," Tarah replied, and avoided the concerned look in his eyes. "Just worried about Jimmy's sister. His mom is scared she is going to die cause she's been fighting anorexia for so many years." That was partially true at least.

"I hope she's okay," William said with sincerity in his voice. "I really do. That's pretty scary."

When Tarah didn't hear from Jimmy over the next couple of days, she attempted to phone his family's home but there was never an answer. She began to worry that Jillian had taken a turn for the worse, but it turned out to be the complete opposite. When Jimmy finally returned home four days after leaving, he was in good cheer.

"She's doing a lot better."

These were his first words when he walked in the door with a smile on his face, Jimmy went on to tell Tarah that Jillian was back in therapy and had actually gained a couple of pounds back "It's not a lot." He sat beside Tarah on the couch. "But it's a start."

"It *is* a lot for someone who has an eating disorder," Tarah reminded him. "I think she's on the right track. You should be hopeful. Maybe Jillian just needs some more counseling to get back herself together again.."

"Man, I hope so." He pushed his dark hair back and out of his face. "I really do. I had a long talk with her in the hospital so maybe that helped."

"I bet it did," she assured him, and just as Tarah began to feel at ease, Jimmy jumped up and headed back to the door.

"I gotta run out for a bit, be back soon, babe."

And then he was gone. Again.

Reluctantly, Tarah picked up the phone and called John. She hated to bother him with her issues, especially now that he was in the midst of wedding plans with Elizabeth. The last thing he'd want to hear about was her problems.

"Hey, Tarah, good to hear from you." John spoke enthusiastically on the phone. "How is Jimmy doing since his surgery?"

"Good, actually but he's having some other problems." She went on to tell him about Jillian's eating disorder and about how she landed in the hospital. "So, we've been kind of stressed. It's supposed to be a mini holiday for us and yet, it's been one thing after another."

"Sorry to hear that, Tarah, but if Jimmy's sister is in the hospital it sounds like she's probably in the best place possible. They can monitor her very closely there and that's exactly what she needs right now," John insisted. "She probably just relapsed, that's pretty normal with eating disorders. I think with the correct amount of support and counseling, she'll be fine."

"I hope so."

"So, everything else is good?"

Tarah took a deep breath and briefly told him the story about Jimmy and the ring.

"Wow! That's quite a surprise." John echoed the happiness she had felt in the beginning. "I take it that he hasn't given you the ring yet?"

"No."

"Well, don't worry about it. A lot has been going on and timing is everything," he reminded her. "You also have to realize that he planned to give you the ring during a really romantic vacation, so he probably is trying to think up an equally nice way to propose here. Just be sure you're ready to get married. You're both still really young."

"I know," Tarah admitted. "I understand your concern. But you know what? I know he's the one. Maybe I always knew that."

"It sounds like it always did with Jimmy," John said. "From day one, there was always something there, Tarah. You know that."

"I have no doubt. Not even for a second." Tarah smiled to herself. "I just worry that he may've changed his mind. The other day we were talking about marriage in general, and he said some shitty things."

"Come on, Tarah." John began to laugh. "The guy is pretty impulsive, but I doubt he rushed out and bought the ring without thinking. It's something he would've given a great deal of thought, which I know from personal experience. I don't think he'll change his mind."

"Hope not," she replied.

"In a way, finding that ring was a curse to you because now it's not only *not* going to be a complete surprise, but you'll be sitting on the edge of your chair, wondering *when* it's going to happen. When he's going to propose."

Or if *he's going to propose*, she thought to herself.

Jimmy returned a couple of hours later and continued to be in good cheer. Tarah was wondering if he had went out to plan something special for them that night, but they ended up just sitting home and watching television. Of course, the mood was light so she was happy; it seemed as if everything was fine again. Jimmy suggested that they return to Thorton the next day to see his sister again. Tarah happily agreed. At least he was inviting her this time. Of course, it meant another day without the sparkly ring she was constantly thinking about. John was right, it was a curse finding the diamond when she did. Now Tarah wish she'd never laid eyes on it.

They went directly to the hospital after arriving in Thorton and found Jillian looking much healthier. Jimmy's sister was excited to see them drop by and gave them each a strong hug. Annette was also at the hospital and seemed much brighter and more cheerful, which alone suggested that Jillian was doing better. When they finally left the hospital a couple hours later, Jimmy seemed like he was back to his old self.

"Hey wanna go smoke a joint somewhere before we head home?" Jimmy grabbed her hand on the way out of the hospital. "Or you want to go see your brother? Dad, anyone?"

"Nah, they'll all be at work today," Tarah reminded him. Being in a rock band automatically put them on a different time clock than the rest of the world. Sometimes they forgot that other people worked during the weekdays. "That's fine. Whatever you want to do is okay."

"Cool." Jimmy turned and gave her a big smile. "Let's go for a drive."

They got back in his car and drove around, talking about their lives in Thorton. So much had changed for them both, that the city they both had grown up in now seemed more like a distant memory than a place they used to call home. It made Tarah smile, looking at all the places they had spent time in together, whether it be with the band or otherwise. She was quite surprised, however, when Jimmy pulled up in the back of her old apartment building and stopped the car.

"Jimmy, we can't smoke a joint here." She started to laugh. "Come on, it's not like I live here anymore."

"You're probably right about that." He started to laugh and opened the car door. She followed his lead and got out of her own side. From across the hood of the car he pointed toward the window that had once been hers when she lived with William. "Remember the first time we really hung out, up in that apartment. Smoking weed and listening to Alice in Chains?" He watched her nod. "That night completely changed my life."

Suddenly it hit her. It wasn't a coincidence that they were at her former apartment building, the place when he first admitted his feelings for Tarah. She bit her lip and took a deep breath. Had he taken her there to propose?

"Let's go sit down for a minute." He gestured toward the back step. She nodded and silently walked with him, hand in hand. Sitting down, she thought back to her breakup with William. It was Jimmy who had waited outside that night in case she needed him. And he had been there ever since.

As if he were reading her thoughts, Jimmy brought up the same topic. "Remember that night when you and Will split up?" He watched her nodding. "I remember sitting out here, not even sure that I should be here or at all. Not even sure you'd come out that door or that you'd want me around if you did. After all, it was my fault that you broke up."

"It wasn't your fault, Jimmy," Tarah spoke softly. "You know that."

"In a way, it was." He seemed to watch her reaction closely. "I just *knew* that I had to at least try to be with you. I'd never felt that way about anyone before, and I decided to put it all on the line. It turns out it was the best decision that I ever made."

"I'm so glad you did," Tarah confessed, knowing that she hadn't exactly made it easy for him in the beginning.

"Me too." Jimmy nodded and gave her a gentle smile. And then he said something she hadn't at all expected. "So, um, I guess it's safe to say that you found the ring?"

He gave her a serious look and for a moment, Tarah feared that he was angry. Her stomach was in knots. How did he know that she had found it? His suitcase had been a mess when she opened it the day before his return from the hospital. He quickly answered her question without her even having to ask it.

"I know because I had it in the pocket of a pair of jeans." He spoke in an even tone. "I wanted to make sure it was hidden really well. When I found it tossed in the suitcase on the day I got home, I knew you must've found it. Why didn't you tell me?"

Tarah fell silent. She didn't know what to say. He actually looked a little pissed off. An ache ran in her heart when she thought of her decision not to tell him about finding the ring. It had only been to spare Jimmy, not to make him angry.

"I'm sorry," she finally managed. "I didn't want you to be disappointed"

"I wasn't disappointed that you found it," Jimmy said. "I'm a little disappointed that you hid it from me."

Tarah was stunned. Was he really this upset with her? Had he brought her all the way to the very place their relationship started, just to end it again? She frowned and fell silent. What else could she possibly say at that point?

"I've been racking my brain for the last few days about all this and wasn't sure what to do," Jimmy continued, and Tarah looked into his eyes and saw a hint of love. It was the only thing that kept her from looking away. "Since the Italy thing didn't work out, I wasn't sure how to propose to you." A smile lit up his face, and she realized that she had been so uptight about the whole situation she hadn't realized he was teasing her. "If you had told me that you found the ring, this whole thing would've been *so* much easier."

Tarah was stunned. She couldn't even talk. Tears filled her eyes as she watched him reach into his jean pocket and pull out the ring she had found days earlier. Suddenly, she was sobbing so loudly that she barely could hear his words.

"Tarah, this is exactly where I was when I knew for sure that you were the one." He reached for her hand and moved closer to her. His eyes studied hers for a few minutes before he slowly continued. "Right here on this step. So I thought it was only appropriate that I bring you right back here, to this very place, and ask you to marry me."

Tarah's hand shook as he slid the ring on her finger, and she barely managed a yes because she was crying so hard. He pulled her close into a hug and she held on tightly to him.

"I love you, Tarah."

CHAPTER THIRTY-EIGHT

▼

Word of their engagement spread quickly. Tarah and Jimmy were ecstatic about their new status and were, for the most part, completely unaware of what the rest of the world thought. Not that they cared. It didn't matter, and it certainly wouldn't change how they felt about one another or their intentions. They were in love and lost in their own little world.

The first people they shared the exciting news with were the members of Jimmy's family. Expecting a positive reaction, Tarah was a bit taken aback when his mother and sister appeared more stunned than anything over the engagement. Although both hugged Tarah and welcomed her as a part of the Groome family, they also warned the couple to not rush into marriage.

"There's nothing wrong with having a long engagement," Jimmy's mother reminded them for the second time that day, just before they left the hospital. "You're young; you've got all the time in the world."

Being in a much more emotional state than normal, Jillian cried when she learned the news and said she already loved Tarah like a sister. And although it was clear that the fragile young woman was very happy about the engagement, she also pointed out that marriage was hard work and that she wouldn't recommend that they take the plunge right away. "Rob and I had a long engagement, and I really believe that was the best idea."

"That was pretty fucking weird." Jimmy referred to his family's reaction to the news as they left the hospital room and headed for the elevator. "Now, I definitely don't want to go see your parents. Jesus, your mom doesn't even *like* me."

"We may as well get it over with," Tarah pointed out. "If anyone from the media spots the ring, it'll be out there anyway. It's not like we can keep it a secret."

"True enough."

As it turns out, David Kiersey was happy about the news. In fact, in the few times they were together, he had gotten to know Jimmy, and he considered him to be a very smart and ambitious young man. The fact that his ex-wife didn't like Tarah's boyfriend may not have not hurt either. However, he also suggested that the couple wait before heading down the aisle.

"There seems to be a theme going on." Tarah referred to everyone's insistence that the couple not marry too soon. "Can't wait to tell mom."

"Whatever." Jimmy shrugged and gave her a quick kiss as they got into his car.

Tarah's mother was difficult as usual and not too happy about the news. That was until she saw her daughter's engagement ring. That's when the mood suddenly changed.

"Tarah, that's a *beautiful* ring." Claire immediately turned her attention on Jimmy. "What a gorgeous ring. Where did you ever find it?"

"I, ah, bought it when we were on tour earlier this year," he said, admitting something that Tarah hadn't even considered. "I had some help because I really don't know anything about rings."

"Well, it is incredible," Claire commented, and Tarah was starting to wonder if the ring was more important to her mother than the fact that she was engaged. "I love it."

"Thank you." Tarah felt awkward and wanted to leave. She was searching her mind trying to think who would have helped Jimmy find her engagement ring. For the matter, she wondered when he bought it.

"Well, I'm so happy for you." And Claire surprised Tarah by hugging her, then Jimmy. Fortunately, she didn't discourage the couple from getting married too soon.

Of all of their family members, Tarah later reflected on how her brother was happiest to hear the news. He'd just returned home from his job at the call center when they showed up for a visit. Bobby was now in management and had a more consistent schedule. As he held his two-year-old daughter in one arm and answered the door with the other, he looked enthused to see his sister and Jimmy. Although Tarah rarely saw her niece, and still wasn't completely comfortable around children, it always surprised her how excited Caitlin was to see her. She jumped around excitedly in Bobby's arms and when he put the child down, she wasted no time in rushing to her aunt.

"I see you on TV." Caitlin put her arms up in the air indicated that she wanted Tarah to pick her up, which she did. Jimmy laughed knowing how frightened she was of children. "I drawed a picture of you. Wanna see it?"

"Okay." Tarah smiled and put the excited child down. Caitlin ran through the apartment as the couple stepped in the door, and Bobby grinned.

"Ever since I pointed you out on television one day, she thinks every blonde on there is you." He began to laugh. "Vanessa was watching an episode of *Melrose Place* one day and when Caitlin saw Heather Locklear, she automatically thought it was you. I told her it wasn't and she said, 'But Aunt Tarah has yellow hair too.' I couldn't seem to make her understand that not every blonde lady on television was her aunt."

"Oh my God!" Tarah laughed. "As if I look as good as Heather Locklear! I'm flattered though."

"You look great," Jimmy insisted.

"Not Heather Locklear great," Tarah smiled. "So Bobby, how are things going with you and Vanessa?" She referred to her brother's new girlfriend. They had been seeing one another for the past few months and it was starting to look like a serious relationship was developing. It was really nice for Bobby, Tarah thought, since the last couple of years had been so difficult for him. Especially now that his divorce with Sara was finalized and sadly she still had no contact with their daughter. Caitlin had been told her mother was 'away' but it never really made any difference. Being a child in a single parent family was all Caitlin had ever known.

"Very well," Bobby replied as he made a pot of coffee. In the background, Caitlin could be heard buzzing around. Eventually she returned with the drawing of Tarah.

"Thank you, Caitlin." Tarah leaned down and hugged her. "Can I keep this?"

"Sure." The little girl's brown eyes danced and Tarah thought how much she resembled Bobby.

"Do you have any pictures of Jimmy?" She pointed up at her boyfriend.

"No." Caitlin giggled. "I make one." And with that she was gone away, running madly through the apartment.

Tarah stood up and continued her conversation with Bobby. "So, you're happy with Vanessa? And so is Caitlin?"

"Yes, actually she really likes Vanessa, which is good. I was a little nervous about introducing anyone into my daughter's life after what Sara did, but now I'm glad I did." He nodded slowly and spoke with confidence. Tarah smiled to herself when she considered how much her brother had grown up in the last three years. "I can really see us together for a long time."

"I'm happy for you." Tarah turned to Jimmy and they shared a smile. "Which kind of brings me to why we stopped by. We've got some news to share with you." Tarah walked over to her brother and showed him the shiny new ring on her finger. "We're engaged."

"Wow." Bobby's face lit up much like his daughter's had moments before. "Congratulations, guys!" He pulled Tarah into a strong hug then walked over to Jimmy and shook his hand. "I really wish you the best."

"Thanks." Tarah felt like the smile would never disappear from her face. "I think you're the first person who didn't tell us to wait because we're too young."

"Hey, if anyone has the right to say that, it's me," Bobby insisted. "But you know what? Sara and I married for the wrong reasons and that has nothing to do with age. Only you two know what's right for you. No one else."

"That's what I say," Jimmy agreed. "It's mostly my family. They're just nervous because I've always been really impulsive and hyper. They probably think I made the decision on a whim and didn't think it through, but trust me, I have. I know what I want."

Tarah and Jimmy traded smiles.

A half hour later, the couple left Bobby's house. Each had a drawing from Caitlin in hand, and Tarah promised that she'd try to drop in to visit again before the tour started, however, there wasn't much time before they would be on the road again.

Once in the car and on the way back to Toronto, Tarah remembered Jimmy's comment earlier that day about having someone help him shop for her ring. She asked him who the mystery person was and he laughed.

"You wouldn't believe me if I told you."

"Was it Michael?" Tarah began to giggle. "Cause I know how much he likes me."

"No, let's not go all fucking crazy here." Jimmy playfully hit her arm and grinned. "No, but still not someone you'd expect. I had Lindsey help me."

"You had William's girlfriend help you?" Tarah was surprised. She didn't think that the woman in her ex's life was much of a fan of hers either. "I can't believe that. So they both know then, obviously."

"Well, she clearly does. I'm sure Will does too. She made several hints that he should be giving her a ring too," Jimmy said. "I just asked her cause she's a model and very stylish and worldly, so I figured she'd have good taste. Clearly she did."

"I think she hates me so I'm surprised she'd help."

"She doesn't hate you," Jimmy insisted. "I think she and Will don't have the best relationship. Lindsey strikes me as kind of insecure. Must be a model thing, because look at my sister. Anyway, she was actually pretty excited to help me out. She knows everything and anything you need to know about rings. And the rest is history."

"That must've been kind of awkward, hanging out with her," Tarah considered.

"Not as bad as you'd think. I told her about Jillian being a model and the anorexia thing, and we were pretty set for the entire conversation to the jewelry store. On the way back, she mostly rambled about everything we saw there. That's about it," Jimmy said, and shrugged. "I think she may seem indifferent toward you because you're still in Will's life because of the band, plus they don't always get along, so maybe she's afraid that you might still have a connection. I mean, it's not such a surprise. I used to worry about that too."

"I know." Tarah recalled her own surprise at his insecurities only a year earlier. Now the three got along fine, as if nothing had ever happened. Time really did heal some wounds after all.

They told the band about their engagement the next day. William was very kind and seemed very sincere in wishing them a happy life together. Eddie admitted that he was cynical on relationships, but did feel that they made a wonderful couple and wished them lots of luck. As for Michael, he just shrugged and said that at least divorce was an option if it didn't work. Tarah noted that both Jimmy and William gave him a dirty at the same time. She didn't care what he thought or anyone else for that matter, Tarah was on top of the world.

It was a good thing too, because once the news hit the media, the response was very mixed. Some people, in fact most fans, were very happy for them. They even started to receive wedding gifts and cards of congratulations through their fan club. Others were less pleased. Some fans who were either smitten with her or Jimmy tended to question their choice of mate. Other people said that they were too young and inexperienced to marry, that it wouldn't last. But the media loved the story, something that delighted Maggie.

"It's simply a wonderful announcement to make before your tour begins. Fans are fascinated by a good love story with a happy ending," she insisted, while Jimmy laughed at the idea. The band had gathered in her office to discuss the new video that had just been released, but instead they tackled other topics. The engagement seemed to be the biggest piece of news. "Hey, think what you want, but your fans are mostly young women, and they love the idea that Jimmy and Tarah are together. It's exciting to them. They want to know all the details. Of course, don't tell them your life story, but throw out a few facts from time to time; they'll love it."

"I think the next song we release should be "One Moment" since it's a love song," Maggie insisted, and Tarah and Jimmy exchanged looks. It was the song he had written for her a year earlier on the day of his birthday and the band's CD release party. "Actually, we'll have to start scheduling that soon. We'll have to work it around the tour somehow, but it's got to be done."

Everyone agreed that that would be a good idea. When they left the meeting, Jimmy suggested that they start writing some new material before the tour began, which was only a week and a half away.

"Already?" Tarah asked, as the band left Maggie's office. "We just released *Another Day in the Sun* and you're already thinking to the next CD?"

"Don't get me wrong." Jimmy directed his comments to all of them. "It's a good CD, very commercial though. I think it'll get us a larger fan base because it has more appeal with radio stations, but still, it's a little too commercial now that I think about it. I'd like our next CD to be a really strong rock album. Just a good, old-fashioned, hard fucking core rock CD, the kind you can have a few drinks to, something that really grabs people. This CD?" He made a face and shook his head. "I don't know man, I liked when we did it, but it just doesn't appeal to me as much. I felt like the producer kind of pushed us into a specific direction, and I'm not so sure about it now."

By this time, they were all in the elevator, and Jimmy had their full attention. Tarah was surprised to see everyone agreeing. Including her. Although the CD was good, it just didn't have the zest that he was speaking about. She knew what he meant and was glad that they were all on the same page. As they headed out of the building that day, everyone was on board to work on some new songs and jump in the studio as soon as the tour was finished, which took them to the end of 1995.

Once in the car alone, Jimmy went into more detail about it with Tarah. "I don't even know where to begin this time, but I just want something with more power to it. Peter was right about the whole grunge thing, remember what he said back when we were signed? It was on the way out? He was right. He and I talked about it the other day again, and I told him my idea; he's totally behind it. He thinks the music industry is getting kind of flaky with all this dance shit, that we need to put something out there to balance it out. It makes sense when you think about it."

"It really does," Tarah agreed.

However, when they actually tried to write something, it was a whole different story. Neither of them could get into the process at all. They ended up just talking about how Jimmy wanted to help produce their next CD as well as do the mixing and anything else he could. He eventually wanted to work behind the scenes in the industry.

"Sure, I love being on stage and doing all this shit, but not many bands are famous forever," he reminded her. "And when this is all done, I want to be in the studio with other bands making *them* famous. Helping them put their best music out. It's what I want."

"That's great," Tarah encouraged. "I just wish I had a plan."

"Isn't there anything else you like to do?"

"I like to write, but I'm not sure if I could ever make a career of it." Tarah thought back to the poems and short stories she had done in high school. "I won a stupid, really lame writing contest once, but it's a lot of work. I don't think I have the focus."

"You might someday," Jimmy reminded her. "You know what you should do? Write in a journal or something? Write about stuff we see and do on tour."

"Good idea." Tarah giggled. "And fifteen years from now I'll write a book about how I was once a rock star in the nineties."

Jimmy grinned and raised his eyebrows.

By the time the tour began, the band was gaining even more popularity. Their first single from *Another Day in the Sun* was quickly moving up the charts. In a time when the O. J. Simpson case was a constant highlight in the media, dubbed "the trial of a century," the topic of domestic abuse was heavily discussed. Talk shows and journalists everywhere were covering this emotional topic, and "Wendy's Song" quickly became the music most often used in their segments. It was Fire's first number one in Canada, and the momentum quickly caught up south of the border and many other countries around the world.

Tarah ended up following Jimmy advice and started to write a journal detailing the events of her life. In the end, each day was fuller than she originally thought. "I never realized so much happened," Tarah would later tell Jimmy. "I suppose I'm so used to all this stuff going on around me that I lose track of how busy I really am." Tarah ended up writing tidbits throughout the day as she had time, because there was simply too much to do it all at once.

After the couple became engaged, Tarah noticed that something changed in their relationship. The physical side that had calmed down slightly since they first got together appeared to pick up its pace once more. It was a new phase in their sex life. It was called anything goes. And for some reason, it seemed to fit in perfectly with their new lifestyle.

Not only did the couple party continually on the tour, they also experimented more and more with drugs. Jimmy, who had once been dead set against Tarah doing anything stronger than the occasional line of coke was often taking speed in order to follow the fast pace on the road. Tarah was intrigued by the consistent energy that Jimmy had and quickly followed suit. They worked hard and partied even harder, and Tarah experienced the most intense sexual experiences of her life during this period. They did it everywhere. In public washrooms, backstage at shows, at parties, and anywhere else they felt they could get away with it. They were rock stars and could do whatever they wanted. No one expected less.

It was during a break from their tour that the band worked on their next video. When it was done, Tarah and Jimmy went to an all-night party. The couple drank, smoked weed, and snorted coke with a small collection of celebrities who were also well-known on the partying scene. The rest of the band didn't join them. They never did.

After the couple finally left the party at four the next morning, they returned home to find themselves wide-awake and as high as a kite. It was then that they began to work on what would later be the band's most popular CD. During the course of the next four days, the couple did shots, smoked weed, took speed or E, and only occasionally slept. During their waking hours, they either had sex or wrote songs. A rare shower or food break was permitted, but that was it. They didn't answer their phone or door during this phase, choosing only to talk to one another. And the music seemed to flow in the most natural way. It was dirty and gritty. But it worked.

Just before the band went back on tour, Tarah and Jimmy presented the fourteen songs that they wrote during that drug-fueled period to the rest of Fire. The couple had done a simple recording on a computer program they recently learned. Everyone was stunned and silent. Unlike the Fire's previous material, these songs were heavier, edgier, and very provocative. In fact, Tarah felt slightly exposed as the others listened to their songs because most were clearly about sex and partying.

William was the first to speak when the collection of songs were played back to them. "I like it. It's a completely different sound, but they're catchy." He looked like he was still in thought as he spoke. "I think we can polish them up, but yeah, for sure. That could be our next CD."

"You know we could write some more songs and make it a double CD. That'll help us get closer to fulfilling our contract," Jimmy pointed out. "Then we only have one left to do and we're out. We can negotiate after that and get a better deal next time around."

"I like that idea too," William agreed. "I like that a lot."

Tarah remained silent because she and Jimmy had already discussed all this in great lengths. It was actually her idea to do a double CD. If they wrote fourteen songs in four days, it was completely possible to write fourteen more in the next six months. Eddie loved the idea too, but remained distracted; Michael didn't respond.

"Then it sounds like a plan." Jimmy shot Tarah a smile. "That's what we'll do."

CHAPTER THIRTY-NINE

▼

"I can't believe we're halfway through November." Tarah spoke thoughtfully on a late Saturday night after she and Jimmy returned to their apartment. The tour had made its way to Toronto, giving the couple an opportunity to drop by their home for a few hours before heading out again early the next morning. "Where did 1995 go?" Tarah collapsed on their couch and watched Jimmy checking out their CD collection. With the lights turned low and the television off, both looked forward to a quiet and peaceful night. It had been a hectic tour, and Tarah was relieved that it would end in four weeks.

"I know. Good question," Jimmy called over his shoulder. "Hey, I found something you might like, it's nice and mellow."

A smile lit up Tarah's face when a familiar song filled the room. It was from the same Alice in Chains CD that they had first kissed to almost two years earlier. Jimmy sat beside her on the couch and they shared a smile. Tarah instinctively snuggled up to him. She closed her eyes and pushed all her worries away. She didn't want to think about the rushed pace of the next few weeks or the upcoming holiday season. Tarah only focused on that moment and how happy she was to have one consistent thing in her life.

"Who knew how much everything would change after that night in my apartment?" Tarah stared at the diamond that sparkled on her hand as she felt Jimmy's arms pulling her closer to him. "Who knew we'd be engaged someday?"

"I think I did," Jimmy admitted, and Tarah looked up and into his face. He gave her slow grin. "Seriously."

"No you didn't," Tarah teased. "You probably thought I was another notch on your bedpost."

"Yes, Tarah." He nodded and rolled his eyes. "This was all part of my elaborate plan to get you in the sack. It just got *way* outta hand."

"I see that." She gave him a quick kiss. "So much has changed since then. Some things were good and some were really bad." The words caught in her throat as she thought about Wendy. "You know it's almost a year since she died," Tarah said softly, but didn't even want to say her friend's name. She wasn't sure why, but it hurt more when the word *Wendy* flowed through her lips. Tarah felt Jimmy giving her a tight squeeze, and she took a deep breath. "I don't know how I'm going to be able to survive the anniversary of that day. I was thinking earlier that it was around this time last year I first found out that she was being abused. There was so much time she was out of my life, and I didn't even know why. I thought she was mad at me. I thought she hated me because I was with William."

"Baby, how could you've known?" Jimmy said in a matter-of-fact way. "No one knew. She didn't want you to know—that's why she wasn't in your life. She was probably embarrassed and ashamed."

"I know."

"Listen, I have an idea," Jimmy said as he slowly turned to Tarah. Looking into her eyes, his face was very serious. "Why don't we get married during the holidays?"

"Jimmy, I don't know—"

"Come on, do you want to spend the rest of your life always associating the holidays with misery and something so horrible?" Jimmy said, his eyes searching her face. "Tarah, it doesn't have to be that way. I'm sorry about what happened with Wendy, and I know it completely broke your heart, but *we're* still alive. And after that really bad panic attack you had on New Year's Eve last year, I … I just think life is way too short. So what are we waiting for? We know we want to be together. So let's just do it, Tarah, let's get married."

"But we didn't plan anything," Tarah said, as her mind raced. "We can't just throw a wedding together in a month."

"Baby, let's just elope." Jimmy shook his head. "Who cares? Unless you want the big extravaganza that the media will be chasing people around and asking questions about, then what difference does it make? It's *our* day and it's about *us*. And when all is said and done, it's not about what dress you wear or what kind of fucking cake we feed everyone, it's just about us. It's our fucking day, and I personally don't feel a need to share it with many people when practically everyone told us that we should wait because we're apparently too young. I don't need the grief and neither do you."

Tarah thought about his words and slowly agreed with him. "You're right. My brother is the only one who was cool about it." In the days since their surprise engagement, most people in both families had casually commented on how there was no rush to tie the knot. The couple felt that people were making the unfair assumption that they really didn't know what was going on or how they felt about one another.

"Then your brother and his girlfriend will be the only people who know. We'll bring them with us and no one else," Jimmy suggested. Tarah knew that her fiancé would've preferred his family be at the wedding, but he was very upset that they were all underestimating his feelings and dedication to Tarah. Even Jimmy's mother had recently commented to him during a phone conversation, that marriage was a lot of work. To that, Jimmy calmly informed his mother that he had not only lived with Tarah for close to two years, but they'd been through some major highs and lows together. Although he hadn't gone into any further explanation, Tarah knew that someone with no real loyalty to her would have bailed long ago. They were together every day; he'd seen Tarah through everything from her best friend's death to her own frightening panic attack that followed. It was actually quite insulting to assume that their age automatically made them ignorant and naïve.

"Okay," Tarah agreed. "Then that's what we'll do."

They discussed the details late into the night, and Tarah called her brother early the next morning to share the news with him. "I know it's the holidays, Bobby, but we'd really like you to be there with us."

"Wow, on New Year's Eve?" He seemed hesitant. "Are you sure you don't want to tell anyone else?"

"Yup," Tarah insisted. "You were the only completely supportive person in either of our families. We can just say we're going on vacation together and then come back married."

"And you don't mind if Vanessa comes with us?"

"Not at all," Tarah said, and smiled to herself. "I actually assumed she would. You can bring Caitlin, too."

"No, that's fine. I'll see if mom will take care of her for a few days," Bobby replied. "Well, if you two are sure that this is what you want to do, then sign me up."

"It is." Tarah went on to explain how Jimmy suggested that it'd be a way to make the holiday season a positive time again, rather than a constant reminder of Wendy's death.

"I agree," Bobby replied, and Tarah could hear Caitlin doing something between a chant and singing in the background. "And if you two are ready, then I think you should just do it. It's like I said before, I'm probably the last person who should be giving you advice on marriage, but it's pretty clear that you're a good match, so I'll definitely be there. I'll talk to Vanessa about it later today when we meet for lunch."

"Thanks." Tarah felt light when she got off the phone. It was really going to happen; she was getting married!

The tour continued, but she was relieved when it was finally come to an end. Although Tarah certainly enjoyed being on stage, she wasn't as enthusiastic about the hectic pace and the constant technical issues. There were a few shows where the lead singer for the other band was unable to perform because he was too messed up on heroin to function. The press were told he had a really bad flu. Everyone in the inner circle knew the truth.

The band had a meeting with Peter Sampson a few days after the tour ended. He wanted to know how the members of Fire felt about doing an acoustic CD featuring some of their popular songs. "A lot of artists are putting out either live or acoustic CDs in the last few years, and the fans seem to like it. I know you have some other stuff you've been working on, but maybe we can put that aside, release a live CD, then work on more songs in the meantime and release the double CD later next year. Then you'll officially be finished with your contract and we can renegotiate."

"Wow, that happened fast," Eddie spoke up, something he would never have done when the band first started out. "Where did the time go?"

"You guys have been working like dogs," Peter said with a smile on his face. "I've got to say that when I saw your band play in bars back in Thorton, I knew you had something different. I knew you'd be a success."

"Thank you," William replied for them all. "Thanks for taking a chance on us."

Of course, Fire had been a great investment for FUTA. CD sales alone were fantastic, and it was expected that things were only going to get better. If the band agreed to release an acoustic CD, it would be followed by their *own* tour, much to Tarah's relief. It would just be across Canada but Peter seemed pretty encouraged that they'd be able to pull it off. Their morale was good and the band agreed to start work on their next CD immediately after the holidays. It wouldn't be too difficult since they weren't required to write much new material, just essentially do a softer version of their original songs. It's something they'd experimented with a few times while on tour, and the fans loved it.

Even though the band was taking a break, they continued to receive media attention. This time it was over William and Lindsey's relationship. People seemed to have an increased interest in the couple since Lindsey signed a contract with a major European designer, pushing her even more into the public eye. Tarah felt that having a rock star boyfriend seemed to be more of an accessory to Lindsey than anything else, and when she shared her opinion with Jimmy, he agreed.

"Will's a smart guy, he'll figure it out eventually," he insisted. "But I'm not gonna lie to you, I've been hearing a lot of stuff about them."

"What do you mean?"

Jimmy shrugged. "I heard they're both cheating on each other. But I don't know if that's true. That doesn't sound like something either of them would do. Especially Will. But that's what the rumor mill is saying."

Even though they had broken up long ago, Tarah still cared a great deal for William. He'd been a friend to both her and Jimmy over the last couple of years, and the last thing she wanted to see was for him to have another girl hurt him like she had. Especially if the circumstance involved another guy—that would just kill him. However, when she suggested talking to William about the rumors, Jimmy shook his head no.

"Baby, don't get involved. I know you care, but it's not your place to say anything. Besides, it's probably just a bunch of bullshit someone is spreading around. You know how these fucking losers in the media are, it's always about who can report the best story. And *story* is the keyword here."

Tarah reluctantly agreed and quickly pushed the thought from her head.

The holidays snuck up on them and Tarah spent a quiet day at home on the anniversary of Wendy's death. She shed a few tears but promised herself that rather than focusing on her brutal murder, she'd instead think about the good times they'd shared. In the end, wasn't that all that mattered? But it did make her see even more clearly, how important every day really was and how much she wanted to marry Jimmy on New Year's Eve. Who knew how much time they all had? Life was way too short, as Jimmy pointed out. They couldn't take a single thing for granted, even their careers.

"Who knows?" Jimmy pondered on Christmas Eve as they sat alone in his family's living room. "Who's to say that anyone will care about Fire next year? It's just one CD to the next; the next one could be on top of the charts or completely bomb. You never know how things will go over. We just gotta keep going and appreciate what we have now."

"Agreed." Tarah took a sip of eggnog and looked up at the sparkling Christmas tree. Jimmy's parents were sleeping, and his sister and husband were expected to arrive for Christmas dinner the following evening. "I hope it does well though. Do you think we can pull off a whole acoustic CD?"

"I do." Jimmy nodded and took a drink of beer. "I really think so. You've got an amazing voice and that works with acoustic. If you were some moron on the charts who can't even sing, then I'd be worried, but you've got the pipes and the emotions for that kind of thing."

"I hope so," Tarah said, and smiled. Jimmy leaned in and kissed her.

"Hey, wanna have sex on my parents' couch?" His eyes sparkled. "We've never done that."

"No, let's try to contain ourselves for one night. I somehow don't think I could really get in the mood knowing your parents are in the same house."

"Whatever." Jimmy shrugged. "They had so much eggnog tonight, they're probably dead to the world anyway."

Tarah glanced toward her ring. "We should save our energy for the honeymoon."

Jimmy laughed. "Baby, I think we've been on our honeymoon for like two years now."

No one thought it was strange or unusual that Tarah and Jimmy had invited Bobby and Vanessa along on their trip to Vegas the following week. In fact, Jimmy's mother made a comment on how it'd probably be an exciting place to welcome in the New Year. His dad just told them to have fun, and Jillian appeared to quickly forget all about the trip. In fact, she spent most of the holidays talking about her life and how well her therapy was going. She'd gained some weight since she was hospitalized earlier that year, but still wasn't exactly breaking the scales.

"I love my sister, but fuck!" Jimmy complained as they left the day after Christmas. "The whole holiday was about her. We put out a new CD and toured North America this year, but who gives a fuck? Not to mention the fact that we got engaged. Not that anyone cares about that." He spoke bitterly as they left Thorton and headed back to Toronto.

"Honey, don't worry about it. At least your sister is doing better. I actually saw her eating Christmas dinner and some candy." Tarah tried to be positive.

"Yeah, I know." Jimmy seemed to calm down. "But did you notice Jillian went to the bathroom right after she ate. My parents are in denial, but I think she went and threw up her food."

"I hope not." Tarah spoke honestly. "I really hope you're wrong."

"Me too," Jimmy replied. "Me too."

Tarah sat in silence and started to wonder if Jimmy's sister had always been the center of attention because of the eating disorder. It had never occurred to her before, but maybe that explained some of Jimmy's issues and attitudes. Sometimes she thought that all the little things that hurt him so much only emphasized more to her just how much he needed her love. Maybe relationships were really about healing all the hurts of your life with someone who loved you unconditionally.

The days flew by, and the next thing Tarah knew they were all on a plane to Vegas. Everything had been booked and planned in advance. Jimmy had rented them the honeymoon suite at one of the nicer hotels, also paying for an equally extravagant room for Vanessa and Bobby. The two couples were giddy and excited as they arrived in the lobby. Tarah was happy to see her brother having fun for a change; the last few years had been hell for him and he really deserved a nice vacation even though it was only for a couple of days.

Both couples settled into their rooms, and later that night went to dinner and had some drinks before returning to the hotel. After spending a few hours with her brother and his girlfriend, Tarah was convinced that the two made a great couple and told him when they were alone.

"You're just saying that because you're all excited and happy about getting married," Bobby insisted. "You want everyone to be in love."

"Maybe a little bit." Tarah laughed. "But I like Vanessa, she's really nice and I guess I'd just like to see everything work out for the two of you. After our parents were divorced, I never thought either of us would have a normal relationship."

"Well, we don't automatically have to follow into their footsteps," Bobby replied. "I guess I sort of did with Sara, but I was also younger."

"Oh, please!" Tarah said as she cringed. "Don't say too young to know better or something like that, I've heard enough of those comments to last a lifetime."

"Well, it's like I said before," Bobby insisted. "No one else knows what is right for you and Jimmy, *except* you and Jimmy. And to be honest, on some level I knew it was the wrong move when I married Sara. I just didn't want to face it. I don't think that's the case with you two. Jimmy is clearly insanely crazy about you and you're just … insane," he teased, and Tarah playfully punched him.

The next day, Tarah woke up with knots in her stomach. She was so nervous about the wedding she couldn't even imagine how scared she would've been if they'd had a large function rather than eloped. Jimmy was already up and around and quickly jumped on their king-sized bed when he saw Tarah's eyes open. "Good morning, it's your last day of being single. So if you want to do anything wild and crazy, I'd suggest you get it out of your system now," he joked. "Otherwise, Tarah Kiersey, tomorrow you'll wake up as Tarah Groome. I don't know why you want to be, but, hey, what the fuck do I know?"

Tarah laughed. "You know plenty." She leaned forward and gave him a slow, gentle kiss. "I love you, and I can't wait to get married today."

"Me too," Jimmy whispered.

The rest of the day seemed to run in fast forward. The couple rushed to get ready, after meeting Bobby and Vanessa for a late breakfast. The wedding was scheduled for two in the afternoon. Just before they left the hotel, Tarah sat on the edge of the tub, alone in the bathroom. She closed her eyes and thought of Wendy. "I wish you were with us," she whispered and stood up for one quick look into the mirror. Neither she nor Jimmy wanted a traditional wedding in any way, and both decided to wear something nice, if not over the top. She wore a long, white, strapless gown that resembled a summer dress rather than something that would be worn for a wedding, however that's what she wanted. It looked perfect on her petit figure, and after a few tanning sessions had given her a beautiful glow. Vanessa had helped Tarah put her hair up with a collection of beautiful antique-looking hairclips. Noticing that the bride to be was having difficulty putting on her makeup because of a shaking hand, Vanessa graciously offered to help Tarah with that too.

"You look beautiful!" Vanessa insisted after they were finished, and Tarah thanked her for the help.

"I don't think I could've done it without you. I'm such a mess." Tarah sniffed. "I just can't believe it's happening today."

"Well, for what it's worth," Vanessa said, putting the finishing touches on Tarah's hair before adding hairspray. "You clearly are more than ready to get married. I know Bobby's said that people have been giving you and Jimmy a hard time about being engaged so young, but what do they know? Really?"

Their eyes met in the mirror that was before them, and Tarah fought back the tears. "If you didn't love him, you'd never be this emotional. And if you weren't ready, this would be when you'd be questioning the decision."

"Oh, now that part I'm sure about," Tarah insisted, and smiled. "And thank you, Vanessa. For being here today with us and just helping me keep together."

"Don't worry about it." She gave Tarah a quick hug. "Now, we've got to meet the boys in my room."

Tarah and Vanessa found Jimmy and Bobby drinking a beer and talking about hockey. "I guess this is how they get ready." Vanessa grinned as they entered the room, and Jimmy's eyes met with Tarah's. He was wearing a suit and tie and looked handsome. She thought back to his sister's wedding, two years earlier.

"Perfect." Bobby jumped up. "Vanessa and I will meet you downstairs, guys." He said as if he sensed they needed a moment alone.

"Okay," Tarah said, and watched them leave, closing the door behind them.

"You look beautiful." Jimmy walked across the room and reached for her hand. "So, are you ready?"

"Yes." Tarah felt tears filling her eyes.

"Are you sure?" A smile crossed his face. "Sure we're not too young?"

Tarah began to laugh and blinked her tears away. "No, not at all."

"Perfect." Jimmy squeezed her hand. "So, let's go get married."

"Sounds great." Tarah nodded as she continued to look into his eyes, before they left the room.

Chapter Forty

▼

"My own daughter got married and I wasn't even invited to the wedding!" Tarah listened to her mother sob over the phone. This was the third call she and Jimmy had made to family members, after the media broke the story. Apparently someone had recognized the famous couple and overheard them discussing wedding plans earlier that day. Jimmy and Tarah had barely exchanged rings when the story leaked. Now they were doing damage control. But it was clearly too late.

"Mom, it was kind of last minute," Tarah lied, exchanging frustrated looks with Jimmy. He had just finished explaining to his parents, then his sister, the same story. Neither of them confessed that the trip was planned around their wedding, but attempted to make it sound like an impulsive decision. Not that this fact improved the situation at all.

"It's still hurtful." Her mother continued to sob. "I only have one daughter and I didn't even see her getting married. I hope at least your brother took some pictures." Bobby had not taken photos. It hadn't occurred to any of them. They only had one picture that was included with their wedding package. Not that it really mattered to Tarah. She was just relieved that her brother was happy to go along with their story of not planning the wedding, so that both families were spared more anguish.

"I was so nervous that I don't remember," Tarah said, and thought that was a reasonable answer. "It doesn't matter mom, it's not a big deal." Thankfully, the media hadn't found them until after the wedding was finished. It was a special day, and she already felt discouraged by the fact that her celebration dinner with Jimmy, Bobby, and Vanessa, had to be cancelled at the last minute so they could make the dreaded phone calls. On top of everything, they still had to check in with Maggie to give their manager a heads up.

"Well, Tarah, I'm very disappointed in you." Her mother sighed loudly on the phone. "What about Jimmy's family? How do they feel about this? You know, I haven't even met these people, and yet our children are married. And you *are* barely older than children."

"You'll meet them soon." Tarah ignored the last remark and nervously played with the phone cord. She hadn't even thought of introducing the two families. It would be a dreaded event. At least, she considered, they could both discuss how disappointed they were in their children for getting married too young *and* in secret. They shared those opinions.

"Were they as upset as I am?" Claire Kiersey pushed on.

"Yeah, especially Jimmy's mom." Tarah hesitated to add fuel to the fire. Jimmy's mother had said many of the same things as her own, except she added how she feared they'd be divorced in no time since they were so young and inexperienced with life. It made she and Jimmy want to scream. Jillian simply cried hysterically and insisted that the couple should have shared their special day with their families. Tarah was surprised that both Jimmy's mother and sister seemed insistent that they remarry again in a church. It was unlikely.

"Tarah, all this pain you brought on two families. Was it really worth it?" The words seemed to sit in the air and stare into Tarah's eyes. Had she committed a murder, it seemed unlikely that the response could've been less favorable.

"Well mom, I didn't really think about how *our* decision was going to affect *your* life." Tarah felt anger rise from her stomach. "And I'm not going to apologize for what I've done. I love Jimmy, and I'm glad I married him. I don't care if the wedding was in a church or if our families were there, I just wanted to do what was in my heart to do. And if you can't understand or respect that, then I'm sorry. Good night." And with that, Tarah hung up the phone and burst into tears. Jimmy rushed to her side.

"This is supposed to be the most wonderful day of my life, and everyone's trying to ruin it." She felt his arm around her shoulders as he pulled her close. "But yet, if we had gotten married with our families, they would've given us shit about getting married young or not getting married in a church or whatever. I feel like we just can't win."

"Baby, don't listen to all this crap," Jimmy firmly insisted. "Don't let them take this day away from you. It's still very special regardless of the media or our families. We did what we wanted to do and that was to get married. They'll all just have to learn to live with our decision." He hesitated for a moment. "I still believe we did the right thing and wouldn't go back in time to change a thing," he insisted.

The next two calls Tarah made were to her father and John. Both were much more happy with the news of their wedding than anyone else had been. Finally, they called William who also seemed sincerely happy for the couple and promised to share the news with the rest of their band. It was the boost that Tarah needed to get out of her funk, and by ten that night, the couple was in bed and not giving either of their families a second thought.

Two days later, it was time to return home. The year of 1996 had officially begun and Fire was scheduled to work on their acoustic CD later that same week. In the meantime, Maggie had scheduled a meeting with herself, Tarah, and Jimmy. She wanted to talk about their wedding and the media coverage it had received. The couple had returned home on the second to learn that their elopement was big news and the reactions were mixed. Although Tarah understood the surprise, she couldn't help but feel that this was something personal that she didn't want to share with the world. Of course, those were the kinds of stories that the media jumped on. It was human nature that people wanted to know about stuff that wasn't any of their business; Tarah understood that as well.

"People absolutely love the fact that you two eloped, especially on New Year's Eve." Maggie appeared to be more excited about the attention the newlyweds were receiving, rather than the happy news itself. That didn't surprise either Jimmy or Tarah. "It's so romantic. People love you as a couple. There was an unofficial poll done online the other day and it seems that 68 percent of people feel that you make the perfect couple. Very sweet."

"Very weird," Jimmy insisted, and Tarah noted that his wedding ring seemed to glitter in the sunlight that poured through the nearby window. "Why do people care one way or another? I mean, it happened, but so what? Slow day for news, as they say?"

"I guess people just love the happily-ever-after stories." Maggie sat forward in her chair and smiled. "That and reports of pregnancy and divorce."

"One is definitely not like the others," Jimmy said with a grin.

"So, do you have an official statement other than to confirm that you're married?" Maggie grabbed a notepad and made eye contact with Tarah than Jimmy. "Anything you'd like to pass on to your fans."

"How about that they should get their own lives so that ours seem less fascinating?" Jimmy said, and continued to grin. "'Cause seriously, people get married every day."

Maggie shook her head with a huge smile on her lips, and she began to write. "The couple are happy to confirm that their marriage took place on New Year's Eve and want to thank fans for their love and support." She sat down the pen and turned to Tarah. "That sounds a little better than what he had to say."

Fire gathered together a few days later to work on the songs for the new CD. Throughout the holidays, when Jimmy and Tarah were getting married, apparently William had been playing around with a few ideas. "I worked on some of our old songs that I felt translated well into an acoustic version. I also started a couple of songs on my own, but I might need some input." Of course, although the band was together in the same room, it didn't mean that everyone was involved in the songwriting process. Michael and Eddie quietly chatted in the corner, while William, Jimmy, and Tarah spent the rest of the day working on the new material. Eventually, as the day turned to night, William's brother and the band's drummer said they were going for a drink.

Much to Tarah's surprise, William looked irritated and snapped at the two. "What the fuck man? We're here, as usual, doing all the work while you guys just screw around. You don't mind taking the credit when the CDs come out, but you don't even fucking help us write the songs." His hazel eyes darted through both Michael and Eddie. It was clear that neither of them had expected that reaction from William, and they stood for a long moment in silence. "Like seriously, I don't think you guys should take any credit for these songs if you don't write them. All along we add you to the list of people who are writing with us, but you aren't helping at all."

"Ah, sorry, man," Eddie finally managed, and Michael remained silent.

"You know what? Just go." William's voice was much louder than normal. "Get the fuck out of here if you don't want to be here." He pointed to Jimmy, Tarah, and himself. "We'll do all the work, as usual." And with that, he turned as if to dismiss them. Eddie and Michael took advantage of this reaction to rush out of the door.

"Lazy assholes." William looked exhausted, with one hand rubbing his face. "I'm just getting fed up with this crap. They never help us, but usually they at least look like they're paying attention to what we're saying. This time they didn't even fucking bother to give us that courtesy."

"You're right, man," Jimmy agreed, and slowly began to nod, glancing at Tarah who was still stunned by William's reaction. It was rare to see her ex show any signs of a temper. She couldn't help but to wonder what was really going on. Maybe Michael had done something else to irritate him, and he had simply used this as an excuse to lash out.

"Anyway." William shook his head. "Sorry about that, guys, just a lot on my mind, and I don't have any patience today."

Jimmy silently nodded, and Tarah wondered if all the rumors about him and Lindsey being on the verge of breaking up were true. Even at that, there was a different look in his eye, one she didn't recognize.

"Is it something you need to talk about?" Tarah approached the subject cautiously, not wanting to be the victim of his wrath if she could help it.

However, at the same time, she wondered if maybe he had made this last comment in the hope of being coaxed to discuss whatever was going on.

"No, Tarah." William sighed loudly and seemed to regain his energy and enthusiasm. "That's fine, I just needed to get that off my chest. Thanks though." A few minutes later the three were back to work.

Things were slowly starting to come together. They were booked to go into the studio the following week to see what they could come up with and to lay the tracks down. Unlike the first and even the second time they recorded, the band would have sufficient time to do whatever needed to be done. Tarah still hoped it didn't take long. She wanted to get in and out of the studio and be finished with it. The acoustic CD didn't really excite her very much, but vocally she felt it was a challenge and a chance to showcase her voice. It was a great opportunity, although slightly boring compared to the songs they had already written for what now appeared to be a double CD to be recorded during the latter part of 1996.

Tarah wasn't sure if it was due to William lashing out at Eddie and his brother during that one afternoon, but there was much more tension during the recording process for that particular CD. Snide remarks were made by Michael, and for a change they weren't being directed at Tarah. Over all, there was clearly a whole new level of tension between the band members that had even surpassed the days when Tarah and William first broke up. It was as if all the time the band spent together was finally becoming too much to bear. Suddenly, everyone's tolerance level was at an all-time low. Morale wasn't good, and Tarah had no idea how Fire was going to tour during that spring, as Peter had insisted they would.

"I just can't see it working out," Tarah would later tell Jimmy as they drove away from the studio and headed back to their apartment. "William is super edgy these days, that's not like him."

"Something is clearly going on behind the scenes that we aren't aware of." Jimmy pointed out the obvious. "This ain't like Will. He wasn't even this bad when he found out that we were fooling around behind his back."

"You make it sound like we were having a ton of sex," Tarah said, and rolled her eyes. "We were just kissing a little bit."

"Yes, while on top of one another and trying to remove each other's clothes," Jimmy added, and winked at her. "That's called fooling around, Tarah. You can pretty it up all you want, but there was at least once that we could've easily crossed that line and you know it."

She didn't disagree.

The CD was finished a few weeks later, and the band decided to call it *Play 2*. Once again, Jimmy was heavily involved in the production side of things. Considering less than half of the material was new, Tarah was surprised that they had spent so much time in the studio. The entire band had seemed to have more than its normal share of bad days, and finally the group decided to take some time off. Even William seemed to mellow out by the time the project was done, leaving Tarah to assume that his relationship with Lindsay must've been in good standing. The entertainment news and tabloids were quiet during the end of January of 96. The media focused on the announcement of Lisa Marie Presley's divorce from Michael Jackson. However, the longer that Tarah and Jimmy were in the industry, the more immune they became to these types of stories. They didn't have time for tabloid gossip.

Tarah occasionally talked to John, who was awaiting his own wedding that would take place in June of that year. The couple had changed their minds a few times but finally settled on a date and time, although at one point John admitted that Jimmy's idea to elope wasn't looking so bad. "There is so much work to preparing a wedding," John complained. "I can see how people get lost in the details and forget why they're getting married in the first place."

"Yeah, that's pretty much how Jimmy felt when we eloped," Tarah admitted. "And although we pissed off a lot of people at the time, they eventually got over it." Although not completely. Tarah and her mother were still barely speaking. Both sets of parents had arranged to finally meet a week after the wedding; unfortunately the couple wasn't available due to their busy schedule in the studio. Tarah suspected that it was probably a bitching session anyway. As Jimmy had joked at the time, the parents probably spent the whole time talking about how inconsiderate they were to marry in secret, not to mention the fact that they were too young to even consider the step in the first place.

"Elizabeth really wants a nice, traditional wedding and I want her to be happy," John said. "But don't think I haven't mentioned the elopement idea to her at least once or twice." He laughed. "It's not working though."

Tarah noticed that her relationship with Jillian became strained after the New Year's Eve nuptials, but she had developed a close friendship with Bobby's girlfriend. The two women talked on the phone regularly, and Vanessa confided to Tarah that she thought she and Bobby would be moving in together later that same year.

"I couldn't be happier to hear that." Tarah smiled on the other end of the phone line. "You guys make a great couple."

As February slowly came to a close, marking the two-year point in her relationship with Jimmy, Tarah was shocked when she went on the Internet one night to learn that William was in the center of a scandal. Stunned, Tarah reread the words in front of her twice and even looked up the story on another entertainment site. It reported the same thing. Rising from her chair, she found Jimmy in the kitchen making a grilled cheese sandwich and eating a bag of chips.

"Hey, babe, want something to eat?"

"No." Tarah shook her head and watched his eyes study her face carefully.

"Okay, what's up?" he asked suspiciously.

"I just read something that really surprised me." Tarah couldn't even believe the words she was about to say. "I was online and about to go play my game when I saw a story about William."

"William?" Jimmy raised his eyebrows. "What did he do this time?"

"According to the site I was on," Tarah said, then hesitated for a moment. "He was dumped by Lindsey."

"That doesn't surprise me."

"He was dumped by Lindsey because she caught him cheating on New Year's Eve," Tarah said, and watched Jimmy's dumbfound expression.

"You're fucking with me, right?" Jimmy flipped his sandwich, which was now turning black and turned off the burner. "You can't be serious."

Tarah didn't reply. She didn't have to, because Jimmy could see that she wasn't joking.

Chapter Forty-one

▼

Every website on the Internet, every channel on television, and all the tabloids on newsstands were talking about the Lindsey and William story. And they all painted the same picture. Lindsey was the innocent victim who walked into a bedroom on New Year's Eve and caught her cheating man in the act. She had bravely held back from announcing their breakup for the next two months, but somehow, a mysterious and unnamed source leaked the story, and now Lindsey tearfully confessed her side. William was nowhere to be found, and Maggie insisted that the members of Fire make no comment. Not that any of them would. Regardless of any tension within the band, in the end, they were still loyal to one another.

Reporters tried though. Tarah and Jimmy were constantly harassed when caught leaving the couple's apartment building. Tabloid programs were only a minor inconvenience in her life previously, but William's ties to a supermodel changed that for the entire band. Suddenly she and Jimmy were caught in a huddle of reporters each time they walked out their door; at times Tarah felt like she could barely breathe, let alone move. It was overwhelming and frustrating. Her heart would race uncontrollably, and she began to fear having another bad panic attack. How did movie stars and major celebrities live like this every day? How could you live a normal life when you were constantly stalked? No wonder William had disappeared. Tarah wondered where he had gone and hoped he wouldn't be spotted.

Jimmy was hardly calm over the matter. He'd told more than one reporter to fuck off, especially after seeing how they attempted to bully the answers out of Tarah. "You guys are fucking losers," he hollered at them one day. "Get a real fucking job and leave us the fuck alone." This appeared on one of the tabloid programs that same night. Of course, Jimmy's words consisted of almost one long beep as they attempted to cover the profanity.

"Fucking trash," he said one day after they got in their car. "No wonder William took off to wherever. Who needs this?"

"Yeah, but he shouldn't *have* to take off." Tarah shook her head as she watched the reporters trail behind them as they drove away. "That's the problem. It wouldn't matter if he stood out here and calmly answered their questions, they'd never leave him alone until another big story came up."

"Fucking savages." Jimmy frowned as they headed onto the street. "It's pathetic. She made William sound like an asshole, and we all know that he isn't like that. I mean if it's even true that he did cheat on her, it's probably the only bad thing he did in his life. And chances are she's no angel either. Trust me, my sister was in the modeling world, it's pretty fucking trashy, no matter how glamorous they make it look on the outside."

"It really makes you wonder." Tarah shook her head. "How many celebrities do we think are total pricks because of a situation like this one. I mean, look at William; he's genuinely a good guy. He always has been, and yet this one incident completely crucifies him in the media. Anyone who didn't know him would think he's a complete asshole and he's not. But they only want to hear one side of the story."

"Well, we could tell them otherwise but it doesn't matter." Jimmy shook his head. "They aren't going to sell papers or whatever the fuck they're selling by making William look like a hero and Lindsey like a skank, although I'm starting to think that she just might be one after all."

"That isn't necessarily true either." Tarah took a deep breath. "But I don't for a second believe that the story was accidentally leaked. She wanted it out there; I'm sure of it. Look at all the attention she's getting. It's insane."

It took a few more days for the story to blow over, and eventually the reporters disappeared. Something else had occurred in the entertainment world and all was forgotten. No one knew where William was, so Tarah was surprised to find him at her door a week after the story broke. He looked tired and miserable and wore a scruffy beard; it was a side of him that Tarah had never seen before. Even Jimmy looked surprised to see their guest.

"Holy fuck, man." Jimmy ushered him in their apartment. "Get the fuck in here before any of those losers track you down." He closed the door behind him, and William gave them both a small smile.

"Thanks." He nodded. "Thanks for not saying anything to the press either."

"Of course not." Tarah felt her forehead wrinkle, and she gave him a sympathetic look. "We'd never do that."

"I know, but it's pretty hard to get away from reporters sometimes."

"No shit, man." Jimmy shook his head. "They were fucking insane. I almost decked one at the end of it."

"It's their job, I guess." William spoke fairly. "I can't really take the high road this time."

"You guys go sit down." Tarah pointed toward the living room. "I'll make a pot of coffee."

"We don't have any, babe." Jimmy replied with a shrug. "Sorry."

"I thought we had some left." Tarah stopped mid-step.

Jimmy shook his head no. "I kind of forget to pick up some." Glancing at William, as he sat on the couch, Jimmy then added. "But, hey, I'll run out and get some for us. You guys, talk." He gave Tarah a pleading glance and rushed out the door. She knew that Jimmy wasn't interested in getting involved in William's problems, but clearly he wanted to talk about them with someone. That person would be Tarah.

"So, where've you been?" Tarah walked across the room and sat beside him on the couch. "You certainly did a great job of hiding. They were all going crazy looking for you."

"Our management company provided a house to hide in for a few days." He grinned. "It was out of town where no one would expect to find me. It was great. I had time away from everyone and everything to think."

"I can understand that." Tarah nodded calmly. "Did it help?"

"A little," William said, but his eyes were full of sadness. "I realized that I was getting too caught up in the celebrity world. That's just not me. All the parties and the fake shit. Lindsey owning purses that are worth more than what I used to make in a month when I was a mechanic; it's nuts how people live."

"I agree," Tarah said softly. "I mean, all that stuff is nice but it's extravagant. It isn't necessary."

"That's for sure." William looked uncomfortable as he glanced around the apartment. "So, I've been doing a lot of thinking, and I guess I owe you an apology."

"For what?" Tarah said, caught off guard by his remark. Was he about to drop some bombshell on her from their days together? Was he about to confess having some sneaky affair behind her back? If so, she really would've been happier to not know, but as it turned out, that wasn't it.

"When we broke up, I really looked down at you because of the Jimmy situation. And I'm not going to lie, I didn't even know for sure what had taken place but regardless, I assumed the worst of the two of you" William said honestly. "I wasn't being fair, especially not to you. I didn't understand how anyone could do something like that to someone they loved. So I stubbornly assumed the worst of you without even asking questions or talking it through. I just threw you out and washed my hands of the whole situation."

"Given the situation," Tarah jumped into the conversation, "I can understand that. I don't think I'd be so calm if the tables were turned."

"But I should've at least let you tell me what happened. At least talked to you about it, but instead I acted like an arrogant jerk and just sent you packing. I had you moved out within twenty-four hours like we hadn't been together at all, and that wasn't right." William took a deep breath. "I owed you more than that."

"Not really," Tarah disagreed. "I think I would've felt much worse if you had been kind to me at that point. I didn't deserve it."

"You deserved a chance to explain yourself." His eyes met with hers and he fell silent. She realized that he was now giving her the opportunity to say whatever needed to be said. "I realize it's been two years and a lot has changed in both our lives since then, but if you want to or have to say anything to me. Then this is the time to do it."

"It doesn't really matter now," she insisted, but judging from the look in his eyes, Tarah felt like he needed to hear the words much more than she felt the need to say them. "I didn't mean to do it. And I hadn't even looked at Jimmy that way before, that's the strange part. It happened when you went to your aunt's funeral." She watched him slowly nodding. "Jimmy dropped in to get you to check out a CD but you weren't home. We listened to it together, and for some reason we started to kiss." Tarah hesitated and was surprised by the difficulty she was feeling in telling this story, even though so much time had passed. "That's all that happened. I was shocked and couldn't believe what I had done. I hated myself for kissing someone else behind your back, and I hated myself for hurting Jimmy, because I knew he had real feelings for me too. I just couldn't seem to win at that point. "

"Anyway, I thought that'd be the end of it but it wasn't. There was a crazy attraction between Jimmy and I that was unexplainable." Tarah could see that William was taking in her every word, and he nodded in understanding. His eyes were full of vulnerability and sadness. "And I hated myself but I just couldn't fight it. And you and I weren't getting along, and I think we both didn't want to face that fact that things were coming to an end with us. I mean, we had just moved in together but the problems weren't going away. They couldn't be ignored. But that's not an excuse for anything." She rushed forward. "I still deeply regret not sitting down and talking to you about it."

"I didn't give you a chance" William insisted.

"No, I mean before that day. I should've talked to you right away, after it happened" Tarah said, staring at her hands. "Not that *anything* really happened with us, seriously. I know you probably don't believe that, but it's true."

"I believe you." William's voice was quiet. "I wish I could say the same in my situation, but I can't. I couldn't even lie about it, not that I would. I just think there can't be anything more repulsive in the world than walking in on the person you're in a relationship with and seeing them having sex with someone else."

Tarah remained quiet. So that fact *was* true.

"But that's what happened," William said, scratching his beard. "Something I never thought I'd ever do. Cheat on someone. Never thought I'd do that."

"Why did you?"

"Because Lindsey and I weren't getting along, and I wasn't dealing with it, just like I didn't deal with us not getting along.." William leaned forward on the couch as he spoke. "Because I thought she was cheating on me. In fact, I'm sure she was cheating. Not to say two wrongs make a right. Because the girl who I was with that night, was someone I'd been attracted to for a long time and vice versa." He fell silent for a moment, then added, "And because I'm an ass."

"I don't think one mistake makes you an ass," Tarah insisted.

"Well, in the eyes of the public, it does." He referred to the many articles that had touched on the subject of his deception. "I'm just the typical dog in a band."

"That's not fair."

"Maybe."

Tarah gave him a sympathetic smile.

"So now, at the very least, I have to apologize to you for being so judgmental toward you when we broke up. I'm hardly in the position to judge anyone considering I did something much worse," William said, and Tarah thought she could've heard a pin drop on the floor the room was so quiet. "So please forgive me."

"I don't think you were wrong," Tarah insisted. "But it's water under the bridge, and I'd like to think we've passed all of that."

"Me too," William said, and fell silent for a moment. "I just have one question." With his head down, he turned his head and looked up at Tarah, his hazel eyes shining. "When do you stop hating yourself?"

Tarah gave him a sheepish smile and quietly replied, "Any day now."

By the time Jimmy returned with the coffee, William was gone, and Tarah was lost in her own thoughts.

"He didn't stick around for long," Jimmy commented as he sat a bag of groceries on the counter. "Or did I take longer than I thought?"

"A little of both." Tarah watched him unpack the items from the next room.

"So, what's the verdict?" Jimmy asked cautiously. She knew that his insistence that such things were none of his business lost out over his curiosity in that particular situation. "Did he tell you anything?"

"Yup. He told me that he did cheat on Lindsey, and she caught him. And they apparently weren't getting along for months. He thinks she might have cheated on him too." Tarah hesitated for a moment. "William feels horribly guilty, and they've been broken up since New Year's but wanted to keep it off the radar."

"Even from us?" Jimmy raised his eyebrows. "That's kind of weird."

"Yeah, I know." Tarah wrinkled her forehead. "The whole *situation* is kind of weird."

William slowly returned to the public eye but had few reporters bothering him. Most had moved on to other controversies. There were rumors that he had a secret girlfriend, but no one knew who it was or if it was even true. Had he gotten back together with Lindsey?

The band began promoting their new CD in March, working on a music video, doing interviews, and all the usual stuff. Meanwhile, Tarah and Jimmy decided to buy a house. A real estate agent was looking through the nicer areas of Toronto and Mississauga. When she asked if there were any specifics they sought out, neither really had an answer. Then Jimmy spoke up.

"I'd like to have a recording studio right in the house, but if that isn't doable, then we'll build one." He exchanged looks with Tarah, who wasn't surprised. The longer they worked in the industry, the more Jimmy talked of doing behind-the-scenes side of recording a CD. "Other than that, just a really big fucking house."

Tarah had no preference. She just wanted a house and to be away from living in an apartment building. "I hope I never live in anything but a house for the rest of my life," she insisted. "No more apartment. I don't care how luxurious or nice they are, it's just not the same as a house."

Fire's tour was due to start in May, and FUTA was still looking around to find another band to join them. Ticket sales began on a small scale with the band only playing venues that seemed pretty minor compared to what they had been doing, but that quickly changed. When another up-and-coming band joined the tour and ticket sales increased, many dates had to be rescheduled into stadiums that sat about three to four thousand. Peter said that their next CD and tour were sure to put them on a whole new level of success. Fire was moving up in the world.

"Not to say an acoustic CD isn't to be taken seriously," Peter reminded them. "But I'm just saying that it's the calm before the storm. Just hearing the material you want to put on the next CD, combined with the media attention and ticket sales now, I think you're on your way to the top."

It was exciting news, but scary at the same time. It was a great deal of pressure put on the entire band to make the next CD the absolute best they'd ever done. It was hard to predict how an audience would react to music, and they were still building their own loyal fan base. That combined with the competition in the music industry made it difficult for newcomers to establish their fans. It was one thing to reel them in, quite another to keep their interest.

Optimistic that their real estate agent was going to find Tarah and Jimmy a new home, the couple began to pack in April before their next tour was scheduled to begin. That way, they'd be on top of things in case a house was found at the last minute. During those hours of organizing their stuff, the newlyweds found many things that carried memories for them. It was a time to throw stuff out and start fresh in a new home. It was exciting and really made them see how far they'd come in a short couple of years. Usually they were just so busy with tours and everything else that neither really had time to sit down and think about what they could now afford. It was a whole new world.

And as they packed, Jimmy found himself reluctantly listening to Tarah's collection of 2Pac CDs. She'd developed a passion for the rapper's music after watching an intriguing and inspiring documentary about him on television. Tarah had a lot of respect for the man and wasn't shy about telling anyone who'd listen.

"Never thought I'd like it," Jimmy finally admitted one day. "But this guy's smart. Not my usual kind of music but he sort of stands out."

"2Pac has been through hell and back, and you gotta respect that." Tarah was insistent and felt that music was taking a shift in the latter part of the nineties. Even in the time they'd been involved in the industry, she'd seen big changes take place and was happy that Fire was still relevant with fans. Her own musical tastes were changing and she found there to be fewer and fewer artists who really grabbed her attention. Jimmy often joked that he could recite lyrics to any 2Pac or Bush song, because Tarah listened to both obsessively.

"There aren't many other bands that I like anymore," Tarah insisted. "There's way too much crap on the radio."

"And it's only gonna get worse, baby," Jimmy insisted. "The tide is turning, and we have to make sure that we turn with it."

CHAPTER FORTY-TWO

The tour for *Play 2* was relatively calm compared to what Fire had experienced with the previous one. There were fewer technical problems, everyone in the band seemed bonded together after the controversy with William, and their opening act was very mellow. In general, everything was going much smoother this time around. Although Tarah found the pace almost a little too slow for her liking, she couldn't deny that it was probably for the best that they all take it down a notch.

William continued to keep tight-lipped about his personal life. However, everyone from inside and outside the band were speculating that he was seeing the same girl he'd cheated on Lindsey with, but he refused to comment. Even his own brother had no idea what was going on. The only reason anyone was suspicious at all, was that he often disappeared when the band had a couple of consecutive days off. No one knew where he went or who he was with, but the entire situation gave Tarah an uneasy feeling, and she wasn't sure why.

"I bet he's back with Lindsey," Jimmy guessed one day. "Maybe he's just too embarrassed to admit it after everything that's happened."

"I don't know about that," Tarah said. "I've seen online that Lindsey is with someone else. Some guy from Europe who is apparently rich, I don't know the details though." Besides, Tarah didn't really think that William would restart a losing battle. It was pretty clear from their conversations that he now knew that the relationship was definitely over, so why would he bother going back?

Fire took a short break from the tour during June 1996, so that Jimmy and Tarah could attend John and Elizabeth's wedding. Fortunately, the weather was fantastic and the big day arrived with not a cloud in the sky. As they sat in the back of the church, Tarah felt a small tear slip from her eye as she watched Elizabeth walk down the aisle, a reaction that seemed to stem from thoughts of her own wedding only a few months earlier. Jimmy, however, took her tears as a sign of unhappiness and questioned if being present at a more organized and elaborate wedding made her regret that they had eloped.

"Not even for a second." Tarah reached over and squeezed his hand as they watched John and Elizabeth say their vows. "I just have a completely different perspective now. A wedding has a whole new meaning to me now that I'm married. It's hard to explain. I just see the whole function in a different light, and I think about how nervous she must be, standing up there right now. I know how scared I was the day we got married and there were just two people with us."

Jimmy gave her a small smile. "But are you *sure* you don't have any regrets about not doing all this." He gestured around the room. "The guests and dress, stuff like that."

"Nope." Tarah smiled. "Not at all."

The day went without a hitch, which made Tarah very happy for John. He had always been such a good friend to her over the years and made her learn a great deal about herself. It was John who encouraged Tarah to join the band, admit her feelings for Jimmy, and deal with every issue in between. He deserved every bit of happiness he could find with Elizabeth, which is exactly what she later told him when they had a moment alone.

"Oh, Tarah," John leaned in and gave her a hug. "I'm just so happy you could make it today. I know how busy you are with touring and everything else going on with the band."

"Of course I made it," she insisted. "After being such a wonderful friend to me for so many years, making sure I was here for your wedding seems like the least I could do for you. God knows, I've always felt that you've helped me through so much, and what have I ever done for you? Except bring you my problems?"

"Tarah, you've supported my relationship with Elizabeth from the get go, and you've been a friend to me," he insisted as they walked back to join Jimmy, who was enjoying some wedding cake at a nearby table. "I've just always been happy to be there for you when you needed it. We all need guidance during certain periods in our lives, and let's face it, I don't mind the fact that I helped to encourage you to join a band that ended up being as popular as Fire. I get bragging rights, after all."

"You definitely do." Tarah gave him another quick hug before joining Jimmy. The couple left shortly afterward, knowing they'd soon have to catch a plane to meet the rest of Fire in Newfoundland. The band was scheduled for an early morning interview at a radio station the next day, followed by a concert later that night.

The couple's search for a house continued but to no avail. Jimmy suggested that they start looking for another real estate agent, but Tarah thought his actions were too harsh. "Let's just wait a bit," she suggested. "After all, we don't have time to move right now. Let's just ride it out until after the summer." The tour was scheduled to end in late October, and the band was planning to return to the studio sometime in November. Ironically, in the midst of all William's controversy, he had apparently written an incredible love song called "Just You" and insisted that he had another one in the works.

"What's the deal with that?" Jimmy would later ask. "He just broke up with someone and he's writing love songs?

"I'm telling you," Tarah said, shaking her head. "He's got someone else, and that's where these songs are coming from."

"It's pretty typical, when you think about it." Jimmy began to laugh. "We get stoned and fuck for four days and write a CD about sex, and William gets stuck in a paparazzi dream, secretly meets another girl, and suddenly is writing a CD full of love songs. So does that mean he's the Light and we're the Dark?" Jimmy referred to their two CDs that were to be recorded that fall, which were to be called *Dark to Light*.

"It means that we're on a completely different page than he is." Tarah laughed.

"Try a different book all together," Jimmy said with a smile.

The tour continued throughout the summer months, and Fire had the opportunity to visit their country from one end to the other, once again. Tarah often remarked how she wished they had more time between dates to really explore the cities and surrounding areas, but every spare moment they had was taken up by either interviews, photo shoots, or taping videos. There was always something else to take their time, and although everyone in the band loved the work, sometimes it felt like being in the music industry consumed their entire lives. Sometimes Tarah envied those who had a regular nine-to-five job and wondered how people in her industry actually managed to maintain relationships with family, spouses, and friends with their busy schedules. If she hadn't been in a band with her own husband, chances are they would've broken up long ago. Her life was just too hectic to even remember even the most minor things, like the date or what city they were in. It sounded ridiculous when she admitted it on the phone to Bobby one day, but he quickly reminded Tarah that she hardly lived a standard life.

"You don't have to be in a commercially successful band to forget stuff like that," Bobby informed her in late August when she called him during the course of the tour. Tarah could hear Caitlin talking loudly in the background to another child and envied the normalcy of his day-to-day activities. "Your life isn't even consistent really, every day is different."

"That is true." Tarah smiled to herself, glancing around the hotel room. Sometimes it felt like she was a nomad, and although it was adventurous and fun, a part of Tarah really missed sleeping in her own bed. "It seems to be getting less consistent by the day." She was referring to the fact that Fire's popularity had grown in recent weeks, which was great for the band, but gave Tarah a sense of instability that she couldn't quite understand or explain. The industry was changing so fast that she often feared one day she'd wake up and it would all be over.

"Things will calm down once the tour is over," her brother reminded Tarah. "So is that when you and Jimmy will be moving in the new house?"

Tarah smiled on the other end of the line. "Yes." She could hear the enthusiasm flow from her own voice. Their real estate agent had finally found their dream home only a week earlier. The couple had flown into Toronto between shows to check out a few listings that were available, neither of them really feeling confident that she'd managed to find anything they wanted. But, as it turned out, they were wrong. "It's perfect for us," Tarah insisted. "It's beautiful, hardwood floors, huge bedrooms and bathrooms, gorgeous property, I could go on forever. You'll have to see it to really understand how perfect it is."

"That's great, Tarah." Her brother seemed to be walking away from the sound of his child's voice, possibly into another room. "Does it have a recording studio, like Jimmy wanted?"

"No, but he's getting one." Tarah laughed. "Don't worry about him, he's already got it all planned out. I can't wait to move in."

"Which will be?"

"Not until November, which is around the time our tour ends, so it kind of works out well." Tarah felt an uneasy feeling. "Bobby, are you okay? You don't sound like yourself today." She had noted that although he was talkative, he was still quieter than usual.

"I am, but there's some stuff going on here that I want to talk to you about." His voice lowered slightly. "I didn't want to say anything with Caitlin in the same room."

"Oh no, what's going on?"

Bobby took a deep breath. "Sara is back, and she wants Caitlin."

"What?" Tarah spit out. "After being gone for so long, she wants the baby back?" Of course, Caitlin was now three years old and hardly a baby any longer, but the entire family still referred to her as such.

"Kinda." Her brother sighed loudly. "She's trying to say that I ripped Caitlin from her when she was down and out. Sara is trying to give the impression that she was in a deep depression at the time, and I took advantage of that to take Caitlin out of her life."

"What?" Tarah frowned. "I mean, she was in a depression, that's true, but I don't understand."

"She was in a depression, but she left us and didn't make any effort to see the baby." Bobby spoke firmly. "But here's the part you aren't going to like. Sara said that since I have a famous sister now, that if I can get her ten thousand dollars, she'll back off."

"She wants to blackmail you?" Tarah felt anger jump into her voice. "She wants to extort money from *me* to leave *you* alone?"

"Exactly." Tarah could hear the sadness in her brother's voice, and she felt her own heart sink. He loved Caitlin, and it wasn't fair to put him through such an ordeal; hadn't he been through enough already?

"Bobby, if you really think that will make her go away, maybe that's what we'll have to do." Tarah hated the idea of being blackmailed, but at the same time, it was just money. She didn't want her brother's family to be ripped apart, or her niece to be used as a bargaining chip. Maybe throwing some money at the problem would be the only solution for the situation. Her brother didn't agree.

"No, Tarah." He spoke sternly. "I'm not going to do that. That's not right, and who's to say that even if we give her money, that she won't keep coming back for more or torment our lives anyway. I'm going to fight her on it."

"Are you sure, Bobby?" Tarah was hesitant, but did see his point.

"Yes, I'm sure," he insisted, and then paused for another moment. "I can handle Sara. The worst part is that this whole situation has caused Vanessa to sort of back off on us lately. We'd been talking about moving in together for months, but something always seems to stop us from going ahead with it. Now, this Sara thing is the latest excuse. I don't understand what's going on, but we're clearly on the wrong track."

Tarah wasn't sure either. Although she and Vanessa had been close just after the wedding, her own hectic lifestyle didn't give her much time to reconnect with friends, especially when she was on tour. "I don't know, Bobby," Tarah admitted. "I haven't talk to her in ages, and when I did, she certainly didn't mention anything being wrong. Maybe you should sit her down and have a discussion about all this. See what's the deal."

Bobby seemed hesitant to agree. But three days later, when Fire was in Vancouver, BC, Tarah called her brother and learned the bad news. He and Vanessa had broken up. Even though she loved him and Caitlin, Vanessa said that she felt that gaining an instant family just wasn't for her. Tarah suspected that there was more to the story than that, but wasn't about to tell her brother who was already devastated by the breakup. He now felt that being a full-time dad was considered "baggage" for women, and he seemed to grow resentful almost overnight.

"I guess that says a lot about women," Bobby snapped through the phone. Tarah recognized the bitterness that her own mother still carried around with her, years after the divorce from their father. "What does she expect me to do? I'm not about to get rid of my daughter, for Christ's sake."

"I don't think she meant it that way." Tarah felt like she was walking on eggshells in this conversation. "Maybe she was just scared and after thinking it over for a few days, she'll change her mind."

"She can if she wants, but I'm done with her." He spoke angrily. "Between her and Sara, I'm starting to think that women are all the same: only looking out for number one and fuck everyone else."

"You know that's not true, Bobby."

"No, Tarah, I don't know that." He spoke angrily, and for a moment she began to fear that he'd blame her for coaxing him to have that particular discussion with Vanessa, even though it clearly had to be done. "Sara didn't care about my daughter and now wants a handout, and Vanessa didn't care enough about me or my daughter to stick around. It really paints a picture for me on how women think."

"That's just two women, it's hardly fair." Tarah spoke quietly.

But her brother refused to listen to her logic, and the two ended their conversation on a negative note. Although she felt horrible for the rotten circumstance, Tarah didn't feel that her brother was being at all fair and hoped that he'd see things differently as time moved forward. She hoped he wouldn't end up with the same disposition toward women that their mother had toward men.

It was during the band's tour in western Canada in early September that Tarah heard some startling news. She was standing in an elevator when two, well-dressed black men got on , deep in conversation. At first, she wasn't paying attention to what they were saying, then she heard the words 'shot' then 'Tupac Shakur.' It hit her like a brick.

"Oh my God!" Tarah seemed to startle them both by jumping in their conversation. Still in the elevator, she felt her heart racing and took a deep breath in attempts to control her emotions. The last things she needed was to have a panic attack right there and then. "Is he dead?"

"No, but it's not looking great." One of the men gave her a small, kind smile, and Tarah nodded slowly. The three began to talk about 2Pac's music and how he had such a promising career ahead of him. It was a somber but respectful conversation. She didn't think that either of the young men recognized her, which suited her well at that moment.

"Did they catch the shooter?" Tarah asked, as the elevator reached her floor.

"No." They both shook their heads and then the taller of the two added, "Drive by shooting, but no one saw a thing."

Tarah nodded, quietly said good-bye to the young men, and slowly walked back to her room. It shook her to her foundation when she considered how much more vulnerable someone in the public eye could be, especially as a target for violence. It wasn't the first time a celebrity was attacked or hurt, and so often it was by obsessed fans. It was a crazy world that she lived in, and there were many days that it was way too much for her to think about. What if she were a target some day? Who knew what kind of unstable person was out there plotting an attack on anyone from Fire, for little or no reason at all?

When Jimmy later returned to the hotel, he had already head the news on Tupac Shakur and said that he felt it was quite suspicious that no one saw the shooter, a license plate, or anything. "Come on now, he's a celebrity, surrounded by people, and no one saw a thing? That's highly unlikely."

"I'm sure they'll find the person who shot him soon." Tarah tried to be optimistic. "And he's still alive, so he'll be fine. If he was going to die, I think he would've right away." A smile lit up her face even though there was a strange feeling in her heart, but she pushed through it. "Watch, he'll write the greatest hip-hop song ever when he gets better, all about this horrible experience. You'll see."

Jimmy looked up from the coffee he was holding, and their eyes met for a long, silent moment. Tarah bit her lip and turned away.

She was wrong. Tupak died on September 13, 1996, and they never found his killer.

CHAPTER FORTY-THREE

▼

"They either want us fucking or fighting. There's no middle ground." Jimmy threw down the national magazine, which claimed the couple that hadn't even been married for one year, was already talking divorce. According to the article, Tarah was constantly frustrated with her husband and wanted an annulment. "And supposedly, this house we're buying is *my* way of trying to keep you happy for the moment. Can you believe this shit?"

"Look, we know that this is how the game goes," Tarah calmly reminded him, but she certainly understood his frustration. If the story had even a shred of truth to it, perhaps it wouldn't have been so troublesome. However, considering that their marriage had been a very happy one, Tarah understood his resentment toward the magazine in question. "This isn't the first time we've had to deal with this and it won't be the last. Unfortunately, this is the way these monsters work. If they weren't saying that there was trouble in paradise, then they'd say that I was pregnant. They can't sell magazines when things are just normal. People don't want to hear about how we're just an average couple who just happen to be in a rock band. They want to hear the dirt, and when there isn't any, they're going to make it up."

"They're saying that their 'sources' tell them that we're miserable." Jimmy raised his eyebrow as he sat across from Tarah in their hotel room. The tour was almost complete, with only a handful more shows to go before being finished and neither had been to their apartment in weeks. A ton of packing awaited them. There was just too much to do and their time was already stretched, but they were managing. "Who the fuck *are* these sources?"

"People they obviously make up." Tarah shrugged. "I mean, some people will say anything for a buck. Haven't you ever noticed that when they refer to people as their 'sources' that the story is absolute shit?"

"Can we sue these fuckers or what?"

"I don't know," Tarah replied glumly. "I don't think we can do anything. And even if we did, it would just bring all this attention to the magazine. That's what they want."

"Maybe I should go on one of those talk shows that I keep being asked to do." Tarah wondered out loud. She had been invited to various shows in Canada, as well as interview requests from some popular American talk show hosts and reporters. Tarah had always declined, choosing only to do interviews with the members of her band so that all the attention wouldn't be focused on her. "Maybe I've got to go on one of these shows and set the record straight."

"You don't think that's maybe why they're doing this?" Jimmy pointed out, pushing a strand of hair from his blue eyes. "Maybe they think if they write enough shit about us that eventually we'll do an interview for someone, and then we've fallen in their trap. You don't think this is part of the game?"

Tarah silently thought about his words for a moment. He was probably right. If there was something she learned about this business in the last few years, it was that it was a manipulative and cunning industry. "Do you ever wonder if it's Maggie or someone from the record company feeding these stories to the media? I mean there were a few times that it was pretty obvious. Like the time you and Michael got in a fight in FUTA's parking lot and the story suddenly was released." Tarah's thoughts jumped back to that morning and the hostility that was between Jimmy and Michael. The tension never completely subsided, but it was clear that the band made more of an attempt to get along for the sake of their careers, if nothing else.

"Absolutely," Jimmy replied. "I have no doubt. We're just puppets on a string to them. We're the way they make money, and they're going to whore us out till there is no more money to be made. It's as simple as that." He took a drink of his coffee. "Not to say they're the only ones spreading these stories, who's to say that the media aren't talking to people who we think we can trust. That's the problem, Tarah. Sometimes I don't know who we can trust anymore. I just feel there are vultures hovering overhead."

Tarah agreed, and after some time, reluctantly made a phone call to Maggie saying that she'd do an interview with a well-known female reporter in the US. Tarah made it clear that she was very hesitant, and Maggie insisted that she'd attend the interview with her, and that in the long run, it might be in Tarah's best interest. "I know you hate doing these kind of things, but sometimes they are a necessary evil." Tarah agreed with the evil part. The interview was scheduled for the following week with Enid Taylor, a strong force in the entertainment world.

The rest of the band didn't seem to care that she was making this step into the media abyss, with the exception to William.

"Tarah, are you sure you want to do this?" He spoke honestly on the same afternoon he learned the news. "She can be a vulture sometimes. I remember Lindsey did an interview with her once and by the end of it, she was crying."

"I'm not Lindsey." Tarah rolled her eyes. "And I'm not going to cry."

"I'm just saying she's out for blood." William wrinkled his forehead. "Enid Taylor will come across as caring and kind, but she goes for the jugular."

"I'll be fine," Tarah insisted, even though she had her own doubts.

She started to feel overwhelmed with everything going on in her life. She was constantly thinking about the tour's end and the start of their next CD; she also was preparing for her and Jimmy's upcoming move. There were so many details to look after that she didn't know where to begin. Things were strained with her mother and Jimmy's family, so she didn't dare ask for anyone's help. Her father was working more than she felt he should, and Tarah often worried about his health. What if the cancer returned? And then there was her brother.

Bobby was still dealing with his own issues. Tarah had hired a lawyer for him that had fortunately scared off Sara from any notions of scamming money from either of them. However, Vanessa was still out of the picture, and it didn't appear she was coming back. Tarah was surprised because her brother's girlfriend had spoken excitedly about their relationship at one time. Had her brother left out details? Was there another guy in the picture? Things weren't adding up.

Tarah began to doubt her decision to do the interview with Enid Taylor a few days before it was scheduled to occur. It'd been an impulsive decision and completely a reaction to constant rumors about her relationship with Jimmy, but it was too late to back down. She decided that it was best to get it over with and move on. Chances were, it wouldn't be as bad as she was expecting. The band had taken a couple of days off before concluding their tour the following week, and that was when the interview was scheduled to take place. Although Tarah was exhausted, she flew to New York to meet Enid Taylor and face the music.

Maggie had already prepped Tarah with some of the possible questions that might be thrown her way, and all but told her what to say in response to each. About halfway through the "dry run" before meeting the reporter, Tarah grew frustrated with feeling as though she had to memorize a bunch of words written by someone else. She thought of Jimmy's comparison between them and puppets on a string and finally told Maggie that rehearsing answers just didn't seem right. "Why can't I just be myself?"

"Because she'll eat you alive," Maggie insisted. "You have to carefully watch how you answer or you risk opening the door to more invasive questions and subjects you don't want to discuss. And you also have to consider that if you word something the wrong way, it can lead to all kinds of trouble."

Suddenly Tarah felt sick. This wasn't what it should be like, she thought. Why was the world so contrived and orchestrated? It reminded her of the days when she worked at Rothman's. How many times had her manager recited an explanation or lecture that sounded as if he were reading from cue cards? Maybe, she decided, everyone was a puppet to someone else. Politicians were the people most often blamed for being fake and rehearsed, but wasn't everybody at some point in their lives? Was life just a series of hoops to jump through?

Tarah was quite surprised when she met the famous Enid Taylor in person. The woman who always looked polished and perfect on television, had about an inch of makeup on her face, not to mention around her eyes. The woman looked like she was sixty years old rather than her claimed age of forty. Enid's eyes were dark, but her skin was so translucent that Tarah almost thought she could see through it as the blue veins popped out on her face, not to mention the ones in her hands and neck. The reporter's hair looked like a wig because it was perfectly styled and didn't appear to move. Tarah would later report the details to Jimmy and describe the woman as "creepy" because she barely looked like a real person. But her husband insisted that this was just normal for the industry and that possibly nothing about her was real.

The interview started off smoothly. Enid flattered Tarah on being so young, yet mature, successful, and responsible. She talked about what a successful band Fire was, and how they were quickly rising in popularity in the US after finding great success 'with our northern neighbor.' But then it started.

"I'm actually surprised, Tarah, that considering how popular your new CD is in North America that Fire only chose to tour Canada with this CD, and not the United States. Why is that?"

Of course Tarah couldn't tell them it was because FUTA didn't feel that the CD had enough commercial appeal to make a US tour worth their while this time around. She had to sound like the CEO of her own business and be ready to put it in the best light, as Maggie had told her many times before sitting down in an interview. Fortunately, this was one of the questions they had practiced before going on air.

"We felt that we wanted this tour to be a little more intimate and something to give back to all our Canadian fans who were with us from day one." Tarah recited her lines. "Our next project is a double CD, which will be followed by an extensive tour, including all across the US. We're all really looking forward to it."

She was relieved when Enid seemed satisfied with her reply, but wondered if perhaps the reporter sensed the practiced answer.

"Excellent, Tarah." She gave her perfect smile. "We sure look forward to that. Now, is it true that you're going to be back in the studio soon? That certainly doesn't give you much of a break, it seems that Fire has been going nonstop since you were signed in 1994. How do you find time for your families?"

"We managed to squeeze in as much time as possible," Tarah answered confidently. "It's not always easy, but we manage."

"What about last year when you and Jimmy were married, I understand that you chose to elope?"

"Yes, we did."

"And that your family members were quite upset because you and your husband didn't let them know about your plans?" Enid asked innocently, and Tarah felt the urge to slap her across the face. Instead, she smiled and played along.

"Originally, we just wanted some time to get away for New Year's Eve and invited my brother and his girlfriend along. It was sort of a last minute decision to get married while on vacation." Tarah felt awkward answering the question. "It just felt like the best possible time."

"You mention that the wedding wasn't planned, but wasn't it true that you in fact had the honeymoon suite of the hotel booked? I also heard that you had prearranged to have someone marry you and Jimmy, is that true?" Enid gave her a big smile, and Tarah fought the urge to lash out. After hiding this fact that the wedding was planned from both their families for almost a year, one interview could create even more tension. William was right; she shouldn't have agreed to speak to Enid Taylor.

"We did book the honeymoon suite to celebrate the holiday and our time off." Tarah answered carefully, and she could see Maggie sitting in the sidelines slowly nodding her head to continue. "As for prearranging the wedding, you've clearly been misinformed." She felt her heart racing and hoped that the reporter wasn't about to pull out some evidence to call her bluff, but Enid just moved on with the questions.

"I guess I was misinformed." She let out a little laugh. "Do you ever regret rushing the marriage and not having a longer engagement?"

"No." Tarah knew that reporters hated these quick and easy answers because it gave them very little to work with, but she should've known there was another question that would quickly follow on its heels.

"Isn't it true that many of your relatives wanted you both to wait because you were so young?" Enid glanced down at her notes. "Is that why you eloped, because of the pressures by both your families to not get married too soon?"

If she wanted to be honest, Tarah could've said yes, but she refused to give in. "Our families would've preferred that we waited, however our choice to marry when we did had no bearing on their preferences. It was an impulse thing and we went with it. After all, we were engaged for a few months at this point, so it wasn't unreasonable that we wanted to go ahead with the marriage, rather than wait."

Tarah could see Maggie nodding in approval in the background.

"And married life, is it what you thought it'd be?"

"I didn't really have a concept of what it would be," Tarah admitted. "However, things are going great. I'm very happy to be married."

"So the reports of an upcoming divorce aren't true?"

"Not at all," Tarah insisted. "In fact, I don't know where they're coming from. We're very happy."

"There must've been a great deal of tension in the band at one time," Enid glanced down at her notes again. "I understand you had a relationship with William when Fire was first discovered and actually broke up around the same time. How did you cope with this situation?"

Tarah took a deep breath and could see Maggie rolling her eyes from across the room. Fortunately, Enid didn't notice.

"I think we handled it the best way we could at the time. I mean, we all had the common goal of making the best of our opportunity with FUTA, and therefore managed to work things out and move forward in order to make a success of Fire."

"But didn't you break up with William to start a relationship with Jimmy?" Enid pushed forward. "That's quite a complicated love triangle."

"I *wouldn't* say it was a love triangle." Tarah spoke sternly, feeling her anger grow. "It's not a soap opera, it's my life." In the background, Maggie shook her head no, but Tarah no longer cared.

"But you have to admit that it was a pretty dicey situation." Enid pushed a little harder. "It certainly couldn't have been easy."

"No, but we dealt with it," Tarah abruptly answered, her heart pounding wildly in her chest. She could feel her face getting hot, a fact that didn't seem to go unnoticed by Enid.

"But, I would think—"

"It's the past," Tarah interrupted the reporter. "And I don't live in the past. We've all clearly moved on."

Enid Taylor looked a bit taken aback by Tarah's abrupt reply, but quickly regained control of herself and the interview. "Of course." She then jumped into William and Lindsey's breakup earlier that year and asked Tarah if she was surprised by his "indiscretion" in the situation.

Tarah felt like the lights that were already beating down on her were becoming much hotter. The room was starting to feel suffocating and she suddenly felt the urge to get up and run away. "I was surprised, but feel that what goes on between two people, should be kept strictly between those two people."

"In other words, you don't want to discuss it." Enid gave her perfect Colgate smile.

"In other words," Tarah corrected her. "I don't think it's any of my business."

"That's fair enough." Enid Taylor seemed to accept the answer. "Clearly you don't want to get involved in that particular situation. But tell me this much, Tarah, before we end our interview. What do you think of William's new girlfriend?"

Tarah shook her head. "I don't know anything about a new girlfriend. We don't discuss his personal life."

"Really, that's surprising," Enid remarked, and fell silent for a moment. "But considering it's Maggie Eriksson, your band's manager, wouldn't you say that this is a conflict of interest?"

Maggie! Tarah was stunned, but hid her surprise the best she could. It was clear Enid was expecting a shocked reaction, followed by an emotional response, but Tarah refused to give her the satisfaction. Although the whole concept was surprising and quite unexpected to her, Tarah kind of liked the idea. So with a big smile on her face, she exclaimed, "That's fantastic! I'm so happy for them both."

CHAPTER FORTY-FOUR

▼

"Things were a little awkward." Tarah admitted to Jimmy over a late-night dinner. Immediately following her interview with Enid Taylor, she hopped on a plane and met up with her husband in Manitoba. Fire was due to play there the following evening. She now wished they had skipped the quaint, little Italian restaurant and just returned to the hotel. Nothing would've felt better at that moment than a hot bath.

"Sounds like a great understatement." Jimmy pushed a strand of black hair from his face and sipped on his beer. "Not only did you have the interview from hell, but then this Enid chick drops a bomb on the whole thing. So, what did Maggie say after you left? Did she explain what the fuck was going on?"

Tarah thought back to first few uncomfortable moments away from Enid, which took place when she was alone with the band's manager in an elevator. Maggie, the same woman who was always fearless and confident, was suddenly self-conscious and awkward in Tarah's presence. "I can explain," she automatically said in a hushed tone. "God, how did that bitch find out about us? We were so careful." Maggie seemed to be thinking out loud. "I feel so awful that you had to find out this way."

"Maggie." She turned to the band's manager, who suddenly seemed much shorter than earlier that same day. Tarah recognized the same deer-in-headlights expression on her face that she herself had carried years before, when people found out about her secret affection for Jimmy. Her heart filled with compassion. "You don't have anything to feel awful about. I'm not angry with you. I just was shocked to find out in that kind of way, but I certainly understand why you wanted to keep things quiet. I mean, especially if you were the same girl William was caught with on New Year's Eve."

And she had been. The entire story came out as Maggie drove Tarah back to the airport, an arrangement that had been made earlier that same day.

"She seemed relieved to be telling me everything," Tarah said to Jimmy as the waitress brought them each a plate of pasta. Glancing over the food, she shook her head. "I don't know what I was thinking, ordering up a big plate of food like this so late in the day. I'll probably fall asleep while I'm eating it."

"Nah, you'll be fine." Jimmy thanked the waitress, and the couple sat in silence for a few minutes while she walked away. He began to dig into his spaghetti and Tarah hesitantly did the same with her food. "So, what's the deal?"

"Well, apparently they had kind of a flirtation going on for awhile." Tarah used her fork to play with her linguine. "They kind of always liked one another. And she was at the same party on New Year's Eve as William and Lindsey, who weren't getting along, a bunch of shit was going down between them and when Maggie saw William, they began to talk. And I guess one thing led to another, and the rest is history."

"I'm kind of surprised that Lindsey didn't blab who it was back when she did the *revealing* interview earlier this year." He rolled his eyes dramatically. "Why wouldn't she mention it was the band's manager?"

"First of all, I can't comment on the revealing interview thing because I just did the same thing today." Tarah finally lifted some food to her mouth. "And believe me, it's sometimes not what you expect when you walk into it. As for not admitting that it was Maggie with William, I guess she had her own secrets she didn't want revealed."

"Like?" Jimmy only looked half-interested.

"Like the fact that William caught Lindsey with his brother."

Jimmy dropped his fork. "What the fuck? Are you shitting me?" His blue eyes looked upward while his head was still tilted down. "You expect me to believe a super model fucked that piece of shit?"

"Yup."

"No fucking way? Wow." Jimmy picked up his fork again. "I guess the title 'rock star' goes far with some people."

"Think of the models who are with creepy, old, *rich* men," Tarah reminded him, suddenly feeling more alert after watching his reaction to the news. "Seriously, it's not that surprising in the end. And maybe she did it on purpose to really hurt him."

"I'm surprised he didn't mention it to you, or did he?"

"Nope." Tarah shook her head. "I suspect, knowing William, they made an agreement to keep each other's dirty secrets. The only reason why she even let on to the media that William cheated on her was because it was leaked from a friend of hers."

"Wow." Jimmy seemed to be shoveling the food into his mouth at this point, but still managing to smile. "That's crazy shit. So, back to Maggie and William, isn't it kind of ironic that he ended up in the same situation with her, as you did with me."

"It is." Tarah nodded and took a drink of her water. She thought of William's apology to her after the whole story had been revealed. "I guess it taught him not to make judgments about other people."

Jimmy fell silent again.

"So, why didn't they tell anyone about their relationship?" Jimmy took another drink of his beer. "I can see at first, but we're in fucking October. Did they want to keep the secret forever?"

"From what she said, I think they were so happy together that they kind of wanted to stay in their own secret world, where no one knew a thing." Tarah attempted to explain what Maggie had told her earlier that day. "Maybe there is more excitement to people not knowing, like an affair. Plus, you know William, very private. I think things with Lindsey taught him that he didn't want another relationship that the entire world watched. It makes sense, when you think about it."

"It does." Jimmy chewed on his food. "You're right. When we were first hanging out, there was something really cool about catching you in a corner secretly, knowing that no one else could knew what was going on between us."

"There was." Tarah nodded and thought for a moment. "But I wouldn't want to do that for months on end. Sounds like a lot of work to hide something."

Jimmy was quiet. "So, what do you think of all this? Do you think it's good or bad? Do you think they're serious?"

"I think they're very serious, and I also feel it's a good thing." Tarah nodded and relaxed in her chair. "I'm happy for them. It was a shock to learn about it during an interview, but I think it's great."

"Me too." He tilted his head.

The interview with Enid Taylor was played a couple of days later, and Tarah wasn't too impressed with the final result. It was edited in such a way that made her appear very defensive, for what appeared to be no reason. Enid looked calm, relaxed, and completely innocent as she asked the questions. But at least Tarah felt she appeared sincerely happy for William and Maggie when asked about their relationship. Everything else in the interview seemed tedious in comparison.

The public finally knew about the secret relationship, and William would later admit to Tarah that it was kind of freeing to not have to hide it any longer. "It's not that I was ashamed of her in any way," he told Tarah the day after the interview was aired. "It just felt right to not display it like I did with Lindsey. I feel a little bad for not telling the band, especially you, but we agreed that if you tell one person, you might as well tell everyone."

"You don't owe me an explanation," Tarah insisted. "I had no more reason than anyone else for knowing or not knowing."

"Yeah, but I like to think that we're pretty open with one another." William spoke honestly. "I feel that because of everything we went through together, whether it was our relationship, Wendy dying, or the band, that we'll always have a different connection."

Tarah smiled and considered how far they had come from the days following their breakup. She never would've guessed back then that they'd someday have a sincere and caring relationship between them. "We do have a different kind of connection, but your private life is your private life, and you were right to keep it secret for as long as you could."

The tour was finished a few days later and everyone was relieved to take a break. Although for Tarah and Jimmy, it wasn't much of a break. The couple proceeded to move into their new home, which Tarah referred to as "the mansion." To her, it wasn't necessary to have such a large house, but Jimmy had his heart set on something elaborate, because to him it was a sign of accomplishment. Plus he was very proud of his new studio, which had soundproof walls so that the neighbors didn't have the police at their door on a daily basis. Tarah had never seen her husband so excited about a project, not since their band was first signed.

Both of their families seemed to be finally losing their grudge over the secret wedding. In some strange way, the Enid Taylor interview seemed to unify them all because both their families were angry about how the interviewer attacked Tarah.

"You poor thing!" Jimmy's mother had exclaimed on the phone the day after it was televised. "What a horrible woman! I always hated Enid Taylor. I wish you'd told me you were planning to do an interview with her; I would've warned you that she's a mean-spirited witch."

"It's fine." Tarah spoke gently in the phone, thinking that perhaps she would've told her about the interview had Jimmy's mother been talking to either of them regularly. "Don't worry about her. We all know the truth."

Tarah noticed that as her first anniversary drew closer, that both families seemed to constantly be making comments on how she and Jimmy were a good match. Although it frustrated her to hear the words that should've been said a year earlier, John pointed out that everyone was just realizing that their own concerns about the marriage were unfounded.

"Your families now see that their apprehension about you and Jimmy getting married was completely tied to *their* own reluctance toward the wedding, it had nothing to do with whether or not you and he were ready. It was about *them* not being ready."

"Such wise words." Tarah sat across from her long time friend in the living room of her new home. "So, where is Elizabeth today?"

"Another doctor's appointment." He grinned from ear to ear. "You know how it goes with pregnant ladies."

The couple had learned that they were expecting a baby shortly after their wedding in June and were ecstatic. The baby was due in February of 1997.

"Not really, but I do believe that they have a lot of doctor appointments." Tarah sipped on her coffee. She was still on her first cup while John was finishing his second. "It won't be long now." She glanced toward the window and thought she caught site of a flake of snow falling. It was mid-November and a cold, Saturday afternoon.

"I know, and it's exciting but kind of scary at the same time," John admitted. "So what about you and Jimmy? Do you think you'll be having babies someday?"

Tarah began to laugh. "I doubt it, at least not any time soon. We barely have time for ourselves or to be together, let alone have a baby."

"There's no rush."

"Besides, our families are just getting used to the fact that we're married." Tarah shook her head. "Let's not push it by throwing kids in the mix."

She later repeated the conversation to Jimmy and laughed while telling the story. But he surprised her by suggesting that they consider the prospect in "a few years."

"Are you serious?" Tarah was taken aback by his reaction. "I didn't think you'd even want kids."

"Not yet." Jimmy shrugged. "I mean, it's not the time for that, but maybe someday, when things calm down, and I finally have my act together."

"I think you already have your act together."

"Yeah, but not really." His eyes scanned a bag of pot that sat on a nearby table. "I gotta work out my demons and get my head together first."

Tarah silently nodded. Although he had come a long way from when he first told her about his sister's rape, she knew it was something he hadn't completely dealt with and wasn't sure how to help him. She just tried to be as supportive as possible. What else could she do?

The band put off working on their CD until the first of December, giving them a break that they all needed. Besides, between Jimmy, Tarah, and William, more than half the songs already were written. By the time the band was ready to record, Jimmy's studio was done. Although the band hired a producer to help guide them, Jimmy insisted on doing as much as he could behind the scenes in order to be completely involved in the project and obtain all the skills he wanted.

"This is going to be the CD that puts us on the map, I can feel it," Jimmy insisted one night when he and Tarah were alone in the studio. "This'll be our golden egg. Not to sound cocky, but there are times I play back some of these songs, and I'm just floored by how good they sound."

"I don't think you're being cocky." Tarah glanced around the room. "I think you're right. There is something very different this time. Even when we're recording the songs, the energy in the room is amazing, and we've all grown up a lot since our first CD."

"True." Jimmy nodded. "We have. We're happy, William's happy, Michael is mellowing out, and even Eddie seems to not hate the world as much as he did a couple of years ago. Maybe we're all finally on the right path—career and otherwise."

"I hope so." Tarah leaned over and kissed his cheek. "In fact, I think you're right."

The dark anniversary of Wendy's murder crept up on them as they were recording the CD, and William suggested that they all take a break for the holiday season. "After all, we're still ahead of schedule, even though we started late." Much to Tarah's relief, the entire band agreed. Even though two years had passed since that terrible day, it still was quite painful for Tarah.

"Mourn her for the day, and then let it go," Jimmy gently suggested to her that morning before they got out of bed. "Don't let it take away all the great things about the holidays, especially our first anniversary." He rolled over and the two shared a long, lingering kiss. "So, what are we doing for New Year's this year?"

"I don't know," Tarah whispered. "I don't think much can top last year."

The couple was surprised when both their families got together and threw a surprise anniversary party for them on New Year's Eve. Neither Jimmy nor Tarah expected such a thing, especially after the reactions to the elopement the year before.

"We decided to stop being jerks." Jimmy's mother rushed over and gave her a strong hug shortly after the couple arrived that evening. They had expected just a quiet night with Jimmy's parents, eating take out and having some wine. Instead, they found a house filled with balloons and Happy Anniversary signs across the wall. A huge cake was on the kitchen table and Caitlin excitedly was inspecting it.

"Tarah, Tarah, look!" she cried out. "Santa brought a cake!"

Everyone laughed, and Jimmy thanked his mom for throwing a party for them.

Both families gathered in the living room, and Tarah saw a small collection of wedding gifts on the coffee table. Exchanging glances with Jimmy, she noticed the humor in his eyes and she already knew what he was thinking. Clearly this was everyone's way of apologizing for the upset the previous year. The only people not there were Jillian and her husband, but they were apparently just running a bit late.

Everyone drank wine and quietly chatted. Both her parents were sitting a distance away from one another, and Tarah noticed that her brother looked slightly depressed. She later asked him what was going on. He told her that since breaking up with Vanessa, he felt like his entire life was just about being a dad and work. He didn't have much time for a social life, and she sensed he was lonely.

"Sometimes I feel guilty," Tarah confessed to Jimmy later that night when they were alone in his former bed. "I have it so great, and my brother's life seems so difficult. I wish there was something I could do for him."

"He has to make his own way." Jimmy turned off the lamp and curled up beside her and stared into Tarah's eyes. "Don't ever feel guilty for what you've accomplished; I don't have to tell you that nothing came easy, and nothing came because you didn't take chances. You've had your battles to fight, we both have."

"I know," Tarah said sadly. "But even tonight, he's alone for New Year's Eve, and here we are together."

"Alone in my old bedroom," Jimmy whispered seductively in her ear. "How fucking hot is that? Did I ever tell you what I used to do in here all the time?

Tarah began to laugh. "Yeah, I believe you mentioned it once or twice."

CHAPTER FORTY-FIVE

▼

The *Dark to Light* CD compilation took much longer to record than the band had originally anticipated. With so many precise details and the perfecting of each song, the members of Fire were insistent that this recording be the most outstanding work they had ever done together. In the end, they were confident that their efforts would pay off.

The first of two CDs would be called *Dark* and would feature songs with such titles as "Lust," "Fantasy," and "From Dark to Light." Jimmy and Tarah wrote it almost entirely in their drug/sex binge many months earlier and it centered around the physical pleasures and desires of a relationship. The music would later be referred to as being dark, aggressive, and was often compared to that of Marilyn Manson and NIN, who both were recognized for a similar sound at the time.

The second CD was simply called *Light* and featured songs mainly wrote by William, with such titles as "Dream," "Flower," and "Light," all centered on the blissful and joyous stage of love that he believed described aspects of the emotion. Each song was beautifully written and appealed to the commercial market, while the *Dark* CD appealed more to the underground crowd, the listeners who some people in the industry preferred to give a blind eye.

Jimmy had decided early in the recording process that he wanted to create a link between each song, leaving no pause from one track to the next. "It just fits," he insisted to the rest of the band, who seemed intrigued with the idea. "Considering each CD has its own individual theme, I think it'd be cool to have each song locked together. Essentially, it shows the listener that each track is very closely connected to the last one."

And he was right. Weeks later when the members of Fire heard the final version of *Dark to Light,* they loved it. And so did Peter Sampson, as well as everyone else at FUTA. The momentum just continued to grow. Jimmy would later be recognized for the band's enormous success following the CD's release. People would often refer to his belief that *Dark to Light* would be Fire's golden egg; after selling countless CDs and winning awards, it would be recognized as one of the best releases of the late nineties. It was an accomplishment that the entire band would share, but in the music industry it was Jimmy who'd be considered the mastermind of the entire project. The few others who helped produce and master the CD would even take their hats off to his enormous insight and instinct on the project.

That was a time when Jimmy felt certain he'd found a place that guaranteed his future success, and that he'd never have to work another dead-end job again. He often confessed to Tarah that he sometimes feared, just as she did, that their days were numbered on both the radio and music channels. The industry was unreliable and fans were always searching for the next best thing; dance music and boy bands were becoming increasingly popular. It was an unpredictable industry and when the couple talked to others who were in bands, they often found that they weren't alone in their fears. Fans were fickle. Even FUTA had this concern.

"That's why it's important to really hold on to your fan base. Keep the ones you already have," Peter Sampson insisted in their meetings before the CD was actually released. "It's a really weird time for music. It's a strange transition, even from a few years ago when Fire was first signed. Not crazy about where it's going, to tell you the truth," he admitted to the band. "The industry just isn't as exciting as it once was. But, hey," he raised his hand in the air, "I'm not getting any younger either, maybe it's just me."

"There's definitely a big draw to this kind of mindless music that's out there now." William spoke diplomatically. "I mean, I know there's obviously a market for it, or it wouldn't be there, but it's such a change from the Nirvana and Pearl Jam days. It's almost like all that music that was once so popular, was just swept under the rug and replaced with a cheap and tacky version."

"In other words, *crap!*" Jimmy added. "There's so much crap on the radio, and I feel like that's what's getting all the airplay now."

"There's a clear change in the air," Peter agreed then moved to another topic. "And it's because of this change that FUTA really wants to go all out and push this CD. We really believe in it and think it can shake things up a bit. We want a big tour—push the airplay on the radio and make music videos that capture people's attention. All in all, I want you guys to work your asses off to get this CD right to the top, because we all know that it's got the ability to do so." He paused and glanced over their faces. "And if there's anything you need to get this one on top, *anything,* then I want you to tell me. Cause we're pushing this baby out of its mama and right into college. No fucking around."

Jimmy would later find out that FUTA's record sales were starting to drop and shareholders in the company were not happy. Unfortunately, it was a very competitive market and the label was only as successful as the bands that they signed. And Fire's *Dark to Light* looked to be FUTA's best hope of rising share prices in the early part of 1997.

The CDs were released on March 31, 1997. Approximately one month earlier, Peter Sampson invited Tarah and Jimmy into his office for a meeting. He wanted to discuss their first video for the *Dark* CD. It was a seductive song with intense sexual overtones called "Touch." Neither of them understood why they were the only members from the band to show up, but Peter quickly brought them into the loop.

"There's an idea that Samuel Lynes and I were playing around with that we wanted to bring to your attention." Peter referred to the director scheduled to shoot the band's new video a week later. "That's why I only asked the two of you here to join me this morning, rather than the entire band."

"Okay?" Jimmy said, and already was appearing very skeptical of Peter's words. "So what's the deal? Why is it just us here?"

Tarah gave a small smile and suddenly felt uneasy. It occurred to her that there was something very unsettling about not including the rest of Fire in their meeting. Why were they excluded? What was going on? She had a bad feeling.

"I wanted to run an idea by you," Peter repeated, and continued to ease into a smile. "We were of course talking about the shoot for "Touch" and how we thought that considering the topic in the song, that it'd be a good idea to feature a couple all through the video. You know, being affectionate." He seemed to stumble over the last word. "We were looking at various actors and models who might be right for the part and then Samuel suddenly had a fantastic idea. He said why don't we just get Tarah and Jimmy to do that part in the video, rather than some anonymous couple that no one cares about." Peter's eyes lit up as if he just had the best idea ever. "What do you think?"

Tarah shook her head to say no and opened her mouth, but Jimmy already beat her to the punch.

"Are you fucking crazy?" Jimmy snapped, and almost flew out of his chair. "Like we *want* that kind of attention on ourselves. If I had my way, no one would even know Tarah and I were married, at least then the media would leave us the fuck alone. Now, you can't even turn on the Internet or open a magazine without seeing some kind of invasive story on us. Not to mention the fact that we aren't that self-indulgent that we want or need a video centered specifically on us. We are *part* of a band after all, aren't we?"

Tarah bit her lip. After *Dark to Light* was released, their contract was technically fulfilled. There was always a good chance that FUTA wouldn't take them on again if this CD didn't do well, there was also a chance that the record company might have some other ideas in mind that were being planned behind closed doors. Tarah hated feeling like she and the other members of Fire were the topic of many conversations in FUTA meetings, but somehow she suspected they were. This specific meeting just proved it.

"And, Tarah." Peter cleared his throat and continued to smile. "I notice that Jimmy is speaking for both of you, but you're allowed your own opinion of course."

"I agree with Jimmy." Tarah spoke quickly. "That's why he spoke for both of us, because he knows I feel the same way about this kind of thing." She resented the fact that on more than one occasion, it was suggested that Jimmy didn't allow her to live or think freely. It was the farthest thing from the truth, but of course, there were certain reporters who implied that he was very controlling in their marriage. Tarah hated the image of their relationship that was presented in the media, but wasn't about to tell them that his tendency to be over protective had a great deal to do with her panic attacks and Tarah's general anxiety issues. Then again, he'd always been very defensive of her when others attacked, even in the days when she was dating William. At the time, she had just assumed it was because he was a nice guy. Of course, later on it became extremely clear that his protectiveness of Tarah related to his general affection toward her. But now that they'd been together for a few years, she felt strongly that a part of him *needed* to feel like he could always defend her, perhaps to somehow make up for the horrible day in his childhood when he wasn't able to protect his own sister from a rapist. He was working out his issues, but weren't they all?

"Well, I'm sorry you feel that way," Peter remarked, still with a dim smile on his face. "I just think the fans would love it. You guys are the real deal and a lot of fans love that aspect of Fire, especially young girls. If you two were featured in the way we're thinking, it would be tasteful and sexy and show a more vulnerable side of your relationship." He shifted his gaze toward Tarah, and she knew it was because he felt that she was the weak link of the couple. If either of them were to say yes, it'd most likely be her. And everyone also knew that Jimmy's wife was one of the few people who'd be capable of changing his mind. "Just a thought."

Tarah shook her head no and her eyes met with Jimmy's. He gave a sad smile.

"So basically they want to whore us out," Jimmy ranted as they left the FUTA building and headed to their car. He climbed behind the wheel and sighed loudly while Tarah fastened her seatbelt. "We just put together two CDs that contain the best music any of us ever wrote and yet the main focus here, clearly, is how they can market us for something *other* than our music. I just don't understand."

"Come on, Jimmy." Tarah gently touched his arm. "You know that's how they operate. I wish I could tell you that it'll change, but it won't."

"I know." He finally relented and turned the ignition. "I just never thought …" Then he stopped, shook his head, and drove out of the parking lot.

The video for "Touch" was shot the following week and was revealed to the band after post-production was completed. It featured two models who greatly resembled Jimmy and Tarah. In fact, they were almost identical. Jimmy's face turned a bright red, and Tarah had tears in her eyes as they both watched the video.

"We should've known something was up when Peter didn't show us the final cut for 'Touch,'" Jimmy fumed. The band was gathered together in his office, but it had been a young intern who was left with the task of giving them the first view of their new video. The young, frightened woman seemed confused when the members of Fire became tense as they watched the results, which featured the couple in a number of erotic and suggestive positions. Tarah also noticed how the intern's eyes glanced from the couple on the screen to Jimmy and Tarah, as if comparing their likeness. It only added to her anger.

"You guys wouldn't do the video FUTA wanted, so they just decided to do the next best thing? And behind all our backs, because we didn't see these actors on set," William said as soon as it was finished playing. "That's pretty messed up. If they're trying to keep us signed on, this isn't the way to go about it."

And with that, the entire band rose from their seats and silently left the room. No one said another word until they were outside in the parking lot.

William gave Jimmy and Tarah a worried look. "That's not right, guys." His eyes shuffled to each band member's face. Even Michael was shaking his head no in response to this turn of events. "I can't believe it."

"It's like a big 'fuck you' to us all, especially me and Tarah," Jimmy replied in a much calmer voice than anyone expected. His eyes were downcast and if anything, he appeared more upset than angry. "Remember Tommy from Confusion 45?" Jimmy referred to the first band they had toured with after being signed. He glanced up toward the boys, then Tarah. "He always said FUTA stood for 'Fuck you Up The Ass,' and he was right because that's what they're doing. I thought he was exaggerating, but I was wrong."

"But does it really matter?" Eddie spoke up. "Would any other record company really be any better? Wouldn't they all fuck us over in some way, if given the chance? I've heard some pretty brutal stories out there at parties and stuff. There are worse companies than FUTA. It's just like you can't win sometimes."

"You know, all any of us wanted was to make it in the business so we could do what we love for a living." William spoke quietly. "And here we are, doing what we want, but there's all this extra crap added on. I know we have to play the game to a certain extent but what they did today, it crossed the line."

"Can we ask Maggie what she thinks?" Michael suggested, and Tarah noticed that William shot him a dirty look. "I mean, since she used to be our manager."

Since the relationship between William and Maggie became public, she had stepped back from representing their band and had someone else take care of them now. Tarah hadn't even met the new rep and didn't even know if it was a man or woman. In fact, she hadn't even seen Maggie since the public announcement about her and William. Their relationship continued to be very low profile, but from a few comments here and there, apparently still going strong.

"Yeah, I'll ask her." William quickly looked away from his brother, and gave Tarah a crooked smile that automatically made her suspect that he knew that *she* knew, about the Lindsey/Michael fling. There was clearly still hostility between the brothers.

"I suspect we can't do anything about it." Eddie shook his head and gave Tarah a sympathetic smile. "They've got a whole legal team behind them, I'm sure they've already checked it out."

"True." Tarah bit her lip in attempt to keep from crying. "I guess there isn't much we can do."

"Yeah we can," Jimmy spoke sternly. "We can shop around for another label after all this is done. This CD is going to be a huge success, we all know it so we shouldn't have an issue getting a better deal elsewhere." Everyone seemed to be in agreement.

William called Tarah later that night and told her that Maggie said Eddie's comment was correct, and that the record label would have a whole legal team behind them. "Also," William continued. "Where the video is kind of raunchy, she thinks they might be looking to get it banned or create some kind of controversy by releasing it. Of course, the fact that the actors look like you and Jimmy doesn't help. She said that they need us right now though, so we can try to fight it."

"I don't think it'll help," Tarah admitted as she played with the phone cord. "I think they're going to do what they want anyway. I wonder if we can talk about it publicly?"

"That, I'm not sure about."

Tarah found Jimmy downstairs in the weight room where he was working out. Since buying their house, Jimmy said he wanted to get in better shape so that he didn't look like a scrawny kid anymore, not that Tarah ever though he had appeared that way. "You're blinded by love," he would always say anytime she failed to see any faults that he saw in himself.

"Babe, I talked to William." She stuck her head in the room and watched him put some smaller weights on the floor.

"Nothing, right? We can't do a thing." He raised his eyebrows.

"Not really." She shook her head. "Maggie thinks that they're trying to get the video banned and that's why it's so over the top, just as a way to create publicity."

"I was kind of thinking the same thing, hon."

Tarah nodded and walked closer to him. Ever since he started working out, his back and chest were quickly becoming muscular. It was very sexy.

"So, whattcha doing?" She smiled.

"Nothing that can't be stopped." His hands reached out and pulled her closer. "You know what, maybe we should've been in the video after all."

"You think?" Tarah watched him stand up, and his hot breath brushed over her forehead.

"Those actors? We could've showed them up."

CHAPTER FORTY-SIX

▼

The video for "Touch" was an immediate hit. It wasn't banned, as some people had speculated, however there were some religious and parent groups that greatly protested it being played during specific time periods. This was something that the music channel generally respected, but it didn't matter because it only made the kids want to see "Touch" even more. In fact, any form of protest seemed to strengthen the song's popularity. Still, not everyone was completely happy.

Tarah cringed every time the video came on television. The similarity between the actors to both her and Jimmy was just too much for her to handle. There was a great deal of publicity about the subject and some reporters even went as far as to claim that Jimmy and Tarah had suggested the idea of hiring these look-a-likes. There were even those who believed it *was* Jimmy and Tarah featured in "Touch," something that greatly upset the couple.

"Jimmy is furious," Tarah confided in John during a late Saturday night phone call. Her close friend was now the father of a one-month-old baby girl called Sydney. In an attempt to distract himself from his daughter's slight temperature that was keeping him awake, John phoned Tarah and insisted that they talk about anything else but his parental fears. That was when he made reference to the new video, which in turn opened a floodgate.

"I don't blame either of you for being angry," John gently insisted, and Tarah could visualize him on the other end of the line, hovering around Sydney's room, one eye toward her crib while his mind was half into their conversation. All attempts she had made to talk about his baby had failed, and Tarah actually felt a little guilty for discussing the trivial matters of her own life. "It really was a violation of your privacy. Even though you aren't the couple in the video, they clearly taped these extra scenes and plunked them in to create the impression that it's you and Jimmy. I really find it a pretty dirty tactic in order to sell records, but unfortunately a lot of people will assume that it was your band's tactic, rather than that of the record company."

"And you hit the nail right on the head," Tarah insisted. "I feel the same way I would if someone broke into our house when we weren't home and proceeded to go through our stuff. They just crossed the line this time. It's just another thing that makes me believe that the business owns us. Sometimes I think signing that contract five years ago was like selling our souls to the devil, but other times I think that I'm being too much of a diva, because look at everything it's given us. We have money; we've had opportunities and experiences that were incredible. Do I have a right to complain?"

"I believe so," John insisted. "This situation kind of crossed the line. Have you ever gotten in contact with the people responsible for this decision?"

"We talked to the director, but he said he was only following the instructions of our record label because they paid for the video, not us this time."

"And they ...?"

"Won't return our phone calls."

Tarah couldn't shake the feeling that the worst was yet to come, even though Jimmy insisted that everything would get better. They just had to be patient.

The next tour was scheduled to begin in late April. Previous to that, Fire was busy doing interviews on television, for magazines, and at radio stations. Their schedule was packed pretty tight as FUTA did more promotion for their *Dark to Light* CD than all the others combined. There were ads on television, Internet promotions, contests, and practically anything that could put Fire and their music on the forefront of everyone's minds. It was amazing and overwhelming at the same time. What if they couldn't live up to the hype? Even though their new CD was the best work the band had ever done together, and Fire had the strongest bond in their careers, there was still a part of Tarah that feared that the sales wouldn't match FUTA's expectations. What if their tours only received a lukewarm reception? However, these concerns were quickly dissolved as the weeks flew by and it became very apparent that everything was on the right track.

"Sometimes I have to stand back and wonder when all this *became* my life," Tarah solemnly confessed to one of the industry's leading magazines. It was a quote that many people both in and out of the music business could relate to. Who hadn't wondered the very same thing about their own lives from time to time? After all, it was attitude, imagination, and decisions that created everyone's world, regardless of status.

On the weekend before the tour was about to begin, Tarah and Jimmy made plans to go for dinner with William and Maggie. It was a rare opportunity to see how the very private couple interacted with one another, something Tarah could never really envision. Even though a great deal of time had passed since their relationship became public knowledge, it was still amazing how little the world knew about the elusive pair. They didn't do public appearances together, and both refused to discuss one another or their relationship with the media, factors that seemed to fizzle out all interest in the two of them. But it was an evening with the two couples together that turned off Jimmy and Tarah from sending out another invitation for the four of them to get together again.

"I feel like we just went out to eat with our fucking parents," Jimmy remarked as soon as they got in the car and headed out of the parking lot. "I mean, seriously, William is our age, and Maggie is what, in her late twenties or something? And they talked to us like we were a couple of fucking morons who needed to grow up."

"Maybe we do." Tarah shrugged, chewing on a mouthful of bubble gum.

"William was never like that when you were together, was he?"

"Well." Tarah thought back while glancing out the passenger window. "I mean he always acted kind of older than me or more mature."

"It's just weird, they were talking about traveling the world and the best wines available." Jimmy shook his head as they flew down the street. "By the way, when did William start drinking? What's with that?"

"It's wine, I don't think they consider that to really be drinking," Tarah said, gently caressing Jimmy's shoulder, as if to calm him down. "*We* drink, they merely have a glass of wine from time to time."

"And clearly, only the best wine." Jimmy sighed loudly. "I feel like *he's* becoming *her*."

"I don't know," Tarah said, and shrugged. It wasn't a big concern to her, but she understood what Jimmy meant. "Maybe he likes the fact that she's really classy. I mean, she's got the Chanel purse and sunglasses; I wouldn't even attempt to guess which designer is responsible for the outfit she was wearing. She's high-maintenance and I guess that William recognizes that, and I guess, he must like it." Tarah stumbled through the words. "Guys like that kind of thing."

"Not all guys, trust me, but William was always different."

However, neither Jimmy nor Tarah could deny the love that existed between the couple. Even though they were hardly exhibiting their desire for one another, it could easily be seen in both their eyes. The little looks that they shared throughout the evening, something much more subtle than the blatant lust that Tarah and Jimmy had demonstrated at the same stage in their relationship. Each couple's ways of displaying affection was clearly completely foreign to one another. But it was clear that Maggie was much more mellow when she wasn't in business mode. The same woman who had spoken to the band sternly at times, who appeared manipulative and sometimes conniving, was the girl next door when sitting beside William. And it was beyond obvious that he was in awe of the band's former manager.

"I'm just happy they're happy." Tarah decided to end the conversation in a positive note. "Regardless of whether they think we're a couple of morons or not. It doesn't matter. We're just all in different stages. Maybe someday we'll get why they're how they are. But like I said, I'm happy that they're happy. "

"Me too," Jimmy finally replied, reaching out to touch her hand. "It's nice."

It wasn't until the twelfth hour that FUTA announced who was touring with Fire as an opening act. It was a promising new group called Distraction. Although there was a great deal of talk within the industry that this particular band was known to be heavily involved in drugs and partying, everyone in Fire agreed that their music was closely related to their own recent CD and would make a nice addition to their tour. They were scheduled to play across North America and international dates were supposed to be announced later that same year. However, touring the entire continent was enough to think about at first, otherwise the future would be overwhelming to everyone. They were just taking it day by day.

"After this tour is done, I think we need to take a long break," Tarah whispered to Jimmy in bed the night before they were scheduled to fly to Vancouver to do their first official performance. They'd be returning to the province of British Columbia in late July to do a huge outdoor show with other rock bands from both Canada and the United States. "I mean, if it's ever done."

"It'll go faster than you think." Jimmy's eyes looked huge in the dark, something she had grown used to long ago. "But you know that. And, sure, when it's done we really do need to take a break. I feel like we've gone nonstop from day one. The few breaks we've had were never enough for the long days we had to put in throughout the years."

Although the new CD and ticket sales were excellent for the tour, all the gossip and reviews weren't as impressive. Although many magazines spoke kindly of *Dark to Light*, there were still just as many that were critical, especially as the compilation gained popularity. Some tried to suggest that with the *Dark* CD they were trying to carefully follow Marilyn Manson's lead on his *Antichrist Superstar*, while others said that the two CDs were so diverse from each other that the contrast suggested that the band was slowly drifting apart in a creative sense.

Then another controversy erupted. It happened when a fan claimed to a national newspaper that she had been coaxed to give sexual favors to one of the band's roadies in order to meet Eddie back stage. Where, Tarah heard through the grapevine, more sexual favors were delivered. It was a seedy part of the industry that she preferred to give a blind eye to, but this was impossible when the story broke.

"Oh yeah, like *that's* never happened before in the music industry." Jimmy rolled his eyes when the news broke. "Give me a fucking break, that guy didn't exactly force his dick in her mouth, she did it of her own free will. Then she wants to blame us? I don't fucking think so."

Jimmy's crass comments didn't seem to go over well with the other members of the band. And although Tarah did see his point, the girl in question was a teenager, which made the situation even stickier. She noted that Eddie fell silent during the entire discussion and everyone knew exactly why.

"True, but it reflects on our band, and we certainly don't want that kind of image portrayed to our fans." William seemed to take a line out of Maggie's promotional dos and don'ts book, Tarah thought as she avoided Jimmy's eyes. "We can't give the impression to people that we condone a teenage girl being used in that way."

"She let herself be used," Jimmy insisted.

"But she's young. You got to remember that, Jim." William spoke calmly as usual and Tarah thought back to how Jimmy recently complained that he felt like the child, while William was the adult. "That doesn't look good on us."

And so the band made a formal apology and fired the roadie in question. It was unfortunate, but Tarah didn't agree with what this employee had done, and in the end they had an image to protect. And certainly, parents wouldn't allow their teenagers go to Fire concerts if they thought that this roadie was still with the band. Not that any member of Fire had a doubt that it was happening with other groups in the industry, but it wasn't those bands that were being reported in the media.

And just as that controversy began to quiet down, there were rumblings that some obscure author was planning to write a book about Fire. Rumor had it that many ghosts from all their pasts were going to be revealed in the most unflattering light possible. Including some of the many women Jimmy had affairs with before meeting Tarah.

"I don't want to think about it," Tarah snapped, when Jimmy attempted to discuss the news with her after it was revealed to the band. Just over a month into the tour and she was already starting to feel the strain of the fast-paced, bad publicity on top of the added pressure of having to make this CD compilation a huge success. Tarah began to feel like she was drowning and knew it was important to regain her strength, but it was getting more and more difficult. "I didn't want to think about all the girls from your past when we met, and I don't want to think about them now."

"I don't blame you and I don't want to think about them either." Jimmy tried to comfort her as she lay in their hotel room bed. She'd been angry all morning. His hand gently ran down her arm. "Tarah, it's the past, but, of course people are going to come out of the woodwork with their stories if some author is offering them money or fifteen minutes of fame, whatever it is."

"It just bothers me. I can't handle anything more," Tarah complained. "Why can't they ever just leave us alone?" She often thought of how celebrity couples broke up and blamed the strain of fame as being a contributing factor. Now she understood.

"Tarah, it's the same problem we keep running into, but it's just a different direction this time." He paused for a moment. "Not that I think it helps very much, but these are girls from a million years ago, and they didn't mean anything to me. It's not like I've been with anyone else since we've been together, so it shouldn't bother you. I don't think about the guys you were with before us."

"Yeah, well I wasn't with God knows how many guys before you," Tarah pointed out, turning around so that their eyes met. He quickly looked away. "I had boyfriends, I didn't have a chain of one night stands. And you never did tell me how many there were."

"Because it doesn't matter," Jimmy insisted, and looked back into her eyes. "Most of them were girls I met when I worked at the bar, or when I was out partying. It doesn't matter how many."

Tarah had attempted to guess his number many times but he refused to say. She knew that the string of women started after breaking up with his first girlfriend at seventeen and had only stopped when he started to date her at age twenty-two. Although logically, Tarah didn't feel that it was likely that he had been with that many women in probably a four-year span, she somehow knew better. The only thing he had ever revealed to her was that the total was well into the triple digits. Jimmy later told Tarah that he deeply regretted even giving her that information and suggested she forget about it. Most of the time she did but other times, it haunted her. Especially now that there were suggestions that Jimmy had been with well over three hundred women and when Tarah asked him, he didn't admit or deny it. To her, that suggested he was guilty.

"I don't understand," Tarah said and closed her eyes. She told herself over and over that it didn't matter. In her heart, Tarah knew Jimmy never had cheated on her, but it still felt like a jab in her chest to think that possibly hundreds of women had been intimate with him before she was even in the picture. It gave her an uneasy feeling even though she knew it was probably not justified. There were women, after all, whose husbands had just as many affairs while they were together. Who was she to complain about his sexual history before they even met?

Not knowing what to do about the tension between them during the upcoming days, Jimmy ordered her flowers and bought Tarah a beautiful ruby ring. But in the end, it was a desperate speech that finally won her over.

"I give up," Jimmy confessed after a week had passed, slumping his shoulders in defeat after another show where their own problems were not even evident to the fans. They were sitting in yet another hotel room, and he watched Tarah having a drink. "I don't know what else to do. Maybe if I was sophisticated like Will and Mags then I'd know just what to say or buy, but I'm just me and I don't know this kind of stuff, Tar." The dim light of the room revealed a tired version of his face. He ran a hand through his hair and gave her a desperate look. "If I could erase the entire past, you know I would. In fact, I'd start with erasing all the girls, and then I'd erase you meeting William first; and then we'd all be fine. Neither of us would ever have to think about who was with who before."

Tarah wanted to say something but the words caught in her throat. Suddenly she saw that all the women in his past were equivalent to the one man in her own past who made Jimmy feel insecure. Suddenly, she didn't feel so justified in being angry.

"You really feel that way?" she finally managed, quickly realizing that it was a stupid question.

"Yes." Jimmy spoke honestly. "All those girls were just girls who meant nothing to me," he reminded her. "You were in love with William. There's a whole world of difference there. All the numbers in the world sometimes don't compare to just one." He held up his finger and she felt chills run up her spine.

"I'm sorry." Tarah felt her heart race as she rushed into an apology, but he quickly cut her off.

"Don't apologize, it's not necessary," Jimmy insisted, his voice now barely a whisper. "If you only knew how many times I've wondered to myself, what if I had done things differently? What if I had been more direct with you about my feelings sooner, rather than standing back and watching William with the girl I wanted to be with? I don't know. Maybe it wouldn't have mattered to you then or maybe it would." He fell silent for a moment and Jimmy tilted his head slightly. "But if you *only* knew how many times I've wondered."

Tarah forgave him that night.

The tour ran through the summer months, and FUTA continued to introduce new promotions to gain more records sales, not that they were doing poorly on their own. It was apparent that any negative media attention wasn't preventing their fans from buying *Dark to Light* and the momentum was only building as the tour went forth. But Tarah continued to feel drained from the grueling days and found herself often ending her night with a drink or a joint. A few months into the tour, both Jimmy and Tarah were accepting frequent invites from the members of Distraction to various parties. Most were centered around drugs. Where cocaine had once been the drug of choice in their circle, now Tarah and Jimmy were introduced to a new world. And although the couple refused to even consider anything as intense as heroin, they certainly had access to it. But it didn't stop them from trying various pills; some to keep them up, others to bring them back down. At the time, it seemed harmless.

CHAPTER FORTY-SEVEN

▼

"I don't like what we're doing. I don't like the people we've become."

These words were on the tip of her tongue, but she couldn't quite get them out. Tarah silently followed Jimmy, hand in hand, as they wandered through the crowd of strangers at a random party that Distraction invited them to that night. Both bands had just been part of a day-long, large outdoor concert that gave Fire the opportunity to play to the biggest audience of their careers. And because Tarah was nervous, the singer for Distraction gave her a pill just before Fire went on stage. She didn't know what it was but mindlessly followed his instructions to swallow the bitter-tasting object. He was right: she sailed through the show like it was nothing. But the pill's effects were still being felt.

When had she become this person? It was the question that Tarah wanted to ask, but her lips wouldn't move. She felt numb and withdrawn from the world. They approached an empty space on a couch, and Tarah felt Jimmy's hand release hers, gesturing for her to sit down. She wanted to tell him that she didn't want to be there, but he turned to talk to someone who was sitting on the other side of him. Tarah couldn't even function enough to see who it was, and in a way, she didn't really care. Every moment was surreal. She just wanted to crawl out of her skin and escape the world around her. Would Jimmy noticed if she died right then? Did he even remember she was there? Had he noticed her acting strange? She felt scared and neglected.

That's when she realized that Jimmy was talking to the guy who gave her the pill. Was he asking what was wrong with her? What if she was never normal again? What if this was permanent? Only a few hours earlier she had been fine. Why was she such a zombie now? Why did people like being this way? It made her feel insane.

Slowly, she found herself coming out of her stupor and returning to the real world. It felt like hours had passed but Jimmy later revealed that it was only about twenty to forty minutes. Neither of them ever found out what kind of pill she had been given. Jimmy was quite angry that she had taken an anonymous drug, making her promise not to take such a chance again. She had been frightened after that experience, and knew it would be the last time she did drugs. It was time to grow up.

Although the band's goal of increased and continual success seemed to be hand delivered, so were the added pressures and stress that quietly accompanied it. But it was the music that kept Tarah and the rest of Fire going. She often reflected on how there was no feeling in the world like being on stage with clusters of enthusiastic fans screaming, dancing, and singing to the songs that *they* wrote from their hearts. It filled her up in a way nothing else could, not even love. It was indescribable, and there were moments when Tarah couldn't believe that she was really doing it, that she was living a dream that most would cut off their left arm to experience for even a day.

In August, the band was told about a fourteen-year-old fan who was dying of leukemia and wanted to see Fire play live, something they were all happy to accommodate. The teenage girl was named Tia, and she not only wanted to see the band perform, she also had a special request for Jimmy and Tarah. Apparently one of her favorite songs was "It's Only Love" by Bryan Adams, and she requested that the couple sing the song together on that night.

"Man, I don't know." Jimmy cringed when he heard the news. "I don't want to sound like a prick, but I just don't like being in the spotlight that much."

"Jimmy." Tarah spoke in a calm voice while gently touching his hand. "She's *dying*. I think you can put your own concerns aside this time. It's a really big deal to her." And after a long pause she added. "Do you think I'm comfortable doing this? Tina Turner is a legend. I can't possibly measure up to her!" She referred to the singer who originally sang the song with Bryan Adams.

He quietly nodded, realizing his wife was right. After all, the teenager had been given less than six months to live. If there had been any doubts about fulfilling Tia's wish, they disappeared two days later after watching an interview featured on the girl's local news station. Small and feeble, Tia smiled brightly to the television camera and talked honestly about the fact that she had accepted her own mortality and that being sick had taught her to live every day as if it were her last. The poignant words hit Tarah particularly hard. Tears ran down her face as she watched a small town television reporter inquire about the fourteen-year-old's difficult journey, and Tarah realized that her own problems were quite small in comparison. Jimmy passed her a box of Kleenex, and Tarah listened to the dying child speak excitedly about Fire's upcoming show in a nearby city and how she was going to be a VIP in the audience.

"And I understand that you had a very special request for the members of Fire for this particular show?" The reporter spoke with enthusiasm. "You asked them to sing "It's Only Love" by Bryan Adams and Tina Turner? I think that song must be as old as you!"

Tarah smiled in spite of herself as the young woman replied by saying that it had been one of her favorites since she was "a kid" and that recently, she'd had a dream where Tarah and Jimmy were singing the duet especially for her. "It was really cool," she went on to say with an infectious smile. "It felt so real, and I think it might be a sign."

" A sign of what?" the reporter asked.

"A sign that they'll always be in love," Tia said dreamily.

Three days later, they were ready to perform the song. The band met the dying fan just before their show, and Tarah knew she had to find it in herself to push all emotions aside. She couldn't think about how it felt to hug a fragile young woman who was clearly fading away, her body so small, yet surprisingly strong, as she tightly clung on to Tarah while thanking Fire for inviting her to their show and especially for performing one of her favorite songs, even though it was by another artist.

"That's fine," Tarah insisted. "It's not the first time we did someone else's song and took the credit," she joked.

"I'm so happy because, like, that will make this a perfect night." The girl smiled and stuttered nervously through her words. She twirled a strand of blonde hair that flowed from the wig that she wore, while her big, blue eyes glanced around at the entire band. Tarah noted that she wore a slight tinge of blush, as well cotton candy, pink lipstick and nail polish. And even though the small crowd that gathered around the teenager was clearly saddened by her fate, the terminally ill girl herself seemed to be in the best of spirits, if not a little shy.

Tarah wasn't sure of how she'd get through that performance. Her thoughts jumped back to the last time she had done a special request in an emotional situation. It had been in memory of Wendy, and she suffered through a bad panic attack because of it. What if this happened again that night? The song they were performing for the sick, young girl was to be at the end of their show, so that helped, but still, what if she couldn't handle it? Had she really became any stronger in the last couple of years?

But the show was a success. It seemed like the entire band put on their best performance in years, on some level knowing that it'd possibly be the last one Tia would ever see before dying. Although the girl had only one specific request, it was clear that every word of every song was being sent out to the enthusiastic fan in the VIP section. It was *her* show that night and no one else's.

When the concert was about to end, Tarah announced that they had a dedication for a "very special fan." The band started to play the song that had topped the charts ten years earlier, and the entire audience seemed to be singing along while a very sick girl cried and smiled at the same time. So did the girl's parents, as they stood beside Tia.

Luckily, Tarah was so engrossed in having Jimmy front and center with her, that she hadn't seen the tears. This was fortunate since she would've been sobbing right along with Tia. However at the time, Tarah's face was lit up with a smile watching a grinning Jimmy making eye contact with her. It was the first time he had ever sung anything but backup vocals for Fire, but he did so with such ease that the song flowed very smoothly. Meanwhile, the audience went insane as they watched the idolized couple singing to one another—it was a rare treat.

Just a little past the halfway point of "It's Only Love," there was a silent pause in the original song that the band had previously decided would be extended for a more dramatic effect. However, they weren't prepared for the overwhelming response of the audience during those few quiet seconds. Tarah felt her entire body turn toward the thousands of fans who were before her and she could hear it. At first, the cheers sounded far away and then suddenly, they were a stampede galloping on the stage. She felt frozen in time as the intense love from the audience flowed toward the band in such abundance that it almost took her breath away. It was like hot sun and cool breeze all at once. The warmth fell across her face and entire body one limb at a time, while a chill ran through her spine. Tarah's throat went dry. It was a second of her life that Tarah would never forget, regardless of what the future held.

The sound of Jimmy's guitar broke the silence and brought her back into the moment. She finished the song with everything she had and it was followed by the most powerful applause of Fire's career. She blew a kiss to the audience and left the stage, only to return for an encore.

Television cameras had been in the building that night, mostly to tape a B roll for the segment following up the original story. It wasn't something that the band had really given much thought to since everyone simply cared about making a dying girl's wish come true. However, this time the story would be presented to viewers throughout North America rather than just locally. Everybody loved the fact that a rock band with a somewhat controversial history, was now giving something back to a dying fan.

Tarah watched the follow-up news story the next evening. She smiled seeing the playback of her and Jimmy singing to one another on stage and a part of her relived the magic of that night. But then they went to the sick girl crying in the audience, and Tarah felt anger rise inside her body. In her eyes, they were exploiting a dying teenager. They wanted to play on people's emotions rather than focusing on the positive in the story. It depressed Tarah. She turned off the television and sank into bed. Beside her, Jimmy was sleeping peacefully.

In the days that followed, Tarah grew more and more depressed. She found herself drinking regularly. However, this time, it was for an escape and not for fun. There was a big difference and a part of her knew that she was on the wrong track when her habits changed so quickly. But another part of her didn't care. She wasn't sure how else to cope. Life flew too many questions at her and Tarah wasn't able to answer them fast enough, if at all. Why did she feel so powerless? Did she deserve all her fame? When did this insane merry-go-round stop? Was she part of the cold, cruel media that exploited people? Was it partially the band's fault that Tia was exploited? And why did kids who hadn't even experienced life yet, get a terminal illness?

Two weeks later, Tia lost her battle with cancer.

As August slowly made its way to completion, the band continued to perform across the country and promote *Dark to Light*. The American leg of the tour was about to begin in two weeks, and all Tarah could think about was when it would end. She loved to perform but their vigorous schedule was growing tiring. It was rare that the band had a day off. There was always a show or heavy promotion to television and radio stations. Fire had done so many interviews that Tarah felt as though she had memorized a script and was repeating it over and over. The questions and answers were always the same. She thought back to when her career began and didn't recall feeling like a puppet on a string as she did now. But it didn't make sense. After all, wasn't this what Tarah had wanted? What the entire band wanted? Yet, when she glanced around at their faces sometimes, everyone's eyes were soulless and dead. It wasn't exciting anymore. The thrill had long disappeared. Now it was all business. Had they been naive before, or were they just unappreciative now?

On their off time, Jimmy continued to explore the partying scene; Tarah tagged along but avoided drugs. Her last experience had scared her way too much. And when Tarah looked around at these parties and nightclubs, it appeared that she was the only one who avoided this lifestyle. The very people who showed optimism and a positive attitude on daytime talk shows wearing their sophisticated and cute outfits, could be found at these parties. Often they were snorting, smoking, or drinking their way out of the illusion in which they lived. Nobody wanted to exist in the fishbowl that they created, but no one knew the way out. It was a side that the rest of the world didn't know a thing about, and clearly, that's how celebrities wanted it.

Not that Tarah was any different. She walked on the television stages, talked to the DJs, and television hosts, only to sit in a dark room with the very same people later that night and watch them snort a line of coke. It happened a lot. It happened regularly. It was a dirty and disgusting world that everyone tried to hide. Partially because it was unacceptable, but mostly because no one wanted to be honest with themselves let alone the fans. It was a shameful secret that had to be kept.

It was during one of these parties that someone gave Jimmy and Tarah Ecstasy. Although she originally said no, she found herself slipping the pill in her mouth after watching her husband do the same only moments earlier. They left the party early, went home and had what they later considered the best sex since they met, and then woke up the following day wishing they were dead. Jimmy was tired and Tarah was depressed. The most depressed of her life. She felt hopeless and weak. All she did was cry; Jimmy tried to console her, but when she looked in his eyes, it was as if he were dead inside. Like he couldn't completely comprehend what was going on. Yet, they had to get dressed and do an interview later that same day. Luckily, both bands had taken the end of August and first few days of September off for Labor Day. Everyone needed it. And Tarah and Jimmy went back to their house that they'd barely seen in weeks.

Tarah should've felt more comfortable waking up in her own bed the following day, but it didn't matter much because she felt like crawling out of her own skin. She stood up and walked toward a mirror. Stopping for a moment, her vacant eyes stared back. She was pale and thin. Ashamed, Tarah walked downstairs to find Jimmy in the living room. He was eating a bowl of cereal and watching television. Tarah felt as though she was dragging her body across the room, feeling as miserable as the last morning but unable to express it. How could she describe the waves of depression that seemed to continually flow over her? But she had to try.

"Jimmy?"

"Oh my fucking God, Tarah!" her husband exclaimed as soon as he saw her standing in the room. Using his spoon to point toward the television, his eyes were wide while he rapidly chewed his food. "Did you see this? Princess Di is dead!"

His words hit her like a brick. She turned toward the television to see the scene of a car accident, then a flash of a crowded memorial site in England. Tears burned her lids but Tarah couldn't stop staring at the newscaster as he spoke of how Princess Diana and Dodi Al-Fayed were in a car that was desperately trying to escape the paparazzi. Feeling her stomach turning, Tarah

Fire

flew to the closest bathroom to vomit. And she couldn't stop. She heard Jimmy behind her, talking, but she couldn't understand what he was saying. His hand was on her shoulder. Finally she stopped, realizing that tears were running off her face and dripping into the toilet.

She cried as Jimmy flushed the toilet and got her a glass of water. Tarah silently glanced down at her blue nightgown with puppies on it, thinking of how she was way too jaded to wear such a child-like piece of clothing. Jimmy sat on the floor beside her and rubbed Tarah's back with one hand, while holding the glass of water with the other.

"It's okay."

"No, but it's not Jimmy." Tarah frowned. "This is what our world has come to; it's just about the next big story to these people. And it's the vultures who will chase a car and cause an accident that kills people, just for a story!" Tarah began to cry again. "And the worst part is that these magazines and papers sell. I don't know what is worse, the people who sell them or the ones who read them."

"I know, Tar. I do. I understand." Jimmy continued to rub her back while speaking softly. "You're right. I was as shocked as you were. Princess Di was a really cool woman who cared about people and this is how she was paid back. I'm angry too. Although we haven't dealt with the media to the same extent as her, we certainly have in our own way. And, I don't know, I can't even imagine what it must've been like to live in such a fishbowl. Sometimes it seems like the bigger celebrity you are, the smaller your world really is and the less air you have to breathe."

Tarah later watched interviews with celebrities who would express sympathy for Princess Diana, disdain for the overzealous reporters, and rant about how the paparazzi made their own lives hell. However, many of the people were often the first to manipulate the media when it became an advantage for them. It was a game. And no one played by the same rules.

But there were also celebrities who shared Tarah's point of view. They felt that the human race had hit an all time low, and that it was only going to get worse. It also shook a lot of people to their foundation. If it happened to Princess Di, who's to say they weren't next? If it wasn't an overly anxious reporter, it could've been an overly enthused fan or a psychotic critic. Anything was possible.

And although Jimmy and Tarah had promised each other to stop experimenting with drugs that manipulated their emotions as the Ecstasy had, there would come a day when Jimmy would forget their conversation. It happened later that fall, just as their tour was about to finish in North America.

Christmas was a little more than a month away, and Tarah felt the happiest of her life. Everything had been going better and she thought nothing could bring her down again. Life was slowly starting to feel right and she wasn't sure why. She should've realized that there would always be some bumps in the roads. And sometimes there were craters.

It was at a party in their hotel in late November that the course of everything would change. Jimmy and Tarah were feeling on top of their game, their CD had surpassed everyone's expectations, and the tour had been an amazing success. They were untouchable. Nothing could hurt them. And it was that night that Jimmy took a mix of drugs without thinking of the consequences and under the assumption that the supplier had any reason to be honest.

And as Jimmy watched Tarah that night, as she stood across the room from him and talked to a famous rock star, he felt his anger and jealousy grow. His eyes stared through her for what felt like hours, assuming that what could've easily been a casual conversation was a grand seduction. And as "Deformography" by Marilyn Manson filed the room and the words flowed through Jimmy's brain, he felt his heart pounding wildly and a rage burn inside of him. Knowing that his reaction wasn't logical, he jumped from the couch where he had been sitting and flew across the room. Grabbing Tarah's arm, he pulled her toward the door. Ignoring her obvious resistance, Jimmy bullied her into the hotel hallway and practically dragged an angry and humiliated Tarah back to their room, which was on the next floor. But what started off as a fight, ended on a completely different note.

CHAPTER FORTY-EIGHT

▼

"Let fucking go of me!" Tarah shook away Jimmy's hand as they got inside the elevator to return to their room. Both seemed unaware or unconcerned with the fact that two middle-aged businessmen were already located inside, waiting for the couple to decide on what floor they wanted to go on. Neither seemed startled so much as annoyed by the impulsive pair. "What is wrong with you? I was just talking to the guy, what right did you have to drag me away like that?"

"I'm not fucking stupid, Tarah." Jimmy shaking hand selected their floor, and the two men who stood back in the elevator exchanged looks. "I know what I saw."

"What you saw," Tarah sternly reminded him, "was me talking to someone I grew up listening to, not some random guy at a party. I just wanted to introduce myself, nothing more and nothing less."

The elevator door opened and the two made an abrupt exit. Both fell silent as they returned to the hotel room and went inside. Jimmy headed to the bathroom, where he bent over the sink and threw cold water on his face. The song "Closer" by Nine Inch Nails could be heard in the next room and suddenly Tarah was standing in the doorway watching Jimmy with interest. She held back, almost as if apprehensive to enter the bathroom, noting that he almost appeared frustrated by the fact that she was there at all. He sighed loudly and grabbed a towel to wipe his face, then threw it over the tap.

"I'm sorry, Tarah. I don't know what I took at the party, but I feel really fucked-up right now," His breathing seemed to become heavier as he gripped the sink and looked down into it. She noted that Jimmy's face was relaxed, but there was something different his eyes that night, something she knew was the drugs. It hurt her to see Jimmy spinning out of control. "I feel like I'm on the edge."

"Of what?"

He turned his head, Jimmy's blue eyes suddenly appeared seductive and enchanting and after a long silence, he finally answered her. "Everything."

Slowly approaching her husband, she felt the weight of his eyes on her own. But he didn't look away, not even for a second. He didn't even blink, just stared.

Tarah's fingers gently touched Jimmy's cheek, and she moved close enough to feel his hot breath against her face. Desire flowed through her body as his soft lips met with her own and one of Jimmy's fingers ran down her back and under the waistband of her pants. Tarah suddenly wanted him with a strong intensity and judging by how his hand was sliding inside the back of her jeans, he felt the same way. Reluctantly letting go of his lips, she could hear his breathing become heavier by the second and she reached for Jimmy's spare hand and slowly took it in her own while the other one disappeared from the back of her jeans.

"Let's go to bed," she barely whispered, her own throat becoming dry as she watched a small bead of sweat form on his forehead. Tarah glanced at the bulge in his pants and her heart started pounding at an almost frightening pace. "Do your worst," she challenged him, turning to walk away, her hand in his, preparing to lead him to the king-sized bed in the next room. But she was barely a few steps from him when she felt such a powerful tug on her arm that Tarah thought it was being pulled out of its socket. Her entire body was swung around, and Jimmy's face was almost touching her own when his breathing turned to panting and boldness entered his eyes.

"Do my worst?" he challenged her, continuing to grip her arm tightly, his fingers digging into the soft flesh causing her to whimper in pain. "You have no idea what you're asking."

And with one sudden move, Tarah felt her entire body thrown against the nearby wall. Her skull made a huge thud as it hit the hard surface, and the wind was almost knocked from her lungs. The beautiful mirror that hung over the nearby sink came crashing down, with broken glass scattering everywhere. Before she had a second to send out a scream from the pain or protest the barbaric actions from her husband, Tarah felt Jimmy's lips roughly take over her own and his tongue dart into her mouth. She could barely breathe and her head throbbed, yet Tarah felt incredibly aroused as his body pressed against her own. She was pinned between the wall and Jimmy, and Tarah felt like her legs were about to give out from beneath her. Her body was begging for him to be inside of her as the bulge in his pants seemed to get bigger and her thong became wetter. If he were to walk away at that moment, she would've begged him. Pleaded. Given him anything in the world. Tarah had never wanted someone more in her life.

So when Jimmy suddenly moved away from her, she automatically felt a huge sense of disappointment. His eyes were full of lust and his breathing continued to be heavy as his fingers traced the outline of her chin. They continued to travel down until reaching the neckline of her T-shirt. It was then that Tarah felt her entire body being pulled forward and he suddenly ripped the material opened, revealing a soft pink bra underneath. His mouth hungrily moved between her breasts, and she heard a loud moan escape her lips; the material from her top fell to the ground. His mouth moved back up her neck and to her chin, where drops of his saliva dripped from her face as his teeth gently grazed her skin. She felt Jimmy's hands running up and down her naked back while his tongue ran down to the place where her neck and shoulder connected. Tarah gasped when she felt his teeth dig into her skin then moaned loudly when he began to greedily suck her neck. His hands ran over her hips, squeezing them; she felt herself being lifted up, and she instinctively wrapped her legs around his body. Jimmy's mouth moved up to her ear and his own gasps of desire only caused her to tighten her grip to his body. He began to kiss her with renewed intensity, and she felt her body being moved down to the floor.

Jimmy's hands ran through her hair and his mouth started to move down her body once again. He stopped briefly, sitting up to quickly remove his T-shirt to reveal his naked and muscular chest. His hands touched her stomach then moved back up, and while one began to lower a bra strap, the other released the clip on the back. He quickly removed the pink material, and his tongue ran over her left nipple while Tarah's hands ran through his hair. She felt a tingling throughout her body and wanted the foreplay to just be over with. How much more of this could she possibly take? She felt like a child who was being tickled continually, with no relief in sight.

He sat up again, this time to remove her jeans. They were fortunately loose and slid right off. Then Jimmy stood up. He slowly unfastened his belt buckle while standing over her, something Tarah found wildly irresistible. Dropping his pants to the floor, Jimmy stood before her wearing nothing but a pair of blue boxers.

Jimmy moved back down to the floor and on top of her. She felt something sticky as his hand ran over her face. Out of the corner of her eye, Tarah could see blood on his arm, she assumed from the broken glass from the nearby mirror. However, his fingers were moving over her body so quickly, that blotches of blood were on both of them including a huge glob on his cheek. The tip of her tongue ran over the spot on his face where the scarlet droplets were collected, and she suddenly craved the taste, her tongue hungrily licking it up like it was the most expensive champagne in the world.

Instinctively, she knew there was something incredibly sick about wanting to taste his blood, but there was something irresistibly hot about it too.

Tarah watched as Jimmy moved away from her and turned her body around so that she was on her hands and knees. Tarah felt the heat between her legs only increasing as she anticipated him to finally move inside her. She could hear him standing up and removing his underwear. They often did it doggy style and he knew she loved it, but as he ran his hands over her ass and spread her legs, Tarah suddenly let out a loud yelp when she felt him push past her thong and into her ass. It hurt, and she cried in pain and begged him to stop, for some reason Jimmy seemed to instead push harder into her anal region. She hated it and started to cry, and his hand reached for her throat; Tarah was surprised when his fingers tightly gripped her neck. He finally let go and the other hand that had been gently massaging her scalp, suddenly grabbed her hair and yanked it back. She let out a scream and finally felt him pull out of her ass. This was nothing like the sex they usually had. Although it was never boring, it was also never this forceful. It scared her. And she liked it.

But almost as if he were reading her thoughts, she could once again feel Jimmy's hot breath in her ear as he gasped loudly. She was still on all fours as his hand moved over her thong and between her legs, squeezing the material and everything beneath it. He began to suck her earlobe and she felt his saliva running down her face and dripping from her chin. His tongue then ran down her back slowly, while his fingers slid past the thong and inside of her, and Tarah felt her body floating toward her first orgasm. It was so intense that she screamed in pleasure while his tongue ran down her back until it reached her hips. He withdrew his fingers, and she felt his hands on each of her thighs, while his tongue fumbled around with the back of her thong. His lips grazed her skin as she felt him start to remove the piece of material with his teeth. Letting go, he slowly turned her over and licked the fabric that had just been nestled between her legs before taking it all in his mouth and continuing. He then pulled it off and threw it aside.

She felt so dirty—and even more aroused by his actions.

He moved back up again, his head swooping in between her legs aggressively where his tongue worked furiously along with his fingers, until Tarah heard herself crying out in pleasure once again. Not that it took a lot of time. She wasn't sure if it was because of the severity of the sexual experience, but her body seemed to be ultra sensitive to every touch, causing intense pleasure from each orgasm, Tarah continued to want more. She couldn't help it. Her desire was overwhelming.

Jimmy moved on top of her and both of their bodies were sticky from a combination of things that included the blood from the broken mirror and saliva that seemed to flow freely every time his mouth touched her. The sex was dirty and degrading. But she liked it.

Their mouths grinded together once again, and Tarah spread her legs far apart. There was no denying that Jimmy was not going to be able to delay things much longer, his dick was pushing into her stomach and she finally felt him moving it between her legs. His pushing himself inside her felt like heaven, and Tarah cried out in anticipation. She wrapped her legs around him and dug her nails into his back.

"Oh my God!" she gasped and arched her back. "Jimmy, I can't! Oh my God!"

Jimmy thrust roughly into her, while noises she had never heard before escaped from the back of his throat. Small droplets of sweat fell on her face as he ploughed farther and farther into her, and she felt a combination of pleasure and pain. But she continued to encourage him to work harder, push harder, and he pulled her hips up slightly. Tarah finally felt herself come, and she experienced an orgasm that seemed to flow through her entire body while Jimmy groaned loudly and somehow seemed to push even farther into her before collapsing on her body. He was drenched in sweat and stuck to her body. Their hearts were both pounding wildly. She couldn't move. Not that she wanted to at that moment. They both lay there in silence for a long time before standing up.

Jimmy automatically grabbed a towel and began to wipe himself off. Tarah turned toward a mirror and was stunned by what she saw. Her hair was in disarray and she appeared wild-eyed. There was blood all over her, including running between her legs, and when she turned around, Tarah discovered more on her ass. And the bruises were everywhere! On her legs, thighs, arm, back, and one on Tarah's neck. She didn't dare say anything to Jimmy, who watched her from the other side of the room, but she resembled a rape victim.

"Hey, it's not just you," he observed, and turned around and Tarah saw scratch marks all over his back, shoulders, and even some on his ass. Had she done that? Tarah couldn't even remember. He had no bruises but more blood than she did. And it was everywhere.

Tarah's legs were weak, and she sat on the edge of the tub. Staring at the broken glass on the floor, she shivered and wondered if there was something completely wrong with them. She felt uncomfortable and didn't know how to get herself back to normal. Not that she regretted the sex. There was just something unsettling about it.

"Baby, we've got to take a shower." He grabbed a robe in the corner and put it on. She shivered and remained quiet. "Actually, you should run a bath. Do you want a robe?" He asked but brought one to her before she could answer. He gently helped her put it on while his eyes quietly inspected the bruises.

"Are you okay?" he finally asked. And Tarah nodded.

"Are you sure?"

Tarah shook her head no. "I feel like I took whatever you had. I don't feel right."

"Me neither," Jimmy admitted, and almost seeming to be hesitant to sit beside her. "I don't think I can do that shit anymore. I can't do those drugs. I know I've said it before, but this kind of freaks me out a bit. And although the sex was crazy and insane, there's something just not right in my head and I can't describe it."

"Me too," Tarah whispered, and she felt him pull her close and kiss her cheek. They both were looking at the broken glass on the floor. There was blood everywhere. She watched as Jimmy stood up beside her and turned on the tub, occasionally checking the water. Tarah was in a daze and watched the water as it flowed out of the tap. When the tub was finally filled, she disrobed and got in and felt some comfort from the water that flowed around her ravished body. It was comfortable.

Jimmy left the room and Tarah just stared into the water, thinking back to her childhood baths. A part of her wanted to escape back to her childhood and start over. But then again, it was said that if you went back in time and changed even the smallest detail of your life, everything in your future would change with it. As much as she sometimes felt like her life was too out of control, there were some things that she'd never change. Like Jimmy. What would she ever do without him? Everything she had dealt with in the previous years would have been unbearable if it weren't for him. The money and fame were wonderful in theory, but love gave you a sense of security and comfort that was amazing.

A tear trickled down her face and she quickly wiped it away. But it was followed by another and then another. She thought about how out of control she felt at times and Tarah realized that it was up to her to make some changes before the industry took over her entire life. They were getting close and she had to stop them. Time went by fast and it was not uncommon for Tarah to not know the day of the week, let along the date she woke up on. It was insanity.

And the drugs had to stop. Jimmy was right about that one. Why had they ever started doing them? Why did they go to those ridiculous parties? Why weren't they just dealing with the stress and frustrations rather than drinking and drugging them away? And even though she was clean, that night had turned into a scene from a twisted movie. The sex had been mind-blowing, but strange at the same time. She had felt so disconnected from Jimmy, which didn't seem right at all.

After her bath, Jimmy took a quick shower and they both went to bed. Curled up and cozy, as if there were no blood or broken glass on the bathroom floor, the two fell to sleep. Nothing was abnormal and nothing was strange.

CHAPTER FORTY-NINE

▼

"I never thought I'd see the day that you'd bake anything, let alone Christmas cookies." Jimmy laughed and grabbed one of the poorly decorated Santa Clauses from a plate of holiday characters. Each sugar cookie had globs of overlapping frosting, a disappointment to Tarah who had intended for her creations to be perfect. "Look at this guy," he held up the Santa Clause and signaled toward his missing foot. "An amputee."

"What can I say?" Tarah couldn't help but join him in laughter. "I'm not very domestic."

Jimmy nodded, biting into his cookie. "Good thing you're awesome in bed or I'd never put up with you," he teased, giving her a quick wink and disappearing from the room. She simply smiled and shook her head. When recently asked in an interview why she thought her relationship with Jimmy continued to be strong even though they worked in an unstable industry, Tarah had commented on how they simply had a lot of fun together. There was a definitely a playfulness between them, something that people like William and Maggie probably wouldn't understand, but it didn't matter. Their relationship was only between her and Jimmy, no one else's opinion or thoughts really mattered. And it was only going to get better.

It was the first year since Tarah's childhood that she really looked forward to Christmas. After her parent's divorce, the holidays were usually divided between time in a dreary bachelor apartment with her dad or an undecorated house of depression with her mom. After Tarah moved out on her own, she rarely could afford gifts for Christmas, and New Year's Eve was a regular reminder that she was either in an unhappy relationship or none at all. When she finally had all the elements that made for a wonderful holiday season, Wendy was murdered. Three years had passed since that horrible day, and although Tarah would always associate her former friend with the Christmas season, the sting was getting slightly weaker. It was an unfortunate tragedy and had been devastating at the time, but Tarah was learning to put things in perspective and move forward. After all, it was also during the holidays that she and Jimmy were married.

The tour for *Dark to Light* was finished for the year and had been a huge success. In early January, the band was scheduled to meet with FUTA reps to discuss their future with the company. It was at that time that Fire would be involved in contract negotiations and discuss their international tour that was supposed to start in late March. However, no dates were written in stone, something Tarah assumed wouldn't happen until FUTA knew for certain that the band would re-sign with them. And although it hadn't been discussed between Jimmy, Tarah, William, Eddie, and Michael recently, there was a mutual understanding that they all wanted to consider their possibilities. Other labels had approached them and everyone in Fire wanted to weigh their options.

There were also rumors that William had been considering a solo career. He hadn't discussed this with anyone in Fire, but that wasn't unusual. Since his relationship with Maggie had started, there was a clear wall between him and the rest of the band. Jimmy suspected that she was working on him, attempting to separate the band's lead guitarist from the rest of Fire. There was a good chance she'd be successful. After all, Maggie knew the industry and could easily push his career in whatever direction she saw fit. To Tarah, it seemed like a complicated situation to get involved in, especially if the power couple were ever to break up. Not that anyone had any reason to think they would, but the two still kept their relationship tightly under wraps. It was understandable, but also kind of weird.

Tarah and Jimmy decided to keep a low profile as well, but for them it was on the party scene. Ever since the previous month when Jimmy took the unidentified pill, the couple decided that enough was enough. It was a dark path that they didn't want to journey down any longer, it was time to grow up. After all, how many of their own idols had died after becoming heavily involved in drugs? It certainly was possible. And they were much too happy to either ruin or end their lives. It was time to turn the page.

Then there the brutal sex thing in November. Tarah noticed that Jimmy seemed to have forgotten the entire encounter, waking up the next morning and having to be reminded why she was full of bruises. At first he appeared very alarmed to learn that he had anything to do with the dark marks that covered her body, but she assured him it was okay. It wasn't like he had beaten her. And the sex had been mind-blowing, even though a little over the top even for them. But there was something very unsettling about that night that seemed to follow Tarah, like a ghost sitting on her shoulder. She attempted to push her uneasiness aside, but it continued to return.

Tarah and Jimmy decided to stay in Toronto for the holidays, opting out of visiting any of their relatives for Christmas and instead having a quiet celebration at their home. Although no one in either of their families seemed to like this idea, everyone quickly forgot it the week before Christmas when the couple returned to Thorton to visit and distribute gifts.

"I think everyone was so excited to see us this happy that they let down their guards," Tarah commented on the way home that night. She was exhausted and could barely keep her eyes opened. "This is the first year that I really can't wait for Christmas."

And there was a big reason why she felt this way. Tarah had just learned that she was pregnant and planned to surprise Jimmy with the news on Christmas Eve. It was her gift to him. The timing was perfect. And although she had never been a "baby person," her pregnancy had introduced her to a whole collection of new emotions that she never would've expected. Suddenly having a baby just felt completely right.

"It's going to be perfect. The stars are finally aligned in the skies." Tarah leaned her head against the window and looked outside at all the cars that flew past them on the highway. Tarah watched the reflection of her own smiling face in the window. "I feel at peace."

"I think they've been aligned since we met." Jimmy spoke gently, his voice suddenly sounding older and Tarah couldn't help but giggle. They'd come a long way since that night they first hung out together, alone in the apartment she once shared with William. There was an unmistakable chemistry between them that had been undeniable.

"Can't believe that your brother finally got out of that funk." Jimmy changed the subject, not realizing that a single tear had slid from Tarah's eye. She quickly wiped it away and it went unnoticed. "Finally, he met a girl that isn't fucked-up in the head."

"Well, in all fairness, Vanessa wasn't fucked-up," Tarah replied. "It just wasn't right. We don't know all the details on that."

"Yeah, you're right," Jimmy agreed. "I shouldn't say it, but after her, he seemed to date a lot of losers."

"True," Tarah agreed, thinking about some of the girls he'd described to her in the past year alone. "I'm happy he found someone who really seems to work for him. Not to mention that she absolutely loves Caitlin." She referred to her niece that was almost five years old.

"Probably more so since she can't have kids herself," Jimmy remarked quietly, and Tarah nodded. Bobby had recently mentioned this fact during one of their phone conversations. Tarah felt awful for the woman she'd just met that same day, wondering how someone would cope with such a heartbreaking circumstance. It wasn't something that every woman was dying to do, but there was some comfort in at least having the option to bear children.

"Either way, I'm happy that he's finally happy."

Unlike Tarah's mother, who was clearly never going to get over the bitterness and resentment she had toward David Kiersey. Even that same day, she'd managed to make a snippy remark about the new woman in her ex's life. Tarah grew exhausted just listening to her mother speaking about any topic. Jimmy had just reminded her again that Claire Kiersey would never change, so there was no sense getting upset about her poisoned comment.

Jimmy's family was much more balanced in comparison. His mother was like a child herself, especially through the holidays, while John Groome remained silent and strong, yet loving toward everyone. Jillian continued to be preoccupied with her weight, something that Jimmy had learned to accept. Even though his sister always spoke of having children, it never happened. Tarah suspected that it created some tension with her husband Rob, but everyone knew that Jillian was too obsessed with her weight to voluntarily get pregnant.

Before leaving town, they dropped in to visit a few friends, including John. He was excited to see them both and apologized for Elizabeth and his baby Sydney not being there, but they were out doing some shopping. After approximately an hour, Tarah and Jimmy left.

"You know, sometime we should go to Springdale," Tarah commented out of nowhere as they continued to drive on the 401. "I want to go back and see Wendy's grave."

"Are you sure?" Jimmy sounded skeptical. "Are you sure you'll be okay to do that?"

"Yeah, I think I'm ready now," Tarah replied quietly. She hadn't been there since the day that Wendy's body had been buried. Since her death occurred during the winter, the actual burial hadn't occurred until months after she died. Tarah had been there that afternoon and almost had another anxiety attack during the brief service. "I need to make peace with her being gone, and I think that's the best way."

Jimmy silently nodded. He understood.

They went the next day.

When she got out of the car and headed toward the graveyard, Tarah wasn't as confident. Walking on the uneven ground that was lightly dusted with snow, she thought about all the times she and Wendy had spent together. She thought about the beautiful smile that always graced Wendy's face, the drunken laughter of their nights out, and the many tears they had shared during difficult phases. She also thought of all the wasted time when Wendy wasn't in her life. How long had she thought her former friend had snubbed her? And all along Wendy was in an abusive relationship. Had there been any signs? Any ways that Tarah could have known? Only three years had passed, but yet it felt like a lifetime since she had seen Wendy's face.

Jimmy was hesitant when Tarah had insisted she go to the grave alone. He stood back, a worried expression on his face, and as he pushed a strand of black hair away, his pale blue eyes seemed to send her a message of support. She turned and walked into the silent graveyard until she found the headstone that marked the end of a young woman's life. Kneeling down, Tarah swallowed the lump in her throat and remained silent for a long time. A tear ran down her face as she touched the cold, gray stone lovingly, remembering all the times they shared.

"I think you know why I'm here. I haven't told Jimmy yet about the baby. But I know that you know," Tarah finally managed to whisper. She silently found strength to continue. "I don't know where you are right now. Is there a heaven? I'm not even sure sometimes." She stared at the lettering on the tombstone. It was Wendy's maiden name, something Tarah hadn't noticed the last time she was at the graveyard. Below it were the dates. Wendy had only been twenty-three when she died.

"I told Jimmy that it was important that I come see you again. Especially with everything going on right now, some big changes." She fell silent again and stared down at her leather gloves. "I don't know if we're going to stay with FUTA, or what's going to happen now. There's so much more to consider than there used to be. Life can be so confusing and so wonderful at the same time."

Tears were flowing down her face, but Tarah didn't feel the usual uncomfortable feeling of her heart racing or her breathing becoming labored. In fact, she felt relatively calm as she spoke. These words would free her.

"I think about you all the time." Tarah hesitated and continued to cry. "I wish you were here to share my wonderful news with or to talk about what's on my mind. I wish you were here to have the life you deserved with someone who deserved you. I sometimes wonder if I had stepped back, if maybe you would've gotten back together with William, if maybe you'd be alive now. Not to assume that either of you might have wanted that, but it crosses my mind from time to time. I wonder if I should've pushed harder to get back into your life, if I could've gotten you away from that maniac. There are so many things that I wonder about. But I have to accept that it was out of my control, and that everything happens for a reason."

Tarah wiped tears from her chin. She finally had stopped crying and attempted a brave smile, and the sun suddenly shone down to light up her face. She saw it as a sign. "I've got to go now, but I'll be back. I promise I'll never forget you. Not even for a moment." She slowly rose and headed back to the car, where Jimmy waited for her. His face was solemn as he took Tarah in his arms and hugged her. Finally, she moved away to show she was fine to leave.

Feeling exhausted by the emotional event, Tarah drifted off on their drive back to Toronto. Jimmy and she then spent a quiet night at home. The next day, Tarah awoke early and decided to head out to do some last-minute shopping. Although she had bought most of Jimmy's gift, there was one thing she had to arrange delivery for on Christmas Eve. She wanted to buy him a huge television set or stereo system for his "office," which was a room beside the studio. Currently it held a computer and various guitars for when he worked on his music. But Tarah knew that sometimes he just went there to veg out and she decided to fill the room with things that would make him happy.

She was relieved to enter the electronics store unnoticed. Tarah really just wanted to browse around with the other shoppers and not be badgered by anyone who recognized her. However, she quickly noticed that everyone was standing in front of a large television at the back of the room. At first, she didn't really pay attention until she saw a flash of herself and Jimmy and then her mouth fell opened.

A reporter was talking about a sex tape.

They were talking about *her* on a sex tape with Jimmy.

Tarah thought she was going to pass out. She rushed out of the store before anyone noticed her in the room.

Outside in her car, Tarah felt an anxiety attack coming on. She started to cry. "No, not now. Please, not now." She put her head down and focused on her breathing. She had to calm herself down and get home to talk to Jimmy. He was awake when Tarah had left that morning, and she wanted to make sure it was her who broke the news. *How did this happen? When did it happen? We never made a sex tape!* Tarah felt the thoughts flowing through her head and suddenly had the urge to vomit. Glancing around outside, she saw no one near her car and quickly opened the door and threw up on the pavement. The bitter taste of vomit remained. She closed the door again and wiped her mouth with a tissue before finally starting to relax. When she felt able, Tarah calmly turned the key in the ignition and drove home.

She felt like a zombie and wasn't sure how she made it, but eventually Tarah was back in her garage. A throbbing headache crossed her eyes, and she slowly got out of the car and headed inside. Her legs felt wobbly as she walked from room to room calling out Jimmy's name, but there was no answer. Going into the basement where his office was, she only found an empty room. Searching the house from top to bottom, she secretly cursed him for choosing such a huge place, but then started to cry for being angry with him. This wasn't Jimmy's fault.

Back in the bedroom, she noticed the computer was turned on. Had he seen it already? Their bed was unmade and a towel was on the floor. She called out his name again, but he wasn't answering. Glancing in their bathroom, where the light was still on, she noted he wasn't in there either. Turning off the light, she returned to their bedroom and sat down in front of the computer. The screensaver was on when she shook the mouse. Looking at the screen, she began to cry. He already knew about the tape.

A huge article talked about the scandalous sex tape that had been released by an "unidentified" source the previous day. The writer explained how the tape displayed some "very rough sexual acts that included one scene that suggested rape." Tarah automatically knew the night in question. The story went on to talk about the blood and bruising displayed on Tarah. It also mentioned that when Jimmy started to have anal sex with her, she screamed for him to stop. The article went on, but she couldn't read it.

Tarah sat back in her chair. Tears were burning her eyes and she grabbed a nearby garbage can as vomit burnt her throat once again. She wanted to die. Filled with humiliation, shame, and anger, Tarah began to sob loudly while pains crossed her chest and she began to shake. Getting off the chair, she sat on the floor and pulled her legs close to her body. She felt her depression slowly turn to anger, and she loudly cursed the media. Such disgusting vultures, heartless creatures, and she hated every last one of them. And then it suddenly hit her like a brick. Jimmy wasn't home. He was missing, and he had just read the same article as her. The one that suggested he raped her.

"*Oh my God!*"

Tarah rose from the floor and searched for the phone but didn't know where to call. She collapsed on the floor in misery and gasped for air. *Jimmy is going to think he raped me! He's going to think he raped me, just like his sister was raped. What if he hurts himself? Where is he?*

Almost as if it were a sign, the phone rang. Tarah was hesitant to answer until she noticed it was William's number. Picking up the receiver, she couldn't speak at first because she was crying so hard and her hand was shaking.

"Tarah?" William's voice was full of concern. "Is that you? I saw the story about you and Jimmy. Are you okay?"

"No." Tarah started to cry again. "I'm not."

"Tarah, is Jimmy there?"

"No!" She began to feel hysterical. "I don't know where he is, but he knows everything."

"Okay, Tarah. Maggie and I are coming over, try to stay calm."

She hung up the phone and curled up in a ball and cried. She was still wearing her coat from earlier that morning. Finally, the doorbell rang. She went downstairs and answered it. William was alone.

"Maggie went to the office to see if she could find out anything else," he said and walked through the door, closing and locking it behind him. Pulling her into a tight hug, Tarah felt some comfort but couldn't stop worrying about Jimmy. When he finally let go, he put his arm around her and led Tarah to the next room where they sat on a couch. "There are reporters outside your house." He broke the news to her. "Did you know?"

"No, I went out to get Jimmy a gift this morning and they weren't there." She watched him grab a box of Kleenex from a nearby table and set it between them. "That's when I found out about the tape and came home. There were no reporters then and Jimmy wasn't home." She blew her nose.

"But he must know."

Tarah nodded. "The computer was on and the page on the screen was about the tape." She hesitated for a moment. "William, I didn't make this tape. I don't know anything about it at all." She felt herself calming down slightly, now that she had someone to talk to.

"I know you didn't, Tarah." William rubbed her arm. "Maggie did some checking and I guess it was taped in a hotel." Tarah nodded. "Apparently someone who works there put cameras in your room, hoping to catch something." He seemed hesitant to reveal the truth. "Tarah, I know this isn't the time but you guys were completely violated. This is a legal matter."

Tarah wiped her eyes again. Her entire face hurt from crying. She understood what he was saying, but it gave her little comfort at that time. "William, he didn't rape me! I can't believe they are saying that."

"Tarah, that's how the media work, you know that," William calmly reminded her. "They don't play fair. They want a story, and they'll edit whatever they want together to make it look worse than it is, you *know* that. It's like them shooting twenty pictures of you then putting the worst one up and saying you are pissed off or something, that's how they work."

"But Jimmy might not know that."

"Of course he does." William spoke gently, attempting to calm her down.

Tarah shook her head and felt another flood of tears falling. She then told William everything. About Jillian's rape, the drugs he took on the night the tape was shot, everything. When she was finished, she felt her body relax.

William nodded. "I can see why you're concerned. But if we start—"

The doorbell rang. Tarah only answered it after seeing a police officer was on the other side. Then she fainted.

CHAPTER FIFTY

▼

It was John who had once told her that every decision she made had the potential to change the course of her entire life. "Especially," he added, "if that decision is something that scares the hell out of you!" And looking back, Tarah knew he was right.

There were two things that scared the hell out of her, and she never regretted either decision for a second. Not even now.

One decision was to get on stage for the first time and sing in front of an audience. It literally was the most frightening thing Tarah had ever done. All eyes stared at her with interest and no judgment, yet she could feel her knees shaking underneath her jeans. Sweat formed on the back of her neck and her stomach turned throughout the entire song. But she had done it.

Of course, it wasn't until weeks later at Jerry's, when Tarah sang "Under the Bridge" in front of approximately two hundred people, that she really hit her stride. She could feel their admiration as the words flowed from her mouth and the genuine applause when the song was finished. And although that night in general had been a disaster, Tarah later would realize that this was one of the decisions she had made that changed the course of her life. This had been the kind of thing that John was talking about in his subtle lecture to her, back when he saw the potential that she herself hadn't recognized yet.

The second decision was to be honest with herself about her feelings for Jimmy. It would've been a hell of a lot easier to stay with William and deny what was in her heart. But she would've been lying to herself. Hadn't there always been something about Jimmy that stood out to her? Even on that first day they met, as she walked down the stairway at William's house to meet the band's new addition, hadn't she known? He was on the chair, gingerly setting down a guitar as his blue eyes watched her with interest. Maybe if she had been living in the moment, Tarah would've noticed. But as usual, her brain was somewhere else, preoccupied with what William did or didn't think of her at the time. She was thinking ahead rather than concentrating on what was going on around her in that moment. But hadn't that always been her mistake?

And here she was again, doing the same thing. Except now, it was thoughts of the past that gave Tarah comfort. It took her away from the reality of that moment.

There was still no word on Jimmy. When the police officer showed up at her door, it was to ask Tarah questions on the sex tape. Apparently the hotel's management had contacted the authorities in order to charge the specific employee involved. According to the officer, the young man worked in maintenance and had cameras installed in both the bathroom and bedroom to tape the couple. Apparently he was an obsessed fan. Lovely.

"I think if I were you, I'd hire a lawyer," William suggested, after the police officer briefly dropped by and left again. They were sitting alone in the living room of her house, waiting to hear from either Maggie or Jimmy. It was after lunch and still, no one had called.

"I suppose." Tarah shrugged, glancing in the corner at their Christmas tree. Another holiday ruined, she thought sadly. Sitting on the couch, both legs beneath her, she wrapped a blanket around her shoulders. "I just can't even think about that now."

"I know you can't." William gave her a small smile from the chair across from her, where he sat. "But it is within your rights. The hotel is responsible for their employees and your privacy was invaded. I'm guessing you'll hear from them sometime soon, they're going to want to rectify this situation."

Tarah nodded, nervously twisting her beautiful, diamond engagement ring around her finger. She thought back to the day Jimmy proposed. She still could remember the gleam in his eyes as he pulled out the ring and asked her to marry him. She loved him so much. And now he was missing. What if he had done something to hurt himself after the media's insistence that he forced himself on her? She knew it was taboo to say so out loud, but there was a bad feeling setting into her heart and she secretly feared the worst. It wasn't like him to just disappear.

And although the phone constantly rang, it was never from him. Most of the calls were from both their friends and her family, but she wasn't ready to deal with them yet. It was too soon. She couldn't even think straight anyway, not until Jimmy made a reappearance. Every time the phone rang, William would announce the caller, and Tarah would simply shake her head no. The messages were growing on her answering machine and most were filled with shock and outrage about the scandal. She just wasn't ready to deal with it yet.

Finally the phone rang and it was Maggie. And she had information that took a huge weight off Tarah's shoulders.

"I know where Jimmy is." William's eyes sparkled as he delivered the news to a relieved Tarah. "Maggie found him at her work. He was there talking to Shannon." He referred to the woman who had taken over for Maggie after she stepped down from managing Fire. "She said he thought the record company or our management had pulled this as a publicity stunt. Maggie said that the agency wouldn't even think of doing something like this unless the specific people involved *wanted* a publicity scheme. And we know that happens with other celebrities." William raised his eyebrows. "But you can stop worrying, Jimmy's generally okay."

"What do you mean by 'generally?'" Tarah rose from the couch, mindlessly dropping the blanket on the floor. Her heart began to race. "Where is he? Why didn't he come home?"

"He didn't come home because Maggie suggested he go somewhere else to stay under the radar." William pulled a set of keys from his pocket. "It's sort of out of town, but I know where it is. It's the same place I went when I had my own scandal after Lindsey and I broke up. It's owned by the management company, they often use it for situations like this one. If we can shake the reporters, I can take you. Jimmy and Maggie are there now."

"Do you mind?" Tarah choked on her words. "Is he okay?"

"From what Maggie said, he's fine. But apparently he's been drinking a bit." William hesitated. "He's pretty upset. Maggie tried to stop him, but you know how Jimmy is, it's not that easy." He hesitated for a moment and stared into her eyes for a long moment. "Anyway, go pack some stuff for both of you and I'll take you."

Tarah followed his instructions and twenty minutes later they were in his car and on their way. Luckily, they had lost all the reporters who had waited anxiously around her house. Now, as they drove in silence, Tarah did a lot of thinking. There was so much to consider. Holding her stomach, she thought about what she'd say to him when they arrived and feared what she'd find. At least Maggie was still there with Jimmy to keep an eye on things.

In the midst of it all, Tarah wasn't even paying attention to where they were driving. They were heading out of Toronto and that was all she knew. Tarah didn't care where William took her. As long as Jimmy was there when they arrived.

Forty-five minutes later, they pulled into the driveway of a small house. It was a simple bungalow, nothing elaborate or fancy, but just average enough that anyone living in it would stay under the radar. It was perfect.

Tarah wasted no time jumping out of the car and flying up the front step. Maggie was already opening the door as she arrived at the top. With a sympathetic smile, she moved aside to let her in and warned her that Jimmy was really upset. "I tried to talk to him, but he won't listen." Maggie spoke quietly and gently touched Tarah's arm. "I don't know if William told you but he went to FUTA to talk to someone, but none of the reps would see him. He seems to think that they had something to do with this tape." She waited to see Tarah slowly nodding before continuing. "Regardless, I plan to get to the bottom of this situation."

Tears sprang into Tarah's eyes when she once again thought about everything that had just taken place. It was like living in a nightmare and she couldn't wake up. It just seemed to get worse and worse, and her emotions were all over the map. One minute she felt calm and the next she would be sobbing uncontrollably. She couldn't wrap her brain around this horrific and bizarre situation. Why was it happening to them? How could she deal with it?

Maggie leaned forward and pulled her into a strong hug, something that greatly surprised Tarah. "It's going to be fine," she attempted to reassure her, but Tarah wasn't ready to accept these words yet. Would it get better?

Maggie released Tarah and stepped back with a compassionate smile on her face. "You have my number if you need me. And I have the number here as well. In the meantime, your fridge is well-stocked so you can stay here for a few days. I'll be in touch either tomorrow or when I have some new information."

And after a few more parting words of encouragement, she was gone. Tarah suddenly felt the house was much too silent. After locking the door, she glanced around briefly at her surroundings before finding Jimmy in the bedroom. He was sitting on the floor, a tequila bottle beside him, with his back to her. When he finally turned around, Tarah thought her husband had aged ten years since that morning. His eyes were bloodshot and his face was drained of all color. The last time she'd seen him this way was the night he spoke to her about his sister's rape. It scared her.

Without saying a word, she rushed across the room and fell down beside him. Her arms greedily pulled him close to her, and she felt every tear that had been held back falling from her eyes. Tarah's entire body fell into sobs as she felt his strong arms hold her. He was silent and that made her nervous. She finally moved away and saw deadness in his eyes. He quickly looked away.

"Jimmy, I was so worried about you," she whispered while her fingertips grazed his face. There were so many things that Tarah wanted to say but she wasn't even sure where to begin. "I didn't know where you were at all."

"I'm sorry. I didn't mean to worry you, Tarah." He turned toward her and brushed a piece of hair from his eyes. She noticed how drained he was and then glanced at the bottle of tequila. Luckily, he hadn't drunk much yet. She had to find a way to get it away from him. It was the last thing he needed right now. "I woke up when you were leaving this morning and jumped in the shower. As soon as I got out, the phone was ringing. It was my sister and she was screaming at me. I had no idea what the fuck was going on. She just kept ranting about some video of me and you and how I had raped you—"

"*What?*" Tarah felt her mouth fall open. No wonder he was so upset. Why hadn't Jillian had enough common sense to approach Jimmy differently and at least consider that the media reports were exaggerated? After witnessing the constant battles her brother had with the press, had Jillian not *yet* realized that they often report wildly inaccurate stories? "My God! What is *wrong* with her?"

"Tarah." Jimmy remained calm and took a deep breath and looked down at the floor, clearly avoiding her eyes. "I went online and found the video. She's right. There *is* one point where I hurt you and you *did* ask me to stop because I was hurting you." His eyes once again met with Tarah's. "But I didn't."

Tarah thought back to the anal sex. That's what he was referring to, and up until that point she really hadn't thought about it again. And she certainly didn't think he was assaulting her. "Jimmy, that's crazy!" She shook her head. "Please, you were fucked-up on drugs that night. It isn't like you were in your normal state of mind to begin with, and second of all, I was just as into having sex as you were. If not more, so forget it. Please."

"Tarah, I can't." Jimmy spoke sorrowfully. "I had to listen to my sister scream, and then cry to me on the phone this morning, and it made me see that I'm no better than the guy who raped her. She's right. I did the same thing." He reached for the bottle of tequila, and Tarah felt anger rise from her stomach. How *dare* Jillian pull this shit on Jimmy? She *knew* how much that kind of comment would hurt him. "And then my mom called and yelled at me and started crying. I just couldn't take it so I rushed to the FUTA to see what the fuck was going on. When they refused to even talk to me, I knew something was up." Tarah watched him lift the bottle to his lips. "I'm sure they were behind this, that was my first instinct from the minute I heard about it, and I stand by it. They always wanted to have us featured in videos or interviews, they wanted all this attention to be brought to us being a couple, and this would just be another thing that would put the band in the spotlight."

Just as Jimmy was about to take a swig from the bottle, Tarah ripped it out of his hands. This was the last straw.

"No!" Tarah screamed, and she felt an anger rise from the tip of her toes right to the top of her head. Never in her life had she felt completely at the end of her rope with a situation. It was the first time Tarah felt the need to jump in and take control of a situation, rather than let someone else do it. "If it takes some yelling to get through to you, then let *me* be the one to do the yelling!"

Stomping into the bathroom, she poured the tequila down the sink. Jimmy was stunned but didn't argue as he watched his wife fly out of the bathroom and stand over him. "Enough is enough, Jimmy. First of all, I don't know who taped this video. I don't care who taped it. Regardless of whether it was FUTA or anyone else, I don't care. I've personally had it with FUTA either way and right about now I'm angry that someone invaded our privacy, then tried to turn this whole thing around as if you are some kind of savage. It pisses me off considering—"

Tarah stopped when an overwhelming pain dug into her chest. She took a deep breath and closed her eyes. This time the anxiety attack wasn't taking over. Not this time. She had things that had to be said, and Tarah wasn't about to stop talking for anyone or anything at that moment. It was time.

Tears formed in her eyes and Jimmy jumped up from the floor and approached her. "Tarah, are you—"

"Please, Jimmy! Just let me finish what I have to say." Tarah began to sob as she spoke, but she didn't care. She wouldn't stop. "It pisses me off considering you've been the one person who's always been there for me. And I've been thinking about that all day when you weren't around, and I was scared that you were somewhere, staring over the side of a building, thinking about jumping, because of this rape accusation because I knew how it would affect you."

"Tarah, I wasn't—"

"Let me finish!" Tarah fought through the tears. "Please, Jimmy, I have to say these things. It's important." She watched him fall silent, and his eyes showed signs of life that weren't there only a few minutes earlier. He nodded for her to continue. "I was going to say that it pisses me off that they're saying all this stuff about you when I know how much you've done for me. From day one, you were always in my corner, even when you had nothing at all to gain from it. Like the times when Michael would put me down, and you'd jump to my defense. How many times did you do that? Or the time some guy in our audience yelled shit out about me, and you flew off stage and attacked him. And the night that William kicked me out—you were *always* there for me. It didn't matter if there was something in it for you or not. You just were there for me in a way that no one ever has been. Not my family or my friends. No one."

Jimmy seemed hesitant to speak but passed Tarah a tissue. "I didn't do those things thinking that we'd end up being together. I just liked you, I thought you were a good person and I didn't think it was fair that they were attacking you."

"Yeah, and now you're the one who is having everyone attack *you* for something you didn't even do."

"I'm not sure about that Tarah," he replied as she blew her nose.

"No, Jimmy. Please stop saying that. You didn't do anything wrong. Please."

"But, Tarah—"

"That's the other thing." She threw the Kleenex in a garbage can. "If *I'm* saying you didn't assault me in anyway, then you didn't. When I told you to stop, it was because it hurt, but whatever. You weren't holding me down and raping me. Fuck, Jimmy! Your sister had some guy forcing himself on her; I can't even believe either you or she would even compare this to *that* situation. That's crazy!"

"But Tarah, it's like Jill says when a girl says stop, she means stop."

Tarah rolled her eyes and sighed loudly. Her head was beginning to ache and she was exhausted from the entire day. "Oh fuck, Jillian!" she snapped, and watched Jimmy's mouth fall open. "I've about fucking had it with Jillian and her constant need for attention. Your entire family has tried to help her for over ten years now, and yet she's still starving herself and puking every chance she gets. I know it, you know it, we *all* know it, and we also know that she doesn't want help. If she does, then why isn't she getting it? How come she still has an eating disorder? Why isn't she being supportive of you rather than barking at you about this video? What's wrong with that picture?"

"It takes a long time, Tarah." He spoke patiently.

"Obviously. It's been over ten years since she was raped!" Tarah snapped. "If she wants to walk around being the victim for the rest of her life, then that's fine. But she's not dragging you down with her anymore. And when this is all done, I'm going to call your fucking sister and tell her that she had no right to accuse you of being like her rapist. That's a horrible thing to say. It's bad enough that the media is painting you in a certain light, you don't deserve to have your sister do the same thing."

"I know, Tarah, but she was upset."

"Right, and she called the house a million times today to apologize," Tarah said sarcastically, knowing that of all the phone calls she had screened that day, Jillian's wasn't one of them. "Sure."

"Okay, I get your point," Jimmy gave in. "I don't think she intended on being so judgmental though. I really don't."

"I don't care." Tarah spoke honestly and took another deep breath. She refused to have an anxiety attack. It was about time she took power over her own body, as well as her own life. "All I ask is for you to stop saying you assaulted me. Then, stop blaming yourself for not stopping your sister's rape. It happened years ago and it was horrible. But you didn't do anything wrong. You were a scared kid who didn't understand what was going on. You were just a kid, Jimmy! Please, please, don't carry this around with you for the rest of your life."

"I'll try not to."

"No, you've got to promise me that you won't. It's so important."

Jimmy silently nodded. "Okay. It's a new beginning."

"It could be."

"Okay." He reached for her hand. "From now on, I'll try my best to forget that day."

"I don't necessarily want you to forget it. I just want you to realize and understand that you were only a kid. You weren't responsible to swoop in and save your sister. And chances are you couldn't have done anything anyway. He could've hurt you." Tarah leaned in close to Jimmy and stared deeply into his eyes. "I think that's why you always want to be there to swoop in and save me. I sometimes think that a part of you regrets not being able to help your sister, so you try to be there for me and I love you for it. But I have to learn how to look after myself."

"No, you don't. I'll always be there for you."

"I know that and I appreciate it." Tarah felt herself calming down, her voice relaxing. "But I still have to look after myself too. It's time I grew up."

"I guess." Jimmy squeezed her hand. "I know I probably need to grow up too."

"You do."

"Really?" His eyebrows rose and his voice took a seductive tone. His slid his arms around her and she put her hands behind his neck. "No more fun?"

"I didn't say that." Tarah smiled. "But we won't have as much time."

"Yeah, I suppose it's time to negotiate a contract." Jimmy's face suddenly lost all of its light. "And we're back on the merry-go-round again."

"Well, maybe, but probably a different kind of merry-go-round."

"Yeah, well isn't one record company just like the next." Jimmy shrugged and his smile warmed again. "If my theory on this video is right, it won't be FUTA."

"I'm not talking about that," Tarah whispered. "I wasn't going to tell you until Christmas Eve but then all hell broke loose today and I decided maybe you needed this news more today, than you will then."

Jimmy looked confused. "What news?"

"I'm pregnant." Tarah bit her lip and a smile slowly lit up her face as she saw Jimmy's eyes widen and the room was suddenly completely quiet. "I know we didn't talk about it but—"

"Oh my God!" he whispered back. "Are you serious, Tarah?"

"Yes." She could tell he was still full of shock but clearly, Jimmy accepted the news. "I found out a few weeks ago when I started to feel like crap all the time. At first, I was worried that we weren't ready to be parents. But the more I thought about it, the more excited I got."

"But are you sure you want to do this? I think it's great but what about you?" Jimmy looked slightly hesitant, and a smile struggled to creep on his face. "You hate kids, remember?"

"I never hated them," Tarah replied as his arms pulled her closer. "I just wasn't ready to have them, and now, I think I am. I think it's time. So, can we move forward and stop focusing on the past?"

"I think you've given me new motivation." He pulled her into a strong hug, and Tarah felt another tear slip from her eye, but this time it was a reflection of something positive. "Oh my God, thank you for telling me today. I so needed to hear some good news."

"So you're okay with it? I know we didn't talk about it or plan it." She pulled away from Jimmy and inspected his eyes. He was definitely happy.

"I'm more than okay with it. I can't believe it, a baby." He gave her a quick kiss on the forehead and then the happiness in his face disappeared. "What about this whole mess, Tarah? I don't know if I want to have a kid living through all this shit with the media all the time. It's bad enough we've got to."

"I've been thinking about that too." Tarah took his hand and led him to the bed where they both sat down. "I was thinking about leaving the band. I love what we do, but this was kind of the final straw today." She watched Jimmy nod. "I don't want to be in the limelight anymore. It's not what I thought it would be, as naive as that must sound. I just want to have a normal life. I love being on stage, but the cost is much too high."

Jimmy agreed.

"So, I've been thinking of trying to get into writing or something else." Tarah confessed. "I've even thought about writing a book about our story as a band, but then I don't know if I'm ready to go over all this again."

"There's lots of time." Jimmy nodded. "You can do anything, Tarah. You're smart and creative. Maybe you just need a break from this business. Maybe someday you'll want to go back to music again."

"And what about you? What do you think?"

Jimmy sat in silence for a moment. "I don't know. Love the band thing, but I really would like to produce music. Ever since the last CD, I've had different artists approach me about working with them, but I never had the time. But maybe I need to make the time. Maybe I'll be good at it."

"Considering our last CD is doing exceptionally well, I think that the odds are good." Tarah smiled. "I think you need to at least try. Maybe we'll just announce that we're taking a break from the band to work on other projects. William was talking about doing other stuff earlier today, some solo work, so maybe things will fall into place. You know it might all work out in the end."

"I hope you're right, Tarah." Jimmy gave her the same perfect smile as on the first day they met in William's basement. The same smile that she fell in love with over and over again. The smile that always told her that everything was all right. And she smiled back.

Breinigsville, PA USA
09 April 2010

235831BV00001B/28/P